SCAVENGERS
ROBERT HOOD

Clan Destine
PRESS

First published by Clan Destine Press in 2022

Clan Destine Press
PO Box 121, Bittern
Victoria, 3918 Australia

National Library of Australia Cataloguing-In-Publication data:

Hood, Robert
Scavengers

ISBN: 978-0-6453168-2-7 (paperback)
ISBN: 978-0-6453168-3-4 (eBook)

Cover Design by © Cat Sparks
Original Cover Art by Cameron Sparks
Design & Typesetting by Clan Destine Press

Clan Destine
PRESS

www.clandestinepress.net

Praise for Scavengers from a host of award-winning authors:

'Robert Hood, master of horror, has turned to crime. In *Scavengers*, he deftly stitches the body horrors of Frankenstein's creation into the fabric of a chilling murder mystery. This archetypal battle between humanity and monstrosity pits a laconic, haunted PI against a psychotic serial killer, drawing the reader into a dark web of alienation, intrigue, and sheer terror. I couldn't put it down.'

JANEEN WEBB, author of *Death at the Blue Elephant*, *The Dragon's Child*, and *The Five Star Republic* (with Andrew Enstice)

'*Scavengers* is a spectral thriller of (modern) Promethean dimensions. A lightning-powered Frankenstein's monster of a novel that stitches hard-boiled noir with classic horror, the hunt for a serial killer with a revenant ghost mystery, the black magic black market with Bulli Pass. Gruesome and intelligent, with a disinterred heart of uniquely Australian grit.'

J. ASHLEY-SMITH, author of *Ariadne, I Love You* and *The Attic Tragedy*

"Why should you read Robert Hood's *Scavengers*? Because Hood, a fantasist of the highest order and one of the best damn wordsmiths working in Australia today, has combined horror and hard-boiled crime fiction into a genre-bending, spine-chilling chimera of a novel that will keep you up all night!"

JACK DANN, author of 70 books including *The Memory Cathedral*, *The Man Who Melted*, and *Shadows in the Stone*.

'Robert Hood is one of the grand masters of Australian Horror writing. Here, he infuses a gritty neo-noir crime story with disturbing, haunted, macabre elements, and to impressive effect.

TIM NAPPER, author of *Neon Leviathan* and *36 Streets*.

'*Scavengers* is smart, dark, riveting crime fiction at its best. This is Hood at the top of his game.'

KAARON WARREN, author of *Slights*, *The Grief Hole*, *Into Bones Like Oil*, and *Tide of Stone*.

'God made the world in six days
and was arrested on the seventh.'

– Ambrose Bierce,
from *The Devil's Dictionary*

PART ONE
THE INSISTENCE OF MEMORY

1

'MIKE? WAKE UP!'

The immediacy of a memory: a birthday party, images of Lucy Waldheim – good and bad – morphed into a different time and place. Mike Crowe woke to find himself partially covered by crisp white sheets in a chic room – too bright, airy and upmarket to be his own. For a moment, he was disoriented. A radio automatically came on, in the midst of a news report about some poor bastard named de Mora who'd been found murdered in a Balmain hotel overnight. No one knew why. Crowe reached over and thumped his fist on the off-button, cursing it. Then he rubbed his fingers along the lengthy scar that had been carved down the left side of his face several decades ago by a since-deceased thug, as though to confirm his own identity. He remembered where he was. In Wollongong, the steel town cum university city on the south coast of NSW, and this apartment, in one of the city's high-rise, beachfront hotels. But memory of Lucy rushed over his mind again and lingered, sharp with sorrow. It felt as though someone had shot him in the chest.

Lucy had been dead for just on 10 years.

He breathed heavily.

'Bad dream?' said a woman's voice. 'Sorry about the alarm. I set it for nine. I have work to do.'

The voice's brunette owner dragged on the sheets Crowe had accidentally pulled away from her. Her name was Gail Veitch. A journalist, yes, but much more. Crowe and she had history, 20 years of it. Years of friendship and conflict, random spates of intense interaction and relative peace, commitment implied but never formalised. The thing was, Crowe had always considered himself a lone wolf, ill-suited to close connections – a legacy from his long-dead father, who had given him cause to distrust letting people get too close. But Gail challenged that and got closer than anyone else. Not that he'd admit it. He couldn't tie her down. He wouldn't tie himself down. Yet she was more important to him than she knew. Perhaps more than he recognised himself.

'I don't dream,' he muttered, sliding out from under the sheets. He walked toward the open window and looked out over Wollongong's main beach. It was a spectacular view, which he got to enjoy whenever Gail had work in the Gong, as she always booked the same room in the same hotel whenever her employers were paying. A handful of surfers dotted the gentle waves. The sun had risen some time ago, and, uncharacteristically for this time of year, was hanging in a calm, blue sky, with only a few ragged clouds visible further up the coast.

'Everyone dreams.' Gail yawned, stretched. 'I've never seen you like that before. Groans and sobs. Sounded like my cat – you remember Jimmy Olsen, right? Dreaming of mice that got away.'

'You've never had a cat.' He didn't turn around.

'Okay. But if I did, it'd be called Jimmy Olsen and would dream of lost mice. So, what the hell were you dreaming about anyway?'

'Doesn't matter. Ancient history.' Crowe walked back, lay on the bed and gently drew Gail to his side, wanting her warmth against his chilly flesh. 'Forget it.'

He could see questions percolating in her mind, even though she didn't voice them. Together and apart, the two of them lay in silence for a few minutes, Gail's breasts pressing against him. He ran his fingers down the smooth curve of her back, feeling her vertebrae as though to check they were all there. As he did, his anxiety over long-lost Lucy faded, replaced by the beginnings of arousal.

'Mike–'

'Don't say it.'

Knowing him well or not, Gail was at heart a journalist, an

interrogator, and always had been. She was persistent in her curiosity. She'd raise the question again, mistake or not.

'It sounded like a nightmare. I've often wondered what scares you.'

'Nothing scares me.'

'Always Mr Tough Guy, eh? You know it'll come back and bite you on the arse if you repress that stuff.'

'Let it try. I bite back.'

She laughed. It was brief and followed by silence. Her head turned toward the open window, but her luminous green eyes weren't studying the sky. He could almost see her mind ticking over and wondered what she was thinking.

An irritating noise that sounded like an anaemic doorbell with aspirations to become a rapper suddenly leapt from the mobile phone on the bedside table. Crowe only answered phones when he was expecting a call. His own was turned off. Not Gail's. He didn't bother telling her to ignore it. She was constitutionally unable to.

'Shit,' she muttered. Her warmth disappeared as she pulled away and reached for the bleating instrument. 'Might be important. I'll have to take it.'

Crowe growled something that wasn't quite agreement.

'Gail Veitch,' she said in her best journalistic manner. 'Speak.'

She listened. Her artificial smile, pinned on as if someone could see her, withered in displeasure. She gave Crowe a side-glance. 'Stop shouting, Charlie.'

Her face went stony. 'I don't know what you're—'

An even stonier silence.

Then: 'Charlie, really? What I do in my spare time is none of your business.' She glanced toward Crowe, engulfing him in her conspiracy. Her black hair overlapped onto her lightly tanned, high-cheek-boned face as though to form a mask.

She really is beautiful, he thought.

'He's an old friend – you know that. We were talking about an article I'm working on.'

Crowe could hear the voice on the other end, no clear words, just the murk of bluster: Charlie Pukalski, pillar of the community as far as the community was concerned, dodgy bastard to those in the know, an old frenemy.

'I'm not yours and I don't owe you anything, Charlie.'

More bluster, louder.

'Yeah, yeah, okay.' Gail held out the phone to Crowe. 'He wants to talk to you,' she said flatly.

He didn't reply.

She mouthed, *Stay cool.*

Reluctantly, Crowe took the iPhone X-something or other from her. He didn't like mobile phones much; they made you too available. He'd given in to the inevitable a year or so back, but few people had the number. He still used a landline and an archaic message-recorder in his office. 'Pukalski? What makes you think I'd want to talk to an arsehole like you?'

Pukalski's tone was twisted tight around a core of anger. 'I'd watch your tongue, *mate*, or you might lose it. I got a job for you.'

'I don't need a job.'

'You always need a job. Least employed PI around, I reckon.'

Crowe's PI licence had long expired, but Crowe didn't bother to remind him. 'I'll rephrase it then. I don't need a job *from you.*'

Pukalski laughed, with no camaraderie in the sound. 'Ill-mannered as ever. Okay, if money's not enough to overcome your scruples, how about I appeal to your good nature?'

'Lost it long ago.'

'Pretend. Be in my office within the hour or that bitch you're screwing ends up in the morgue.' By this stage his usual, carefully acquired Aussie accent had lapsed into the more European mode that only appeared when he was totally pissed-off. 'I imagine you prefer your meat warm.'

Words came of their own accord, and Crowe regretted them immediately, not because they weren't true, but because they were. 'Touch her and I'll make sure you never touch anything again.'

Charlie was silent for a moment, but when he spoke it was in a more reasonable manner. 'Look, Crowe, you don't like me, I don't like you, but I have an offer. If you don't want it, you can walk away.'

Crowe listened to the pounding of his own blood, felt its reluctance to calm down. Stupid. He needed to be cooler. Calmer. Crowe had been involved in Pukalski's past enough to know the jerk was more than capable of taking the low road just for fun. He said nothing.

'Be here within the hour.' Pukalski sounded smug. He knew he'd won this round.

The connection went dead. Crowe was ready to fling the mobile across the room but stopped himself. Gail took it from him and carefully put it on the bedside table.

'That seemed to go well,' she said.

Truth be told, Crowe didn't understand why she was still massaging Pukalski's ego, why she let him boss her around, pretending she was the 'media contact' bimbo he kept in addition to a little wifey. *Investigating*, she said, *a big story*. As far as Crowe was concerned, Charles Pukalski was an arsehole and not to be trusted. But it was a touchy subject; saying anything about that might bring up issues about his own relationship with Gail and his commitment or otherwise.

'What's up?' she said.

'Just a meeting.'

'He'll hurt you, Mike.' She stared at him, using her eyes to good effect. 'He's pretty agitated about something.'

'You think so?' He grunted, knowing the chances of getting her to do what he was about to ask weren't great. 'One thing, though. Once I've gone, head back to Sydney, hole up someplace Pukalski doesn't know about.'

'Hole up? That's rather melodramatic, isn't it, Marlowe?'

'Just a precaution. Make sure no one's following you. Lay low for a while.'

'Lay low? Even ignoring the dire overkill of all this, I can't afford to right now. Too busy. Anyway, it'll just make him more pissed. He'll take it out on you.'

'I don't give two fucks about me. *You* need to go. Okay?'

She said nothing.

'Okay?' he repeated.

'Whatever, Mike. If you insist.'

She was lying, of course. He knew that, and she knew he knew. Crowe slid out of bed, but she reached up, grabbed his arm and pulled him back. 'When's your appointment?'

'An hour.'

'You've got some leeway then, haven't you?'

'Some.'

'One last time then?' Even Crowe recognised irony when he heard it. Once again, a smile flirted around the edges of her mouth.

He stared into her eyes. Determined, amused, an attitude he couldn't quite read. There was always an undercurrent. She worried him sometimes.

But he had to admit he admired her recklessness, even as it provoked dread.

Later, as Gail showered and prepared for work, Crowe lay on the bed and recalled the dream that had haunted his sleep. Oddly, it remained clear in his memory.

Sunlight splashes over distant bush and the closer textures of house and surrounds, turning the scene into a spectral landscape. Crowe blinks, momentarily dazzled by the brightness. He makes out a sprawling two-storey mansion with pseudo-Doric columns at the front – a prime example of late '80s nouveau riche pomp-and-circumstance in white brick and glass. A glimpse of water through lines of uniformly manicured trees looks familiar. Ah, he thinks, Gregor Waldheim's lakeside retreat. He pats at his coat pockets but hasn't brought his shades. So, he squints some more.

It all comes into focus, revealing society types in jackets and dresses that no doubt cost a shitload more than Crowe could afford even when he managed to get regular work. They move with tense nonchalance. Few are having fun; they're playing a part. Most, beneath their bravado and expensive clothes, grapple with a deep, unsettling fear. Crowe can almost smell it emanating from them, like stale food scraps left in a kitchen refuse bin too long.

What the hell is he doing here?

He can't make out what anyone's saying. Just a dull murmur, even when they talk at him. It's as though the vocal track has been turned down, their words too insignificant to matter. Musical accompaniment wafts around him. West Indian. Crowe raises one hand to block the glare rising off the surface of a large in-ground pool. A gaggle of gaudy Hawaiian shirts play steel drums, sax, guitar and mandolin.

'Hi there, Mr Crowe. Enjoying the band?'

A young woman appears out of the crowd. A name springs immediately to mind with a poignancy that causes disturbance deep in his chest. Lucy. Waldheim's daughter. Unlikely heir to this house and Waldheim's fortune. She's vibrant in a fuchsia and pink off-the-shoulder dress that fits like it was made for her. Which it probably was. When you're in Lucy Waldheim's presence, it's easy to believe the whole world was made for her. She's certainly the focus of this scenario; he recognises it then as a memory that's playing out beneath the present. It's her sixteenth birthday. Her tawny brown hair, usually dangling over her shoulders, has been trimmed back and curled. It suits her.

A chill pushes through his muscles, despite the sunlight.

'I guess so, Lucy. You?' he says.

'They're okay. I was hoping for some death metal.'

'Really?'

Her smile glows with good-humoured irony. 'Thanks for coming anyway. I know it's not your thing.'

'Why would you think that?'

'Well, you don't like these people much.'

'And you do?'

She shoots him another sly glance, and in that instant, spiked by bright innocence and canny youthfulness, his body fills with a mix of anger, pain, sorrow. He doesn't know where the emotions are coming from. He has always liked Lucy. Smart kid. Personable. Why should her presence here make him feel so miserable?

'They're mostly Dad's friends,' she adds.

'What about yours?'

'I…I don't really have any.'

Crowe stares at her in playful disbelief. 'How could you possibly have no friends? You're everything anyone in their right mind would want in a friend.'

She smiles, apparently pleased to have provoked such a positive reassurance. 'Maybe I've never come across anyone in their right mind.' She touches his arm. He can feel a chill right through the leather of his coat sleeve. 'But I'm glad you're here, Mr Crowe. You'll do as a friend.'

It rises again, the deep and poignant sorrow. Crowe senses he's forgotten something important.

'Call me Mike,' he says, stepping back so her hand drops away from him.

'You've told me to do that many times. But Dad wouldn't like it. He says I shouldn't get too familiar with—'

'Older men?'

'Well, any men actually. He's very protective.'

'He worships you.'

'Like a princess.' She wrinkles her nose, as though catching a whiff of something foul. 'But princesses aren't real. At least you treat me like a human being. I like that. I like you. You make me laugh.'

She glances away, rubbing her hands down her dress as though to remove unwanted wrinkles. It makes Crowe uneasy. He has watched her becoming a woman, having known her for more than a decade now, and he doesn't want her teenage hormones to fixate on him. But there has always been a sadness in her he hasn't been able to define.

'You're anxious,' she says, and laughs. 'Don't worry. I don't intend to ask you out on a date or anything.'

Crowe tries to look as though the thought had never crossed his mind.

'That'd be too much like going out with my father,' she continues, smirking, then adds in a lower, sadder tone, 'Only you'd look after me better.' As she speaks, the words seem to twist, adopting a barely audible distortion that unnerves him. He doesn't remember having this conversation.

'You must have quite a few boyfriends by now?'

She shakes her head. As her hair wavers gently around her ears, reddish streaks he hadn't noticed before appear among the tawny curls. Then her eyes latch onto his with an icy intensity. They are strangely dark now.

'I'll never have a boyfriend, Mr Crowe. You know that.'

'You're kidding, right?'

'It's true.'

'Of course you will.'

'Don't you remember what happened to me?'

He feels his heart stop. It's a moment of transition as the threads of time begin to drift apart. Tears pool in her eyes, red and viscous droplets spilling out over her cheeks.

'What the hell, Lucy—'

'I'm lost.' Her tone is hollow now. Her face withers, becoming increasingly gaunt. Crowe can see the skull beneath her suddenly ragged skin. 'They won't let go.'

'They? What are you talking about?'

Suddenly the pitch of her voice drops, drawing away from him. 'I'm trapped in a dark place, Mr Crowe – a terrible place. Help me, please.'

'What are you—'

'I can't tell you…I can't speak it…but it's bad. You have to stop them.'

As skin shreds from her face, she falls forward, leaning on him, spilling bloody tears over his shirt. Her words fade to a whisper. He leans down to hear what she's saying.

'The world is full of scavengers,' she whispers. 'They're drawing closer. I don't know what they want.' But Crowe can't feel her breath.

There is none.

Then her body goes limp in his arms.
She's cold and dead.
Long dead.

Memory, but not a memory. There'd been a party, but it hadn't happened like that. What was his mind trying to tell him?

2

FOR THE MANY YEARS SINCE HE'D LAST SEEN LUCY WALDHEIM ALIVE CROWE had wanted to remember her as she'd been then – a spunky kid, 16 years old and hyper-charged with the sort of irrational energy that makes anyone over 30 rather edgy. Intelligent, kind and opinionated, yet never pushy or irritating – that was the Lucy he wanted to hold onto. But immediately after the events of that September, it had proven impossible. Instead, Lucy had become a corpse. Even the good memories of her were tainted by that knowledge. Impulsively, he saw her now as he'd found her then, slumped in the back of an old shed in the middle of nowhere, floor a glistening black-red pool.

The torch pulls away, revealing meaningless splatter on the wall behind her. He throws light across her face. Her once-bright eyes are dull, flesh leached to wax. Blood has dried in runnels on her cheeks as though she's been crying. His guess is, she's been dead for several hours at least.

He raises the beam and for a moment the meaningless splatters seem to morph into words.

But it's a message he can't quite read...

He pushed the memory aside. He'd seen death before, more than enough for any one man in the course of even a less-than-respectable life outside a warzone. But for some reason – maybe pure, irrational sentiment of the kind he fought to avoid – Lucy Waldheim's was different. It saddened and infuriated him. More than he would have expected, more than was warranted by his previous interactions with her. During the time he'd worked on and off for her father, he'd watched her grow into a young woman and a good person, one of the few genuinely good people he knew. She cared about stuff, stuff she didn't benefit from, stuff she wasn't trying to scam. She was totally different to her father. A ring-in. Crowe had come to like her more and more. Perhaps she reminded him of his sister before the latter went cold. Or perhaps not – he'd never been overly fond of Tara, whom he hadn't spoken to for nearly a decade. Unexpectedly, though, the feelings he had for Lucy haunted him and made him think of his alienated sibling.

He'd failed Lucy. He'd failed Tara too. Worse still, perhaps one day he'd fail Gail as well.

That feeling had become so insistent he'd been forced to not think of Lucy at all. It was hard, but, after a while, other priorities had taken over and it had been only now and then that she entered his thoughts. When it happened, he mostly saw her violated corpse. But this latest vision had been the worst. Why the horror-movie imagery? Why had his psyche tossed up that particular scrap of mental detritus?

What if she was still alive?

He'd been the one to discover her body, sure. That it was murder and she was dead had seemed obvious to him at first sight. But then the corpse had gone missing and hadn't been located since. It had simply disappeared. Blood still marked the spot where she'd lain. Perhaps Crowe believed, at some level, she was alive and waiting to be found. Perhaps he should be looking for her.

Find me.

He slammed his hand against the steering wheel. Morbid analysis of old failures was a bad habit to foster. As he turned toward the Wollongong industrial area where the offices Pukalski maintained for his less salubrious business dealings were located, Crowe pushed these thoughts aside with impatience. Right now, he had more pressing problems.

Charles Pukalski himself.

Pukalski was the densely packed source of a large slice of the region's economic activity. Apart from a reputation for being legitimately successful, he was also known in certain shady quarters for having fed his success on a diet of shonky business dealings and well-hidden criminality. His undue influence over the city council was occasionally poked at by some zealous journalist, who'd inevitably find themselves stalled by lack of 'proof' – or in hospital. The few overtly ethical councillors who'd tried to cut Pukalski's ties from the inside were unceremoniously removed from office, either by way of revelations regarding their own corrupt goings-on, whether genuine or fabricated, or through back-alley intimidation.

Pukalski had a knack for making his enemies underestimate him. He came over as a hearty hail-fellow-well-met type, open-faced, good-humoured, ripe for the picking by sharper minds. But his latter-day career indicated that a much keener, more ruthless persona lurked somewhere inside this man who looked like he was asking to have his pockets picked, as some of those 'sharper minds' had found out to their cost.

His apparent invulnerability was why Gail had ingratiated herself with him: to get at the dirt that filled his pockets. As an investigative journalist, she was a crusader by nature, if not always an altruistic one. She recognised the potential for a good story when she saw it.

Or so she reckoned. Sometimes Crowe thought that maybe, just maybe, she'd peered beneath the man's double façade and had seen something Crowe was blind to.

He took a deep, calming breath.

Outside the door of Pukalski's office, a couple of over-zealous minders frisked him for weapons as though their 'Boss' was some sort of head of state. They didn't find any; his favourite Beretta 92FS was safely stowed in the boot of his old BMW.

'I got a job for you,' Pukalski said, thick lips twisted into a sneer, after the goon squad ushered Crowe in. He was ensconced behind a big oak desk, elbows leaning on a blotter that had never seen ink, authoritative upper-management demeanour set to 'smarm'. Unlike Crowe's jacket, Pukalski's charcoal suit looked swanky enough to have been delivered by a high-class tailor that very morning. It fitted him perfectly and was immaculately pressed. Pukalski wasn't tall, but he dressed with class. Sometimes it enhanced his stature. Other times it merely emphasised his pretensions.

'So you said.'

'I'm not mucking around. This is a sensitive matter.' Pukalski prodded his index finger on the desktop. 'It's business, okay? And I want my arse covered. Officially, no glitches. But it'll happen my way. Not theirs. Right now, though, there's nothing I like about it. But $200 million is at stake. $200 bloody mill.'

Crowe found himself getting more and more interested. There was a good chance Pukalski might set him up to take the heat, ending with Crowe in a shithole, but it sounded intriguing. $200 million's worth of intrigue.

'A pay-out, I'd guess. What're you paying out for?'

'None of your concern.'

'None of it has to be my concern, Charlie.' Crowe gave him a shot of cold Bogart-esque disdain.

Pukalski, meanwhile, looked like a man trying to place Crowe onto the chessboard of a game that had already started – and deciding whether it would be worth the trouble.

The thing about Crowe was his usefulness. Once upon a time he'd had a valid private investigator's licence, but that was just play-acting. In reality, he'd consider anything, legally valid or not – within limits, of course. No killing. No physical or financial harm inflicted on the innocent. He was proficient at getting jobs done and in the past had got things done for Pukalski with admirable efficiency. But one time Pukalski had left him hanging and it had been all Crowe could do to extract himself from the clutches of Sergeant (now Superintendent) Douglas Pirran. Pukalski had tried to talk Crowe into working for him again – taunting him that he'd lost his edge – but he'd refused until now. Until Pukalski had found some leverage.

Pukalski's grey-blue irises clouded over and his accent thickened. 'I hope you're not going to be shitty about this. You owe me, and you'll listen nicely.'

Ah, here it comes. 'I don't owe you a thing.'

Pukalski stood, which might have made him intimidating to anyone who wasn't Crowe. He turned and took two paces toward the window. He gazed back at Crowe for a moment, then turned away again and looked out the pane of glass. What was so riveting about that particular slice of industrial wasteland, Crowe didn't know, but Pukalski continued staring while he spoke.

'So, you've already forgotten the circumstances of my call this morning, eh?'

'You interrupted some important negotiations, Charlie. Indiscreet of you.'

Pukalski turned and scowled. 'Don't get smart with me, Crowe. I'm not in the mood.'

'Isn't *smart* what dumb arses like you hire me for?'

The Unappreciated Boss Man took an involuntary step toward Crowe then tried for Hard-As-Nails Gangster instead.

'Surely you know what she is?' One hand had made a fist. He looked as though he was about to grind it into the palm of the other.

'You mean Gail Veitch? Sure I do.'

'She's a whore.'

'She's a journalist.'

'That what you were doing with her? Being interviewed?'

'She gives great interview.'

Pukalski squinted at him. After a moment, he laughed. 'So how long've you been shagging her, then?'

What could he say? All of Crowe's answers, from toss-off humour to the truth, had consequences. The expression on Pukalski's face suggested none of those consequences would be pleasant.

'Just this once,' Crowe said, flatly, hoping to minimise the damage for Gail. 'Honest.'

Several moments went by as their eyes locked in a game of chicken. Crowe let Pukalski win. He'd been pushing his luck and didn't think he could gain much more traction from doing so. 'This banter is all very pleasant, Charlie,' he said in a conciliatory manner, 'but what's the problem?'

'The problem is this, Crowe,' Pukalski said, 'whoever owned it in the past, Gail's arse is mine now.'

'Yeah?'

'Yeah. Arse, tits and any other accessory.'

Crowe felt impatience boil up again despite himself.

'Tits and arse? All yours, are they?' Crowe said. 'Must check Gail's copyright branding more carefully next time.'

Pukalski began bouncing his fingernail against his teeth. Click, click, click. An irritating nervous tic. 'You know what you are, Crowe?' He held up his hand in a stop sign. 'No, I'll tell you. A bottom-feeder, that's all. You hang around the arse of my business and feed off the corpses

I shit out of it.' He nodded thoughtfully. 'But I'm not a petty man. I recognise talent and its uses. That's why I don't want to dispose of you, terminally, like I should. Know why? Much better to use you. You're the perfect janitor to clean up messes.'

Crowe sighed. 'Can we skip the foreplay? Gail and I have known each other for years. Old friends from back in the day. You know that. What we do is none of your business.'

'We had an understanding, Gail and I.' Pukalski almost whispered it as he returned to his desk and sat in the big leather swivel chair. His eyes were cold blue now, like the sky reflected on ice. At that moment, he looked genuinely dangerous.

'Understanding? What understanding?' Crowe said. He primed himself to fight his way out of the room.

But Pukalski simply offered him another puppet smile and leaned back. 'It's you who's been disrespectful, Crowe, but I'm a forgiving man under the right circumstances. It's an easy job. It'll be to your benefit in the end. And Gail's.'

Why the hell was he now bargaining instead of putting a chair leg through Crowe's skull? 'I'm only interested in benefits that take monetary form, Charlie.'

Pukalski smiled with a contraction of his thick lips that made it look as though he'd eaten a bad olive. 'That's what I like to hear. I can trust people who only work for money.' He coughed, clearing the olive out of his throat. 'Yes, there's a payment I need to make, an exchange for goods and services. Big one. But the arrangements suck 'cause they've been imposed on me, and it's all a bit sus. I want you there to look after my interests.'

'As I obviously care about your interests so much.'

'Obviously. Let's face it, you're good at this shit.'

'Come on, Charlie. You've got an oversized grog cellar full of apes could strong-arm a deal like that.'

'The apes in the cellar are dumb as planks. I need someone who can evaluate the situation on the fly. I want you.'

'I'm flattered.'

'Don't be. I just like working with people who owe me.'

Crowe looked at him, understanding dawning. 'Okay, so you want me to steal back the payment, don't you? Your bloke will hand it over and get the merchandise, and you want me to take it back? That way you get the goods and the money both, and you know I won't blab about it.'

Pukalski grinned. 'And that's why I want you on the job, Mikey. None of my other blockheads would have figured that out.'

Crowe sighed inwardly. 'Ten per cent,' he said.

Pukalski glared. 'You've got to be kidding. You're not worth $20 million.'

A man could dream. 'Take it or leave it.'

Crowe could see Pukalski's brain turning over, flopping about like a whale in the shallows. He was still hoping for a better way off the beach, evaluating what further advantage he could gain from Crowe's acquaintance with Gail.

Maybe he rightly sensed there wasn't any.

'Twenty grand, Crowe,' he said, then added, just because he couldn't help himself, 'To sweeten the deal, I'll agree to leave Ms Veitch alone – as long as you do the same.'

Crowe decided not to push his luck...or Gail's.

3

THE SKY WAS CLOUDING UP, BUT FOR THE MOMENT CROWE BARELY NOTICED. He headed toward his suburban hideaway over at Mangerton in a sour mood despite the unexpected monetary enticement, taking a roundabout route in an attempt to calm down. Not a great idea. The traffic aggravated his sense of being some sort of patsy. Sure, he knew he'd have to go along with Pukalski, for the time being anyway. And he could use the money. But being under the man's thumb made Crowe very grumpy. Pukalski's psychic stink was already clinging to him and it was far from his favourite cologne.

He slammed on the brakes, barely missing some kid with Bluetooth headphones that covered his ears and squeezed his attention away from the realities of morning traffic. Crowe leaned on the horn.

Calm down, mate. Just let it happen. Do whatever it takes.

On an impulse, he headed back to Marine Drive, where he stalked up and down the beach for god knows how long, letting the waves, the sun and the general lack of people settle him. At the Five Islands Brewery, he sat with a Fat Yak beer or three and some fries as a surrogate breakfast, stared at the islands, snarled at overly jolly young folk who had the gall to challenge the grumpy atmosphere he was trying to spread around, and discussed the meaning of life with a seagull. The latter's take on the issue consisted of ontological guff that somehow involved the equitable distribution of deep-fried potato.

Eventually he went back to his car, tore up a parking infringement notice that had optimistically appeared under one of his windscreen wipers and headed off down Grand Pacific Drive toward Mangerton.

Crowe's house was a typical non-descript suburban residence, built circa 1960, fake bricks and all. The suburb had once been the locale of senior executives from the steelworks at Port Kembla, and this governed the grandiose nature of the homes they built. The houses had since been bought by a wider economic demographic but still retained some prestige value. Except for Crowe's place, which was considerably more downbeat than most. It could have done with a touch-up to its paintwork and guttering, the slate on the front steps was cracking at the edges and had broken off in places, and the yard was clogged with out-of-control foliage. But he liked it. Reminded him of the place he grew up in. Recollections of his family's Western Sydney home were the only nostalgia he still retained from his childhood.

He found the front door unlocked.

Gail was waiting in his lounge room. She was dressed in black slacks and a cream shirt that hung on her like a layer of translucent mist. She looked out of place on the battered brown three-seater. Her hair was shorter than it had been that morning. The starkness of the bob emphasised the sensuality of her features and the lustre of her eyes. She'd had her hair done while he was gone. Probably making sure she looked her best for his funeral.

'This isn't a hideout in Sydney.' He tossed his coat over a chair.

She shrugged and leaned on one elbow. 'I wanted to make sure you were okay.'

'Bullshit.'

Her immaculate eyebrows bent into a frown. 'I'm hurt. But okay, if it makes you feel better, I never do what I'm told. You know that, right? So why expect me to start now? Anyway, I figured there might be a story in it and I don't intend to let Pukalski keep me from doing my job.'

'Your job will get you killed one of these days.'

'I've survived *you*.'

'Yeah. So far.'

Crowe gave her a theatrically deadly look. It made her laugh. 'How the hell did he find out?' he asked.

She rose, walked toward him. 'Not from me.'

'So how'd he know then?'

'Had me followed, I guess. I thought I noticed something odd– '

'When was this?'

'Week before last.'

'You should've told me.'

'I wasn't sure. He's been a bit more distant than usual. But generally okay. He must've been saving it up.'

Crowe huffed and went to brew coffee.

'Is that all he wanted to see you about?' she said, following him.

Crowe filled the percolator with water, poured coffee grounds into the filter and flicked the switch. The mechanism began to drip. 'You want coffee?'

'Sure.'

He rinsed two mugs. Gail had bought them for him. Pictures of Bugs Bunny and Daffy Duck decorated the sides. Both Looney Tunes characters were dressed as gangsters.

'You going to tell me, Mike? Or are we just going to play games?'

'Depends what sort of games you've got in mind.'

She shrugged. 'Whatever you like. Detective and femme fatale? You're fond of that one.'

For some reason her casually flirtatious air annoyed him. He raised a sceptical eyebrow. 'What kind of deal do you have with that dickhead?'

Some of the playfulness that had been skirting around her features suddenly departed for more comfortable climes. She frowned. 'I have no idea what you're talking about.'

'He said you and he had an "understanding" of some kind.'

'He's just provoking you, Mike.'

'Not going to tell me about it, are you?'

'There's nothing to tell.'

He grunted. 'Yeah? Well, either way, I'm bloody sure chasing around after Pukalski is–'

Before he could say any more, she snapped, 'And don't bring up what I'm doing with Charlie again.' She glared at him. 'He sees me as a trophy, thinks I'm his tame journo. I make him look good and write him articulate speeches when he needs 'em. Maybe that's what he meant by an understanding. There's nothing in it.'

'Expect me to believe that?'

'Does he act like a man in love?'

'He's the type that sees ownership as love, and he's jealous. So yeah, he does.'

'The only jealousy around here is yours. With Charlie, it's not love or jealousy. It's leverage. And clearly it worked.'

'So you're telling me you and he never–'

'Do you really want to go there, Mike? I never promised I'd be *faithful*. And neither did you.'

She was right, and yet it wasn't quite true. Some promises are implied rather than spoken. But if that were the case, Crowe had probably broken the unspoken promises as often as she had, though not for some time. He wondered if he was being sexist again. She frequently accused him of it. It was something he didn't have much of a handle on. Watched too many old crime movies, Gail reckoned.

Crowe sighed. 'To tell you the truth, it's not really about you. It's about me. And you're right, it's leverage. He wants me to do what I assume is a dubious job. And he knows he can use you to get to me.'

'I'm your weak point, am I?'

'You know you are.'

Her gaze was like a grenade that was about to go off.

'Nice haircut, by the way,' he said.

She huffed.

When the pot was filled, he poured the coffee into the Daffy mug and passed it to her. She held it in both hands as though she needed its warmth. He took a few sips of his own and let the caffeine tartness settle in his chest while he studied her.

The first time he met Gail, several decades ago, had been dodgy as hell, to say the least. In fact, he'd been hired to 'off' her, as they used to say in the pulps. In all honesty, he'd been a headstrong dickhead back then – after all, it *was* the '80s. But even so, he didn't make a habit of killing. The day he and Gail met had involved a number of violent deaths, but he'd never *intended* to murder anyone, least of all Gail. He'd known all along – especially once he met her – that he'd find a way to avoid it. If he hadn't anticipated it'd be a hassle, he might've let their brief encounters get less brief right from the start. But Pukalski had been part of those early days, too; at the time, Gail, barely out of her teens, was having an affair with him, using him. Years later, she was doing it again.

It was dumb and Crowe didn't really understand why she felt so driven to nail him. The first time it had fallen apart quickly, though bloodlessly, at least for her. This time he wasn't sure such a happy ending could be guaranteed. Pukalski was older, meaner, more demanding.

'Do you need a story that bad?' he asked quietly.

She shrugged. 'The story of a gangster-wannabe's downfall? A man who's been bleeding the city for years and getting away with it? Sure. Why not? But I suspect there's even more to it. Behind-the-scenes stuff. Intuition tells me there's something brewing, something big. I just can't quite put my finger on it.' Her eyes narrowed and became inward looking, as though she was close to seeing what she was after.

'Outing celebrities is safer,' he said quickly to bring her back.

She returned from her reverie. 'Nearly came up with a sensational story featuring our Kylie, but it was both bullshit and totally boring. Seriously, Mike, I'm getting tired of falling back on celeb dirt-wrangling to feed the bank account. It's demeaning. I need a better reason for doing what I do. I'm convinced Pukalski is involved in something big. Something that matters.' She stared at him. 'There's someone behind him, propping him up. Someone higher up the food chain than him. I need to know who.'

'And yet these months of humiliation have produced no proof, right?'

'I can feel it. It's close.'

For too long Gail had been the sort of journalist that digs up filth on pop-culture idols, or makes it up, and gets it published on cheap but glossy pages filled with lurid headers and drab paparazzi shots. Celeb scandals fascinate everyone, but no one takes them seriously. On and off she'd produced some *real* journalism, investigative stuff, rather successfully, too. She even won an award for an article on post-9/11 security scandals. Various pieces she wrote in 2013-2014 about the misogynistic campaign that had unseated Prime Minister Julia Gillard, and the aftermath of that as it related to women in Australian politics, got her into the bad books with some of the larger newspapers and saw her unofficially ignored. That sort of reporting was where her passion lay while the fluff paid the bills. She was, however, determined to make more serious stories her main focus, and perhaps Pukalski was ripe for the picking.

When she'd turned up in Wollongong about a year ago, the Boss Man had recalled the good ol' days and gradually drew her back into his life. But after two months as an undercover 'trophy' journo, she still hadn't got what she wanted, and Crowe was sure she was whipping a dead horse. Personally, he thought Pukalski was just a cog in someone else's machinations, though normally he didn't give a shit.

'Pukalski didn't say what he was planning, if anything,' Crowe said. 'Didn't mention your future at all. It was me he was trying to intimidate.'

'I'm sorry, Mike.'

'Can't you investigate something safer? Like serial killers? The bloke the rags are calling the Scavenger is all the rage.' She laughed and Crowe shrugged. 'Ah, well. Got some paid work out of it.'

She arched an immaculate brow. 'What sort of work?'

'A no-honour-among-thieves sort of thing.'

A smirk slipped across her lips. 'Details?'

'No details. He was real coy about it. Odd, actually. Some chest-beating, but after a while he didn't seem to care what we'd been up to.'

'So are we going to call it a day?'

'God, no. But I reckon Sydney's a safer locale than here.'

'It's nearly midday. Can we get some lunch first?'

Crowe shrugged. 'I've just had breakfast.'

'Chips and beer, right?'

'I gave the chips to a gull in exchange for information. He got the better end of the deal.'

'Real food then?'

'If you insist, but you leave for Sydney straight after.'

She grabbed his hand then dragged him behind her as she moved toward the door. 'Don't just stand there, I'm hungry.'

'*Then* you go, right?'

'I have no desire to hang around here and get reconciled with Charlie anyway. I think you're right. I think my time with him is probably up, but whatever this new scam of his is, it might be just what I need. Will you keep me informed?'

'You'll go back to Sydney? For a while?'

'I'd do anything for you, Mike.' She reached up and, as she often did, ran her fingers down the scar on the left side of his face.

Once again, as always, her beauty made him indifferent to the lie.

Crowe still didn't believe a word she'd said, but she looked so bloody gorgeous as she said it.

Sometimes I remember. I welcome such moments, even though they don't last long. All too soon they fade. Like me, they exist in an in-between state.

I've been trapped here too long.

Right now, out of nowhere, I remember the first time we met, the man and I. My father had known him for years – Mr Crowe was his name – before I was old enough to notice the strangeness of Dad's day-to-day activities. By the time I was nine, interacting with other girls at my private school, sometimes staying over with the few friends I made, seeing their families interact, I was starting to get that my father wasn't normal. It was the way people tip-toed around him – people who visited him in his elaborate and rather sinister study, being noticeably deferential to him. Often they'd just sneak in across the back lawn, or, if coming through the front door, were ushered in without a word said to any members of the household. I once asked about them and my father nearly bit my head off, telling me to mind my own business and if he ever caught me spying on him again, he'd be very cross.

It shocked me, because otherwise he took little disciplinary action at all, leaving that sort of thing to my mother. Once, I asked her about them. 'They're business clients,' she said. 'What business is Dad in?' I asked. She paused, staring at me as though weighing up my capacity to understand. 'He's a high-level financier, dear,' she said at last. 'He funds many enterprises.' 'But he doesn't go to an office or anything,' I pointed out. 'He likes to work from home,' she replied then added seriously, 'Best you don't ask too many questions, darling.'

So I never mentioned the visitors again, though I did watch them surreptitiously from my bedroom window. Mostly, I didn't like the look of them, and it was several years before I fully realised what Father did. He controlled people.

One afternoon after school – when I was 11, I think – I was sitting near the pond in the front garden, trying to write a story about ducks and what they got up to when we weren't looking at them. It was a school project that I'd deliberately misinterpreted. My imaginary ducks were planning a coup to take over the house because they were sick of living in the pond, sick of never being part of what went on under the humans' roof. I wanted it to be sort of like George Orwell's Animal Farm, *which I'd just finished reading. I didn't look up when I heard a car stop outside the gate, but something drew my attention to the man who entered through the side entrance and walked purposefully toward the house. He wasn't someone I'd seen before. He was tall and heavy-set, with the sort of three-day growth beard that somehow didn't look like the result of laziness. He was dressed in grey trousers and a black leather coat, and nothing about him was particularly tidy or businesslike. His dark-brown hair needed a trim. He glanced at me, paused and came over the lawn. I felt nervous; Mum had warned me about strange men. But he was friendly enough, with a pleasant smile and eyes that were only critical for the first moment of evaluation.*

'You must be Lucy,' he said in a gravelly voice.

'Do I know you?' I asked.

'I wouldn't think so,' he replied.

'How come you know me?' I responded.

'Your father's mentioned you more than once. A bit besotted, I'd say. It's so unlike Waldheim, I took notice.'

That surprised me. 'Really?' I frowned and tried to remember when my father had ever given me significant attention. He sometimes helped me with my homework when he had the time and often came into my room at night to kiss me good night. On occasion, he'd linger there. Was that a sign of besottedness? We hardly ever talked much. I really wanted to. But all there was were his visits.

The man saw my confusion or embarrassment or whatever and thought he understood. 'Working dads can be a bit distant, can't they?' he said. He leaned toward me and whispered, 'Doesn't mean they don't care about you and talk about you to friends and acquaintances.'

My curiosity got the better of me. 'What does he say?'

He took a step back. 'Good things, of course. How beautiful you are. That sort of thing. But I'm not really a friend of his – barely an acquaintance.'

I demanded he tell me what he was then, and he explained he did jobs for my father, on and off. Odd jobs, he said.

'Do you like him?' I queried.

He thought for a moment before replying. 'I don't know. He's a bit hard to fathom. I'll let you know when I come to a decision.'

I thought it was a strange answer to give.

I stared at him then, trying to peer through the image he clearly liked to project, but could detect nothing sinister. Quite the opposite. I've always been good at seeing through the masks people like to hide behind. Everyone's mask except my father's. Suddenly I felt uncomfortable and looked for something else to say. I'd already noticed a long scar that ran down the left side of his face and blurted out, pointing at him, 'How'd you get that?'

He smiled at my lack of propriety and ran his finger along the scar. It was barely noticeable but fascinated me. 'A rather stupid mugger with a knife took me off-guard, a long time ago, back in my errant youth.'

'What did you do to him?'

'Let's just say he regretted the decision.'

'Did you kill him?'

He paused before saying, 'I've done lots of things I've come to regret.'

I nodded knowingly but was unsure what he meant. 'You know doctors can remove scars like that now.'

'Can they really?' he said, amused by my dumb innocence, no doubt.

'Yes! I'm sure my father would know someone.'

'I prefer to keep it, to remind me to pay attention. Don't you like it?'

'No, it's fine.' I felt silly and childish, which I guess I was.

After a moment, I noticed him looking at what I'd been writing and felt a bit embarrassed. 'Sorry,' he said, 'just curious.' He glanced at his watch. 'I guess I should be going. He's expecting me. Nice meeting you.' He began to move off but stopped and looked back. 'My name's Crowe, by the way.'

'Can I call you Mr Crowman?'

'Not if you want a long life.' He smiled mockingly. 'Mike's preferable. And I hope things work out for your ducks.' He gestured at the house. 'Though I don't think they'd enjoy living there.'

That's when I knew I liked him.

Crowe was nudged awake by a sound that might have come out of a dream. *Whispering.* Gail lay with her back against him, breathing gently; she'd inevitably failed to leave for Sydney. He touched her, comforted by her soft warmth and her familiar scent.

Someone moved in the gloom.

He glanced in the direction of the movement and, in that instant, the someone was bending over him, features obscured and sculpted by shadows. A young girl's voice distorted by distance or trauma said, *Remember me, Mike. It's important you remember.* He felt a cold hand touch his forehead. For a moment, shock blocked any attempt to leap up or cry out, and Crowe's head filled with images from the past.

His flashlight avoids the spot where Lucy's body lies and illuminates a path around the barely visible interior. A few rusty tools hang from nails so corroded they look like gravity should snap them. Several empty spaces indicate recent use.

What's missing from that line-up? Ancient markings on the wall suggest shears. Had there been shears there until sometime yesterday morning?

What's that sound? A shoe scraping on the concrete floor? Pulse racing, he glances around at a chaos of interwoven shapes: crates and boxes, several free-standing metal shelves full of bric-a-brac, a wheelbarrow…all barely visible in the dim moonlight coming through a high-up and very dirty, web-curtained window. For a moment, he thinks he sees a human shape – someone hunched down near a ride-on mower. He turns the beam on it. The space flares then settles. Nothing. His imagination is starting to play tricks on him.

Taking a deep breath, he moves the torch back toward Lucy's corpse. Most of her clothes have been torn off, evidence of sexual molestation. Injuries all over her body and head indicate a sudden and violent frenzy. Who could've hated her so much? He feels numb.

He locks the shed as best he can and trudges through bush toward the main bungalow. It'd been deserted barely 15 minutes ago when he'd gone there looking for Lucy, and no doubt still is. He'd let himself in and found evidence of her presence: a suitcase with some clothes that were very Lucyish, female toiletries, her diary, a couple of books – The Dance of the Happy Shades and The Progress of Love. He knew Lucy had been reading them, because at her birthday party she'd spent some time telling him how great Alice Munro was. 'I've just read The Beggar Maid, Mr Crowe,' she'd said. 'It's really cool. Sort of sad and transcendental at the same time. You should read it.'

'Sad and transcendental? You sound like some wanky reviewer for the weekend literary supplement.' He'd shrugged, holding up his hands to ward off comment. 'I'm a yob, Lucy. Pure and simple. Pearls before swine.'

'What do you read then?'

'Beer labels and the occasional Playboy. And not for the articles.'

She'd smiled. 'You've got this tough-guy image, but I know better. You'd enjoy these books.' Teens like Lucy are romantics, always looking for humanity in the heart of the monster. But who has time to read?

The bungalow is still unlit and empty. No electricity and no telephone either. No one has lived in the place for a decade or more, Waldheim had told him. Apart from anything else, it's maybe a dozen kilometres off the nearest trace of a decent road, and Lucy didn't drive. How had she got there?

He makes a more thorough search of the house this time, wiping down anywhere he might have touched earlier. The place isn't very big. It had been a holiday retreat for the Waldheims, back when Lucy was a rug rat, and is in a poor condition, with evidence of unauthorised entry. Local kids probably. Waldheim's increasing wealth and business pressures had made holidays of the kind they'd used to have less and less frequent, and anyway, Lucy and her stepmother could afford to go to Bali or the French Riviera on a weekly basis, so why the hell bother with Merryvale River?

Lucy had bothered. Looking through her stuff back in Bowral, the family's main home, Crowe had come across an old diary in her bedroom. 'Last night I dreamt I went to Merryvale again,' she'd written less than a year before. 'With Mum. It's no Manderley, but we had good times there. Maybe I'll go back one day. I miss her so much.' He'd thought maybe she had gone back to the place. Waldheim put shit on the idea, but Crowe had decided to look anyway.

But when he spies a recently opened can of Tooheys, he knows she hadn't been the only one there in the past day or so. Lucy hated beer. 'The smell's cheap and common,' she'd always say. The can is lying on the floor and a close inspection of the wall above it reveals a new dent in the plaster. So maybe there'd been an argument. As well, the butt of a cigarette has been crushed into the tight-pile once-cream carpet — one of those foul exotic brands that smell like recycled camel turds. Muddy, still reasonably fresh scuff marks decorate the floor here and there.

Crowe spends some time going through the rooms with his torch, finding dust, more scuff marks, items belonging to Lucy. He keeps none of them. He takes care not to leave evidence of his presence.

Unwilling to go back to the shed to say goodbye, he sends silent regards as his car rolls across compacted ground fronting the bungalow, headlights off so he won't accidentally draw attention. Not that it's likely. The isolated structure is a decaying relic surrounded by walls of bush. Darkness closes in like depression. No one for many kilometres, he'd guess.

But suddenly someone's standing right in front of the vehicle. Crowe slams on the brakes, barely in time. Whoever it is doesn't move. Crowe flicks on the headlights.

It's Lucy. She's standing there, staring at him, a mess of torn flesh and crimson. Blood that should have stopped flowing hours ago pools around her feet. Crowe feels his heart jump.

Lucy's hand — several fingers completely severed — reaches out toward him.

Help me! she says.

Then he blinks and it's gone. Trees, car, Lucy. All that blood. Everything.

What the hell? It had happened again.

His memories of Lucy were morphing into something else.

4

CROWE WATCHED A SMALL BLOKE CALLED SKARRATT HANGING ABOUT IN the umbra of the old, decommissioned lighthouse on Wilkinson's Breakwater. At least, Pukalski had said it was Skarratt. Crowe had only been in the same room as the man once or twice, and they'd never exchanged business cards or indulged in small talk. Not that he could see his face – at the moment, Skarratt was just a featureless silhouette and Crowe was crouching a few hundred metres away, beside a boatshed in Belmore Basin, where the fishing fleet was moored. Neither he nor Skarratt was very active. The wind moved though, buffing over Crowe's face and squeezing down through his coat collar, filling his bones with after-midnight chill. He hunkered against the concrete wall.

Crowe had watched Skarratt and a taller, stockier bloke arrive and stroll alongside the wall of randomly interlocked concrete blocks that kept the walkway safe from the ocean's more furious moods. Skarratt had lit a match, presumably to smoke, and then made himself comfortable.

'Hurry up, you bastards!' Crowe growled, scaring a seagull that had come around looking for scraps.

The night was gloomy. The moon was having a hard time being seen behind the low, greyish cloud cover, though there was an erratic wind in the upper atmosphere that kept the clouds in motion, just enough to allow for patchy visibility around the harbour foreshore. Mist shifted about in the air, too, and it was beginning to condense. Just drizzle right now, but Crowe had no doubt it would turn to full-on rain before too long. So far, the job had been easy. But the wait was making him cold, and his already sour mood was getting sourer.

Skarratt was Charles Pukalski's official courier. Something in the order of $180 million dollars (the other 20 mill. having been deposited in a holding account as a show of good faith) was stuffed into a leather-covered briefcase made of steel with reinforced locks and chained to his wrist. His bodyguard looked like the product of a wrestler's romp with a she-bear. Earlier, while they were momentarily illuminated by their Mercedes' internal light, Crowe had noticed the guard was failing to conceal something under his calf-length coat. A weapon. Probably a mid-range automatic, from what Crowe could make out. When they got to the rocky face of the breakwater, the bodyguard disappeared into the deeper shadows as though he and his gun wanted to be alone.

And they were alone. At this time of night, the restaurant near the main carpark of the foreshore tourist area – in fact, the entire building, including the fish market – was murky and unoccupied. Whether it was normal practice or just a by-product of the bad weather, none of the fishing boats showed any sign of human life either. Crowe had looked around when he first got there, about half an hour before Skarratt was due to arrive for the drop-off. He found that everything was graveyard quiet. He'd hidden behind the boatshed to wait for the show to start, after he'd made sure Burger was in place. Crowe's own rogue element, Ross Hooper, aka Burger, was an old mate, not very ambitious but good at sitting in cars and staying awake, perfect to keep watch on the main road in case the deliverers needed to be tailed.

None of it made him feel comfortable. Why were they doing this here, now? It felt very wrong.

Crowe didn't like it. Not one little bit. It didn't make sense.

Yet he watched and waited.

An hour passed slowly. He'd moved from boredom into aggravation. The clouds had thinned somewhat, and the moon was making its presence felt a little more effectively. But the wind was colder than it had been, and Crowe's fingers were beginning to complain.

Skarratt and his sidekick hadn't moved. The former might have been looking toward something on the bleak face of the ocean off the end of the breakwater. Crowe peered around the shed wall to see if he could get a better view. Nothing. He could hear a motor though, a deep rumble as though something in the water was hungry and keen for dinner to be served. From the sound it made, it was a motorised dinghy of some sort. It was stupid of him, but he hadn't even considered that because the drop was happening on the breakwater some sort of sea-going vessel might be involved. Taking Pukalski's word on the matter, he'd been waiting for a car to turn up and had positioned himself to keep the entrance road in view. Pukalski hadn't said anything about a boat. Quite the opposite. Crowe cursed, thinking the scenario through: the boys in the dinghy would take the money from Skarratt and hand over their cargo – suspiciously, like kids swapping lollies. Both sides would check their respective packages and back off. The dinghy then motors off toward somewhere unspecified. Maybe a larger ship further out to sea. Skarratt takes his score back to Pukalski and whomever he's working for gets what he wants. Everyone's happy. Well, almost everyone.

Trouble was, Pukalski was driven by greed. He didn't like handing over so much cash, even if it was someone else's. And that's why *he* was here. Crowe was supposed to be a surprise trump card, turning the game back in Pukalski's favour. 'Follow them, do whatever you have to, Crowe,' he'd said. 'Get that money back. Just don't spoil it. But make sure Skarratt's got what I'm payin' for first.'

'How can I make sure he's got the stuff if I don't know what the stuff is?'

'Never mind what the fuck it is! Doesn't matter. It'll be a parcel of some kind. A box maybe. That's enough. I don't want anyone to know I'm involved. Not even Skarratt. And if the bastards end up dead, I won't be cryin' too hard.' Wasn't me, he'd be able to claim, having established an alibi. An outsider did it. A bottom-feeder. God knows who. Most likely, Michael Xavier Crowe.

Crowe dodged quickly across an open space, heading toward the breakwater. Maybe if he could get to the point where the wall of concrete blocks bent out of Skarratt's likely line of sight, he could work something out on the way. He'd been hoping to tail the couriers with Burger's help and deal with them when the opportunity arose. Maybe even find out who was running them. But the boat? That changed the scenario. He hadn't been prepared for it, though he should've guessed.

'Getting sloppy, Mike,' he muttered under his breath. After all, why else have the rendezvous here?

He reached the seawall without being spotted. It was like a giant's game of Tetris that had collapsed in on itself. From behind the barrier of odd-shaped concrete slabs, he couldn't see the ocean, but he could hear it beating hard on the artificial shoreline. The increasingly agitated swell sent a spray of water through gaps and, occasionally, right over the top of the giant lumps of concrete. Crowe edged closer to Skarratt's position, where there was a beacon on a pole, albeit a somewhat ineffectual one in this weather. It wasn't very strong, just enough to be noticeable while making shadows for bodyguards to hide in. From where he was, Crowe couldn't see Skarratt at all now, but he thought he could hear shouting over the roar of the waves. A gull screamed somewhere above him.

Then rapid gunfire cracked in the night. Running forward, Crowe spied a series of flashes and heard someone cry out. Another gun, something smaller, fired. Twice. He abandoned any attempt at stealth and ran full tilt. The stench of old seaweed hung in the air, indistinct under the fumes from the dinghy's exhaust. Moving out from the wall of geometric rocks, he caught a glimpse of Skarratt, leaning over the metal fence at the end of the walkway and looking down toward the water, a black, rectangular object that was no doubt the briefcase dragging on his arm. Crowe couldn't see the bodyguard.

Someone shouted through the puttering of the idling engine, but Crowe couldn't hear them properly over the roar of a wave hitting the rocky barrier near him. A voice replied. He moved along the breakwater, remaining invisible as best he could.

'Get in, Skarratt!' someone yelled. 'Hurry the fuck up!' The boat engine was gunned. Skarratt disappeared over the edge. Crowe leapt into the open. He ran the last few metres to the point where Skarratt had been, dodging around the warning-light pole that he'd forgotten about until he'd almost ploughed into it.

The bodyguard was still in attendance, though not playing an active part. In fact, he wasn't guarding anything anymore and would need to apply for a new job when he reached the over-heated gates of Hell. His killer's semi-automatic had cut him to ribbons. He was lying among the rocks where he'd tried to duck behind cover. It hadn't helped. The briny air smelt like the draught from an abattoir.

What's going on here? Who's double-crossing whom?

Out across the blackish, shifting waves, Crowe could hear the boat sputtering away. It was a darker patch on the perpetually moving ocean, barely visible under the moonshine. Spume was a spectral movement in the gloom. Was it a tinny? He had no way of following. Momentarily he lost sight of the moving shadow and its trailing waves as the dinghy headed further eastward, blocked from sight by the seawall. What had they done with Skarratt? Taken him with them? Was he part of it? Crowe picked up the dead man's dropped weapon – a mini-Uzi submachine gun – and scrambled about to find a convenient hole in the wall. When he caught sight of the boat, he poked the muzzle through the gap and worked the trigger. Flashes lit the air without revealing anything. Water pocked. A cry. Denser noise and more cries between the tiny explosions jerking the gun in his hand. Everything was strangely disconnected.

Crowe released the trigger and pulled back as someone returned fire. Bullets pinged off the rocks near him, but the loosely interlocked blocks protected him while providing plenty of embrasure-like slits to shoot through. It was like being on the battlement of a very damp and crumbling castle.

A distant, barely audible voice started to say something, but stopped when Crowe leaned around the sharp edge of a boulder, just enough to let him make out the shadowy boat. They hadn't got very far out to sea, if that was the aim. He released a burst in the boat's general direction.

Then he heard the engine miss. When it missed again, he grinned and sent off a thank-you to the fickle gods of fortune as it fell silent. Someone on the boat swore and shot rather randomly in the general direction of the spot where they thought Crowe might be. They weren't even close. Furious discussion in indecipherable whispers followed until waves battering the rocks blocked them. Then he heard the sound of the engine refusing to start. Crowe emptied what was left of the magazine at them. Their return fire glanced off the dark surfaces and splashed into the water like hailstones. He fell back to search the dead guard's pockets for a spare magazine. He didn't find one, but he did score a handgun – as luck would have it, a H&K USP45, fully loaded and unfired. He wiped down the Uzi as best he could to erase his fingerprints and tossed it over the barrier into the sea.

The general noise level diminished for a moment, but Crowe did nothing. Neither did the others. All parties were listening for tell-tale sounds. Mutual silence jacked up the volume on the natural ambiance – the sea shifting restlessly, waves smacking on rocks, the wind like a wheezing breath. Curious gulls flapped overhead in the darkness.

A voice whispered something at last. They still weren't far from shore and the wind was blowing in the right direction to help carry the sound to him.

'Shut up!' came another, more loudly, just enough to allow the words to be heard.

Crowe used the voice to get a general line on them and watched without moving. The wind had picked up and a large break in the clouds had increased visibility. Suddenly there was a gleam out in the gloom; some fool had switched on a torch. For a moment, Crowe could see exactly where they were, maybe 60m beyond the rocks. From memory, the H&K was supposed to have good accuracy up to 100m. He could just pick out the three occupants of the boat: one, Skarratt maybe, staring toward the shore; another with a rifle waiting for Crowe to move; a third, with the torch, bending over the engine. None of the three looked like prisoners.

Crowe stepped into the open to get a better view and aimed carefully. Their dinghy was small and as far as he could tell made of fibreglass or even old-fashioned wood. It had been pushed toward the rocks by the waves. Could he hit them in this wind and from this distance? Only one way to find out. He fired. Three times. In quick succession. The bloke with the rifle jerked backwards and fell into the sea with a cry. The light spun off into obscurity, but Crowe kept firing. Maybe he got the others – at least the one near the engine. He couldn't tell for sure.

'You still out there, Skarratt?' he yelled after a moment.

'Who the hell is that?' Pukalski's unreliable courier shouted.

'I've been keeping an eye on you. You've been a naughty boy.'

'Go to buggery!'

'Entirely the wrong attitude, mate. Unfriendly. I've still got plenty of ammo–' he was lying, of course '–a spare magazine, plus what's in this one. What've you got, eh?'

Skarratt didn't reply, but Crowe could hear a sort of rapid splashing sound that told him Skarratt was trying to paddle the crippled boat further out to sea and further around to the right, so they'd be out of

Crowe's sight and out of range. He scrambled up the nearest block and peered across the water. Ignoring the waves splashing high enough to wash him away in the event of a big one, he fired at random. He couldn't go for accuracy, so coverage would have to do.

Sparks erupted in the gloom. A bullet or two had struck the boat's metal fittings at a glancing angle. Water seemed to whisper alight, and suddenly the boat itself was on fire. A superficial fire, thin and blue. Petrol. Skarratt screamed something and tried to beat at the flames. They flared higher and he backed off. Then the whole thing went up.

For a moment, all Crowe could see was the flames sweeping across the water surface like a fiery wind. Detail was lost in the glare. But once it settled back, he could pick out movement. Skarratt had jumped into the sea. He pushed himself toward the rocky platform around the base of the headland. Soon he was totally lost in the heaving waves.

But Crowe knew where he had to go.

5

A LONE FIGURE, HUNCHED UNSEEN ON THE TOP OF THE HEADLAND NEAR the bay's second, functional lighthouse, watched as events unfolded across the restless waters. He was here because something of significance was to take place – the transfer of an object of legendary portent. But he was getting more than he had expected.

He was a scientist, of course, a rationalist. However, though it was an old adage, he believed that 'magic' was just science we didn't yet understand. And knowing what this thing could be used for, could he not himself put it to far better use than the one who had orchestrated this event? Fate, it seemed, was in his favour.

Unexpected interference by a wildcard could be seen as a gift. A reward for his diligence and the righteousness of his deeds.

Momentarily less interested in the sole survivor of the explosion, he gave his attention to the one who'd caused it, though the man was barely visible amid the angular shadows of the rocky breakwater. The watcher was intrigued. The audacity! Was the man familiar? Too far away to tell, even with night goggles.

A voice slithered across his ears. *Why are you so interested in this gangland shit? It's beneath you. Why are you even here?*

'Be quiet. I don't want him to know I'm watching.'

This is not part of the plan. You have more important things to–

The man felt fury boiling up. 'Do *not* question me, if you value your existence. Having an Igor is only of value to me if Igor is neither stupid enough to deviate from my orders nor fool enough to question my actions. That proved to be the downfall of my predecessor. I will not make the same mistake. You will be silent by choice or vivisected by my hand.'

No reply. Was his assistant even there? The man was suddenly unsure. He shook his head.

'Are you there? Answer me!'

Reality was a slippery thing, prone to wild deviances from conventional logic and temporal consistency. It both fascinated and appalled him. He had dedicated his life to creating order, yet always he had to function within a framework of chaos. Sometimes he suspected this 'Igor' was a construct of his own passionate mind, desperate to follow a pattern that had been woven into the world's zeitgeist long ago. He needed an Igor. It was decreed so. But had he brought such a one into existence himself?

No matter. This was an opportunity given to him as a reward, a sign from the god to whom he was seeking to give new life that he could gain redemption.

He scanned the ocean then glanced toward the rock platform, hoping he'd not lost his target. The man was running back along the road that led up from the breakwater and the fleet of moored fishing boats, clearly intending to intercept the survivor where the rocks were less jagged, the water less turbulent. He disappeared behind a concrete wall then reappeared, scampering over a grassy slope below the headland and down onto the rocks.

Good. The man would prevent the swimmer from escaping, while he himself watched, and then perhaps an opportunity would present itself.

He had not chosen this place, but he recalled there was an old Catholic cemetery nearby. And the man carrying the briefcase was roughly the right size to warrant his notice. These elements might be enough to fulfil the necessary requirements. Such spontaneous, unplanned action was not something he was comfortable with, but surely Fate was showing him the way? The one time he had lost his self-control, it had proven disastrous. But *this* time, it felt right. Almost exhilarating. What had seemed not so long ago to be a failure might in fact be more serendipitous than he'd imagined.

The unbelievers called him the Scavenger. It was insulting, a trivialising of his Task. But he would embrace their scorn and scavenge what he could from this evening's events.

Takeaway food, aging and a severe aversion to gyms didn't seem to have affected Crowe's ability to run down the occasional bad guy or disappear quickly when the cops were on the way. Perhaps it was giving up smoking that did it – and not having been blackout-pissed for years.

He reached the base of the headland fast, by running back along the breakwater, across the interconnecting walkway and a neatly grassed slope, and clambering down to the edge of the rock platform – all under the looming presence of the Flagstaff Point Lighthouse at the highest point of the promontory.

Skarratt had to come ashore along here somewhere. He wouldn't be able to make it further, especially not with the briefcase cuffed to his wrist. Crowe needed to get to Skarratt before he could scramble ashore and take off around the reefs below the lighthouse. If he made it to land at all. The waters were heaving restlessly and the rocks were slippery and dangerous. Skarratt's clothes would drag him under unless he was a good swimmer. Suddenly Crowe wondered what had happened to the merchandise Skarratt was supposed to have paid for. Maybe it was at the bottom of the sea. Or had it burnt along with the boat? Neither possibility would make his employer very happy. Oh, well. Maybe he could get Pukalski's money back at least – thank God Aussie dollars were made from plastic, assuming the briefcase Skarratt was carrying it in wasn't waterproof. And he could give the Boss the traitor in his organisation as well. That would have to satisfy him.

Crowe peered across the flat rock platform. Tidal movement swept over its entire expanse. To the side, the shadows of the seaward face of the platform jutted out into the ocean, decorated with white streaks of breaking waves, the fading glow of the burning boat bobbing about restlessly in front of it. But no sign of Skarratt. Could he have reached the shore already? Further around at the base of the cliff, scrub gave way to a shallow slope, then a sharper drop over compacted earth and stone to a tangle of vegetation. From memory, he reckoned there was little more than a sliver of sand and rock fragments on the other side, leading around to the southern beach. If Skarratt made it up from the beach to the main street, he could easily disappear through the cluster of hotels and car yards and on into the houses and business premises beyond.

Crowe ran as fast as he could across the slippery rocks, tore through a stretch of weeds and low reedy bushes, and stumbled down a natural stone ramp, nearly falling headlong into a deep-cut channel that was currently surging with an influx of waves. He squinted through a sudden drizzle, looking for movement that wasn't natural.

He would have missed it if he'd blinked at the wrong moment.

It had to be Skarratt. He'd made it further than Crowe had anticipated, having already reached the beach. Crowe watched as he moved up a rough track that had once given access to a swimming pool and a small clubhouse, long since demolished. Skarratt's movement had become rather awkward. The briefcase was slowing him down, banging against his thigh as he stumbled upward. Crowe dodged quickly in that direction, sticking to the more shadowy places so that if Skarratt looked back he mightn't see his pursuer. The going wasn't easy. The rocky platform was uneven, and when Crowe's feet shattered pools of water, the sound was startlingly loud even against the wind and surf. As Crowe reached the base of the roadway, Skarratt crested the top. Crowe considered shooting him, but at the moment, Skarratt was likely still oblivious to his presence and Crowe wanted to have a chat. He headed up the slope.

Something snapped underfoot. Skarratt glanced around. For a moment, Crowe wasn't at all sure if the man had seen him. Then Skarratt turned away quickly and ducked over the hill. Running. Crowe followed.

By the time Crowe reached the spot where he had last seen Skarratt, the bastard was hightailing it across an open space on the left. Further on, a road led out of obscurity into an avenue of dim streetlights. Moving cars groped about through the rain.

Crowe fired once, but missed, then ran hard as Skarratt ducked into a brake of low she-oaks. Crowe followed.

'Skarratt!' he yelled. 'If you stop, I'll play nice. I promise!'

The thug ignored him, of course. He knew Crowe was lying. Rain had begun to fall again, hard enough that the streetlights ahead became phantoms and the bush turned treacherous. A branch slapped Crowe in the face.

'Skarratt! Give it up!' Crowe yelled as he dashed through a thicket. Beyond Skarratt, low silhouettes, unnaturally straight, stood like a series of pillars and short walls. But he didn't have time to make anything of it. Skarratt was just ahead. He'd slipped on a piece of muddy grass and collapsed onto his arse.

'Who are you?' he shrieked.

Crowe didn't answer.

Skarratt fumbled about, trying to regain his feet, but the bag cuffed to his arm was awkward. It brought him down again.

'No need to rush,' Crowe said, standing over him now while the rain fell on them both. 'Just get up nice and slow.'

'You gonna kill me?' Skarratt whimpered, watching the gun in Crowe's hand.

'I don't know yet. Depends how cooperative you are.'

Skarratt nodded resignedly. Swivelling around onto his knees, he clawed at the surrounding grass to gain traction. His big, stupid '70s porn moustache drooped as though it was slipping into his mouth.

'You got the key to those cuffs?' Crowe asked.

'Hall took them. You shot him before he had a chance to unlock.'

He made it to less treacherous ground, pulled himself up and kept his balance by holding onto a bottlebrush.

'I take it Hall was one of the blokes screwing Pukalski over,' Crowe said. 'Who else? You?'

Skarratt swallowed. 'Dunno what you're talkin' about,' he muttered.

Crowe grabbed him and pulled him out of the bushes. They moved into the open. 'Did you get what Pukalski was after, eh?'

'Sure.'

'Where?'

He started to reach into his coat. Crowe stiffened. Something moved off to his right. Was there someone else here? Maybe whoever had set up the con-job on Pukalski? Wind rustled through the trees. There was something – something that looked barely human, glimpsed briefly as it disappeared from sight. It looked odd – sort of awkward – though, really, it was hard to tell for sure. A low snarl drifted to him out of the gloom.

Then Skarratt hit him with the briefcase.

Crowe staggered. He slid on the slimy grass and fell to one knee. In the process of regaining his balance, his finger tightened on the trigger and a bullet coughed into the ground. It was probably his last.

Skarratt had fled again, scared shitless and not thinking, knowing even if Crowe didn't kill him, Pukalski would, now that he understood who Crowe was working for. Crowe cursed and got up. But before he'd regained his balance something came out of the gust of rain and leapt straight at his chest. He caught a glimpse of a face wearing what appeared to be night goggles. Heard a grunt as he and the phantom collided. Whoever it was raked something sharp down the front of Crowe's clothes. Crowe was forced back. A whiff of dead flesh and mint reached his nostrils, even threw the rain and ocean wind. The thing smashed into him again and this time Crowe caught sight of a wet, open mouth surrounded by a balaclava, screeching incoherently. The attack had caught him on the arm. His leather jacket was cut and watery blood leaked onto his fingers and the grip of the gun. Crowe thrashed out, still unbalanced. His knuckles merely brushed across his attacker's chest. He tried to re-orient himself and shoot toward where he thought the man was, but the gun clicked empty. There was a buzzing sound and the bloke slashed at him again. Crowe backed into low foliage and long grass, trying to gain some distance.

The phantom sprang at him, a featureless shape materialising from the night.

For a moment, Crowe felt fear like a drug-hit tightening his muscles. Whoever this was, he was strong with an intensity Crowe didn't understand. Energy leapt from the unnatural speed of his attacker's movements. Crowe threw the empty gun at him and pulled away.

'Big man!' a voice declared.

Crowe had lost both the rhythm of his defence and his equilibrium. A fist connected with his right cheek. The ground disappeared from under him. He stumbled, trying to grab at the bushes, which were tangling his arms and undermining his attempt to steady himself. Instead, he fell backwards and down. He grappled for a hold. Vegetation tore away, splattering lumps of mud on him as he tumbled. Something hard – a rock perhaps – slammed against the back of his skull. He rolled and his face ploughed into sand.

6

No spectral Lucy stops him this time.

The drive along Kilcairn Creek Road in the night is tough, the trail almost non-existent in places. As Crowe emerges from the off-road and turns toward the township, he passes an old house with a porchlight on and a large bloke standing under it. A van with a ladder strapped to the roof partly obscures him. He watches as Crowe drives into the night. The man wouldn't be able to identify him. Crowe's car is little more than a dim shadow.

He needs to find a phone. Luckily, Kilcairn Creek consists of a country-town main street that hasn't yet been redeveloped by the post-colonial yuppie design squad. It boasts a population of over 900, according to a sign he'd passed on the way in. Where they all are, he doesn't know. An ancient phone booth is leaning against the convict-sandstone wall of a post office.

'Found her,' he says when Waldheim answers the call.

'You're at Merryvale?' Waldheim asks. He demands Crowe bring her back. Not dwelling on details, Crowe tells him the bad news quickly. Waldheim, in near-hysterical anger, calls him a liar at first, then breaks down and cries. The sound of his distress drops away after a bit, and for a few minutes Crowe simply listens to distant sobbing.

'Waldheim?' he says, trying to break through the man's grief. 'You there?'

Someone picks up the receiver. 'You say you found Lucy? Dead?' a woman asks. Eleyn Farnestine is Waldheim's second wife – his first, Lucy's mother, had died of cancer a few years back.

'Murdered,' he says. 'At the Merryvale River place.'

'I see.'

Silence. Farnestine's reaction confirms Crowe's impression that she hadn't cared much for Lucy.

'What do you intend to do?' she continues.

'Report it.'

'You can't bring her back yourself?'

'It was juvenile murder. Looks like she was raped and stabbed to death. You can't pretend she died in her sleep.'

'But a police investigation...it'll be in all the papers.'

'That's the way of things. Any attempt at a cover-up will only create unnecessary suspicion.'

There's more silence. Crowe frowns, wondering what she's thinking.

'Mike?' says Waldheim as he comes back on. He sounds like he's keeping calm only through a superhuman effort of will. 'Find the bastard and do to him what he did to my little girl. You hear me?'

'Sure.'

'Whatever it costs,' he growls. 'The man who could do that to Lucy doesn't deserve to live.'

Crowe agrees, but he says nothing.

Waldheim hangs up and Crowe follows suit. As he turns to leave the phone booth, a wave of delayed nausea hits him, making him stagger out into the night. He takes a moment to regain balance, keeping his eyes shut to suppress the vertigo he's feeling. A sudden gust of wind takes him by surprise. Moments ago, the night had been still under a cloudless sky, the full moon bright against the universe. Where had this come from? He opens his eyes again.

Kilcairn Creek has gone, carried away by the furious weather. Instead, Crowe is in an open space, standing in mud and surrounded by rain and thrashing bushes against a starless backdrop of cloud. To his left, down a rugged slope, rock platforms struggle to escape the pounding ocean swell.

'You must stop him,' says a familiar voice. He turns. It's Lucy, still broken and covered in blood. Eye sockets filled with blood stare at him. Crowe tries to speak, but he can't form words.

Lucy reaches out to him, her hand little more than a white smear.

'Stop him...and find me.' Her lips aren't even moving as the words reach his ears. While he watches, helpless to move, the wind begins to sweep her away, as though she is disintegrating. 'I need your help. Please, Mike, you're my only—'

The words disappear as a stronger gust drags her away.
Crowe slips and falls.

More dreams of Lucy. Recollection mixed with…with what exactly? Fantasies? Delusions? Crowe felt he was at the end of his tether. He didn't know whether or not he'd been unconscious or for how long he lay wedged into the angle between a wind-gnarled tangle of vegetation and the sandy slope. Somewhere beyond, waves roared and savaged the beach, sometimes far away, sometimes so close he could almost feel them spattering him, tugging on his ankles.

'Lucy,' he whispered.

No one answered.

Bugger Skarratt! This was his fault. Though Skarratt hadn't known Crowe was going to be there to interfere with his double-cross, Crowe found it hard not to take the matter personally.

Stop them…and find me. You must help me.

It was clearly Lucy speaking, but it seemed to resonate from all around. Illogically, he closed his eyes against it. It had been very clear this time. Was he going mad? When it didn't repeat, he opened his eyes again. Nothing.

The hard rain had changed to drizzle. Cold water still dribbled down the slope in thick, clay runnels. He pushed himself up on one elbow and glanced around, but the night and the misty rain made his surroundings too obscure. Couldn't see anything clearly.

Stop who? Skarratt? Pukalski? The maniac who'd assaulted him? If it really was Lucy talking, what did she want?

But how could it possibly be Lucy? Lucy had been dead for a decade.

The alternative felt like a cold fire in his gut.

He wondered if Skarratt was still nearby. However long Crowe had been mentally drifting about in his own addled psyche, it was long enough for the shitbag to have cleared out. He and his demented mate were probably at a pub somewhere, chuckling over how it all had panned out. A few glitches, sure, but the loss of two partners meant they'd come out of it with their own lives and a bigger cut of the cash.

He swore into the wind. He hated being taken for a fool.

Apart from the noise of the wind, the area seemed quiet now. Peering through the weeds and tangled kikuyu grass, Crowe looked for signs of human movement, but there was nothing. How long had he been lying in the scrub and sand? It felt like minutes, but it was probably longer. Could have been hours.

He crawled out of the undergrowth and away from the slope, into the open. Still nothing. Stood and looked around. As far as he could see, left to where the she-oaks were still blurred out by rain, and down an incline toward the main road, there was nothing – not Skarratt, nor his mate. Crowe walked in the direction of the carpark, hoping for sign of Skarratt but, failing that, planning to make his way out of the place.

Of course, he didn't expect Skarratt would still be around.

He was wrong.

The clouds cleared for a moment and the moon's death-white light turned the world into a shadowy waxwork display. Skarratt was suddenly visible, lying against a tussock of grass.

Or most of him was.

Both his arms were missing, but Crowe wasn't sure if that or the slash across his throat had killed him. Then there were the hunks of his chest that were gone. It was his left arm Crowe was most concerned with, as it was the one the briefcase had been handcuffed to. But neither arm nor briefcase was in sight.

The smell of blood – as well as the urine and shit Skarratt's body had released as he died – was so strong even the wind couldn't smother it. Gore and blood must have been everywhere, but the drizzle made it hard to tell. Crowe moved as close as he could, stepping on clear patches to avoid leaving footprints in the blood, then he leaned over the corpse and slipped his hand into Skarratt's soggy coat pockets. Nothing. The poor sod's wallet was gone, and there was no sign of whatever Pukalski had been paying for.

The undertaking had been quick and dirty, a vivisection the Scavenger held in contempt. He'd thought it an offering from Fate, but there'd been no time to do his work properly. Besides, all he'd truly wanted was the arm with the briefcase. The object he sought would surely be in the locked metal case.

He had taken both arms as a gesture, nothing more, along with the man's wallet, of course, and a few other fleshy bits and pieces. Naturally, he suspected none of the amputated body parts would be of any use.

They had been spoiled right from the beginning, conditions being what they were. The spiritual groundwork had not been laid beforehand.

Very careless, whispered Igor's voice into his ear. *You condemn me for taking inappropriate action, yet you do this. There was no dignity here. Just a mess.*

He couldn't argue. Igor was right.

But what Igor could not know was that in the tussle, he had seen the big man's face. He'd recognised him. They had crossed each other's path before, years ago before his Great Work had begun. The big man had also been there on the night of his greatest shame, when the love of his life left him. The man had witnessed the aftermath; from his hiding place in the darkness, he had seen the big man's face. The horror and sorrow painted there had haunted him ever since.

It was a revelation, to see him again. So much had aligned tonight that he felt even more certainly there was greater significance in it. He felt more than ever that the path ahead had become clear. The harvest had not been good, but this – *this!* – was a gift.

This man would once again be a witness, not to shame this time, but to apotheosis.

Perhaps, he would be forgiven for his sin.

Perhaps, then, the one who was destined to be his lover would be returned to him.

7

'WHERE IS IT?' SAID PUKALSKI, ARMS CROSSED AGGRESSIVELY, AS CROWE strode into his house and slammed the door behind him.

Crowe had returned home to find his lights on, the telly blaring and his lounge room once again hosting uninvited guests. He really needed to do something about the locks. A large bloke who resembled a mutant cane toad, only bigger and uglier, was on the couch, watching what was no doubt the music-video show *Rage*. Some cookie-cutter model was lip-syncing a bland song while showing off her heartfelt sexuality. The cane toad glanced at Crowe, sneered then went back to the video.

'Brought your lap dog along, I see,' Crowe growled at Pukalski.

Crowe knew from past experience this was Ed Jonwood, otherwise known as The Banger, a nickname he'd acquired because of what he supposedly did to other people's skulls. His suit was a bit too tight for him, so it opened wide across his shoulders, exposing his thick neck and making his head look like an afterthought. He was big, more so than Crowe, and heavier. Pukalski liked having him around – for his muscles rather than his conversation, Crowe guessed, because if he'd ever had any brains, he'd banged them into mush long ago.

Pukalski glared at him.

'You're an idiot, Pukalski,' Crowe said to fill the awkward gap. He stripped off his jacket, which had been soaked by dirty rain and covered in ochre smears. The right sleeve was slit open for half its length. He tossed it on the floor in front of him. Pukalski stared at it as though it might bite. Then he looked at Crowe and the cut on his arm, as defined by congealed blood. The scratch marks on his chest were visible through the tears in his shirt.

Pukalski frowned. 'The couriers give you trouble?'

'Not them.' Crowe flicked off his shoes and headed for the kitchen. Banger stayed in the lounge room, watching the telly with an intense frown, as though it demanded high-level analysis.

'Who then?' Pukalski followed along behind him, like an agitated puppy. 'The merchandise? Did Skarratt get it?'

Crowe began making coffee, barked out a laugh. 'Skarratt got it alright.'

Pukalski kept on. 'Did it go according to plan, Crowe?'

'Depends what plan you mean.'

'The money, Crowe. Did you get it? Quit playing games!'

'Games?' Crowe glared at him. 'What sort of game were we supposed to be playing, Charlie-boy. Doing the deal on a *breakwater* in the middle of the fucking night? What sort of playing field's that?'

'Had to be low profile, that's all. Lots at stake. It's what *they* requested.'

'And who the hell is *they*?' Unsurprisingly, there was no answer. 'I think someone was playing to different rules to the ones you'd been given. I don't know what the deal was all about, Charlie, but the two blokes who came to do the pick-up shot the bodyguard and took off with Skarratt *and* the money. Went out to sea and Skarratt went with them – by choice. Were they really supposed to leave something in return? Or was that part of the game?'

Crowe thought Pukalski was going to choke. 'What? You're kiddin' me?' He stamped about, smashing at the walls with a clenched fist. 'You let 'em get away, I suppose?'

'Not really. I blew up their bloody boat.'

'While they were in it?'

'I asked them nicely to get out, but they begged off – none of them had their budgie smugglers handy.'

Pukalski's cheeks went all flushed and angry. 'Any survivors?'

Crowe poured himself some coffee. 'Skarratt, like the cockroach he was. Swam ashore with the money. I tracked him, caught him. My intuition tells me the merchandise was never anywhere near the action. Like you, Skarratt wanted the money for himself.' Crowe glared at Pukalski. 'Incidentally, what was the merchandise supposed to be, Charlie? Some new designer drug? Seems a few different parties were after it.'

'You don't need to know. Woulda been in a container, I guess… maybe *this* big.' He held his hands apart slightly less than the width of his body.

'Pizza delivery, was it?'

'Shit, Crowe, did you *see* it?'

'No containers, no boxes, nothing.' Crowe poured Pukalski some coffee and handed it to him. 'Damn you, Pukalski – I was very nearly killed because this job was so badly organised. I thought you'd know better than to buy into an arrangement this out of whack.'

Pukalski glared at his coffee as though it might be poisoned. He sipped and swallowed nervously. 'What about Skarratt then? He's got the merchandise as well as the money, right?'

'Don't you get it? Am I being too subtle for you? Skarratt was in on the whole con.' Crowe's repetition of what he'd already said sent Pukalski into a further paroxysm of fury that sent his coffee flying over the kitchen floor. 'Calm down, Charlie,' Crowe urged. 'He got his comeuppance. Some crazy bastard sliced him up.'

Pukalski glared. 'Crazy bastard? What crazy bastard? What the hell are you talking about?' Before Crowe could answer, Pukalski turned suddenly toward Banger and yelled through the open doorway, 'Shut that fucking crap up, Jonwood!'

Banger looked up calmly, shrugged and did what he was told. Then he went back to watching the flickering images on the screen.

Crowe walked through into the lounge room. Pukalski followed. Neither of them sat down. Leaving out the more hallucinogenic aspects, Crowe gave Pukalski the main details of the night, making sure his description of the state of Skarratt's injuries was particularly vivid. As he finished, he dropped into a chair. His skull ached and he was out of Panadol Forte. Hopefully the coffee would help. 'Whoever that crazy bastard was, he took everything with him – Skarratt's arms, the money, the lot. It was no normal killing. More like straight-out butchery.'

'Shit, shit.'

Crowe glanced at Pukalski, who was looking white and sickly.

'Someone else must have known about the fucking deal. You see the attacker? Anyone we know?'

'Too dark. And he took me off-guard.' Crowe made a gesture like a frustrated teacher. 'Come on, Charlie. Can't you see it wasn't some rival of yours?'

'What do you mean?'

'The hack-and-slash MO? The whole souveniring of body parts? Isn't it obvious?'

Pukalski looked as much bemused as angry.

'The Scavenger, for fuck's sake! The Scavenger's been stalking the South Coast for months. Cutting up his victims. The media's been obsessed with him and the cops are getting nowhere.'

'A serial killer?' Pukalski scowled. 'You sayin' some random serial killer stumbled on my business deal in the middle of the fucking night?' He cursed some more and struck the wall so hard the plaster shook along the room's cornices.

'Go easy! I'm renting. Want to get my security deposit back.'

'It was some random nutcase that took everything?'

'That or someone trying to deflect our attention.'

'So an inside job?'

'It already was an inside job, Charlie, with Skarratt doing the old double-cross. How often do I have to say it?' He sighed. 'So who else, besides you, knew about the money?'

'Just Skarratt. Even the bodyguard didn't know.'

'You sure?'

'Yes, for fuck's sake!'

Crowe shrugged. 'Well, Skarratt could've told anyone.'

Pukalski scowled.

'But the murder,' Crowe reiterated. 'It didn't feel *normal*. Look what the bastard did to me. Does this look like part of anybody's plan to you?'

'This Scavenger bloke couldn't have known, could he? And from what I've heard, he only collects body parts. Why would he take the briefcase?'

'Curiosity? A souvenir?'

Pukalski stared at him, squinty-eyed. 'What a fuckin' mess! You really blew this whole job, Crowe.'

'The hell I did. You stuffed up with your misinformation and withholding. If I'd known about the boat, I could've prepared for that, at least. It's all on you, Charlie. I guess your employer won't be too happy, eh?'

Pukalski stared at him with the sudden realisation of some terrible fate.

'How did you–'

'I guessed. Who is he anyway?'

Pukalski moved toward the slouching form of Banger – who kept staring at whatever soundless performance was currently taking place on the telly – and stood with his back to Crowe. Pukalski was trembling. No one said anything for a while. Crowe wondered who the hell the poor sod was going to have to answer to.

While Pukalski seethed, Crowe went back into the kitchen and poured himself a refill. 'Want another cuppa to chuck around?' he shouted to Pukalski, who grunted in the negative. Crowe sauntered back into the other room, and with strained goodwill, they discussed the finer points of Skarratt's betrayal and culpability. Without much conviction, Pukalski took a stab at accusing Crowe of running the whole deal. Crowe just laughed at him.

Pukalski glared, then blinked and looked away. 'Any idea how we can find out who the fuck was behind it?'

Crowe sighed wearily. 'I'd love to say Skarratt, but I doubt that's true. He doesn't have a rep as a logistics genius.'

'Well, whoever it was, I want the money back,' Pukalski said, 'and it's vital I get what we were paying for. It's important. Big-time important.'

'What was it? What's worth 200 million bucks, fits in a box a bit smaller than your ego, and has to be picked up at the end of a breakwater in the middle of the night?'

'Doesn't matter to you *what* it is,' Pukalski growled. 'I want to know *where* it is, that's all. I want it. Here.'

'What can *I* do?' Crowe sipped his coffee and exuded indifference.

'Do what you're supposed to be good at: investigation. Find it. Get it all back. If this disaster takes me down, you're in deep shit, too.'

Crowe just stared at him.

'And I don't buy this Scavenger crap,' Pukalski added. 'Doesn't make sense. Someone else was after the money – and the merchandise. You don't find them, you're done, Crowe. But I'll skin Gail first while you watch, then I'll do the same to you. Understood?'

'Oh, sure. I understand alright.' Crowe came closer to him, exuding a completely false conversational ease. 'But I want the details – all of them.'

Pukalski scowled, scratched at his neck. 'All you need to do is track whoever killed Skarratt and took off with the money, and hope like hell he's got the other stuff, too. Nothin' else.'

'I'll want to know how the deal was set up. And what the merchandise was.'

Pukalski shook his head in a stupidly dramatic manner that made him look like a pantomime doll. 'You don't need to know. That's my business.'

Crowe had gravitated toward Banger while talking. The big man glanced up just as Crowe's coffee mug smashed against the side of his head. Stunned, he tried to reach for his gun, but Crowe pounded on his temple, then reached inside the thug's coat and pulled out the weapon. It was like him – huge and unsubtle. An older Smith & Wesson Magnum by the look of it. Who the hell did he think he was? Clint Eastwood? Pukalski had produced a smaller handgun by then. But Crowe had been quicker. He'd drawn his Beretta out of his shoulder holster and pointed it at Pukalski, even though he knew it was empty, while in his other hand the Magnum stayed locked on Banger. Pukalski swore and dropped his gun on the floor. 'Shit, Crowe!' he whined.

'Okay, enough of this buggerising about.' Crowe shoved him onto the lounge next to Banger. Pukalski flopped, seeming to shrink as the cushions sank under him.

'What the hell?'

'Tell the Not-So-Incredible Hulk to stay right where he is.'

Banger appeared to have cleared his head enough to react. He was pulling himself up, glaring fiercely. Pukalski gestured for him to sit. As soon as the big man did, his eyes edged back toward the telly.

'What do you think you're doing?' said Pukalski indignantly.

Putting his own gun back in its holster, Crowe moved closer and let the muzzle of Banger's big gun press against Pukalski's temple. The Boss Man went glum and defensive.

'I haven't enjoyed the past week much.' Crowe pressed hard on the barrel, feeling the skin yield. 'Getting pushed around makes me a bit touchy and having someone refuse to tell me what I need to know makes me even grumpier. So, listen close. I've got a theory. Want to hear it?'

Pukalski scowled.

'Fine. I knew you'd be keen. Here's what I reckon. Someone – someone who has you well and truly in their pocket – wanted whatever's in the box and got you to broker the deal. I'm guessing he's not a workaday inhabitant of the criminal world, right, but some powerful outsider. Politician? Movie star? Internet über-genius? Whatever. So, he gives you the money then waits for you to do your bit. But you, being a useless and greedy bastard, can't resist the temptation. Why just get your agreed retainer? You want it all. Sure, you've got to get your hands on the box, but once you've got it, why let all that nice money disappear? Instead, you bring in a freelance scapegoat – me – so he can do the deed for you and take any flak that might arise. How am I doing?'

Pukalski's left eye twitched, but he remained silent.

'So the long and the short of it is: your greed's landed you in deep shit, and the free-range lunatic compounded it. Your employer is going to be expecting to get the whatever and will want to know why there's a delay. I guess you can hide your personal culpability for a while, but he'll start asking embarrassing questions sooner or later, and then things might go very pear shaped indeed.'

'It's bullshit, Crowe.'

'I tell you what, Charlie. I'll find your bullshit money and your bullshit "merchandise", whatever the hell it is, not because you worry me in the slightest, but because I'll be damned if some nutter is going to get the better of me. By the way, I'll expect not just the 10 grand, but another 50 grand on top.'

'No chance.'

Crowe raised one eyebrow at him. 'Really?' He leaned closer and lowered his voice. 'I'll need information, too. Particularly about whatever you were paying for and how the delivery was organised. And I need to be left alone.' He pulled back and shrugged. 'Or I can just pull the trigger, here and now, if you'd rather. Save me a lot of grief in the long run, I reckon. In fact, maybe that's the best option.'

Suddenly Pukalski looked worried, but not about Crowe's threat. 'It's dangerous knowledge, Crowe, honest. And personal.'

'Getting kicked about, shot at, stabbed and clawed is pretty personal, too. I'm listening.'

Pukalski resisted for a moment, staring at Crowe, weighing his meagre options. After a few long, drawn-out seconds, he breathed out and gave up. Crowe knew it by a loosening of his shoulders. 'Okay, okay. Just take *that* bloody thing away from me!'

Crowe emptied the bullets onto the floor and tossed the gun onto Banger's lap. The big man didn't even move, eyes still on the screen. *Jesus*, Crowe thought, *talk about a one-track mind*. He walked over to where Pukalski's gun had landed and picked it up.

'It's locked,' he said, unlocking it. 'That wouldn't have been much use.'

Pukalski sat like a deflating dummy, his body adopting the contours of the lounge chair. He began rubbing at his temples.

'Well?' Crowe growled, waving the gun at him.

'Okay, okay, for fuck's sake.' Pukalski's eyes had lost most of their fire. He looked like a man on the edge of an abyss. 'This could ruin me, Crowe. To be honest, I'm in a lot of debt to the client I'm acting for. If he finds out what I did and loses the merchandise, he's not likely to be very forgiving.' Pukalski made a gesture meant to convey the unfairness of fate. 'He doesn't want his name connected to this and I don't intend to tell you anything more about that.' He shrugged. 'He still trusts me right now, but...I was looking out for Number One. As long as he got the merchandise, he wouldn't have given a shit what happened to the money. If I don't get it back...'

He must have found Crowe's stare rather cynical, because he scowled, screwing his jowls into mutant donut rings.

'You wanna hear this or not?'

Crowe made a faux-helpless gesture. 'I'm all ears.'

8

Parts of Pukalski's story made sense: it involved one of the biggest celebrity scandals of the past few decades, a dream scoop for the gossip mags. Gail would have been thrilled to hear it. Crowe, not so much.

On the 21st of September 2015 a navy 1997 Panoz Esperante GTR-1 took a corner badly while negotiating a particularly mountainous part of the Deutsche Alpenstrasse in Bavaria. Despite its sleek, aerodynamic beauty, the car lost its grip on the road and plunged to its destruction. Officially three people died that day: the driver, a male passenger and, most significantly, Marika Kucera, the US-born singer and movie star. As far as cultural icons went, Kucera was at the top: at least three of her albums were well on the way to selling more copies worldwide than Fleetwood Mac and Michael Jackson combined, and her recent Oscar-winning performance in the Hollywood blockbuster *The Last Queen* had her name on everyone's lips. She was both famous and infamous – the subject of endless column inches for her affairs, real and imagined, with politicians and movie stars, both male and female, on top of a hectic schedule of high-society events and promotional appearances. Then there was her extensive human rights work as well.

She was deeply loved and jealously reviled by a massive worldwide audience. Her stunningly beautiful face and fashionably dressed body regularly graced the covers of magazines and journals. If that wasn't enough, she was also descended from one of the royal families of a certain European state. A unique nexus of beauty, brains, breeding, money, status, and privilege.

After the accident, barely alive, she was delivered by helicopter to a hospital in Salzburg where doctors fought to save her. A few hours later, Queen Marika was pronounced dead.

This much was common knowledge. What was not known, although it *was* the subject of the usual cyberspace controversy, was the fact that someone else had been in the car that night: her unborn child.

Crowe looked at Pukalski impatiently. 'Why are you feeding me this celebrity bullshit, Charlie?'

'Isn't it obvious?' Pukalski's attempt at superior intellect came over as an amateur theatrical rendition of severe constipation. 'That's what I was acquiring for my client.'

'Marika Kucera's kid?'

'Her *never-born* kid.' Pukalski rubbed his forehead, as though he was so weary his head needed remodelling.

'You're joking? You mean, someone pinched the foetus, pickled it or whatever and put it up for sale on eBay?'

'Not eBay. The acquisition channels have been deep. The deepest. And very dark.'

'But why would anyone pay millions for some shrivelled thing?'

'It's a hot item, Crowe, a *thing* like that…for the right person. Good investment.'

'It's not like gold bars, is it? Don't see it myself.'

'Well, my client does. Five million bucks worth of *does*. So, I guess you're gonna have to get interested, too. 'Cause I want it back, Crowe. You intend to get on with finding it or what?'

Crowe said nothing. He'd been expecting conflict diamonds or a valuable painting – say, a newly discovered da Vinci *Madonna and Child*. Something predictable – maybe the plans to a government superweapon. But this? He felt like he'd been plunged into a comic netherworld and his bearings were somewhat off-kilter. Did it make any sense at all? A dead celebrity and her dead baby? What did one do with a foetus? Put it on the mantelpiece, use it as a hood ornament?

'It's bullshit,' Crowe muttered.

'Crowe?'

Crowe glanced at Pukalski, who frowned imperiously. 'I got a family,' he said, and it struck Crowe as a bit late to remember this when Charlie had been so intent upon banging Gail. 'A wife and kids, you know. I don't want them to get involved. If I don't get that withered runt of a thing back, my client *will* involve them. He'll involve *me*. I could lose most of my business concerns. My life wouldn't be worth shit.'

'Must really be nasty, this mystery man, to get you this worried. I assume he's some sort of businessman dash hoodlum, hiding behind piles of money. A bit like you, only better at the game.'

Pukalski gave a cynical laugh. 'Nah, in fact, he's pretty clean, according to the law. No mobster.'

'What then? He's rich enough to get you killed? Can't you off him first?'

'Sure, though he's got it set up so he'd ruin me no matter what.' He grunted. 'Everything would go to hell. I'd be worse than dead. Apart from holding me to ransom, this guy's a...' He paused. 'He's not overly stable.' He melodramatically lowered his head to his cupped hands. 'He wields a lot of power and influence. Power largely hidden but known to those of us he has...let's say *adopted*. If he finds I've played him false...' He paused again, uncertain. 'I'm not a religious man, Crowe, but he would eat my soul for breakfast!'

'You've got a soul?'

'We all have, Crowe,' he said without acknowledging Crowe's facetious tone. 'And he knows how to make it burn in hell. Literally.'

Crowe's indifference to his own post-death fate was almost overwhelming, even if it meant his soul would get fried, but he suppressed the urge to say so. 'What is this bloke? Some sort of sorcerer?'

'Exactly. In some circles, both loved and feared.'

Crowe shook his head. Sometimes he found the stupidity of people exhausting.

'So, okay, what was the deal? They give you the mummified foetus in a miniature coffin for five million bucks?'

'Something like that.'

'In the middle of the night on a darkened jetty in Wollongong of all places?'

Pukalski shrugged. 'Why not? My employer won the auction.'

'There was an auction?'

'Of course.'

'And I take it he lives nearby.'

'That's no concern of yours.'

Crowe huffed. 'Well, none of it sounds very likely.'

'I assure you, Crowe, it's the truth. And it's important.' He squinted at Crowe.

'Then why the hell would you trust Skarratt to do the job?'

Ignoring the question, Pukalski leapt up and began to pace. Banger glanced at him briefly, grunted, then let his mind drift back to whatever it had been doing, which had the appearance of nothing at all. *Rage* had finished and he had moved on to infomercials on a different channel.

'How do you know they even had it?' Crowe added. 'Seems clear to me you were set up from the beginning.'

Pukalski glanced at him. 'I was told they did. It was guaranteed. Impeccable source. It's not something you joke about.'

'And you believed them? You don't even know who the buggers are.'

'My employer does. He took care of the initial contact.'

'Then it's his fault. Tell him so.'

'Fuck!' Pukalski kept pacing. It was like being in a room with a chimpanzee on speed. 'I know the deal wasn't airtight, but what choice did I have? It was that or nothing.'

'They sure knew a sucker when they saw one.'

'At the very least I have to get the money back, right?'

'Right.'

He collapsed into the first chair he came to, as though his puppeteer had gone off for a pee break. 'You can't trust *anyone* anymore,' he growled.

'Either way, you're pretty well screwed,' Crowe remarked, handing him his gun.

Pukalski and his giant cane toad went home as the eastern sky was beginning to lighten. Pukalski lost his temper at Banger about the TV, allowing some of his frustration and fear off the leash. Amused, Crowe saw them out then had a shower.

So: Crowe's task was to find whoever had killed Skarratt and taken the money and a dead celeb foetus. He didn't believe the last item existed. It made no sense. It was like something out of an old pulp novel. Pukalski had to be lying. Crowe could see it and hear it clear as a bell. Some other dumb-arse business was being played here and it involved something, and someone, more important to Pukalski than a lost foetus. For five million, he could buy any number of dead babies and pickle them to his heart's content. Pukalski's employer wouldn't have known the difference. Unless he did a DNA test. On second thoughts, maybe that's just what he *would* do.

His phone rang about six. He picked up, thinking it might be Gail. But no one spoke, there was just the hissing of the telephone lines, then a click as someone hung up.

9

'— HOPE.'

This place I'm always dragged back to…it's lightless. Probably cold, too, though I've lost the ability to feel that much. Sometimes I walk up and down the corridors – not looking for a way out, because I don't think such a thing exists, but hoping to meet someone, anyone. Why am I trapped here? I ask the Darkness. Why can't I get out? Why am I alone? Then, for a moment, I remember why. Dry tears well up, and I call out, aware of the horror that lies ahead of me. 'Let me go!' I cry. 'I don't want to stay here forever.'

Looking through the small, barred windows in the doors of each empty room I pass, I see no other inhabitants. In some, at various times, light flickers on the dank walls. A dull, sickly light. But it draws me toward it and I try to go in, just to soak up whatever light there is, but I can't. The doors resist my every attempt to open them.

Soon, the past slides away from me, and once again I can't recall why I'm here. Time passes slowly. Or quickly. I can't tell which. Perhaps it doesn't pass at all.

Then a man slips into my thoughts, and with that memory, others appear that are combined into an unstable and erratic story. A terrible story, a fearsome one, rich with violence and betrayal. Only slivers of light inside it give me hope. But then the light itself, wanting to claim me, becomes a source of fear.

The man stands before me.

'Help me!' I call to him, the man whose name I sometimes remember. 'Don't let him have it.' Then, 'Find me! Find me…please!'

I think, occasionally, I face him for real, in the outside world, not just in a dream.
I have a feeling it happened recently. Maybe this time, too.
 But the man turns away, fading from view, and soon I have forgotten him.
 Soon, for the moment, I forget myself.
 But never for long…

The story of Skarratt's murder didn't appear in the next day's tabloids but only because his body wasn't found until about 5 am., too late for the early edition. Local news on Radio National was full of it, however. The newsreader deadpanned over the mutilated corpse of a male about 35 being discovered near Wollongong beach, its arms cut off. Not far away, near the historic Belmore Basin lighthouse, he said, another body was found, identified by police as a known offender whose death was likely the result of gang rivalry. There was no mention of the burnt-out boat or any other bodies. And no dead foetus in a bottle.

'There has been speculation that the mutilation of the first man is the work of the so-called Scavenger, although it has not been confirmed by police,' the newsreader said. 'The previous serial murders have not shown evidence of criminal association. At present, no one is sure whether this latest incident throws new light on investigations or whether it is simply unrelated.'

Like most folk, Crowe knew only what the headlines trumpeted about the killings: that people were dying. Unlike everyone else, however, he knew the criminal underworld was as ignorant about the so-called Scavenger's identity as the police. He also knew that ordinary crims had no liking for serial killers: they messed everything up for everyone, brought heightened scrutiny from both media and cops, made politicians more vocal about zero tolerance on crime.

Someone like the Scavenger was bad for everyone's business.

Seeing the state of Skarratt's body, Crowe had immediately thought of the so-called Scavenger, and the weird violence that had been directed at him in the lead-up to the messy dismemberment pointed him toward the same conclusion. But the more time that passed, the more he liked the alternative possibility: Skarratt's death was really the calculated work of someone who knew what was going down that night, knew what was in the briefcase, and had hacked off Skarratt's arm to get it. That would make for a more straightforward investigation.

Gail rang about two.

'How'd it go, Mike?' she said.

'Complete wash-out.' Crowe explained what had happened. For the time being, he skipped the weird shit about Queen Marika's unborn baby. He didn't know what to make of that, and until he was sure it wasn't just some con invented by Pukalski to muddy the waters, he'd keep it to himself.

'The police have been busy with the Scavenger almost exclusively,' said Gail. 'They're not happy about it.'

'Well, now it might be my turn to be unhappy.'

'To be fair, you're an unhappy guy.' Her tone shifted to serious. 'You're going to keep working for Charlie then?'

'I don't like leaving things unfinished,' he said. 'And there's stuff here I don't understand.'

'Pukalski's heavying you?'

'If I don't do this for him, I'll be fighting off his gorillas until one of us is dead. And then maybe someone else, someone who's yanking his strings, someone he's extremely wary of. That'd be a bugger. But that's not the point. I want to do the job anyway. Skarratt's not going to cheat me.'

'Cheat you? He's dead.'

'Till I find the money, he's cheated me. Scavenger or not, I'll find who took it – and take it back.'

She said he was crazy, but what the hell? It was his life. Right?

PART TWO
ROADS TO REBIRTH

10

CROWE DECIDED HE NEEDED A BETTER GRASP ON THE SCAVENGER CASE before looking elsewhere, and that led him eventually to the Wollongong University Library and its access to assorted databases, not the least of which included the State Library of New South Wales' collection of newspapers. He had to go through a registration process, though as an inhabitant of the Illawarra he was granted guest membership without anyone raising a suspicious eye. Digitalisation had certainly made it easier to access public information.

First mention of what was referred to as the Scavenger's work was in the *Illawarra Mercury* of 9 October 2017. Two kids scrabbling about in the rubbish depot at Helensburgh came upon a headless body dressed in a tracksuit but no joggers – and no feet to put them on. His right arm was gone, too. The corpse had been there for some time, buried under a heap of old tyres, but eventually it was identified as James McEnoy, 36, an electrician. McEnoy had been reported missing from his home near Knowslay Park a couple of weeks before. As always, he'd gone out late for a jog. What was less usual was his failure to return. Everyone, including his wife, thought he'd run off with another woman. Apparently, he occasionally did that.

It was only when reports of other mutilated bodies were unearthed that talk of a serial killer began. The newspaper report listed two previous mutilation murders.

In early July of 2017, the body of Shane Williams, 38, had been discovered near the railway station at Bombo Beach, just on the Wollongong side of Kiama. Williams, who hailed from interstate, was some sort of writer and had wanted to visit the blowhole as 'research'. The body had suffered the same kind of mutilation – in this case the careful removal of both arms and his head, along with random bits and pieces. At the time, the cops had thought the beheading might have been an ill-considered attempt to hide the identity of the victim, but if so, his killer wasn't very smart – Williams' notebook was found nearby, full of identifying information.

A month later, Cecil Stambridge, 45, had been murdered sometime after losing a round of golf at Shellharbour course, where he played regularly. Friends discovered his mangled corpse at the edge of the swamplands. He'd kept his head, but both legs, a quantity of skin and assorted other body parts were missing, including his ribcage. His throat had been cut first, police thought, though it hardly seemed to matter. Even then no one was making any connection between the two killings.

McEnoy's murder made the link obvious and a few days later, police were forced to admit they had reason to suspect that all three killings – and another uncovered on the same day McEnoy's was hitting the headlines – were the work of one man. Reporters claimed to have already been seeing patterns. Three murders: one at Kiama, one at Shellharbour, one at Helensburgh. Each victim had had bits of his body removed and his wallet pinched. Robbery then, but of body parts as well as property. Each was male and roughly the same age and of similar build. No attempt had been made to conceal the bodies. Only in one case was there evidence that the victim had not been both killed and dismembered in the same place: the first one had had his throat cut just beyond the entrance to the station, but his body had been dragged to a secluded spot on the beach for decapitation. No women, no sex murders, no ethnic or indigenous victims, no kids; but what the reporters were onto still looked like something with potential, even if no one had any ideological interest in Caucasian males. The press was having a field day.

Then Jerry Stoneman was found on the beach at Wombarra. He'd been killed a month after McEnoy, to the day. Stoneman's fingers, both feet and large sections of his torso, including his backbone and some ribs, had been removed. He was discovered among rocks but had probably been killed elsewhere. The tide had sucked him into the sea, and he might have floated some distance. He wasn't in good shape.

After that, everyone got very nervous. Police were starting to look harassed. Journalists everywhere were using the term 'The Scavenger' by then. The papers were full of amateur psychological profiles and police were appealing for help from anyone who'd noticed an acquaintance acting in an odd way. That resulted in half the population being dobbed in. Otherwise, they didn't seem to have a clue.

But then nothing happened until 2 January 2018. No one knew why the Scavenger missed December – maybe the body was simply never found. But apparently, he wanted to start the year as he meant to go on. Garry Hants, a middle-aged pool attendant at the Croome Road Sports Complex, Albion Park, was discovered in nearby Frazers Creek, minus his legs and, again, bits and pieces of his torso, this time with most interest directed toward the pelvic region.

In early February, John Donau, 30, was found in Ocean Park at Woonona. He'd lost patches of skin, most of his chest and back, some fingers, one hand and his left leg.

This was followed by Paul McCartney, late of Emu Plains. Mr McCartney – who was said by friends to have resembled a shorter Ringo Starr rather than his namesake – had been on holidays with his wife, Janice, in a caravan at the Bulli Holiday Park. McCartney was found in the morning of March 3, floating face down in the swimming pool on Waniora Point at the northern end of Bulli Beach. He was missing one leg – his right – and one arm – his left, including the shoulder blade – and again, large slices of flesh and skin.

Suddenly Crowe sensed a looming presence. He glanced around at a tall figure in a tacky grey overcoat.

'Doing family research?' The bloke's nose looked like a turnip. Most of his face was covered in a brown and grey beard. 'Tracing ancestors, eh? More people doing that now than I've ever seen before. What d'ya think it means?'

He leaned over Crowe, squinting at the image of the newspaper on the screen in front of him and puffing like he was on his last legs.

'Social dislocation. That's what I reckon,' he added.

'You're in my light,' Crowe said.

'Old papers are really somethin', eh?' the intruder said. His breath smelt of Victoria Bitter and something more rancid. He brushed dangling tufts of sticky-looking hair out of his eyes. 'They use ta report murders in detail back then – twenties and thirties. All the details. You can get transcripts of whole trials, ya know.'

'It's not an old paper.'

'No? Whatcha doin' then?'

'Reading,' Crowe said.

'Why?'

'Are you a student here or something?'

The man grinned. 'You could say that, but you'd be lyin'.'

Crowe's tolerance, such as it was, had had enough. 'Look, I hope I'm not keeping you from something more important,' he said between clenched teeth.

'Hey, I'm retired. Nothin's so important anymore.'

'Just go and do nothing somewhere else, okay?'

Crowe returned to scanning the database index for more Scavenger references. The next murder, if there had been one, would appear around the end of March, beginning of April sometime, if it followed the rather loose pattern. The dero was still there, peering over Crowe's shoulder at the notes he'd been making. He was wearing a pair of wire-rim glasses now.

'Piss off, mate,' Crowe said, not as affably as last time.

The old guy grinned and Crowe kept reading, ignoring him. There was nothing in the rest of March and April was a dud.

'Maybe they didn't find the one he did that month,' the man said. 'Like December last year, and September, too.' There was considerable conjecture in the newspaper about just such a possibility. It was also thought, optimistically, that the killer might have stopped, even though expert opinion was unimpressed by this idea. 'A psychopathic sadist so far into a series of public, and obviously attention-seeking, crimes is unlikely to go back to some normal lifestyle,' a psychologist was quoted as saying.

'Try the 30th of May,' the old man muttered. 'Or probably the next day or so, depending on when the body was found.'

'What?' Crowe glared at him.

'There was a full moon on the 30th of May,' the dero said.

'Full moon?'

'Sure.' He stuck his lips out from the bristles of his ragged beard in a knowing manner. 'All those others – most of 'em, anyways–' he indicated Crowe's notes '–they were around the full moon.'

'You think he's a werewolf?' Crowe said, emphasising the sarcastic tone.

'Ain't no such thing as werewolves.' The man looked at him with equally obvious disgust. 'Don't believe in that crap, do ya?'

'What's the moon got to do with it then?'

The old bloke giggled. 'Look, werewolves didn't *need* the full moon, you know. That was a Hollywood addition to the legends. Lycanthropes were magicians. Could choose when the hell they changed.' He laughed to himself. 'It's real-life loonies that like the full moon. Levels of family violence rise around then. Increased psychological pressure, they reckon, caused by the moon's proximity. But in mystic circles, it's an auspicious time.'

Auspicious? Crowe scowled up at him. 'You're an expert, eh?'

The man smiled. 'I just keep track of the lunar phases. And the Scavenger kills around the full moon. So, he's either a werewolf, he's reacting to subconscious urges created by tidal pressure, or maybe the full moon holds some special importance for him. You know, something important happened then. Anyway, check it out for ya'self. Go on! The 30th.'

Crowe clicked on the link for the *Mercury* of 31 May 2018. He was pretty sick of staring at the computer screen by then and it was affecting his mood. If the old bloke's suggestion proved a bust, he was likely to take it out on the smartarse. But the headline read: 'New Scavenger Killing. Man skinned in park.'

'You were right,' he said.

'Sure. Used to be a crime reporter.' The old bloke lowered himself into a chair next to Crowe's.

Crowe looked at him. 'A crime reporter?'

'Used to be.' The man shrugged. 'Gave the killer his name. Scavenger. Wrote a lot of the early articles. Wrote this one.'

Crowe huffed sceptically then read the article without looking at the journalist's name.

Lester Henry, 33, had been killed on Monday night on his way to or from the golf course, where he used to go for walks after working late.

His body was found in J.J. Kelly Park behind bushes near the creek. His throat had been cut, large sections of his chest stripped away, and his entire ribcage removed. Apparently, his sexual organ had been carefully amputated – the Scavenger must've been impressed by it.

'Nasty, ain't it?' commented the old man.

Crowe looked up. 'So, you're a journalist?'

'Was.'

'Name?'

'It's there on the by-line. Bugden. Leonard Bugden.'

The old codger was a pest, but Crowe had started to like him, even if he doubted the man was a journalist. He reached into his pocket and extracted $5. 'Here, *Len*,' he said, handing it to his unofficial research assistant, 'go get yourself a cup of coffee!'

The old bloke took it but didn't get up. 'I'll wait for ya and we can have a beer together.'

Crowe frowned.

'I wanna help,' the man added. 'And you can skip June and July. No bodies were found.'

'None?'

'The papers were stuffed with speculation he'd gone or moved on or some such wishful thinkin'. But he was just markin' time, or maybe he took the bodies home with him. Any rate, his next victim was found in August, about the 26th, I'd guess.'

'Yeah?'

'Yep, check it out.'

The old guy was right. Victim number nine wasn't found until late August – on the last day of the full moon. His body, or what was left of it, had been found cut up at the back of the Grandstand at Kembla Grange Racecourse. His head was missing. So were both his arms. The Scavenger had filched bits of intestine, and bone and skin from all over Charley Kevens' body, which had been sawn into lots of little pieces.

'Minor parts,' Crowe's audience commented.

'What?' Crowe said.

The old bloke leaned back in his chair. 'When you do a major reconstruction of, say, an old car, you get big parts like new doors or an engine or wheels. But ya also need stuff like bits of metal for mending rust holes. Valves and bits of wiring. You know?'

He looked at Crowe expectantly. It was bizarre, but Crowe had to admit it made some sort of grotesque sense.

'You heard what went on last night?' Crowe asked.

The old bloke sang a few bars of a song, rather badly.

Crowe frowned at him. 'What?'

'Beatles.' The man grinned, showing his yellow teeth. '*Sgt Pepper's* album. Heard the news, you know? *Oh, boy.*'

Crowe said nothing, puzzling about why he was bothering to talk to this bloke. Maybe he felt sorry for him. He seemed so eager.

'So, when was the full moon this month?'

'Couple of nights ago.'

Of course it was. The night of the Belmore Basin fiasco. With the moon mostly obscured by clouds, Crowe had never had its phases in mind. 'You reckon this latest murder was part of the Scavenger thing then?'

'Exactly the same, 'cept for the shootin' that went down.'

Crowe looked back over his chaotically scribbled notes. 'What he's taken looks pretty random to me,' he said. 'Filched more than one of some things: two heads, lots of legs and feet; he took both Skarratt's arms. He already had arms. Why would he want more than two?'

The old man shrugged. 'Spares?' he said, his light brown eyes glinting behind his glasses.

11

CROWE HAD ONLY TURNED A CORNER OR TWO ON HIS WAY BACK FROM THE university when he twigged to the undue attention being paid to his movements by a scrappy Falcon ute. It had been firmly ensconced in his rear-view mirror. Suspicion fixed itself in his mind and shoulders and he kept glancing back, taking a long way home. The car was still following him by the time he crossed the railway bridge at Coniston. Same distance behind. He couldn't make out the driver's features – the Falcon's windscreen was grubby, and the setting sun was flashing off the dirt, obscuring his view. He made a few more unnecessary and unlikely turns, approaching Mt St Thomas via Heaslip Street and Mangerton, and the ute stayed with him the whole convoluted way. Nothing subtle about it. It was like being tailed by Batman and Robin trying to be incognito while driving the Batmobile around Gotham City in broad daylight.

Crowe led his stalker back to Gladstone Avenue and kept going until he came to a stretch of road away from houses and with a bit of privacy. Then he stopped. There wasn't much the ute could do. Even if he were a complete amateur, the driver would realise that pulling up behind his target would make his intentions ridiculously obvious. As he passed, Crowe got a good look: his old mate from the uni library.

Crowe shoved his BMW into first and went after him. He overtook, cut in front of the man's heap and jammed on the brakes, hoping the old guy had the presence of mind to do likewise. He did, and his pile of junk stalled. Crowe was out of his car and yanking open the driver's side of his stalker's car before he could start up again. The bloke bared his yellowing teeth as Crowe pulled the Beretta from his belt holster.

'What the hell are you doing, old man?' Crowe growled.

'I'm not that old.' Suddenly Bugden (if that *was* his name) garbled some lines of a song. Something about someone shooting his brains out at traffic lights.

'Let me guess. Beatles, right?'

'Yeah. Great song that.'

'Bit grim for the Top 40. Never catch on.' Crowe pointed the barrel of his gun toward him.

The man pulled away, more surprised than afraid. 'Hey, Mr Crowe, what's that for?'

'So, you know me, eh?' Crowe said. 'Then you must have some inkling as to what I do to people who spy on me. What do you mean by following me around?'

The old bloke grinned. The bits of his face that didn't have hair on them wrinkled up like crumpled tissue paper. 'Hey, told ya. I was a reporter. I recognised ya in the library, from the time maybe three years ago when you got mixed up in that council hotel deal–'

Crowe wished, not for the first time, he could wipe out all newspaper references to himself in one fell swoop. 'So?'

'So, I was curious. Goin' after the Scavenger, aren't ya?' His oddly youthful eyes narrowed.

Crowe pulled back. There was no meaning in this. He wasn't some ploy of Pukalski's. Just a random factor. 'What's it to you?' He re-pouched the gun.

'It's what reporters do. I wanna help.'

'Help?'

'I already did, didn't I? Told ya about the full moon. I done a bit of study of psychopaths and that stuff. Read *American Psycho* and ev'rythin'.' Crowe sensed a touch of sarcastic humour in his tone. 'Ya know *Silence of the Lambs*, eh? Bloke in that collected skin. Based on Ed Gein, like Hitchcock's *Psycho*. No? What about *Halloween* then? Don't know nothin' about serial killers, do ya?'

'If you're such a shit-hot expert, go write a book.'

The bloke tapped the side of his nose with his index finger. 'That's the plan. A book about the Scavenger.'

'Piss off and get started then. Do your own research. My business is something you need to stay out of.'

'How old ya reckon I am, Mr Crowe? Seventy? Eighty?'

Crowe was getting impatient and simply frowned.

'Just turned 52, that's all.'

Hard life, Crowe thought.

'Younger than you, right?' the man added.

'Wrong,' growled Crowe. Crowe was only a few years younger than that but wasn't about to admit it.

'Yeah? How old then?'

'Also none of your business.'

'Whatever. I still got years of work in me. But the bastards retired me,' the self-proclaimed ex-journo said. 'For medical reasons, they reckoned. I wanna do somethin' to show 'em I'm still in the game. This Scavenger thing's a godsend.'

'Yeah? So, go read the papers.'

The pest smiled secretively and picked at his nose. 'I remember you, Mr Crowe. Bit of a maverick. A loose cannon. An outlier.' He nodded as though it had just occurred to him. 'Followed your career for a while, though most of it seemed unproven. Editor said you were a nobody, a common thug.'

'He was right.'

'He was full of shit. I think if you're goin' after the killer, you'll find him. That's the story I want. I wanna interview the freak.'

'Yeah? Dangerous business, Len. Chasing freaks.'

'Call me Blowie. Just that and nothin' else,' he added, tapping the side of his nose again. 'Len Bugden's dead an' gone.' His dark-brown eyes became a pool of sardonic expectation. 'You gonna ask me why *Blowie?*'

Crowe glanced at the stains ground into the man's thick, woollen coat and blue track pants and could think of at least one reason. But he said nothing.

''Cause I've made a livin' offa other people's shit.'

Crowe breathed out, reached into the bloke's car and pulled the keys.

Over the other side, beyond the safety rail, a slope, then flat, grassy land ran off toward the southern freeway and the outer suburbs. Crowe considered pitching the keys as hard as he could into the scrub.

'What'd ya gonna do with those?' Blowie asked, following the trajectory marked out by Crowe's eyes.

'Down this road a bit there's a bus stop. I'll leave them there. Hidden in the grass.' Blowie started to protest, but Crowe ignored him. 'I don't want you following me. Where I'm going is my business.'

'But how will I find ya?'

Crowe ignored him and walked back to his own car. As he drove off, Blowie was swearing vigorously and shouting something about freedom of the press. Crowe watched in his rear-view mirror as the bloke leapt about, shaking his fist and making futile threats.

Then something else caught Crowe's eye – a glitch in the mirror that gave an impression of someone in the back seat. A young girl with dark straggly hair, in places matted into clumps by...

...blood?

'What the–' he yelled, slamming on the brakes and looking back over his shoulder. 'Lucy?'

Something wakes me in the depth of the night. I say 'wakes' though I never sleep, say 'night' though night and day are completely meaningless when you're stuck in a gloomy, unchanging place like this. But consciousness does return at times, in a fragmented and hard-to-hold-onto form, teasing me with memories of a life I used to have in a world I'm finding it harder and harder to recall.

But something's changing. I'm getting more flashes of memory. With them comes hope. Most often I remember a particular man and why I need his help. He's a good man, rough but kind. He would talk to me like I was important, like I was worth talking to. He'd joke with me, make me feel I was real. He didn't ignore me like all the other adults. Didn't patronise. His face is clear before me at this moment and I reach out to touch him. Then I'm out of my prison. It feels like the outside world. I can feel the leather seat I'm sitting on, smell petrol and the remains of a pizza in a box beneath my feet. The world is moving past, but I'm there, in it...and I see the man's eyes, seeing me, though he has his back to me. He begins to turn. 'Lucy?' he says. Is that me? Am I Lucy?

I feel my memory beginning to come back and try to answer, but the shadows consume me again. They drag me away...

I'm Lucy.
And I'm back in the near-dark.

The back seat was empty.

He was starting to imagine things now. It was Lucy again, but not just at night, not just in his dreams. What was going on? If this was some manifestation of his psyche, what was it trying to tell him?

Could she possibly still be alive?

Noticing Blowie through the back window, running toward him waving his arms, Crowe hit the accelerator and continued down the road.

12

Unsurprisingly, Superintendent Douglas Pirran – a Homicide Squad heavy known as 'Piranha' (or at least he was to Crowe, who had interacted with him when Pirran was a lower-grade cop in the Gong) – was in charge of general operations related to the Scavenger case within the relevant local commands. Pirran was not only a trifle too honest for Crowe's liking but was also largely responsible for both times Crowe had nearly ended up in the slammer. Crowe didn't like him, but he respected him. The dislike was mutual, but Crowe wasn't too sure about the respect. Luckily Crowe had as little to do with homicides as he could manage, which mostly kept him off the Piranha's radar, and that was how he liked it.

On the other hand, the media spokesperson for the Wollongong District was Sergeant Joe Carson, who just happened to owe Crowe a favour. Not to mention the fact that Joe's scruples were nowhere near as ironclad as Pirran's. He called on Carson at the station and was told by a perky-sounding young constable that the sergeant was unavailable: would he like to leave a message? No, Crowe bloody well wouldn't, but he didn't really have a choice. 'Tell him to call Mr Raven. He's got my number.'

Carson would figure it out. And he'd be in touch because he knew that Crowe's wallet was always open to help grease the flow of information. Crowe just had to wait.

He decided he'd wait in Sydney.

Gail's unit, on the thirteenth floor of the Millennium Tower building in the middle of the City, was neat and modern, like a showroom in a yuppie trade fair. It had pastel-toned walls, soft-grey leatherette sofa, post-modernist paintings by some arty mate of Gail's, and indoor palms that were real but looked so like plastic you couldn't tell the difference. Gail was dressed in a red tracksuit, zipped open enough to reveal her cleavage, and bright-white-with-red-gel-striped joggers. Her earrings were large, oval disks – black with a slash of canary yellow across them. She and Crowe were drinking coffee from hand-made ceramic mugs, which were angular and asymmetrical and bloody difficult to hang onto. The only thing in the room that lacked style was Crowe. He'd been quizzing Gail about the deal Pukalski claimed he'd been paid to broker.

'He didn't mention anything specific to me,' she said, 'though it's the sort of thing he often did. What was he supposed to be buying?'

'I was hoping you'd know. All I got from him was bullshit.' Crowe was feeling a little distracted by Gail's youthful appearance; she was just over three-quarters his age and today, for some reason, looked only half. Her skin was immaculate. Any sign of age was gone; she was a dab hand with foundation.

'I haven't heard a thing,' she said. 'He's been amazingly wired lately, even for a guy partial to amphetamines. I haven't been seeing quite as much of him, though. I thought that was because he was losing interest. To be honest, *I've* been losing interest – he hasn't been as free with information as he used to be. Frankly, the gross-out factor of being pawed by him is starting to outweigh the benefits.'

Crowe slouched back into an uncomfortable designer chair. He refrained from commenting.

'Has he been dealing with any particularly rich bastards? Secret meetings? Whatever?'

'Not that I know of. A few local councillors, but they're hardly big-time.' She turned suddenly, eyes widening with inspiration. 'Waldheim. I heard him talking to Gregor Waldheim on the phone one evening when he didn't know I was lurking about.'

Ah, Waldheim. Lucy's father.

Help me!

Crowe jerked at the sound of Lucy's voice, so violently the chair shuddered.

'What?' Gail frowned, mug paused halfway to her mouth.

'Did you hear that?'

'Hear what?'

'That voice—'

She laughed, completing the movement of the coffee cup to her lips. 'No, I didn't. Must have been from upstairs. I filter them out.' She swallowed then said, 'You're a bit jumpy.'

'Yeah.' Crowe glanced around, listening hard, but there was nothing. 'What'd they talk about?'

'Who? The neighbours?'

The room seemed to darken, so marginally Crowe wouldn't have noticed if his senses hadn't been on high alert. What the hell was going on?

Flashlight catches on something. Violated flesh. Dull eyes in a lifeless face. Brown hair, blonde streaks matted with blood.

For a moment, emerging from the memory flash, Crowe sensed a human figure standing in the far corner of Gail's starkly modern room, draped in its own shadows – shadows that shouldn't exist in that well-lit, open space.

A young girl.

Lucy?

At the thought, he blinked and the delusion was gone.

'Mike! Snap out of it. You're drifting. What was who talking about?'

Crowe glared at her. 'Pukalski and Waldheim. Who d'you think?'

'Right. I don't know what it was about. Only caught the end of it. Does it matter?'

'Maybe. Two arseholes in conference, one of them filthy rich. Big money transfer. Mightn't be coincidence.'

'Waldheim's been quiet for a long time now. He was a big player once, but he withdrew from circulation. I haven't heard much about him for years, though as far as I know most of the companies he owns are still big money earners.'

'Yeah, he slinked off and hid under a rock, the bastard. After...'

When Crowe didn't continue, her eyes narrowed in suspicion.

'So, you know Waldheim? Not a fan?'

'Worked for him a few times. Years ago.'

'Doing what?'

'This and that. Strong-arm stuff he didn't like doing himself.'

'His daughter was murdered, right? That's why he became a hermit.'

No doubt about it, Gail had a mind like a bark spider's web when it came to storing newsworthy snippets for later consumption.

'He hired you to find the killer, I suppose.'

'I failed.'

'But the killer was caught. Bloke who lived near where she was murdered, if I remember correctly.'

'Wasn't me who got him.' Crowe frowned thoughtfully. 'If he *was* the one. You know the body disappeared, right?'

'I don't remember that being general knowledge.'

'I was the one who found her in the first place – and no, that's not in police records either. After I reported the whereabouts of his daughter to him, Waldheim sent one of his minions to confirm and then call the police. But all they found was a lot of blood and tissue scraps. Identified as hers, sure. There were apparently forensic indications that the body had been moved post-mortem. But the clues petered out by the end of the road, where the bloke who was charged with her murder lived. They found a couple of her fingers in his house. The suspect denied knowing anything about it at first but eventually confessed. I wonder how much persuasion the cops used. He claimed he'd left the body in Waldheim's place where I'd found her.'

'Who'd want to steal the mutilated body of a teenager? That's pretty sick.'

'Speculation was it might've been some scheme to suck money out of Waldheim. But no proof was forthcoming, and the cops let it drop. I kept looking for Lucy's body but failed at that, too. All I ever did was fail her.'

'But she was definitely dead, wasn't she?'

'I've seen dead, and yes, I was sure she was dead.' He paused, staring inward. Gail waited for him to come back. 'I *was* sure,' he continued. 'Lately, I'm not so convinced.'

'Really? Why?'

'Wishful thinking probably. When I found her, I didn't look too closely. It just seemed…obvious. Maybe I was in a hurry. I wasn't at my best. Anyway, it's ancient history. Forget it.' Crowe rubbed at an ache in the left side of his skull. 'We have more pressing issues to deal with. Whoever Pukalski was working for, it can't be Waldheim. The man was a sorry piece of human excrement then, weak for all his influence and all his money, and I have no doubt he still is. Charlie-boy's totally intimidated by the phantom he's working for now. Waldheim's not that scary, in my experience.'

'Who then?'

'That's the question. And why spin so much bullshit?'

'Bullshit, eh?' Gail smiled. 'Sounds normal for Charlie. Tell me all.'

Crowe glanced at her, considering. With her in front of him like that, it seemed like the smartest thing to do. 'It's right up your alley, too.'

Her face tilted in a gesture of curiosity.

'He reckons whoever's running him is after a certain pickled foetus – Queen Marika's unborn kid actually, cut out of her and spirited away just after she died.'

That got Gail's attention. 'Marika Kucera. The superstar? Really?'

'Ever heard of anything like that?'

She shrugged. 'The gossip that Marika was pregnant was around on the net from the beginning. Various family members even lent it credibility. Some say that's why she was…disposed of.'

'For getting pregnant? Who'd do that?'

'Well, I guess it depends who fathered it. Doesn't sound likely to me but makes for a nice conspiracy theory. Royal families have a tendency to be inbred.'

Crowe pointed out that Pukalski had seemed sincere enough when he told him about Marika's unborn, but surely no one would pay that much for an artefact so far on from its mother's death that it could be anyone's. Two-hundred million was a lot of money for a dodgy souvenir, whatever the potential scandal value attached to it.

'Let me show you something.' Gail practically leapt for her laptop and in a few seconds was connected to cyberspace. She tapped a few buttons, nails making a business-like sound on the keys, then gestured for him to come look. 'This is a site that tracks conspiracies and rumours.'

The mortuarial imagery that framed the page was dark and suggestive. A header read: 'FOETAL MAGIC?'

Crowe shot Gail a sceptical look. 'Why the hell do you even know about this?'

'I like to know things. Just read it,' she said.

He got as far as the theory that a dead foetus, taken straight from the womb, held untold magical power and offered an unprecedented opportunity to those familiar with less rational aspects of human and nonhuman life, when Gail, impatient with his reading speed, began her own summation.

'Many cultures share the belief that an unborn child is the strongest concentration of life forces known to Man. Birth serves to focus the possibilities that reside in the foetus and hence to drain its inherent power. But until then, it's very strong. Taken straight from the womb a dead foetus can be used to draw in and then control supernatural powers. In China magicians use them to trap ghosts.'

'Ghosts?'

'Empty vessels that spirits can inhabit and through which they can be controlled.'

'Sounds ridiculous.'

'Since when did that stop anyone?'

Crowe huffed. 'I suppose because of Marika's royal bloodline and fame – all the power that comes from the world's attention – her foetus would be considered even more potent than your average unborn?'

'You've got it. That little hunk of unclaimed humanity becomes a rich nexus of vast sociological, political and religious forces.'

Crowe laughed, a bit uneasily, though he was unlikely to admit it. 'Nice Z-grade fantasy, but we're talking real money here. Who in this day and age would think a deceased foetus was useful for anything, especially at that price?'

'A lot of people believe in magic and the power of the afterlife. And how often does a dead über-celebrity foetus become available? Even if you didn't actually believe it held real power, its esoteric value would be immense in some circles and, in the end, could be worth a shitload more than 200 million. Don't discount the significance of gullibility. It's humanity's defining characteristic.'

She had a point. But even if the superstition wasn't bullshit, how did that help track down the client?

'The initial approach came to Pukalski via email,' Crowe continued, on the off-chance it'd spark some neural activity in Gail's hyperactive brain. 'The message offered Pukalski a sizable commission to set up a deal to acquire the foetus and to follow through using all necessary force and/

or discretion. He reckoned he wouldn't've had anything to do with it if it hadn't been for the influence of the enquirer. Let's call him "Mr X".'

'If he's the ruthless kind, "Magneto" would be more appropriate,' Gail retorted.

'How would an electrician help?'

She laughed.

Anyway, Crowe continued, Mr X had replied to Pukalski's tentative interest with an immediate non-refundable payment of $250,000 into a specified 'hidden' account and a name. The name had led Pukalski through a maze of criminal contacts in Germany and the US and eventually to a financially desperate doctor, who claimed to have stolen the foetus from the bowels of the hospital during the hours of chaos immediately following Queen Marika's death. He would sell it to Pukalski for US$200 million. Pukalski, ever the pragmatist, beat him down to $200 million Australian – one million upfront as a gesture of good faith, the rest on delivery – and demanded proof.

'Was there any?' Gail asked.

'Obviously I didn't see it, but Pukalski reckoned the surgeon produced tissue analysis that proved the foetus was the real thing – to the satisfaction of Mr X anyway.'

Subsequently, Pukalski was put in contact with agents within Australia. They – whoever they were – kept him on the back foot right from the start and wouldn't allow any modifications to the terms of the agreement. They dealt with him only from a distance. That was smart as Pukalski could've snowed them if they'd dealt direct. They played him with surprising ease; in the end, Pukalski went along with their instructions simply because they didn't give him time to organise anything better. Hindsight, no doubt, but the whole thing seemed totally dodgy to Crowe.

The penultimate message had read: 'Courier should go to Belmore Basin and stand at the end of the old lighthouse breakwater at 2 o'clock on the morning of the 28th. Someone will arrive by car and walk along the breakwater to where your man is waiting. Your courier will have the money. No surprises. You will be watched. If you do your part without trying to con us, your courier will be given a padded metal box that houses a hermetically sealed, shatterproof preservation jar containing what you're after. We'll be watching for any tricks. No marked bills, only non-sequential serial numbers. You can trust us. We hope we can trust you.'

Pukalski had wanted to pay by electronic transfer or PayPal or some dark web equivalent, but they wouldn't be in it. So, he bargained with them to allow a guard. He didn't want street kids pinching his money. They finally okayed the plan, though they didn't like his amendment.

'How much of all this did you tell Skarratt?' Crowe had asked Pukalski.

'Not much,' he'd said. 'As far as I was concerned the bastard didn't even know what was in the suitcase.'

'So, he found out from elsewhere. Presumably from someone in your employ.'

'But why all the bloody shooting? I was following their instructions. I wasn't conning them.'

'Sure you were. You sent a second bodyguard – me.'

'They couldn't have known that.'

'Maybe they guessed.'

It seemed more likely to Crowe that Skarratt was in on the con from the start. They'd been prepared to deal with the bodyguard. The local agents at least had always intended giving Pukalski zilch, whatever the intent of the original seller. Perhaps the foetus didn't exist. Take the money and run was the go, or maybe try for another bite of the apple later, if the foetus *was* real after all. The Scavenger and Crowe had cruelled it for them.

'What went wrong? You screwed us,' the next email had read.

Pukalski had replied: 'You dumb bastards. Someone in your own group did the screwing. Your lot killed my man and stole the money. Left no container. What the fuck are you playing at? Where's the foetus?'

They didn't reply then. An hour later they called him and discussed the matter at length. Pukalski recorded the exchange and gave Crowe a copy direct to his phone. Gail and Crowe listened to the mp3 on her laptop.

CALLER: Pukalski?

PUKALSKI: Yeah. Who's this?

CALLER: The man with the goods.
    (The voice was deep and slurred, electronically disguised.
    Crowe thought it sounded familiar but couldn't pinpoint
    from where.)

PUKALSKI: Listen, you bastard, you've really stuffed me around. Your life isn't worth shit.

CALLER: We've still got what you want.

PUKALSKI: Well, what I've got right now is a lot of aggravation. What the hell are you goin' to do about this mess you've made, eh? You know your blokes did you over, don't you?

CALLER: What happened to them?

PUKALSKI: They're all dead. Read the bloody newspapers. You can read, I take it.

CALLER: The papers didn't mention anyone else. What happened?

PUKALSKI: Boat got shot up in a gun battle while your boys were trying to piss off with the money. Skarratt was with 'em. My bloke got wasted, but so did your bozos. Skarratt might've made it if that bloody Scavenger hadn't carved him up. I followed your instructions, dickhead, and you screwed me I'm out 200 million bucks. You think my employ–I mean me – you think I got that much money falling outta my arse every day? If I ever catch up with you scum, you're dog-meat.

CALLER: We've still got the item. The deal's still the same.

PUKALSKI: I'm not gonna pay double for a lousy shrivelled corpse.

CALLER: You want it or not?

PUKALSKI: Get stuffed.

That last bit was stupid, of course. He should've kept them going by pretending to go along with a new payment, to get them to make a mistake, anything that might have given Crowe a chance to track them down. But a man like Pukalski would only play the victim for so long. These blokes had pushed him beyond his breaking point. They'd blown it.

After further abuse from Crowe, Pukalski had given him everything he knew about the local agents and some contacts for getting in touch with the guy who reckoned he'd pinched the foetus in the first place. It wasn't much.

Crowe's only other clue was the couriers who'd come to the breakwater. Before he got carved up, Skarratt had mentioned someone called Hall.

'The name "Hall" mean anything?' Crowe asked Gail.

'Jerry...and Town,' she replied. 'Fashion and Musica Viva concerts. That's all.'

Flippancy. She'd lost interest. No more time for business.

'How are you feeling?' he asked.

'Fine.'

'Glad to hear it.' He put his hand on her leg. 'Shall we test the waters?'

'I'm not really in the mood.'

Crowe removed his unwelcome fingers. He recognised that tone. 'Fair enough.'

She gave him a weak smile then looked away. 'Sorry,' she said in a whisper.

Crowe watched her in silence for a moment. He was about to tell her he didn't hold a grudge when she turned toward him, her face almost expressionless. She just stared.

'What?' he said.

'Do you ever wonder if we're doing the right thing?'

'Right thing?'

'The life we lead. People our age have usually settled down by now. They don't try to deal with crims and professional arseholes, never staying in the one place for long. The world has changed since we were youthful drifters, Mike. Since 9/11, crime has become political. The bad guys seemed to be getting weirder and more dangerous.'

Crowe didn't know what to say.

'I'm not the person I was when we first met,' Gail continued, failing to notice or ignoring his impatient scowl. 'I've changed. I think you have, too.'

'Well, I've gotten slower.'

'It's more than that.'

If truth be told, this sort of soul-baring frightened Crowe. Made him think that one day Gail would leave him. At these times he was forced to admit – at least to himself – that he needed her. She was, after all, the only person he *had* to have in his life, whatever the cost. His parents, his sister – they'd all failed him. Or he'd failed them. He wasn't clear on where the blame lay. Gail was right. He was different from the man he'd once been. He felt more vulnerable for one thing.

Later, in the depth of the night, he heard her voice come from the darkness like words from a dream. 'How many people have you killed, Mike?'

'A few,' he replied, not wanting to think about it.

'Any women?'

'Not intentionally.'

'Anyone I know?'

Crowe didn't reply. Memory of Lucy's bloodied, mangled body was still with him, even after the years between and despite intervening deaths. Why? He hadn't killed her. Yet he felt responsible. If he was actually hearing her voice and seeing her ghost, why was *he* the one being haunted? He'd liked Lucy a lot and disliked her father even more.

Of course, there was also the disappearance of her corpse.

'I don't want to discuss it,' he said at last.

'It might help.'

Her or him? He didn't want to know. He turned over with his back to her. Silence took over.

Eventually he slept. The last thing he remembered was hearing Gail muttering softly in her sleep. He didn't know what it was about, but she sounded distressed, reminding him that one of these days he had to put Pukalski in his place.

13

CROWE WOKE EARLY. TOO EARLY.

They reckon good sleep is the product of a mind at peace. His had never been all that peaceful, but usually it didn't keep him awake. That night, however, the restlessness was profound. It threw up images of torn body parts and enveloped him in a sense of darkness so corporeal it took on a life of its own – not simply absence of light, but the presence of an entity that roiled around him, constricting like a gigantic ethereal anaconda. He remembered, too, standing at the brink of a cliff, staring out across an ocean formed of a deep and sentient darkness, feeling sick at heart and fearing not for his own life, but for that of someone else...someone he had once known. He couldn't recall who it was at that moment. Oddly, he *knew* this person was dead, yet he feared for them. Then a low hiss came from behind, and he turned, and there was a shape, human but distorted, standing a few metres away, materialising out of the shadows. He felt its stare, and the knowledge of its awareness of him filled his gut with dread. The shape came closer, slowly. He couldn't move, a totally unfamiliar terror rooting him to the spot. Its face was shrivelled and ancient, mouth sewn together with bloody twine.

'Who are you?' he said.

Then a ragged slit opened in its forehead, as though a jag-bladed, invisible knife had slashed across it. Flesh around the gash pulled back, forming grotesque lips.

This new mouth said: 'I am no one.' Then it shrieked.

Awake now, Crowe extricated himself from the sweaty sheets, crawling out of bed and away from Gail, who was sleeping fitfully. Her shoulders twitched and as he moved, she moaned. What was she dreaming? Not about spectral horror, he hoped. He was doing enough of that for both of them.

His legs felt like their bones had turned to rubber, and his heart thudded erratically. What the hell was wrong with him?

After flushing the mental chaos with a few shots of scotch, he pulled on his clothes and headed out the front door into the corridor beyond. No way was he getting any more sleep, might as well head back to the Gong. The hallway, starkly painted and with rigid chrome trim, was empty but bright, its openness somehow more threatening than if it had been swathed in shadows. The hollow reverberation of his feet echoed around him, tumbling in pursuit like auditory dust as he passed door after door. No one emerged from any of them. At the central lift bay, he pressed the DOWN button and waited, staring dully at his distorted reflection in a shiny wall panel.

Help me.

He snapped back to full awareness so roughly he had to avoid falling by reaching out a hand to steady himself against the wall.

Help me.

'Who's there?'

The voice had been distant yet somehow close by. No one was visible and he could see clearly in both directions, right to where the hall turned at right angles, maybe 100m away, with nothing in between for anyone to hide behind.

The lift door pinged and slid open.

His first impression was that someone was in the carriage, waiting against the rear wall. He registered darkness where there was only light – a woman's shade, slight, perhaps youthful.

I'm here, Mr Crowe, and I need your help.

Lucy again. Her voice was directly behind his left ear and he fancied he felt the touch of something coldly ethereal drift across his skin. He jerked around. No one. Chill slithered into his bones. What the hell was going on?

He glanced back into the lift cage. It was empty and free of shadows.

Crowe was not a superstitious man, but for a moment he could almost believe something spectral lurked invisibly in that corridor. His mother had always cautioned against an easy dismissal of such things – advice he'd never heeded as she had been, generally speaking, totally unreliable. Surely Lucy Waldheim's voice was a faded auditory scrap hung over from the dreams he'd been having, and his conversation with Gail had made it worse. But it was so immediate, it had felt like a physical presence. He shivered. And how often had he 'seen' her over the past few days? Was she trying to contact him or was this the first sign of a brain tumour? Then, annoyed at himself, he stepped determinedly into the lift and jabbed at the ground-floor button. Enclosed in that metal-and-glass box, the trip down seemed uncomfortably slow. The circumstances of his investigation into Lucy's death came unbidden.

Reading the girl's diary doesn't take long; it'd been found at the bungalow when her body had not. Only goes back a month. Most of the entries are naively adolescent, with a heavy dose of anxiety over conflict in the Middle East and the effect of natural disasters on those she'd never met. 'We live such privileged lives,' she wrote. 'Yet we are destroying the planet.'

Several people are mentioned. Her father, of course. She's worried about him. 'We were close once, but he's become so difficult. Last night he got angry over nothing. I thought he was going to hit me.' She'd started to write something at one point – must have been the day before she ran away. Crowe can pick out the words, 'I'll never tell' and 'my friends wouldn't understand', but they've been scribbled over, thickly, and the next page ripped out. There are no entries after that. Her stepmother, Farnestine, is there, too, though mostly as a side note. Someone named Sara gets several paragraphs. Lucy makes her affection for this...girl? woman?...seem so intense Crowe thinks it goes beyond infatuation. But young girls are like that. She also mentions some bloke, in guarded terms, who's been bothering her since her birthday party – 'He thinks I led him on! I was just being friendly'.

Of herself she writes things like: 'I feel like I'm never just me' and 'Why can't they leave me alone?' Adolescent identity-crisis stuff. Makes Crowe remember his own growing up but without much fondness. 'I feel like I'm being consumed,' Lucy notes.

Crowe wants to talk to Waldheim as soon as possible, but police and the media keep the man busy. Instead, Crowe corners Eleyn Farnestine. She's tall and elegant, like a fashion model only recently past her prime. Tension boils beneath the cool exterior, residue of something disagreeable that has left her depleted and defensive. Might be grief, though he doubts it. She studies him through the smudges of her hastily applied eye shadow, the artificial lengths of her lashes.

'I wasn't aware of any problems between Gregor and Lucy, Mr Crowe,' she says stiffly, sliding her forefinger along a neatly plucked eyebrow.

'No teenage rebellion stuff?'

'Nothing. Lucy was a darling girl.' Her tone is flat. She doesn't mean it.

'What about you?' he presses. 'Did you fight with her?'

'Of course not.'

'Did you like her?'

Farnestine's hand begins rising and falling on the armrest of the lounge.

'I adored her,' she says as, unconsciously, her hand bangs harder against the burnt-umber Italian leather.

'Adored? Isn't that a bit like overkill?'

The thumping stops. 'You go too far, Mr Crowe.'

He shrugs. 'Found a diary.' He plunges on. 'She mentions someone called Sara. Can you tell me who that is?'

'I don't know anyone of that name.'

He gives her a sardonic look.

She frowns. 'I think we've got nothing more to discuss. I'm leaving now.'

He puts his hand on her arm to halt her. She laser-stares at him.

'You're not being very helpful, Ms Farnestine—'

'Missus Waldheim, thank you.'

'What's your problem?'

Her hazel eyes sweep over him then ricochet off to the side. 'Gregor wants you to investigate this terrible tragedy, Mr Crowe, but I think it a mistake. This is not some sordid standover job. A young girl has been brutally murdered. Her body stolen. It's police business. Only police business.'

'You've changed your tune.'

Her grey-blue eyes touch on his again. She says nothing.

'One more thing,' Crowe continues. 'Lucy said she'd been getting hassled by someone since her party. A man. Any idea who?'

She smiles but not with good humour. 'She was an attractive girl. Attractive in an obvious sort of way.'

'Are you implying she flirted—'

'Of course not. She was an angel.' Her tone is bitter.

Crowe frowns. 'No one in particular then?'

She stares at him for a moment. 'I don't know. Why don't you ask Siegel?'

'Siegel?'

'Jimmy Siegel. Gregor's driver.'

'Why? Has he shown interest—'

'Hardly. He's way too shy and a bit wooden. But he drives — drove — her around when she went shopping or to meet friends. Drove her to school, too. Gregor doesn't approve of public transport.'

'So she might have talked to him, you think?'

Farnestine grunts sardonically. 'I see where you get your reputation as a detective, Mr Crowe.'

With that she stands and strides out of the room.

Crowe wasn't in the mood for stalkers, real or ethereal, not with the past weighing on him the way it was. His memories and the fact he felt like he was being haunted were enough to deal with. And Sergeant Carson had not returned his call.

Failure to understand why it was happening was what was irritating him the most. Pukalski, the Scavenger, Lucy's insistent voice, grotesque hallucinations, maybe even ghosts, and not just Lucy's...He didn't have a clue what it all meant. One thing was for sure — he didn't need any added irrelevancies. He wasn't sure if he believed in ghosts or not, but it had occurred to him that his subconscious mind might have been trying to tell him something, though how current events might be connected to Lucy Waldheim he had no idea. *It's wrong*, the voice had said. Just what was wrong, in a world where wrongness was endemic, was an intuitive insight Crowe hadn't managed to clarify.

Maybe he just needed to *believe*.

The sun was striving to make the city cheerful, and failing, because a thin layer of smoggy cloud spread out from the direction of the steelworks. There was more than enough light, however, to show Blowie's purple Falcon ute with its patches of rust parked on the street in front of Crowe's Mt St Thomas home. In the cab was Blowie, head tipped back, and from the movement of his lips it looked like he was snoring. Fair enough, it was about seven in the morning, but not on Crowe's bloody front lawn.

Crowe rented the place under the pseudonym 'Ed Rice' and an office at the cheaper end of central Wollongong in his own name. No big deal, but it shouldn't have been easy to find him at the residence. He had a fake driver's licence and other paraphernalia in the name of Ed Rice. Ed was a sales representative for Jackson Electronics Pty Ltd, a small company that did, in fact, have an Ed Rice on its rep list. Ed worked on a commission and strictly part-time basis. Occasionally Crowe made a sale just to improve his record. He wasn't a very dynamic salesman, but the cover should hold for a while yet.

He parked behind Blowie and down the street a bit, got out and walked toward him carefully. What was it with this bloke? Crowe had given him plenty of discouragement, but it didn't seem to matter. Did he have to beat the pest up to get him to mind his own business?

Blowie appeared to be wearing a different sweatshirt from the one he'd had on last time Crowe saw him, though it looked just as dirty. Unshaven jowls puffed out as he breathed. Dead to the world. Life had got complicated enough without obsessive derelicts hounding his every step. Or was Blowie's presence part of some conspiracy? Was this down to Pukalski? Crowe banged on the driver's side window.

Blowie woke up with a start. He flailed his hands about, as though boxing with an invisible assailant. 'No!' he shrieked, 'I'll get it done!' Obviously chatting with one of his inner demons. Suddenly reality focused and he saw the cause of the disturbance. He stopped his histrionics. 'Michael?' he said. 'Ain't this a pleasant surprise!' The glass muffled his words.

Crowe tapped at it to indicate that he should unlock the door. 'Sure thing,' the man said and pulled up the sun-cracked knob.

He looked even worse without the filter of the dirty glass.

Crowe grabbed his hairy face and forced him to look squarely into his eyes. '"Mr Crowe" to you. You don't get to call me "Michael", "Mike" or anything else that implies you know me. Right?'

'Sure thing, boss.'

Crowe let go of the bearded jaw. 'How'd you find my place?'

'I have my methods,' Blowie wheezed, then broke into a fit of coughing.

'You going to keep this up?' Crowe asked. 'Annoying me?'

'I don't mean to annoy you. No. No. Not at all. But I gotta see this through, ya know. It's gonna be big. It's my way back. Can't ya understand that? I wanna be there. When you find him.'

Obsession churned around in his eyes and it looked utterly authentic. Once again Crowe felt sure he wasn't from Pukalski. He was a side issue. A red herring. A failed journalist who wanted to exploit whatever it was he'd stumbled into by recognising Crowe. Or just a self-deceived loony. He stared into the voids of the man's pupils and watched the desperation boiling there.

'Come inside,' Crowe said, giving in to a welling sense of pity. 'We'd better talk.'

When Crowe pulled into the driveway, Blowie was waiting on the back path, leaning from one foot to the other and jiggling. When he saw the look on Crowe's face, he said, 'I gotta pee!' Crowe said nothing, and Blowie hurried down the back past the shed, turned side on, zipped open his pants and released a voluminous yellow stream over the tangle of struggling weeds beside the fence. He flicked off the drops, zipped up and came back. 'Better out than in, eh?' he said and farted loudly. He giggled. 'Always get windy first thing in the mornin'.'

Reluctantly, Crowe gestured him inside and followed – not that being in a confined space with a man who'd slept overnight in a filthy car appealed too much. The smell was not pleasant. He noticed Blowie didn't look around at all, as though he was already familiar with the house.

'You gonna let me help you?' the man asked eagerly.

Crowe got coffee under way. Then he fetched a couple of apples from the fridge and offered Blowie one. The latter shook his head, running his hand over the grey stubble of his chin. Crowe left one apple on the bench and ate the other, watching him.

'Ya not talkin' much,' Blowie said.

'I'm trying to decide whether to break both your legs or leave you one to hop on out of here.'

Blowie didn't look nervous. Instead, he nodded knowingly. The percolator began spluttering. 'Pour the coffee?'

'I'll do my own.' Without thinking, Crowe pushed him away. The chest he felt under the dero's clothes was hard and sinewy, and the shove didn't have any effect. He was sturdier than he looked.

Crowe poured himself a mug of coffee, relented and poured Blowie one, too.

'Got sugar?' the man said. Crowe gestured at the cupboard; Blowie found the sugar and tipped a large quantity in without using a spoon. 'Any scotch?'

'Not for breakfast.'

Blowie nodded and sipped at the coffee. 'Passable,' he muttered.

That was it for small talk. Crowe got him into the lounge room and told him to sit. Once he had, Crowe towered over him. 'Okay. Now one of two things will happen.'

'Yeah?'

'Either you agree to stay out of my business, or you get yourself seriously injured.'

Blowie sipped. 'You won't hurt me,' he said.

'I might.'

'Sure, you've shot people before,' he said, 'but you won't beat me up or murder me in cold blood. Not someone like me.'

'You seem pretty confident.'

'It's just what I reckon.'

He was crazy. So was Crowe, to be sitting drinking coffee, discussing this shit with an old loony who'd named himself after the blowfly, one of Australia's most annoying pests.

'Look,' Crowe said, still reasonable, 'just assuming I'm going after the Scavenger, I can't have some mad geriatric trailing around after me, scaring the wildlife and getting underfoot—'

'I'm not useless,' Blowie said intently.

'Oh, yeah?'

Blowie got up and began pacing. Something oddly intense and muscular suddenly infused his motion. He'd set the coffee mug on the edge of the chair so his hands were free to gesture, which they did with nervous animation.

'Look,' he said earnestly, 'I'm not geriatric or mad. And I'm not a dero either. I told you, I'm a retired journalist.'

Something had changed; it took Crowe a few more sentences to realise what it was. He was no longer speaking with a semi-educated laziness. Suddenly his words had a flow.

'You assume I'm an idiot because I'm so unkempt,' the newly articulate Blowie said, 'but I'm not. I can be whatever I have to be. I can put on a clean shirt and one of your leather coats, and I'll pass as a working reporter. I still have my union card. Was registered as a freelance, even though the bastards wouldn't support me when management gave me the bum's rush. But I've still got contacts.'

'Who did you piss off?' Was he schizophrenic? Crowe wondered, noting that Blowie didn't answer. This was a different man to the one Crowe had met in the library or who'd peed on his back fence. 'Look, your contacts won't help me much.'

'You're wrong. But I know about serial killers. We haven't had that many Down Under, not post-colonial and not that have been identified anyhow. But we've had some. I've studied them. It's God's truth that I'm writing a book. The Granny Killer bloke, you know about that? A while ago now. And the backpacker one – Milat. I want to find others, you know, ones with *style*. *Gravitas*. New ones. Given a chance, I could be onto a Ripper or an Ed Gein. Something iconic. Someone original. This bloke, this Scavenger, he could become the Aussie boogeyman, a cultural *legend*. He's already killed more people than, well, Jack the Ripper say. And just as gruesomely. I can depict him to the masses as something fascinating and terrifying, and he can help me get back in the game. You could go down in history as his nemesis. I wouldn't be a burden, just an observer. But I could help, too. As an ex-journo I still have important contacts.' He reached into his pocket. 'Check this out!'

It was a piece of folded paper, grubby and crinkled from having been sat on so much. He handed it to Crowe, who opened it with tentative curiosity. There was handwriting on the page, which was a photocopy.

'What's this?' he said.

'Read it.'

The calligraphy wasn't very clear, but with a bit of effort Crowe could make it out. A cursive script, but very tight, so that it almost became printing. There was little by way of ornamentation, no swirls, no blurring of the letters into one sweeping line. Each letter was precisely formed and was only made difficult to read by the compression it had undergone and the poor quality of the copy.

Dear Detective Pirran,

I have just read in the newspaper that one of your pet psychologists thinks I am a socially maladjusted recluse who has trouble finding women. She suggests that I am afraid of the female sex. She thinks that I kill these men (my colleagues, as I think of them) because I see such as these as a threat to myself and by cutting them up I am disfiguring them and making them less than human. She makes a lot of Mr Henry because I removed his male organ.

She is mistaken. She does not know what she is talking about.

I do not hate women and never again will I hurt them. Only once did I lose my temper with a woman and it cost me my one true love. Since that regrettable incident, I have learnt why I am on the Earth, how I could truly change humanity for the better. My goal is simple. I am not making my colleagues less than men. I am transforming them, helping them and myself to become something much greater. Your psychologist will realise this in time. Through this work, I will be made worthy of my true love. She will return to me. I will be seen as the saviour of humanity, not a mad scavenger. I merely seek to make amends for past weaknesses by creating a better form of Man and to once more bring my loved one into the light.

Below this was printed in larger letters: DID I SOLICIT THEE FROM DARKNESS TO PROMOTE ME?

'The Scavenger wrote this?' Crowe asked Blowie, who was looking very smug and nodded.

'It was sent to the cops,' he said. 'Obviously. Local bloke I got an agreement with, he copied it for me. Cost me in bribes, natch. But it'll be exclusive to my book. Good, eh?'

'Who's the insider?'

'That would be confidential.'

What his story sounded like was bullshit – possible, Crowe guessed, but rather unlikely. He let it pass for now.

'How do you know it's real?' Crowe said.

'It looks real. Don't it look real to you?'

It did, but that meant nothing. Conmen and weirdos could be competent enough to make a fake letter look 'real'. Crowe got a piece of paper from a drawer and handed it and a pen to Blowie. 'I seem to recall the Jack the Ripper letters were fake. Write out the first sentence.'

Blowie smiled languidly. When he spoke, the Old Dero had returned. It sounded unconvincing now. 'Thunk I mighta bloody done it meself, does ya?'

'You might've.'

He wrote. His scrawl was uninhibited, even extroverted. It didn't look anything like the Scavenger's note but appeared quite natural to him.

'It's his,' Blowie said, once more in his journalist voice.

'Well, it's unlikely to be yours anyway.'

Blowie shrugged and sat down again, knocking his mug to the floor. It sent him into a sudden panic. Coffee splashed over the carpet and he shrieked. 'Sorry! Sorry, Mr Crowe!' He knelt and began brushing at the stain with the sleeve of his sloppy joe.

'Leave it!' Crowe said. Blowie looked up, manic with anxiety. 'Has the Scavenger sent the police any other notes?' Blowie's face twisted through emotions like fear, hate, incomprehension. 'I don't care about the carpet,' Crowe growled. He gestured with the note. 'This, Blowie! Put your mind on this, right! Has he sent the police other notes?'

Blowie crawled back onto his chair. 'No.' He spoke emphatically, his odd mood past. Then he glanced at Crowe and moderated the statement with: 'Well, one more. Accordin' to my contact.'

'What was in it?'

'Dunno.'

'You sure?'

'Yeah. Reckoned it told 'em bugger all.'

'What's this bit, written at the bottom? "Did I solicit thee from darkness to promote me?" It sounds like a quote from something old. The Bible?'

'Close,' Blowie said, looking like he was thinking about something else. 'It's from *Paradise Lost.*'

'*Paradise Lost?*'

'One of the greatest works of poetry ever written, man. By John Milton. Ain't ya got no culture?' He grinned. 'Seventeenth century religious epic. Fall of Satan and that. You know, Adam and Eve...' His gaze sharpened. 'The origins of evil.'

'Why's the Scavenger quoting it?'

'That's the sort of thing I need to find out. Get into his head.' He glanced up at the ceiling, as though he expected something to be written there. 'In the full quote Adam's chatting with God,' he said. 'After he's stuffed things up in the Garden of Eden.

'Did I request thee, Maker, from my clay
To mould me man, did I solicit thee
From darkness to promote me, or here place
In this delicious garden? As my will
Concurred not to my being, it were but right
And equal to reduce me to my dust—'

'What's it mean?' Crowe said, rather unsettled by Blowie's sudden ability to quote whole slabs of poetry from the distant past straight off the top of his head. Evidence was mounting that Blowie was not your run-of-the-mill idiot.

'Adam's whingein',' Blowie went on, 'Whingein' about havin' been made at all. It's God's fault, he reckons.' He shrugged. 'Some people think God's got a lot to answer for.'

'You think the Scavenger's one of them?'

Blowie looked at Crowe. Crowe imagined his bloodshot eyes to be multifaceted, like those of a fly. 'Maybe.' Blowie pointed his long, yellow finger. 'See? I'm helpin' ya. I can give ya all sorts of advice. I can get info from places where crims like you'd be told to rack off. A lot of my journalistic contacts are still hot.'

'Crim, eh? I'll have to clean up my act. Or my critics. One or the other.'

Blowie grinned so that teeth showed like bits of graffiti on a cracked wall. 'So I can help ya?'

'Maybe I won't beat the shit out of you anyway.' Crowe figured he wasn't going to get rid of him short of homicide, so controlling his movements would probably be the best bet. And you never know, he might be useful after all. Could he assume the letter from the Scavenger was genuine?

'Sure,' Blowie said. 'Sure thing. You won't even know I'm around.'

14

Stopping for a beer at the *North Gong Hotel* mid-afternoon probably wasn't the best way to work out his next move. But beyond the letter supplied by Blowie, the day hadn't been very productive, and Crowe felt he needed the distraction. He also needed to recover from being in Blowie's company. The man made him feel depressed, the way he swung from one extreme to the other, his mental illness writ large in his actions. He'd sent the journo away with a promise he'd have work for him soon, then headed off to a smaller local library.

Crowe had flicked through a stack of local newspapers – editions dated between the murders – and had found features on the psychology of serial homicide and detailed reports of community outrage and paranoia, even semi-historical accounts of other such murder sprees from other times and places around the world. Most of them were by-lined to Leonard Bugden, as Blowie had claimed. So he *was* a journo, assuming he hadn't simply adopted the name. Meanwhile, information given out by the cops had become oddly generalised; Carson and even Pirran were talking more, giving more press conferences, but they were saying less. Morbid and panicky interest in the activity of this serial killer remained at a high level throughout South Coast communities resulting in increased pressure on the police taskforce. According to public perception of such things, grotesque violence such as this just didn't happen here, in God's country. In general, they were right, but not totally. Most people only read histories that emphasised the area's more bucolic, tourist-focused qualities.

Crowe needed to talk to Carson and soon, so when he got to the pub he called the station again, using the pay phone to avoid being recognised, and left a message with a different youngster: that Mr Raven would be waiting at the *North Gong Hotel* for the next few hours. It was risky, but case files would give him addresses of potential witnesses, the results of forensic tests and a range of information not handed over to the press. Right now, he had more or less sweet bugger all to go on. Blowie was starting to look like Crowe's only other possible source of information, and that wasn't ideal.

With a schooner of Toohey's Old to talk to, he found himself a corner table. At least the seats were padded.

'So, what now?' he muttered to his beer. Information gathered by the police squad had obviously been little help to the official investigators, but you could never tell what a different set of eyes could make of the same information. Hopefully, Carson would respond soon.

As he pondered his limited options, his attention was drawn to a movement at the edge of his field of vision. He glanced up, past a couple of blokes chatting lazily at the bar. A teenage girl appeared in the mirror wall behind the bar itself, partially obscured by bottles, signage and beer taps. Something was wrong though. The image shimmered, as though a signal was being interrupted. Yet only the girl was blurry. The rest of the pub and its visible occupants were crystal clear. Then Crowe realised that for the reflection to be where it was, the girl herself would have to be right next to him – but there was no one. The image began to come into focus.

Blonde-streaked brown hair. That face.

Shock struck him hard enough to make him gasp out loud. 'No!' He pushed himself up, knocking his glass over. What was left of the beer splashed across the table and onto the floor. Nearby patrons turned to stare. The barmaid appeared, eclipsing the figure in the mirror.

'Are you okay?' she began.

Crowe rushed over to her. 'Move!'

But the figure caught in the mirror was gone.

'Hey, mate!' said one of the water-buffalos leaning on the bar. 'What's ya beef?'

Ignoring him, Crowe glanced around frantically. No sign of anyone even remotely like Lucy.

'Something the matter?' asked the barmaid tentatively.

Crowe took a deep breath. 'Sorry. I thought I saw…someone I knew. Someone I haven't seen for a long time.'

'Well,' she said, 'Looks like you lost your beer, too.'

'Um, yeah. Careless of me. If you've got a rag, I'll clean it up.'

She gestured indifference. 'Never mind. Happens all the time. I'll get someone to deal with it in a moment. You should relax.' Her eyes evaluated him. 'You want another schooner or have you already had too much?'

'That,' he said, 'was my first for the day.'

She raised one eyebrow. 'If you say so. Why don't you sit over there?' She gestured at a different but equally empty booth. 'And I'll bring another…Toohey's Old, wasn't it?'

'Thanks. And again, sorry.'

She gave him a just-doing-my-job smile and held out her hand for his money. He gave her a tip.

Around the time his fourth schooner went down, marginally slower than the first three, Crowe had just about stopped brooding, but he was still scanning the crowd as it drifted in and out and grew larger and noisier with the after-work influx. He was somewhat surprised, though perhaps he shouldn't have been, to see Superintendent Douglas Pirran come through the smoky glass-panelled doors. The cop cut through the press of patrons as though he expected them to know what he was – an out-of-uniform cop in his crumpled sports coat, white shirt, slackly knotted tie and law enforcement-blue slacks. His closely shaven face, in profile, was like a sugar banana: large forehead, flat nose, big jaw sticking out aggressively. His lips twisted up at one side in a sort of permanent sneer. In one meaty hand, he clutched three voluminous green recycled shopping bags. They looked heavy.

'Mr Raven, I presume.' He shook his head, put the bags under the table and stood staring at Crowe. 'We've got to talk.'

'Don't just stand there. Pull up a pew,' Crowe said.

The superintendent slid into the booth opposite Crowe. 'Who are you waiting for?'

'I like it here, Piranha,' he said. 'With the common folk.' He'd spent most of the time looking for Lucy to reappear and for Carson to materialise. Neither of those things had happened. Instead, he had a member of the NSW law enforcement upper echelon staring at him like a father who couldn't quite decide how much of a disappointment his kid was or how much trouble he was in. His own father had displayed the same look. Often.

'I'm afraid to tell you Carson didn't get your messages – either of them. I've felt he's not been pulling his weight for some time and so made sure he's been very busy. To help out, I've been taking his messages, for I am a New Age Boss.' He eyed Crowe's beer. 'Raven? Really?'

Crowe flushed in spite of himself. He wasn't going to admit Pirran was right. So far, all the man had was suspicions. 'What is this? Police harassment?'

'You should be so bloody lucky.' Pirran pulled back with a sharp laugh. 'I'm afraid it's far worse than that, Crowe. I'm here to ask for help.'

It took all of Crowe's self-control to keep his jaw from falling open. But it wasn't like he was going to be a pushover. 'Why should I cooperate? What've you ever done for me except give me grief?'

Pirran sniffed, as though he thought there were a couple of obvious answers Crowe was too dense to appreciate. His jaw stuck out further than usual. 'Remember those charges no one's ever bothered to pursue? Several counts of disobeying an officer of the law? Engaging in public brawls? Umpteen unpaid parking tickets? Using offensive language in–'

'Okay, okay, I get it.' Crowe sighed. 'You want a drink? Or are you on duty?'

'Scotch and Coke.'

Crowe fetched that and a straight Coke for himself – time to clear his head.

'Look, Mike,' the cop said, relaxing back against the padding of the booth. He paused to take a few sips of his drink. 'You *know* why you get harassed.'

'Sure,' Crowe said, 'it just doesn't make me feel very cooperative.'

Pirran sipped at the scotch again. Then: 'Granted. But damn it, you bend the law like it's made of chewing gum. I'm not a fool.'

'Can we get to the point?'

'The point is, while I don't approve of your behaviour sometimes, I also acknowledge you're good at what you do, which is ferreting out secrets.'

'Why, Doug, you'll make me blush.'

Pirran ignored him. 'So, I get these messages from my well-trained young constables, and I think, *Who is this Mr Raven, calling two days in a row? Could it be a cunning pseudonym?* I have a chat with the good Sergeant Carson who, by the way, gave you up like unwanted virginity. You really need to pick your confidantes with more care. He's a weak man, is Carson.'

Crowe frowned. What was the Pirran up to? 'Not that this isn't a lovely chat, but is it going somewhere?'

'What were you going to ask Carson for?'

Crowe remained silent.

'I'll tell you what I think: I think you were going to ask him about the Scavenger.'

Crowe tried to keep the surprise from his face.

Pirran suddenly became very intense. 'Do you know him?'

'Who? Carson?'

'The Scavenger. Do you know who he is?'

'Unfortunately, I don't,' Crowe said.

'Were you there when Skarratt was killed?'

Jesus, how did Pirran know that? 'On the spot and conscious? No. How—'

'A semi-automatic handgun was found in the underbrush near where the Scavenger killing took place. It wasn't registered to anyone, but they managed to pull a partial fingerprint from the barrel. Matches at several points to your prints on file. Not enough to make a case, if I'm honest, but enough to start me thinking.'

Yet Pirran hadn't had him hauled off to lock-up. A few years ago, he'd have done it so fast Crowe's head would have spun for days. Pirran was being reasonable, even pleasant. What was the bastard up to?

'So, you were there. Did you see him?'

'Not well enough to make an ID.' Crowe decided to give the man a break. 'Look, I've been asked to find him. Not officially hired, as I'm no longer qualified to act as an investigative agent, you might recall. I'm doing it as a favour.'

'For who?'

'Client confidentiality.'

'The other killings that night? The Scavenger interfered somehow. Took something off Skarratt?'

Crowe shrugged but said nothing. He didn't feel like getting into tales of unborn babies and millions in cash in the wind.

'Some sort of deal went down on the breakwater, something to do with Charles Pukalski, I'd bet. Rousch – the one that got shot up – he had connections with Pukalski. One of the others was Hall, Nathan Hall – an old friend of ours. The third body was Irwin Suleman. A petty crook.'

'So Hall and Suleman, were they working for anyone you know of?'

Pirran shook his head. 'Must have been some party, though, four bodies and a burnt-out boat, signs of a struggle. Got anything to share?'

Crowe said nothing.

'It doesn't matter.' Pirran shrugged. 'I'm not interested if it's not connected with the Scavenger. Someone else can deal with *that*.'

'And you're convinced it was the Scavenger?'

'Skarratt got thoroughly mutilated. Messily and in a, let's say, less calculated way than is usual for the Scavenger. That fits if the killer rushed because he was being hunted. But I reckon he took something Skarratt had. I reckon Pukalski wants it back. That's where you come in.'

He looked at Crowe expectantly. He was doing well, but Crowe only offered him a poker face.

'Well, Crowe, am I close? I've got to know. If I thought you actually knew who the Scavenger was—'

'I don't. But I intend to find him. Can we leave it at that, eh? For the time being. No use bringing Charlie-boy into it. I have no love for him, but right now I have to pretend.'

'Yeah. I'd give half my rather pathetic pension to nail that bastard, but he has too many friends.'

'He has no friends. Nobody likes him, trust me. And have some faith. You'll get him one of these days. I promise. But you've got to keep focused, Pirran. One thing at a time.'

'Focused? Yeah.' The superintendent turned and stared out into the deepening twilight. 'You're a pain in the arse, Crowe, but you've got redeeming features. This Scavenger thing, you should see what that bastard does to the bodies. And mostly, we reckon, he lets his victims know what's going to happen to them. He likes to watch them die. Several of them, he hacked off their limbs, or skinned them, before he slit their throats. I've never seen anything like it.' He drained his glass. 'And what does he do with the bits, eh?'

Crowe shrugged. 'Take-away dinners?'

'Maybe he's a cannibal. Why not? It can't get much worse. The point is, this isn't some rancid underworld shit. Who gives a damn if crims waste themselves? Well...' He shrugged. 'I'm a cop, so *I* do. But this...this is ordinary, decent citizens getting butchered. Family men, most of them. Except for Skarratt, none had much of a record. Nine that we know of. Nothing like this has ever happened before around here.' Pirran sighed. 'In a world created by 9/11 and the resulting Iraqi War we loyally signed up for, both the public and the pollies are keen to keep things under control. To quickly staunch any hint of terrorism is our highest priority.'

'The Scavenger's no terrorist.'

'Not of a political nature, no. And less spectacular than the new breed. But there's no doubt the killer provides his own kind of terror. Stopping him is my responsibility. And I don't know where to bloody go from here.'

A body lying in the gloom of a tool shed. Blood on the walls.

Help me!

For a moment, Crowe struggled to hold back his shock at the image of Lucy's death and hearing her voice yet again.

'So?' he managed.

Pirran frowned at him. Then said, 'So, I have to do something. My career's already on the line. The victims' wives and families, they need closure. And this fucker needs to be taken out.'

Crowe raised his eyebrows.

Pirran grunted. 'There's a couple of suspects, but we can't make anything stick. One of them – one that seemed a real goer – was in custody when the Scavenger killed that bloke at Kembla Grange. But neither of them fits the bill. Not really. We've got hair samples, skin samples, stuff that might belong to the killer or might not. Probably there's enough to convict him if we find him. But unless he makes a big mistake, how do we do that? The shrinks reckon he'll go on and on and on till he blows a gasket. Or makes a major mistake. How many have to die before then, eh?' He ground his teeth together. 'I want him.'

'How can I help?' Crowe said.

Instead of saying anything, Pirran reached below the table and fetched the shopping bags. He pushed them across the table to Crowe.

'That's most of it,' he said.

'Of what?'

'Of what we know about the Scavenger. Written reports. Received letters. Expert analysis. Interview transcripts. Copies of otherwise unattainable digital files—'

'You're giving it to me?'

Pirran stared. He was trying to read Crowe's mind. Crowe could almost feel the fear scratching at his skin. He wanted Crowe to be something he feared the ex-PI wasn't. He didn't want to trust Crowe, but he was hoping he could.

'Of course I'm not. I wasn't even here.'

'That's a relief, because, you know, that would be a serious breach of duty.'

'Get whatever it is you're after,' Pirran whispered, 'but help me find the bastard. I don't want to know what you're doing for Pukalski. That's your problem. I don't care how you do it, just get the Scavenger.'

'I'm touched, Doug.'

'Don't be. You're just the best way I know to fuck up someone's day.'

'And all outstanding fines dropped?' Crowe asked.

The superintendent sighed. 'Find this bastard and I'll get you a bloody sainthood.' He gave Crowe a piece of paper with a number on it. 'Ring me there. Any time. No names. If anyone else answers, say you're Philip Marlowe.'

'Philip Marlowe? Cute.' He paused, staring at the green bag. 'Has the killer sent any messages? You know, taunting stuff. Anything like that?'

Pirran squinted, suspicious. 'Why do you ask?'

'Just curious. These sorts of lunatics generally like to be heard.'

'A few letters that might – I stress the "might" – be genuine. A few. Copies are in the file.'

'All of them?'

Pirran paused. Not for long, but enough to tell Crowe that his next statement was going to be a lie. Pirran realised Crowe would know. He sighed. 'All I'm willing to show you.'

Crowe considered complaining, but there was no point. He let it pass.

'Look, Mike,' Pirran said, 'I don't want anyone else to die. You understand that?'

Crowe nodded.

'If anyone pins you down, you got the files from an unknown source.'

'You worry too much, Piranha.'

Crowe remained in the pub after Pirran left, thinking over these new developments and the fact that a police superintendent had been willing to bring him so far into an official investigation. It had never happened to him before. Was it a good thing? Only time would tell. It certainly reeked of desperation.

A shadow loomed over him. 'Excuse me,' said a deep, very tentative voice.

Crowe glanced up. The bloke standing there, leaning on the padded divider between Crowe's booth and the main expanse of the pub, stared nervously at him. He wasn't tall, but his build was solid, and it gave him presence. He held a fedora in one hand and wore light-brown trousers and a zipped-up, dark-red jacket. He looked vaguely familiar.

Crowe said nothing.

The man swallowed and smiled. 'Um, Mr Crowe, isn't it?'

'What if it is?'

'No doubt I've changed over the past decade. I was in here having a coffee before heading home when I noticed you. I was going to come straight over and say hi, but that other bloke beat me to it. So...' His voice faded nervously.

'Siegel, isn't it?' Crowe said. 'Jimmy. I didn't recognise you without your beard.'

The man smiled. 'Yes, I decided it was no longer suitable.' He gestured toward the padded seat opposite Crowe. 'May I? Just for a moment?'

Crowe shrugged. 'Sure,' he said.

As Siegel edged himself into the space between seat and table, Crowe found himself remembering the last time they'd met. Given the circumstances, his presence here and now was rather fortuitous.

Getting at the truth, exposing the lies, hunting any given target. That's what Crowe is supposed to be good at. But he must admit he often just works thoughtlessly, acting on impulse, keeping his eyes open for anything that makes his instincts itch. When he was younger his mother used to say he was lucky, finding what he was after by chance, escaping injury through sheer, mindless serendipity. Apparently, it was a gift from the Dead, she reckoned; she often claimed that ghosts helped him, whispering in his ears to guide him, whether he believed in them or not. They wanted him to be better than he was, she said. He'd always dismissed his mother's beliefs. He preferred to think of it as astute intuition and inbuilt cunning.

When he finds Siegel, Crowe remembers seeing him during at least one of his past visits to the Waldheim mansion, but he'd never taken any real notice. He's the kind of guy who just melts into the background, like a ninja, albeit a semi-conscious one. Not very big and when sitting in Waldheim's Mercedes he melted into the upholstery. He's doing that as Crowe approaches, parked at the rear of the house near the garage, which is bigger than Crowe's entire house.

Crowe taps on the window. Siegel stares straight ahead but sees nothing. He looks in his mid-20s, with black hair cut very close, and sports a thick but well-groomed beard. His uniform is a tight fit on broad shoulders and what have to be strongly muscled arms. He appears to be in a coma. Crowe knocks again, several times.

Languidly the man turns. When he registers Crowe's presence, he taps a button on the inside of the door and the glass automatically descends.

'Ah, Mr Crowe?' he says in a near whisper.

'You know me?'

'I've seen you around. After all, you're a big man.' He smiles. 'What can I do for you?'

'Your boss has asked me to investigate his daughter's murder.'

Immediately, the driver looks away, his facial muscles tightening around his cheeks and mouth. His eyes close for a moment and when they open again, there's moisture in them.

'Sorry,' he says, surreptitiously wiping at his face, embarrassed. He turns back. His sorrow is much more genuine than anything Farnestine managed.

'You were fond of Lucy,' Crowe says. It isn't a question.

The man nods. 'She was...' He swallows, abandoning the rest of the sentence. Finally, he manages, 'She was really nice. Kind. What happened is...tragic.'

'You saw a lot of her?'

'Nearly every day, to and from school. Occasionally other times.'

'Did she talk to you much?'

'A bit. Nothing very personal. Just small talk. She'd enthuse about books she

was reading. Alice Munro, Mary Shelley, Tim Winton, Margaret Atwood. Even Tolstoy. Sometimes she'd ask me about my studies.'

'Studies?'

The man smiles grimly. 'I don't intend to be a chauffeur all my life. I have things I want to achieve. Lucy encouraged me to better myself.'

Interesting guy, in a dull sort of way, Crowe thinks. He could see the chauffeur felt for Lucy the way a man should feel about his sister – the way Crowe didn't feel about his own. She was someone he cared about. His intuition was telling him the man's feelings were genuine…and innocent.

'Did you drive her to Merryvale that night?'

'What?' Siegel sounds genuinely shocked. 'No, how can you think–'

'Just asking. I don't think anything. How would she have gotten there, I wonder?' Crowe ploughs on. 'Any thoughts?'

'I don't know,' Siegel mutters. 'Taxi?'

Crowe has already checked with all the taxi companies. Bugger all.

'Are you aware of anyone who was interested in her?' he asks. 'You know, inappropriately. Anyone with overactive hormones? Anyone I should talk to?'

Siegel's face goes stony. 'Dale Walker, maybe.'

'Who's Dale Walker?'

'Young guy. Twenty-one or 22. He does menial jobs for Mr Waldheim. Part-time. He's being groomed.'

'Fancied Lucy, did he?'

Siegel makes a sound that suggests disgust. 'I see him in the kitchen sometimes, scavenging food for lunch.' He looks slightly guilty. 'We're allowed to.'

Crowe shrugs indifference.

'He told me he was going to ask Lucy out. I tried to discourage him–'

'Why?'

'He's not a nice guy. Unreliable. There's something very weak about him. He lacks the ability to genuinely care about others. No vision. She declined, of course, but he reckoned he wouldn't take no for an answer. I got really angry with him at her birthday party. Inappropriately, perhaps, but I couldn't help it.' He glares into Crowe's eyes. 'He was an obnoxious prick to her that afternoon and at other times. I didn't like him.'

'Are you still working for Waldheim?' Crowe asked.

Siegel's body twitched, as though the mere thought had disturbed his equilibrium. 'No,' he said. 'Without Lucy, the job felt meaningless.

Besides, I was accepted into a study program and left to concentrate on it.'

'Really? Good on you. What sort of program?'

He looked glum. 'I was interested in medicine in general, though I couldn't get into any of the universities. The college I finally enrolled in focused on paramedical training. I used the redundancy package Mr Waldheim generously gave me to pay for it. But it proved to be rather conservative and in the second year I couldn't see the value in it for me and left.'

'That's too bad. What do you do now?'

'Nothing much, I'm afraid. Driving, as always. But for Uber. Mostly part-time.' He was silent for a while, introspective, perhaps embarrassed. Again, his body trembled. He shook off the emotion and stared into Crowe's eyes.

'I just wanted to say hello,' he stated with an air that was almost pleading. 'I've wanted to speak to someone who knew Lucy…someone who hasn't been able to get over…over what happened to her. Others I've talked to seem to have forgotten. To have moved on, careless. And the world, humanity, seems sicker, weaker for it.' His eyes were begging Crowe to do something, to make things right. Crowe knew the look. '*You* haven't forgotten, have you?'

Glimpses of recent moments when Lucy had appeared to him, ghostly and demanding, flashed though Crowe's mind. 'Have you been hearing her? Seeing her?'

Siegel's eyes became moist, his hands trembling.

'Yes, yes, I have. I dream about her every night. I dream about her… dream that she's alive. You do, too, I can tell. If we keep remembering, maybe we'll get her back.'

Crowe didn't answer. He didn't know how to.

After a few minutes of silence, Siegel pushed up and out from behind the table.

He paused and said, staring down at Crowe, 'For what it's worth, I wanted to tell you something that may be important. I don't know, but you…you're a detective. Maybe you care enough. About a year after… after everything that happened, I became convinced her killer – her real killer – had *not* been caught. It tormented me. I even visited in prison the guy who was arrested and found guilty. I looked in his eyes and I could see it. Clearly. He didn't do it. He didn't murder Lucy.' He paused and then added, 'This is not the end, Mr Crowe. I believe there will be redemption. Lucy's killer *will* be found.'

Crowe watched as Siegel pushed through the growing crowd, burdened with his failures, until he disappeared into the grey, dreary evening. Crowe could sympathise with him. They both suffered the same regrets.

But Crowe was in a better position to do something about it.

15

MOST OF THE TIME, I DON'T REMEMBER WHAT SORT OF PERSON I USED TO *be. With the same randomness that throws me out into the world now and then, sometimes it all comes back to me, usually in ragged snippets.*

At this moment, it starts flooding into my mind.

I was young, sure. A bit naive, no doubt. I'd had a privileged life. It wasn't until my mother died that I understood how privileged I had been and how much I had depended on her emotionally. She'd always been there, not just feeding me and keeping me well-dressed, but encouraging me to do the things I'd come to love: reading books, talking about them, listening to all sorts of music and not just the kind that was most popular among my school friends. She taught me there was beauty in the world, enough, if we paid attention, to keep the darkness at bay. She didn't ignore the bad things, simply offered alternatives. She taught me to believe I could succeed without being a drain on others and never at their expense. I could help people. I could, and should, change society for the better, in however small or grand a way I might aspire to. She told me I didn't need to be confined by the fact I would grow up to be a woman in a patriarchal society. Everything was possible. Her vision of life was one of optimism.

It didn't last.

When she died of cancer, I was devastated. For a while I felt like an empty shell, drained of meaning. Even my father was deeply affected. He lost interest in everything, and whatever good humour he had had previously was sucked from him. For a while, he was broody, angry and weak in a way he'd never been before.

I rarely saw him during this time, and when I did, there was little real communion between us. But as the weeks passed, he began to push his mourning aside. His visits to my room, late at night, became more frequent, and the love he had always claimed as the reason for them seemed harder and more demanding. He wanted more from me than I wanted to give. Gradually, the pain of his demands wore me down and I felt desperate. I even contemplated suicide.

When he remarried, it felt like the final betrayal.

His new wife did not like me, no matter what she claimed to the contrary. Calling her 'Mother', as my father demanded, was a violation of all my memories. I tried, but there were so many barriers in her, and a coldness so deep it frightened me, that I had to force myself to interact with her at all. My grades at school worsened and the next year or so before I could escape to go to university was a chasm so deep and uncertain I felt it was impossible to endure it. When my father subsequently declared he didn't want me to go away to uni but to stay and look after him, I couldn't take it anymore, and I...I...

Ran...

...ran...

But that's when I was lost...

The images slide away, overwhelmed by a fog that engulfs me and makes the memories first blurry and indistinct, and then obscures them totally. Once again, I can't see the details of my past with any clarity. My present remains an enigma. I languish in the near-darkness, and in that darkness the fear and sorrow linger.

Though he knew from long experience that Siegel's claims regarding Lucy's murderer and the emotions that drove the ex-chauffeur's conviction that Lucy might be returned to the world were obvious signs of the man's grief, Crowe couldn't help wondering if the ghostly visitations, the distorted memories, the doubts he was experiencing were telling him the same thing. At the very least, he could keep his eyes and ears open for anything that might support the belief, even though he was bogged down in a very different case and was making little headway on tracking down the Scavenger. He decided he would follow his original plan and start by examining the background to some of the killings.

That evening, ensconced in his inner-city office, he began his reading of the Scavenger files with the summary report. A taskforce had been set up and there was a forensic psychologist on board, the one who'd been quoted in the papers, Crowe guessed. A Dr Meera Banerjee, from Melbourne University, a specialist in psychopathic serial homicides. She'd studied in the US where serial murder was a growth industry. The Scavenger killed on a lunar cycle, just as Blowie had claimed. Victims had their throats cut, but only *after* anatomical bits and pieces were removed – and something not revealed to the press: every victim had their heart missing. Implements most likely used included but were not restricted to a hatchet, a scalpel, and a tungsten carbide circular saw with an inbuilt battery to do amputations; all commonly available. The Scavenger left plenty of traces behind but as he'd not been in the legal system there was nothing to match them to.

So far, so standard. The devil, Crowe knew, would be in the detail, and the detail would be buried in the mountains of paper before him. He was less than pleased when there was a knock at the door.

Ross Hooper, known as Burger to his mates, was just bright enough not to run into doorways if you gave him instructions to the contrary. He was content to eke out a living as a heavy for hire, willing to go along for the ride if the job paid okay and didn't involve the cops. It was one of the reasons Crowe had hired him to keep watch the night everything went to shit out at the breakwater. He reminded Crowe of a badly shaved panda who wore T-shirts with beer ads on them, summer and winter. As frustrating as Hooper's propensity for making dumb decisions was, Crowe liked him.

Accompanying him was a young woman whose presence suggested Hooper's decision-making skills had not improved. Her face was pleasant, despite a nose bent enough to show it had been broken once or twice and a few eruptions of acne down one cheek. Long, straight, dirty-blonde hair lay over her shoulders, which were bare above a purple tank top.

'Where've you been, Ross?' Crowe asked. In all honestly, he hadn't thought about Hooper since the shooting started at the lighthouse, and he was annoyed to have him turn up right now.

Hooper pushed past through the doorway into the office. The girl hung back, pouting while she took in Crowe and his habitat.

'Had a job out west over the weekend,' Hooper said. 'This is Sandy.'

'Hello, Mr Crowe.' She reached out her hand and Crowe shook it. Then she followed Hooper inside.

Crowe had set Hooper up on the main road on the night of Pukalski's job to latch onto Skarratt if need be, follow him and let Crowe know where the courier went so he could be dealt with after Crowe had dealt with the others. Yet here he was – four days later.

'I cleared out when all the shooting started,' Hooper said, pulling in his belly. 'You didn't say there was a war on.'

'Forgot all about you,' Crowe said.

'When Skarratt didn't show, I figured something must have happened and pissed off home.'

'Haven't you seen the papers?'

Hooper had gravitated toward Crowe's desk. He idly poked at the open file that lay there. 'What's this? You workin'?'

Crowe nudged him out of the way and shut the file.

'None of your business. Want something to drink?'

Hooper shuffled over to the nearest chair and lowered himself into it. 'Sure.'

'You?' Crowe asked the girl. She shook her head.

Crowe fetched his friend a glass of orange juice from the small fridge next to his filing cabinet. Hooper was meant to be on a strict diet but still ate burgers like they were going out of style. 'Some things are worth dying for,' he'd say. Sandy was wandering around studying the décor, such as it was. A makeshift bedroom lay off to the side and she disappeared into it. Having a stranger poking around his place, unasked, was making Crowe antsy.

'Why am I only hearing from you now?'

'Had a job on out west.'

'Naturally,' muttered Crowe, knowing it wasn't worth pushing the issue. Hooper would get around to saying why he was here in his own time. No use getting mad at the poor bastard just for going around with his head up his arse. Crowe gave him a brief rundown on what had happened and suggested it'd be best if Hooper kept his head down for a while. Pukalski didn't know about him, and it might be wise to leave it that way.

'What's the matter?' Hooper said. 'Don't you trust him?'

'If I don't find this Scavenger and the money and the goods soon, Pukalski will get impatient. I think he half suspects me of organising the double-cross anyway.'

'You didn't, did you?'

'You need to ask?'

Hooper sat nodding, as though his mind had wandered off somewhere.

Sandy came back from the bedroom. 'You don't live here, do you?'

'Sure. Why not? Bed, fridge and dunny down the hall. What more could I want?'

She shrugged and sat on a chair near the window that looked out over Atchison Street.

Hooper was watching her. 'Nice, ain't she?' he said.

'Don't know how you do it, Ross.' Sandy's tank top and her present posture emphasised those aspects that might be termed 'nice'.

'Do it?' Hooper said, looking at Crowe quizzically. 'Do what?'

'Seduce the girls. For Christ's sake, Burger, you're an ugly blob.'

Hooper laughed. 'I got character but.'

'Well, this one's a bit young, isn't she?'

'Young? Nah. She's 24. She told me.'

Yeah, right, Crowe thought.

They talked about nothing in particular for a while, Crowe getting more and more edgy as his mind returned to the Scavenger files. Conversations with Hooper tended to be convoluted, rambling things that almost inevitably led to reminiscences of his imaginary time in Iraq. He was most easily tolerated when there was a job on. So long as he knew exactly what was going to happen and none of it was overly threatening, he was reliable enough.

Usually.

'Geez,' he was saying, 'That other night at the Basin...when the munition started goin' off, I thought I was back in the desert. Sorta panicked. Thought you were dead, Mike.'

'You didn't feel like investigating?'

'Panicked.' He looked down at his crotch and pouted. 'Sorry, Mike. But it was...you know, the dark and all that...you know what it was like, mate?'

Crowe did, because he'd heard the story before, and he knew he was in for a replay.

Sandy glanced up, caught Crowe's eye and smiled rather coyly.

'I've really got a lot of work to do, Ross,' he said.

Hooper didn't hear him. He was off like a race-caller, blathering on about Al-Basrah and the Yanks and the bloody snipers and the bombs, and how the government had let him down. Crowe knew he hadn't been to Iraq, not in a combative capacity anyway. He was too old for starters. But it was a fantasy Hooper couldn't be talked out of. Crowe suspected he actually believed his own fantasy after all these years. It gave him meaning. Sandy grinned. Crowe shrugged. She got up.

'Ross?' she said, interrupting Hooper's flow. 'I'm hungry.'

He spluttered, tripping over his own thoughts.

'Hungry,' she went on, leaning over him and stroking his cheek. 'Go and get us some burgers or something, will ya?'

'Burgers?' Hooper tasted the word.

'Any takeaways around here?' she asked Crowe. 'Any that'd still be open?'

He gave Hooper some directions and some money.

Hooper kissed Sandy on the forehead and disappeared out the door.

'I had to interrupt, Mr Crowe,' she explained, sitting in the chair Hooper had been occupying. 'That was gonna be his long version. Would've gone on for hours. This way you can pack us off as soon as he comes back.'

'Call me Mike. Or Crowe.'

'Which do you like?'

'Crowe.'

She gave him a knowing smile and went to the window. She looked out for a moment.

'So, you and Ross are close mates, I take it?' she said, turning back.

'I like him okay, but he has a tendency to get himself into unnecessary trouble. And his conversation is even more limited than mine.'

'Were you both in that war he's always talking about?'

'Not as such.'

'So where did you meet him?'

Crowe tried to remember, but nothing, not even a witticism, came to mind. 'I wouldn't know. Probably on a job. Feels like he's always been around. What about you?'

'Me?'

'Yeah, what's your deal with Ross? Girlfriend?'

She shrugged. 'I love him, sure. But he's like a father, you know. We don't do it. Sex, I mean. You know how old he is?'

'A good few years older than you.'

'Exactly.' She paused and her general look turned into one of slight embarrassment. 'Okay, I admit I get real horny sometimes. So, we do it. It's okay, isn't it?'

'How long have you known him?'

'Years. He took me in off the street.'

'Years? He's never mentioned you before.'

She pouted. 'Okay, not years. Since last June.'

Crowe settled on 17 as her age while hoping it wasn't less than that. It made him sad; she reminded him of Lucy. As Lucy had been, Sandy was young and abused. Unlike Lucy, though, this one was no innocent and had not had anything approaching Lucy's privileged social background.

'And you don't have boyfriends a bit younger than Burger?' he asked.

'Nah.'

He stared at her for a long moment. He could tell she was lying. But so what? It wasn't his business.

'What about you?' she said. 'Who do you get off with? Or are you past it?'

He laughed. 'Look, as much as I'd enjoy giving you a full R-rated rundown of my love life, I have work to do. Can you occupy yourself? Quietly.'

'Got a telly here someplace?'

'No. This is an office, not a fucking cinema.'

'Can I use your computer?'

'It's not connecting to the internet,' he lied. 'I've been meaning to get it fixed.'

She glanced about the room with a look that was almost panic. 'Can I go lie on the bed then, till Ross gets back? I'm bushed.'

Crowe nodded and she smiled wanly. 'How long will it take him?' she said.

'What? To get the burgers?'

'Yeah. How long have I got?'

'Fifteen minutes maybe.'

She glanced around again. 'I haven't washed for days,' she said. 'There a shower someplace here?'

'Sure, out the door and to the right, just down the hall. Clean towels in the bottom drawer of that filing cabinet.'

She said nothing, just fetched a towel and strode out like she owned the place.

When Hooper got back, clutching a swag of hamburgers in a brown paper bag with the usual logos on it, Crowe was where he'd been when his house-guest left: glancing through the Scavenger files. He had discovered that the files contained three letters from the Scavenger, the one Blowie had shown him being the first. Maybe Blowie *did* have connections and if so could be more useful than Crowe had given him credit for. Crowe cast his eye over the others. One was clearly fake, with handwriting that was nothing like that of the first letter, and a note pointing this out was attached to it. The third was a computer printout – another fake, Crowe guessed. Disappointed, he put them aside for later consideration.

'She's down the corridor,' he said as Hooper glanced anxiously around the room. 'Having a shower. She reckoned she was due for one.'

Hooper began silently munching on a gigantic egg burger, letting the juices drip from the corners of his mouth onto the papers on Crowe's desk. Crowe gathered them up, wishing he'd get lost.

Hooper offered him a burger, but Crowe shook his head.

'She makes me feel real good,' Hooper said suddenly through a mouthful of mush.

Crowe smiled his understanding.

'Yep, real good.'

What was he up to? Lots of undercurrents had filled the room since the two of them dropped by.

'She's nice to you, is she, Ross?'

The big man nodded, took a big bite of hamburger bun, tomato sauce and meat patty, still looking at Crowe over the top of it.

'Does she play with other blokes?' Crowe asked.

Hooper's jaw stopped chewing and slid outward like the drawer of a filing cabinet. 'What d'ya mean?' he spluttered.

'She looks rather lively to me.'

'She doesn't do nothin',' he said defensively. 'She's a good girl.'

'Sure,' Crowe shrugged. 'That's what I figured.'

Hooper studied Crowe's eyes for a moment, then returned to what he knew best. Chewing. Crowe stared back, and, when no more words were forthcoming, began flipping through the Henry folder. Lester Henry, victim number seven, had lived on Kenny Street, near the cemetery, only a few minutes away. The victim had been 33 years old. Born in Geelong. He'd lived in Wollongong only six months, having recently moved from Fitzroy in Melbourne to take up a job with BlueScope. Played golf a lot and had gone for a stroll on the course. As odd as that might seem, it being the middle of the night, it was a habit with him after a late shift. According to his wife, Glenys, he'd come home just after 11 and, unable to sleep, had headed out to walk off his tensions. She'd assumed he got there, because he always did, and he wasn't likely to get lost, was he? What happened after that was unclear, except that he was sliced up. There was a statement from someone called Elly Dernshaw, who claimed she'd seen Henry talking to a bloke on the corner of Cemetery Avenue and Keira Street. She described the bloke as 'taller than poor Mr Henry, who was quite short, you know'. Apart from 'He wasn't fat', she had nothing more to add. Police assumed that, if this bloke was the killer, then they were looking for someone with a bit of height. Not much, because Henry was a shrimp, but tallish. Maybe 170cm. But Crowe's interaction with the killer suggested he hadn't been 170cm. He'd guess 150. Overall, he thought it might be worth talking to Mrs Henry.

'Mike?' Hooper's voice eased itself into Crowe's thoughts.

He glanced up. Judging by the look of anguish on his face, Hooper had finished his burgers long ago. There was only one left. Sandy's, no doubt. He was being restrained.

'What, Ross?'

'You know, Mike, I...um...need, like, a favour.'

'More burgers?'

Sandy entered. She was dressed, with Crowe's towel wrapped around her hair. She and Hooper exchanged glances.

'Nah, somethin' else,' Hooper continued. 'You see, we're...Sandy and me...we're in a bit of trouble.'

'The sort of trouble that involves the cops?'

Hooper nodded. 'Bastards sprung me on Saturday. Petrol station job.' He stood and began wandering around, not meeting Crowe's eye. 'Bit of a blow-out. Got away with 200 or somethin'. Between four of us. Stupid.'

'Petty robberies *are* stupid, Ross. Nearly as stupid as big ones.'

'Yeah, I know. You always say that. But they made it sound like a good idea. Everyone got away, but I think the cops know it was me.'

'You forgot about CCTV surveillance, right?'

He nodded glumly.

'Were you wearing a balaclava?'

'A what?'

'No, of course you weren't. So what do you want from me?'

'Can you put us up for a couple of days, Mike? I'm bust.'

'What, here?'

He laughed. 'Come on, Mike. You'll have somewhere else with a bit of room. Always do.'

Crowe shut the file. Hooper's face was like a bag of used sports shorts: damp and sort of droopy. 'Sorry, mate, I'm too busy to wet-nurse a burger junkie and a teenager—'

'We won't bother you, honest. Coupla days till I can sort somethin' out. You can get to know Sandy better?'

Crowe stared at him. 'Get to know Sandy better?'

'Yeah, she knows how ta make a guy feel good.'

'A couple of days, eh?'

'That's all, Mr Crowe.' Sandy smiled nervously. 'A day or two. I'd be willin' to...' Her voice faded into an awkward silence.

Crowe looked from her to Hooper. 'You pimping her out for rent, Ross?'

'It's not like that,' Hooper muttered without conviction.

Crowe leaned close and whispered, 'That was insulting, old friend.' Crowe pointed. 'Insulting to me and to Sandy here.'

Hooper hung his head, as if waiting for an axe to fall.

Crowe took his spare keys from the desk drawer and tossed them to him. Hooper missed the catch and had to scramble around to fetch. Crowe told him the address.

'Three days, Ross,' he said. 'No more.'

16

THE WOLLONGONG CEMETERY TOOK UP A WHOLE BLOCK BETWEEN SWAN Street and Cemetery Avenue. Part of it spilled over the road into a fragmented corner full of broken monoliths and tilting crosses. Its dead were ancient and forgotten. The suburb, too, was old, with conservative houses that had probably been there since the '50s looking defiantly across Kenny Street toward a field of tombstones and graves. New fencing had been put up not long ago to keep the vandals out – or the dead in. The road itself was wide, like a river of bitumen, forming a barrier between the homes of the living and the dead. A thick perimeter of trees further cut the graveyard off from its potential inhabitants.

Crowe had decided to embrace the gumshoe ethos and check out some of the crime scenes, talk to a few of the Scavenger victims' family members and friends – PI stuff like that. The police files were very thorough, but you never knew what random face-to-face interviews might bring to the surface. Lester Henry's wife seemed a good start.

Unexpectedly, Crowe found himself more on edge being there than he might have thought. Though he was reluctant to buy into the possibility that he was being haunted, there was no doubt that something abnormal was going on. The row upon row of old gravestones played to his unease. He pushed it aside, determined to take what came and deal with whatever it might mean later.

According to the report, Henry had strolled down Kenny Street that

Sunday night, eating a banana and carrying a can of beer. He'd made it to Cemetery Avenue, turned left, crossed Keira Street and entered J.J. Kelly Park about 12.15. The moon had been full. No one knew if he'd reached the golf course; at some point, he'd been seen talking to a 'tallish' man on the corner of Keira Street and Cemetery Avenue. This might or might not have been the killer, maybe someone he knew. Or both.

The only certainty was that the Scavenger took a hunk of Henry's chest – ribs and all. A bit after the carve-up started, the poor bastard died.

Standing in the ditch where Henry's body was found, where the forensic experts believed he died, didn't give Crowe any ideas. Cold wind whipped across the open park. It was a long way – 500m or more – from the spot where Henry had been seen talking to another man. So, had he just strolled this way or been lured? If the latter, how? And once the killer had him here, how had he immobilised him? There were no rope marks on the corpse, though there was bruising consistent with a strong grip. The experts reckoned he'd still been conscious when the killer began slicing him up; the level of some drug in his blood was consistent with that horror story.

Crowe shivered, pulling his coat up around his neck.

A pair of fluffy slippers with teeth yapped at him from behind a wire-screen door. Crowe knocked on the wooden frame again. Its rattle sent the dogs into a paroxysm of rage.

'Shut up,' he muttered, banging his fist hard on the jamb. The two terriers, or whatever the hell they were, chewed at the mesh.

'Yes?' said a female voice from further inside the house. Very subdued. As though it belonged to a ghost afraid its appearance would be too much for anyone to bear.

'Mrs Henry?' Crowe asked. She didn't open the door. The security grille made visibility difficult, hiding her in a web of fine grid lines.

'I'm Glenys Henry,' she said. 'What do you want?'

'I'd like to ask you a few questions, if that's all right,' Crowe said, peering through the mesh. The dogs jumped and snapped.

'Quiet!' Mrs Henry told them. The suppressed anger in the command sent them scampering away. She stood close on the other side of the door and looked out at Crowe – he could see her a little better that way. She looked attractive and aware. According to the files, she was only in her mid-30s, but she had the air of an older lady. 'What sort of questions?'

'I'm working with the police,' he said, flashing his wallet and hoping she wouldn't look at it. She didn't.

She seemed to shrivel then. 'It's about Lester, isn't it?'

'Yes, ma'am. Some follow-up.'

'Your name is?'

'Crowe. Michael Crowe.'

She nodded as though it meant something to her. Then she unclipped the lock and opened the door. 'Come in!'

Lester Henry's widow was of medium build, wearing neat, somewhat old-fashioned clothes – long-sleeved, cream blouse with a high neck line, pleated skirt that fell halfway down her calf, long tartan socks, and black 'visiting' shoes (as Crowe's mother used to call them) – even though she hadn't left the house and clearly didn't intend to. Her chestnut hair was cropped evenly and her make-up was precise. Crowe followed her through the narrow entrance hall into a tidy lounge room. The dogs scampered around his feet. They wanted to bite him but were aware that Mrs Henry didn't want them to. Not yet.

'Sit down, please,' she said wearily, gesturing at a pile of hand-woven cushions. The old lounge creaked under him.

'I've talked to the police,' she said. 'But I suppose you know that.'

'I've read the transcript.'

She nodded. 'Would you like something? A beer? Coffee?'

'Not necessary, Mrs Henry.'

She studied Crowe for a moment, silently, unsure how she should respond. 'I think I'll make some coffee anyway.'

It didn't take her long, which was just as well as the dogs watched Crowe hungrily the whole time she was out of the room. Their black noses, like large ticks poking through a mass of straggly hair, made him want to squash them under his shoe. Crowe glanced around instead, smelling the combined fragrance of Gamawash, Mr Sheen and floral perfume. The lounge room felt abandoned. There were no magazines lying about; no flowers, dead or alive; no pictures of Lester Henry on the side table or the ornament cabinet, as if he had been absent from this place even before death. There was a space where there might've been a TV once and an aerial socket in the wall behind it, but no TV.

'I took a guess,' Glenys Henry said, entering the room with two coffees. 'Black and no sugar?'

'Spot on,' Crowe replied and took the offered mug.

She gazed down at him. 'You look exactly like a private eye, right down to the scar. You are, aren't you?'

Crowe shrugged. Not quite yes, not quite no – nicely deniable.

'Do you have a gun on you?'

Crowe was carrying, of course. Half his life was taken up fulfilling a stereotype. But he smiled condescendingly. 'This isn't a TV show.'

'Why are you investigating my husband's murder anyway?' A whine crept into her voice. She struggled to control it. 'If you're a private eye, someone must have hired you.'

'The police are...well, short-staffed. Sometimes I get work doing the unprofitable stuff. Looking for needles in haystacks. They hope I'll come up with something just by covering old ground. Something they missed. You could describe me as a consultant.'

She sipped at her coffee. Crowe sipped at his. It was instant, but he persisted.

'What do you want to know?' she said suddenly.

'Well, who killed your husband would be desirable?'

The question took her by surprise. She blinked, then frowned. 'How should I know, Mr Crowe? If I knew that, don't you think I would've told the police?'

'Maybe you just haven't remembered.'

'Remembered? I think of nothing else. I go over and over it in my mind, trying to make sense of it. If there's someone who wanted to hurt Lester, I didn't know about it.' Tears welled in her eyes, emotion becoming a flush across her cheeks.

'Take a guess,' Crowe said.

He watched her, waiting for her to talk. She bit her lip, squirmed on her seat as though it had suddenly become lumpy, and finally groaned, very low and sad. 'I can't think of anyone.'

'Try to imagine what his killer would be like.'

'I don't know.'

'Would he be big?'

'Probably. Lester wasn't very tall, but he was strong. He was a manual labourer until about a year ago.'

'He retrained?'

She nodded.

'What did he want? Was there some...weakness in him that would make him vulnerable?'

'Weakness?' She looked confused. The dogs sensed her anxiety and were snuffling around Crowe's feet, growling so quietly they could barely be heard. 'He'd been unhappy, I guess.' Her awareness of Crowe, of the room and the situation, was thinning, loosening its grip. 'Perhaps he wanted something. He'd been restless, unable to sleep, for months before. I thought it might be me, but he said no. It was nothing, he said. A sign of age, he said. But he was only young. I don't know.' Her thoughts leapt outward, grabbing Crowe's attention. 'I just don't know. It was as though he felt unfulfilled.' She began to sob. Lowered her head and placed a hand over her face. Her shoulders quivered. After a moment, she glanced at Crowe again. Eyes swollen. 'We've been married since I was 17. I don't know any other way to live.'

'Children?'

'A girl. She's passed, too. An accident.'

'A while ago, I take it.'

'Just over six years ago. The 28th of May, 2012. Why is life so cruel, Mr Crowe?'

He shrugged. 'Life's just a passing phase. Everyone dies.'

Emotion bled out of her face. 'It's not right.'

Giving comfort was not Crowe's strong suit. He couldn't think of anything to say. Maybe it wasn't right. The dogs didn't care. They were standing near his feet, waiting intently for their cue.

'Did Mr Henry have any enemies?' he asked.

She stood up suddenly. 'Why are you asking these stupid questions? It was chance, pure chance. There was no connection between my husband and the other men who've been killed by this maniac. None. Why do you think Lester might have known him? Why do you think it has any meaning?'

'I just hope it does. Otherwise we may never catch him.'

'You're just like me. Fumbling around in the dark.'

'Sure. It's the only way. Sometimes you knock your shin on things you didn't know were there.'

She gestured him away and turned toward the door. 'Go somewhere else and fumble. There isn't any hope of making things better. I just want to forget.'

The dogs were growling again. Like Crowe, they knew there was no hope of her doing that either.

'Okay,' Crowe said, deciding to leave her to her grief. He stood. 'Thanks for the coffee.'

Despite the useless and somewhat melancholy nature of his interview with Mrs Henry and her dogs, Crowe spent two days visiting – or attempting to visit – other survivors of the Scavenger's victims. After a while it was simply too pointless and too depressing to use a verbal stick to dislodge some theoretical clue from their responses. He was abused several times and cried on at least once, so he decided to give the Scavenger-victim side of the case away. Instead, he spent some time visiting the places where the Scavenger's victims had been found. Most told him very little, but one stayed with him for some time.

Bulli Beach reserve was an exposed green expanse next to a bitumen carpark, dolled up with treated-wood borders and lots of neatly trimmed grass. A brick, aluminium and glass clubhouse overlooked the ocean, its front plastered with ice-cream signs. Crowe looked down on the rock platform that held the Waniora pool. Beyond it, the sea was grey and choppy. Neither body of water looked inviting.

The pool was where Paul McCartney had gone for one last, involuntary swim. Crowe imagined Holly Newcombe – the 20-year-old bank clerk who'd found the corpse – jogging across the reserve and casually glancing down, the dimming sun catching the figure in the water. Normally, she wouldn't take any notice, but he wasn't dressed for swimming. And was face down. She'd eased herself closer to the pool, where she could make out a diffused stain surrounding the body…and that there was a ragged stump where one of his legs should have been.

When Crowe had tried to question her further at her bank job, all he'd succeeded in doing was driving her into hysterics. He'd been walked out of the building by the manager.

The cops had questioned people staying in the caravans at the nearby park, but no one had seen anything, or admitted to it. Time of death was supposed to be about two in the morning, so the lack of witnesses wasn't surprising.

'Poor Paul got up to go to the toilet,' his wife told the cops. 'His bladder's been a bit wonky. I dozed off so I didn't notice he hadn't got back.'

Crowe walked around the pool, looking for inspiration, but nothing came. The wind got worse as he hit the open beach. He walked westward, retracing the killer's possible route.

The Bulli Beach Holiday Park was entrenched between a large brick shower block and distant residential houses. Concrete paths and bitumen roads marked out a pattern of vans and cardboard cut-out bungalows. No movement today, except for flapping canvas. It was like a ghost town. And Crowe could see where the ghosts came from. Behind the park, high on a rise of ground and half-hidden by trees and bushes, was a cemetery – a flat, orderly series of tombstones cut off from holidaymakers by a rusty chain-link fence with gaps at ground level where itinerants could squirm through to meet the locals.

He wondered where the McCartneys had been staying, relative to the cemetery. He tried to remember whether that information had been in the police report, but wind blew all rational thought out of his head. He grumbled to himself then walked across grass and gravel, over a footbridge that spanned Wharton's Creek and along the bike track skirting the park. There was a good view of the cemetery.

He's there, said a young girl.

Startled, recognising the voice, Crowe glanced around.

It was her. An involuntary shudder spasmed through his body, clawing right to the tips of his fingers.

'Lucy?'

She stood a few metres from him. Blood ran down her cheeks and limbs, soaking through her torn clothes. He could see her hand with its missing fingers. She was standing side on to him, staring up toward the cemetery. Despite the wind that gusted over them, there was little movement in her hair and clothing, though a visual instability blurred her edges.

Crowe staggered, his legs weak with shock. 'How can you be here?' He made his lips release the words. It was almost painful.

She turned to look at him, her face shimmering uncertainly. Her eyes were lost in shadows that should not have been there, even given the cloud-filtered light.

Her violated hand reached out.

'G'day,' came a gruff voice from behind him.

Crowe looked around. An old bloke in shorts and a green windcheater sat on the grass just off to one side. He held a fishing magazine.

Crowe turned back to Lucy. She'd gone. He placed his palm on his forehead and pressed it hard, hoping the pressure would make it all go away and he would regain perspective. The vision had been so real.

'Lousy weather,' the old bloke said. He was gazing out over the sea.

'Did you…did you see…' Crowe managed, his flesh still tingling from the sheer unearthliness of the vision.

The old bloke stared at Crowe for a moment, evaluating him. He said nothing. Crowe was unable to finish the sentence. They continued like that for long, uncomfortable seconds.

'Sick of this bloody wind,' the man said suddenly, turning back to the sea.

'What—'

'The weather. Not too good, is it? Not for people on holidays, eh?'

'I…I don't know.'

The old man looked at Crowe side-on. 'But that's okay. Bloody tourists are a pain in the arse.'

Crowe took a deep breath. He had to pull himself together. 'You live around here then.'

The man jerked his thumb toward the caravan park. 'In there, mate. On-site van. During the friggin' hols, it drives me crazy. All the yobbos and their kids. Nothin' but trouble.'

Crowe climbed over the railing and sat beside him. Close up, the man looked at least part Aboriginal. Spiky beach-grass didn't offer much shelter from the wind, which scoured over them belligerently. Sitting there was an odd thing to be doing. It made Crowe feel foolish. He needed to get back to the business at hand.

'What about that Scavenger bloke?' he said after a moment, a head-on assault. 'Were you staying here then? When it happened?'

'Too right!'

'You knew the victim?'

The man frowned. 'I talked to him about, I dunno, maybe half an hour before he got killed. Shit, eh? It coulda been me.'

'You talked to him?'

'Yeah. I was goin' to pee. Can't sleep much at night anymore and tend to wander about. He was in the bog. "Bloody cold night, eh?" I said. He agreed and we talked about the wind, just like you and me.'

'What happened when you finished pissing?'

'He went back to his caravan.'

'You saw him go back?'

He looked at Crowe with sudden suspicion. 'You a cop?' he said. 'Askin' a lot of bloody questions.'

'I'm not a cop.' Crowe took out his wallet and showed him there was no badge in it.

Crowe pulled him back to the night Paul McCartney was murdered, doing his best not to sound like a copper. 'Seems funny to me that no one ever sees the bastard. Okay, so it happens in the middle of the night, but people are around even then. You were.'

'Maybe someone seen him. Maybe I did. Who the hell would know? I see lots of things.'

'You remember noticing anyone else that night? Anyone at all.'

The bloke sucked his upper lip, making an odd insect noise.

'Someone was in the cemetery,' he said suddenly, pointing back over his shoulder at the neat rows of sculptured rock, half hidden by the trees this side of it.

'Yeah? Who?'

'Buggered if I know. Someone was up there before I went for a piss. Saw 'im. It was pretty cold and I remember thinkin' he must be mad. Geez, paying his damn respects in the middle of a bloody freezin' night!'

'What was he doing?'

'Didn't take much notice. He was just there, you know.' He chuckled.

'Did you watch for long?'

'Why should I? It was bloody cold. The weather's crazy.'

'What about later? After you spoke to McCartney?'

'Looked up the hill, but there was nothing.'

'And McCartney? What happened to him?'

'Got himself killed, I guess. He went off in the direction of his van, but I reckon the Scavenger bloke got him before he made it. Poor bugger.' He looked at Crowe. 'His caravan was way back. Mine's facin' the beach. You think it was the bloke in the cemetery did it?'

Crowe shrugged. 'Can you tell me what he looked like?'

'He was a fair way off, you know. Just a blob. Might not've even been there. Like I said, I see lotsa stuff.' He stood.

'Did you see something just now? When you first spoke to me? A young woman?'

The man stared at Crowe for another long moment, long enough to feel awkward.

'I might've,' he said. 'Might not 'ave. Can't tell with these things.'

'What things?'

'Better go now,' he said. 'Hope you don't mind. Gettin' tired.'

It was over. Whatever had opened him up to Crowe had closed off again just as abruptly. He was looking elsewhere now, away from the caravan park, right through Crowe. His cheeks trembled, maybe with cold.

'Sure. Nice talking to you,' Crowe said.

The man went a few paces then stopped.

'I hope you find 'im,' he said, looking back. 'I been feelin' a bit guilty, not talkin' to the cops. And blokes like him, they need to be found. For everyone's sake. Reckon you might have a chance.'

'Why?'

The old guy nodded, as if agreeing with something. 'Ya got interestin' friends,' he whispered through the wind.

'What friends?'

But Crowe's erstwhile companion hopped over the railing and shuffled away.

A sense of foreboding comes over me again. It crawls from obscurity like something insidious, nipping tentatively at my extremities before reaching my heart and then biting into it as though starving for whatever emotions might lie dormant in there. I don't know what it wants of me.

But I have seen its desires.

'Please,' I whisper. 'Leave me be. I haven't got anything for you.'

But I fear what it wants is my soul and it has no intention of leaving until it can feast upon it.

I hunker down and attempt to cry, but there are no tears. I am incapable of tears. Until I'm rescued from this place, this evil will probe my past and bite at my flesh — and if it manages to eat away every memory until I am left empty, it will simply wait for the door to open and take everything it has stolen from me into a new existence. The real me will be left here forever, trapped between light and shade, empty, beyond everything. Beyond the end of the world.

'Please help me!' I cry.

But on this occasion, no one hears.

17

NEXT DAY, CROWE DECIDED TO GO UP TO SYDNEY TO SEE IF HE COULD DIG up anything about Suleman, Hall and Rousch from any other available scumbags who might have knowledge of what had gone on that night on Belmore Basin. He hadn't been getting very far when he found himself at a small weatherboard dump in Newtown, in Sydney's inner west, where Irwin Suleman had lived. It looked like it had been home to no more than vermin for a long time. Gail had made discreet enquiries and the address was, among other things, what she'd ferreted out. As Pirran had intimated, Suleman was a petty crook. His main claim to fame was getting busted fencing stolen goods to a cop. The department had told reporters the cop was undercover, but said cop quit the force not much later and lived well – for a while – off a nest egg that had been laid in one of his bank accounts. The proceeds of horseracing and wise investment, he claimed. The cop's name was Nathan Hall, and Gail reckoned he'd been skint for some months, ever since a drunken night playing cards with dubious characters from Melbourne. Glassing was involved.

Suleman hadn't got off so lightly. He'd served 18 months of a three-year sentence. He'd been working off and on as a barman since he got out the previous November. Sure, he'd been renting, so it wasn't his responsibility to paint, but he might have done minor cosmetics. If he'd cared. Which he obviously hadn't. It wasn't a place to live; it was a place to hide out in – or to hang yourself in.

Crowe pounded on the back door, just to make sure there was no one home. It was mid-afternoon; no one was out on the street, but he doubted anyone would have cared even if they'd seen him break in.

Getting through the door took about three seconds because the lock was broken. But that wasn't a recent thing. Suleman was using a brick to keep the door shut. As it slid open, Crowe thought he saw a figure in a hazy corner of the room. He tensed, focused on the spot, then relaxed as he realised there was no one.

Please…help me!

The words shot through him, reverberating in his bones once again, taking him by surprise. Clear and powerful this time. He closed his eyes and concentrated on calming his nerves. He wasn't used to this sort of thing. It was starting to drive him crazy, assuming he wasn't crazy already.

When he looked again, the room – a sort of enclosed verandah – was filled with over-stuffed boxes. Rubbish, it looked like. He went through into the house proper.

It wasn't as stuffy as Crowe had expected. Suleman had been away for over a week, most of which time he'd spent in the morgue. But someone had opened the door and got the air moving. Maybe the cops, if they'd been able to find out where Suleman lived. The place was so untidy – untidy in a way that suggested long-term bad habits – that Crowe couldn't have detected their presence unless they'd left a business card. If the police had already been here, there probably wouldn't be anything that could help him. If they hadn't, there might be a clue. God knows what, but he was ever hopeful. No record of a police search appeared in the file.

Someone had thrown up in the bedroom. Recently. The smell was overpowering. Crowe held his breath as much as possible while he poked around through the grubby clothes dumped on an old chair near the window and in the room's only cupboard – a small plywood box painted purple. A few mangled copies of a cheap-looking porn magazine. A small envelope of dope, nearly empty but for a few stalks, and a stained bong made from a plastic OJ container. Other bits and pieces of a life that hadn't really been worth much – about $3 in change and a credit card, stolen no doubt, belonging to someone who wasn't called Irwin Suleman.

In the kitchen, which was filthy, he found a few cracked plates, some bent cutlery and lots of Mars Bar wrappers. Nothing much in the ancient fridge except for sour milk in an average-sized carton, a half-full container of yogurt and a few pieces of shrivelled pizza. The place was some sort of visual cliché screaming 'low-life'.

The lounge room was more interesting. There'd been a TV, because the aerial connection was still draped across the bare wooden floor and a few old TV guides taken out of the local newspaper decorated the corners. But it had been removed recently. Crowe could see where it had stood by the relative cleanliness of the floor at that spot. He remembered Mrs Henry's missing set but guessed the absence of this one meant something different.

The room had an old three-seater, too, and there was someone sleeping on it. Goldilocks, perhaps?

He couldn't tell straight away. The someone was covered in blankets without even the top of their head showing. Skinny fingers with short, chewed nails peeked out from one edge. Crowe pulled the blanket up a bit, noted the arm was male and pitted with needle marks. Some days Crowe reckoned his life was full of losers. What did that make him?

'Hey? What?' The arm was yanked away and a pale head with a skull cap of short hair emerged. Its stare was glassy, like someone had been using its eyes as marbles while their owner slept. 'What? Fuck! What?' the youth muttered again. Maybe 20. Maybe not. Crowe tried to look unthreatening.

'Afternoon,' he said.

The bloke stared at him aghast. Towering in his leather coat, tall and solid, Crowe might have been a cop.

'Who?' the zombie managed, swivelling around and placing his bare feet on the floor. A pair of heavy-soled black shoes stood at the end of the lounge. He kept the blanket around himself, probably as protection. No clothes except for a black jumper were lying around, so Crowe hoped that meant he was still wearing pants.

'Byrd's the name,' Crowe said. 'I'm a friend of Irwin's.'

Something like hope entered the young bloke's eyes. He let the blanket drop. He'd been sleeping in a pair of boxer shorts, very crumpled now. A cut-up T-shirt left a lot of hairless, sallow skin showing.

'Irwin? Shit, you know where he is?'

'Sure,' Crowe said. 'Who are you?'

'Jude.' He wobbled uncertainly to his feet then sat down again. 'I feel terrible. The bastard was supposed to be here four days ago. I had to flog the TV to get food.' He lay back, putting an arm over his eyes. Crowe noticed the empty Jim Beam bottle on the lounge chair.

'How long have you been here?' Crowe asked.

The bloke looked out from under his arm. 'Since Sunday. That's what we arranged. The place looked like someone had been through it. Didn't know what to do, so I waited. Irwin always told me if he wasn't here, I should wait. Did he send anything for me? Any stuff?'

Crowe ignored the question. 'Why aren't you sleeping in the bedroom?'

'Did, the first night. But I threw up in there and it stinks.'

'You could've cleaned it.'

'Why? The place is a shit heap. Needs to be firebombed.' He frowned and shrank back into glumness. 'Why're you here anyway? Where's Irwin?'

Crowe sat on the arm of the lounge. Stench of stale sweat and cheap whiskey drifted over him. He put his hand on Jude's shoulder so the bloke couldn't get up. His skin felt clammy. 'Dead.'

Jude's eyes widened. 'What?' He tried to get away from Crowe, but Crowe pulled the young man back.

'Just hang about. We need to talk.'

'What'd you mean dead? How did he get dead?'

'He was shot a little over a week ago. On a job. What's your relationship with him?'

The young bloke turned suddenly and sneered at Crowe. 'You a cop?'

'You his partner?'

'What's it to you?' He tried to get away from Crowe again, but this time Crowe pushed him back into the sofa's lumpy padding with some force.

'Look,' he snapped, 'I've got a job to do, and right now that involves finding out what Suleman was up to when he was killed, and who he was up to it with. Either you're going to cooperate, or I'll break your arms. Okay?'

Whatever warmth was in the bloke's face flushed away. His lips trembled and tears threatened. 'Shit, man, don't hurt me. I don't know shit. Honest.'

'What did Suleman tell you?'

'Nothin'.'

Crowe pushed him hard. He jerked back into the corner of the lounge, more shocked than hurt.

'What did he tell you about Thursday night?'

'He had something on. Double dealing.' The young man snuffled so much Crowe could barely make out what he was saying. 'He sent me to a friend's place, told me to come back Sunday. It'd be over then, and he reckoned we'd be rich. Bullshit, I guess.'

'If it'd worked, you would've been.'

'Yeah? Went wrong, did it?'

'Irwin was a fool. The whole set-up was stupid, and he was a sitting duck. Just a patsy, I reckon. Who was he working with?'

'I don't know. Honest.' The young man glanced at Crowe's stony face and a muscle twitched in his cheek. 'He knew some ex-cop. I'm pretty sure he was in on it.'

Hall. 'Yeah, he was. Who else?'

'Look, mister–' he turned to talk earnestly at Crowe '–with Irwin we were just mates, you know. Sometimes we'd muck around. We drank together, he got me ice when he could. Occasionally we'd do some B&E. But this thing, this job…he kept it to himself. A big bloke came over once, pushed Irwin around for mouthing off down the pub. Don't know his name, but I reckon he was running things.'

'Describe him.'

'I was a bit smashed that day, but I remember he was about your height, bit less maybe. Pretty good-looking, sort of like, um, what's his name? Actor?' He shook his head. 'I forget.'

'Go on.'

'I didn't like him. Bad vibes. And he talked in a nasty sort of way. Growly.' He shot Crowe a questioning look.

'You're doing fine,' he said.

The young bloke's expression sparked, more life in him than Crowe had seen so far. He was enjoying this suddenly. 'Irwin did call him Dick, I remember,' he added eagerly. 'Dick's short for Richard, right?'

Dick Tansey, one of Pukalski's tame monkeys? Tansey was tall, well-built, looked a bit like Richard Gere in his heyday but sandpapered around the edges and not as sexy. Crowe wondered if Suleman could've been working with Tansey. Surely not? 'Does the name Tansey ring any bells?' Crowe asked. 'Dick Tansey?'

Jude went meditative for a moment. 'Yeah, that's him.'

Crowe stood, releasing his grip on Jude's arm. As he reached into his coat, the young man cringed back against the lounge. Crowe produced his wallet and handed over a 50 dollar note. Jude took it tentatively, as though it might bite him.

'What's this for?' he whispered reverently.

'I shouldn't have shoved you around.'

'No sweat.'

'Don't let bastards like me shove you around.'

'Not if I can help it.'

'I mean it. You do, don't you? All the bloody time. It's no way to live.'

Jude looked at Crowe, letting a sardonic grin creep over his lips. He held up the money. 'You're not much good at being a bastard.'

'You don't know me very well.'

'S'pose not.'

'Anyway, Suleman's not coming back. But Tansey might. Or the cops. You'd better get out of here and stay away. Buy yourself something to eat with that.'

'I haven't got nowhere to go.'

Crowe did, so he turned and headed for the door.

After a mostly pointless day spent in Sydney, Crowe returned to Wollongong and found Sandy waiting in his office. She and Hooper had been in Ed Rice's house for nearly three days now and doubtless wanted an extension. She wore a loose-knit cream top and black jeans.

'I brought our rent payment.' She smiled suggestively.

'No charge, I said.' Crowe glanced around the office, but everything looked to be where he'd left it. 'How'd you get in?'

'Key was among those spares you gave us.' She tossed it to him. Crowe caught it and put it in his pocket.

'Where's Ross?'

'Sleeping off a headache.'

'Hasn't been drinking, has he?'

'No.' She shrugged. 'Well, a bit. But we had some trouble the other night. This old bloke turned up.'

Blowie, no doubt. He should have thought of that. 'What happened?'

'Went totally spare. Wanted to know what we were doing in the place. Ross tried to throw him out, but the freak smashed him over the head with a plate that was lying around. Seemed to know you, Crowe. I told him you let us crash there.'

'What did he say to that?'

'Shouted a lot of crazy stuff about bludgers and demanded to know where you'd gone. I didn't tell him. But I thought you might like a bit of warning.'

'Thanks.' It wouldn't take Blowie long to find his office, Crowe figured, if he thought to look in the Yellow Pages. The entry wasn't all that clear, if you didn't know where to look, but it wasn't too much of a mindbender. Crowe was there under 'Investigators', sandwiched between 'Invalid Aids' and 'Investment Advisors'. CROWEMAGNUM SERVICES, it said. Blowie struck him as someone who would get the joke.

'Crowe?' Her voice was lower, cunning. 'Are you sure—'

He waved her away. 'Get lost, Sandy, I'm busy.' She sighed, looking more relieved than anything, and backed out the door.

Something has come unstuck. Up until a few moments ago, I was in my prison as usual, staring at the near-dark that lay docile all around me. Now the gloom is moving, churning into knots as though trying to take shape — though the shapes so far make little sense to me. I thought at first it was a sign of my past returning to me, fighting its way through the oblivion that is my normal state, desperately seeking release. But there is no familiarity at all, no meaning in any of it.

Then the vague areas of shadow slowly become identifiable as a man and a woman standing rigid before me. The man is large. The woman is younger, a bit older than I was. Who are these people? I don't know. I don't remember them. They stare at me but say nothing.

'Who are you?' I ask, but neither of them replies. They drift closer.

As the images clarify, becoming more than solidifying darkness, as though they exist before me and inside my mind at the same time, I realise they are splattered by dark colourations. Deep-red streaks that shift and squirm. Blood? It drips from cuts in their naked skin, forming patterns across the floor.

'What do you want?' I cry.

They don't answer.

I close my eyes, desperate for the moment to pass. This is a new torment, and I understand it even less than the usual fractured moments that come upon me suddenly out of the gloom. This is not memory and was never meant to be. It is something else...

A premonition?

Finally, I open my eyes to confront them, but the figures are gone.

18

WITH A BIT OF PHYSICAL ENCOURAGEMENT, ONE OF SKARRATT'S MATES TOLD Crowe he'd seen Skarratt drinking with Dick Tansey. 'Week or so back. They were up to something,' he said. 'Trust Tansey to get the poor bugger killed.' Wasn't proof of anything but a pretty good indication that Tansey might be behind the double-cross on Pukalski. It'd explain a lot. An inside trader.

According to Gail, Tansey lived in a block of flats at Dapto, a suburb just south of the Gong. Crowe sat in his car a few hundred metres from the front entrance and waited, wondering if he should simply take a chance that Tansey wasn't in there. It was a working day, after all. Luckily, he didn't act on this dubious plan straight away, partly because there was a car parked in front of the flats that looked like one he'd noticed in the carpark outside Pukalski's office building. A new Mustang. Not common to the area. Sure enough, after about half an hour, his target stormed out of the building, got in the Mustang and drove off at high speed.

Once Tansey's car had disappeared in the direction of Wollongong, Crowe headed into the building, gaining access thanks to a teenager who politely held open the self-locking front door for him before taking off down the street. Tansey's name and room number were conveniently on the mailboxes in the vestibule. No one met Crowe on the stairs, and it was still quiet as he stood listening outside Tansey's third-floor flat. So far, so fortuitous. He knocked. No answer.

It took him about a minute to pick the lock. Inside, the room stank of some foul tobacco, but, unlike Suleman's, the place was well-furnished and tidy. Just a few newspapers lying around and several loose DVDs and Blu-rays. Tansey liked his action flicks. *Die Hard* and the Rambos were there, with lots more in a cabinet next to the reasonably large plasma TV and attached player.

In a room that might have been a bedroom, but which Tansey was using as a sort of junk-storage area, Crowe found a camera. Digital. Small, but upmarket. A quick flick through its saved pics showed a few shots of Wilkinson's Breakwater. Groundwork? Nothing very useful, but he pocketed the camera just in case. He rummaged through piles of papers and general rubbish – envelopes, old cards, a screwdriver, gun catalogues, copies of *Firearms* magazine, outdated credit cards, folders with stuff in them that obviously related to Pukalski's business, and some freight invoices. The invoices were addressed to a no-doubt fictitious character who ran an equally fictitious import business. This was clearly how the foetus had been shipped into the country. For the first time, Crowe wondered how one would go about getting an item like that past Customs. The answer was obvious. You didn't. Illegal immigrants might be easily caught sneaking on-board, but there were plenty of ways a boxed-up foetus could get in undetected.

He'd just shut a drawer that contained receipts, no doubt collected for tax purposes, when someone said, 'Looking for something, Crowe?'

It was Tansey. He must have snuck in while Crowe was absorbed, because he hadn't heard a thing. Tansey had a Colt .38 in his fist and a smirk on his lips. Crowe didn't go for his gun.

'You should park somewhere less obvious,' Tansey said. 'What're you after?'

'Just wanted a chat, Dickie,' Crowe said. 'You know I'm doing some work for Pukalski?'

'Does it involve rifling through my flat?'

'Might. Depends what you've been up to.'

Tansey sneered, stepped back and gestured Crowe through into the room with the TV, keeping well away from him, making sure there was no chance for Crowe to jump him. 'Empty your pockets,' he said. 'Gun first. Nice and easy.'

He was usually a cool customer but something was making him

nervous. Crowe could see it in his intense watchfulness and in the movement of his tongue, which would pop out suddenly and run along his upper lip. Crowe liked to think it was him that was making Tansey nervous, but probably it was the possibility that he'd already revealed his suspicions to Pukalski. For a moment, he debated whether or not to try something he'd regret afterwards, but he doubted Tansey's anxiety would affect his aim much, and his finger was already twitching against the trigger. Crowe removed his Beretta with two fingers and dropped it onto the floor.

'Kick it over here!' Tansey snapped.

When Crowe did, Tansey bent cautiously to pick it up, then stuck it in his coat pocket.

'Now we can talk,' he said.

'About what?'

'You know what.'

'Enlighten me.'

It was obvious Tansey didn't know how to handle this. As yet, he wasn't sure what conclusions, if any, Crowe had come to, and he didn't want to ask any questions that might give him away.

'For a start, why're you doin' over my flat, eh?' he said at last.

'I was brought up bad,' Crowe replied.

Tansey scowled. 'No jokes. I could claim you were a burglar and just shoot the crap outta you.'

'Wouldn't work. The cops would find out there was a connection between us and come to different conclusions. They mightn't give a rat's arse I'd moved on to greener pastures, but they'd love to pin it on *you*.'

Tansey licked his lips even more frantically. 'You haven't emptied your pockets yet.'

Crowe began doing so, fastidiously casual: Tansey's camera, a box of matches, comb, a spare clip for the gun, keys. He bypassed the invoices, hoping Tansey didn't know he had them and wouldn't be game enough to check Crowe's pockets.

'What do you want from me, Crowe?' Tansey said.

Crowe shrugged. 'Love and understanding.'

He glowered, chewing his lip. 'You're dead, Crowe. You know that, right?'

Crowe gestured at Tansey's gun. 'You intend to do it with that thing?'

'I might.'

'Noise will disturb the neighbours, you thought of that? Lose your standing as a good tenant.'

Tansey considered it for a moment. Getting Crowe away from there was going to be a problem.

'Turn around!' he said.

Crowe smiled sweetly and turned, moving to the right so he was standing facing the TV. It was nice and shiny.

'Lean on the telly,' Tansey said, 'At arm's length.'

Really? Crowe thought. *Bad strategy! How's he still alive?* He leaned, which gave him an even better view of the TV screen's dully reflective surface.

'Don't move or I'll stick a bullet up your arse,' Tansey said.

Crowe watched the man's blurred reflection come forward and tried to judge distances and angles. It wasn't easy as the perspective was uncertain. But he could hear the shuffling of Tansey's tread, the creaking of his leather belt and the seams of his coat. He didn't divert to pick up anything else, so he was going to use the stock of the gun. His presence was close, a mix of bad vibrations and body odour, and Crowe imagined his arm rising. Tansey was right-handed.

Crowe dropped suddenly, down and to the left. As he did so, he kicked up. Tansey squawked something obscene as the impact unbalanced him. Then Crowe was rolling, hoping he could avoid any bullets Tansey might feel constrained to send his way. He was still trying to get his balance. Crowe threw himself blindly at him. Tansey tumbled, fired the gun. A bullet slammed into the ceiling, showering plaster on them. Crowe's fist ploughed into his gut. Tansey yelled more obscenities and fired again. Crowe felt the wind of a passing bullet cut across his hand. Blood spattered onto the carpet. Another close call.

'You've had it, Crowe!' Tansey screamed.

Crowe dove for the nearest doorway as a bullet gouged into the floor at his feet. He ended up behind a short wall that divided the corner of the lounge room into an entranceway. A lump of hot metal and plaster exploded out of the wall a few centimetres from Crowe's head. He could hear his attacker coming.

No time for heroics. Crowe had him off-balance, but he wasn't a complete klutz, and he had a gun. Two guns. Crowe reached back, flung open the door and jumped into the corridor. 'Crowe!' Tansey shouted.

The stairwell was perhaps 20 strides away. Crowe knew he'd have to be quick to get out of the line of fire before Tansey emerged from his flat. He ran. As he did, a door squeaked open, and an old woman peered through the crack. 'What the dickens is going on?' she said. As she spoke, she stepped in front of Crowe.

Crowe was moving too fast to avoid her and they collided. The woman swore in a most un-grandmotherly manner. On the edge of his peripheral vision, Crowe registered Tansey; he had Crowe in his sights. Crowe grabbed the woman and swung her between himself and Tansey's gun. She shrieked and squirmed as she noticed what was pointed at her. Crowe held tight. 'Now, now, Dickie!' he said. 'We don't want to shoot the neighbours, do we?'

Tansey swore. Crowe backed toward the stairs then nudged the woman forward. She stumbled across Tansey's path as Crowe leapt down the stairs four at a time and around the first bend. A bullet smashed into the wall about a half a metre behind him. The noise was like thunder in the confined stairwell.

Adrenalin pushed him forward. He could hear Tansey behind him and the old woman screaming, which gave him a twinge of guilt, but he kept ahead of Tansey to the bottom of the stairs. And out the front door. His car was about 200m down the road. Tansey's was straight ahead, on the gutter in front of the courtyard formed by the horseshoe building. A bunch of school kids were wandering across the open lawn. A red Hyundai sports wagon drove past. Two women appeared, carrying bags of groceries.

Tansey must have hesitated at the front door. Being seen waving his gun about by the old lady would be enough of a problem, but out here there'd be too many witnesses. Crowe would've got to his BMW easy, but his keys were back in Tansey's flat, on the coffee table where he'd dropped them as he emptied his pockets for the bastard. He would've had to run for it if Tansey, in a fit of idiocy, hadn't left the keys in the Mustang in his rush to catch Crowe in the act. Crowe opened the door and jumped in.

'Crowe!' Tansey screamed, the sound of it echoing through the courtyard. He'd put his gun in his coat and was running toward Crowe. Crowe hit the starter. The engine turned over immediately, as was only right for a new car like this. He put it into gear. His foot hit the accelerator as Tansey's hand slapped against the driver's side window. Crowe sped away while Tansey shouted something incoherent and waved his gun. But he didn't shoot. Maybe he was afraid he'd put a hole in his car's nice blue duco.

Crowe had to ask the building supervisor to unlock his office when he arrived, which the man did with ill grace. There was no love lost between them, and it was clear Mr Trognon wished for some excuse to have his unwelcome tenant kicked out. Today, however, was not going to be that day.

As soon as the super stalked away, Crowe slammed the door behind him and headed to the bedroom. He had an unregistered handgun in a safe hidden in the back of the wardrobe there – an older model of his Beretta. He loaded it, made sure the safety was on, stuck it in his empty holster and grabbed an extra magazine. Next, he put the Scavenger files and the invoices he'd liberated from Tansey in the safe and locked it.

Then he rang the managerial suite of Pukalski's office and asked to speak to Pukalski. The secretary replied that Mr Pukalski wasn't in the building.

Crowe sighed. 'Where is he then?'

The woman's tone stiffened. 'Can I take a message?'

'I need to speak with him *urgently*,' Crowe said. 'Important business that can't wait.'

Her silence remained intransigent.

'It'll cost him if I don't speak with him now,' Crowe added.

'Your name is?'

He told her and the phone started singing a bad '90s serenade at him. A moment later she came back on the line. 'It seems Mr Pukalski has given his PA quite specific instructions regarding you, Mr Crowe.'

'That's heart-warming.'

'Mr Pukalski is having a lunch-time meeting at the *Harbourview*. He left about five minutes ago.'

'He'll be at the restaurant?'

'He had some other business to attend to on the way, but I think you'll be able to find him there at 12.30 or so.'

'Thank you.'

'It would be best,' she added stiffly, 'if you talked to him as soon as he arrives. He'll not want his guest kept waiting.'

Crowe asked who Pukalski's guest was and she replied that it wasn't information she was authorised to hand out.

'I understand,' he replied. 'Listen, maybe I won't bother Mr Pukalski right now. Can you pencil me in for a brief meeting with him this afternoon?'

She checked Pukalski's diary and confirmed that a brief meeting could be fit in at 3.30 – no longer than 20 minutes, though.

'That's enough time. One other thing. Mr Tansey should come to that meeting as well. Very important. I assume he has a mobile? Yes? Good. I assume you have his number?' She indicated she did. 'Can you ring him for me and let him know we can further discuss the, um, problem we identified earlier this morning at that time?'

She said she would. Crowe hung up. Hopefully, Tansey would get the message and do what Crowe expected he would. And all Crowe had to do was arrive at the *Harbourview* before him.

19

CROWE GOT TO BELMORE BASIN IN ABOUT EIGHT MINUTES, RIGHT ON 12.30, parked Tansey's car in a side-street where he'd be unlikely to see it, then sprinted toward the restaurant, which was in a modern building that for some reason always reminded him of ice-cream. It hung balanced over the water – trawlers to one side, a newish, tarted-up plaza on the other. Lots of idlers climbed the public stairs into the building. Some, dressed more expensively than those looking for fish and chips, veered off into the restaurant. None was Pukalski.

Crowe waited out of sight. Crowe wasn't about to expose himself unless he was sure Pukalski hadn't already met up with Tansey. The end would be the same if he had but probably messier.

A few minutes later a Mercedes drove up, piloted by Banger. The big bloke parked it in a reserved spot then got out, glanced around indolently, nodded. Pukalski emerged from the back seat, frowning but looking more in control than the last time he'd spoken to Crowe. Trailed by Banger, he went through the front door, to be greeted by the maître d'.

Crowe came at the restaurant from the back, along a walkway that led in from the headland. The odour of fried fish and hamburger wafted around him. Inside the restaurant, the ambient smell was more like garlic and coriander. Pukalski and Banger had already been shown to a table overlooking the harbour. Charlie-boy sat facing the door, with Banger to one side.

'Crowe?' Pukalski rumbled. 'You got something?' A waitress coming to take their order frowned at his aggressive manner as he waved her away.

Crowe lowered himself into a spare chair, turning it slightly to face the main entrance. 'Sure,' he said. Then, 'Hi, Banger.' Banger was studying the menu with puzzled intensity. He glanced at Crowe and nodded, no sign of comprehension changing his tough-guy expression.

'Well?' Pukalski said.

'Can't we eat?'

'Not likely. You know who's behind the business?'

Crowe gestured toward Banger. 'You want him to hear this?'

Pukalski looked at Banger, who appeared oblivious to everything except the menu. 'He doesn't hear anything he's not supposed to. That's what I like about him. Now say whatever you've got to say. I'm expecting someone important, and I'd rather you weren't around when he gets here.'

'Ashamed of our obvious intimacy, eh?'

'Get on with it, for fuck's sake!'

Crowe gestured for him to come closer.

He leaned toward Crowe, his mouth pulled in tight.

'I did some poking around among the friends of Irwin Suleman. You know Suleman?'

'Should I?'

'He was one of the two blokes Skarratt was meeting that night. The other was Nathan Hall.'

'How'd you find that out?'

'Friendly cops. What I also discovered was that they'd been in communication, on and off, with a third party. Someone in your immediate employ.'

As Crowe spoke, Banger looked up. He was frowning. He was suddenly more interested than his boss thought.

'Who?' said Pukalski.

'I'll get to that. Anyway, I had a hunch and broke into this third party's unit. While I was there rifling through faxes and crap addressed to you, the suspect came home, got the jump on me and more or less spilled his guts. I escaped, of course.'

'Who is it?'

'Bear with me, I'm playing for suspense here. Hitchcock once said–'

'I don't give a fuck what Hitchcock said!'

'Okay. Fair enough.' Crowe smiled, amused by Pukalski's impatience. 'I've made a few guesses about what they did.'

Pukalski's face screwed up with suppressed annoyance.

'How'd you receive your instructions about picking up Queen Marika's foetus?'

Pukalski gestured urgently, glancing around to see if anyone might have overheard. 'Shut up about that, Crowe! We're in public here!'

Crowe shrugged. 'How was the pick-up organised, Charlie?'

Pukalski sighed. 'Email from OS. But then an anonymous intermediary took over. Reckoned email was too easily traced, despite all that security stuff, encryption, false trails, all that tech crap. Began sending faxes from untraceable numbers, never the same one twice–'

'And what if someone was intercepting the real messages and sending on false ones? Playing you, Charlie.'

Pukalski's face hardened, his thick lips puffing into red slugs on his chin. Looking over his shoulder toward the restaurant's entrance area, Crowe caught a glimpse of Tansey through the logos on the plate glass door. Just in time.

'Who?' Pukalski hissed.

'Someone you trusted.'

Pukalski frowned, then glanced at Banger, as though considering him as a candidate. The door of the restaurant pushed open.

'Ah, here he is now,' Crowe said. Tansey entered, just as Crowe had hoped. He looked suitably anxious but less murderous than would've been likely if he'd thought Crowe would be on site. He ambled past the head waiter and began scanning the restaurant for Pukalski. What he found was Crowe. Who waved.

Tansey should have taken off, assuming his prospects to be hopeless, but he was working to a different script. Instead, the stupid bastard sprang aggressively toward Crowe and Pukalski, no doubt planning to take out Crowe. He reached into his coat. His movement in their direction was so sudden and its aftermath so chaotic, Crowe couldn't tell for sure what he'd had in mind. Banger at any rate was convinced Tansey's intent was malicious. He cried out something inarticulate and stood up. The table tilted and fell. Cutlery clattered on the floor and plates broke. The waitress, who had just wandered over to try again for their order, shrieked as Banger's Magnum appeared out of the big man's coat. Crowe pulled her aside, seeing Tansey's eyes widen.

'What're you doin'?' Tansey said. His hand emerged from his coat. Holding his gun.

Banger fired. The noise was deafening and started a frenzied domino effect that sent customers in every direction. Tables and chairs crashed aside as people threw themselves to the floor, or, less sensibly, ran for the exit.

Tansey jerked under the impact. His eyes were like billiard balls, staring at the muzzle of Banger's gun even as his body flew backwards, collecting a table and bringing down a storm of food and utensils on himself. For a second, big streaks of blood lingered in the air.

But Tansey wasn't finished. 'Bastard!' he gurgled, scrabbling at the overturned table in an effort to get a bead on his attacker. His .38 discharged loudly. The shot scored into the polished wood of the table. He collapsed and fell back. Pukalski was standing to one side, frowning and making fists so tightly his knuckles had gone as white as the tablecloths. The waitress was crying, pulling on Crowe's arm and keeping him unbalanced.

'You...' Tansey began, raising the gun for another go.

Crowe jerked his own gun out, but Banger was closer by then. He fired a second time, directly at Tansey's face. Most of it went in a different direction to his corpse, which thudded back against the carpet.

Someone started screaming hysterically. Crowe felt the waitress's hand latch onto him again.

Pukalski walked over to the huge man standing less than a metre from Tansey's shattered head. He grasped Banger's shoulder. 'Go!' he whispered. 'You know what to do.'

Banger nodded expressionlessly, turned and then ran for the door, dodging past a startled-looking man who'd just entered. 'Shit!' Pukalski growled, moving rapidly toward the pinstriped business-type. The man's expression was one of vapid incomprehension.

Fingers Crowe assumed were the waitress's grasped more tightly. Despite the coat that put a layer of leather between her hand and Crowe's skin, it felt as though she'd made direct contact with him. Her touch was icy and began to hurt.

Crowe turned, reaching with his other hand to pull her off. Though he could understand her terror, this was ridiculous. But his hand found nothing to push away, and he discovered that the space around him was devoid of waitresses. Of anyone, in fact. He glanced around, scanning the few straggling diners. With that icy touch still lingering in the flesh just below his elbow, he realised that none of them was close enough to have been the cause.

A smudge passed across the corner of his left eye. He tried to follow the movement, to focus on what had caused it, and found himself staring at the newcomer Pukalski had gone to intercept. Pukalski had his back to Crowe. He was talking earnestly, gesturing. The guest stared over his host's shoulder, sight locked on Crowe. He was frowning. Did he know Crowe? For a moment, Crowe couldn't tell. But there was something familiar about the sour twist of the man's lips, the arrogant tilt of his head. In that instant, still aware of that phantom touch on his arm, Crowe realised who it was.

It was his old buddy Dale Walker, Lucy's unwanted suitor.

He'd cleaned up his act sartorially, but the trendy short-cut red hair and wispy moustache brought back memories. The chill in Crowe's flesh spread through the rest of his body.

Walker swallowed and glanced away.

Walker looks set to leap through the nearest window when Crowe enters the electrical store where Lucy's unwanted suitor reportedly earns a living when he's not doing odd-jobs for Waldheim. He's the manager apparently; the store franchise is owned by one of Waldheim's many companies. Deciding perhaps that his fancy pants will get dirty on the window ledge, he ducks out a doorway at the rear of the shop instead. 'Can I help you, sir?' asks a young dude who looks like he should be on a surfboard rather than in a store trying to convince customers he knows the difference between the $29 toaster and a $420 Snackmaster Prime.

'I'm after the manager,' Crowe growls and shoves him aside.

Crowe gets to the back room in time to see Walker fumbling with the lock on an exterior door. Two steps and Crowe slams him against the closest wall. 'What's the hurry, Walker?'

'Leave me alone!' he says.

'Or what?'

His eyes flick over his shoulder. Crowe follows his glance. The surfie hovers undecided on the far side of the doorway. Crowe holds Walker with one hand and wrestles his out-dated PI licence from an inside pocket, flashes it at the intruder. 'I'm a cop,' Crowe says. 'Undercover. I'm asking Mr Walker a few questions about fraudulent tax returns. Run along and serve a customer or something.'

'Sorry,' the kid says and dashes off.

'I don't know anything about Lucy,' Walker splutters. His face is thin with prominent cheekbones. He shakes his head to get a rather long curl of red hair out of his eyes. 'Honest. Nothing.'

Crowe gives him a 'you're-a-lying-scum-and-I-might-just-beat-you-to-a-pulp' frown. 'So what makes you think I wanted to talk about Lucy?'

'What else?' Fear dilates his pupils. 'I saw last night's news.'

'The cops haven't dropped by for a chat then.'

'Why should they? I don't know a thing.'

Crowe relaxes his grip on Walker's shirtfront and smooths out the crumpled material. Straightens his tie. Smiles. Wisely, Walker doesn't try to move.

'A reliable source tells me you'd been harassing Lucy,' Crowe says.

'It's a lie!'

Crowe presses him into the wall. 'A lie?'

'Give me a break, man. I just thought she might like to go out with me, you know. She seemed interested enough at the party.'

'You mean she talked to you without throwing up?'

'Her father thought it a good idea.'

'Did he? You're really stretching credibility now.'

Walker hunches awkwardly, combining grim hurt with worldly nonchalance. 'So I rang her a few times, but she was always too busy. Then I was put on to some bitch that told me Lucy wasn't interested. I didn't believe her.'

'Why not? Sounds likely to me.'

The young man wants to stand up for his manliness but is too scared. 'I decided to forget it. I didn't want to cause a fuss. And I heard ...' He gulps the words back and looks at Crowe as though he's afraid Crowe will ask him what he's heard.

'Heard what?' Crowe asks.

'Nothing.'

Crowe grunts. 'You know the difference between me and a real cop?'

'What?'

'Cops get fired if they beat up suspects.'

Walker scowl-grins, as though Crowe has made a bad joke. 'I heard Lucy was, you know, a dyke.'

The look on Crowe's face makes him barrel on quickly. 'I'm not saying it was true or anything. It's just what I heard. Probably a lie.'

'Who told you?'

'Mr Waldheim's driver. We were buddies.'

'He said she was a dyke? Those words?'

'Well, no. I asked if he could take a message to Lucy for me. He reckoned I'd just be wasting my time 'cause she preferred chicks.' Prefers them over you anyway, Crowe internally translates. 'I know she hangs out with a dyke.'

'Name?'

'Sara Rampen. Works in Mittagong. She's a chemist or some shit.'

Crowe pats his cheek.

Yet again, it felt to Crowe as though Lucy had been trying to tell him something, and if he had to accept the reality of her preternatural whisperings, this scumbag's presence, signalled by a ghostly touch, might well have meaning. Impulsively, he strode toward the huddled group. 'Walker,' he said, ignoring Pukalski's displeasure, which was manifested as a scrunching-up of his facial muscles and an unsuppressed obscenity, 'we need to talk.'

A look of mingled surprise and apprehension crawled over Walker's features. It was quickly sent on its way by a well-practised stare of defiant scorn. It was rather convincing. Crowe was impressed.

'Get the fuck away from here, Crowe!' growled Pukalski.

'I just want to talk with good ol' Dale. We're buddies from way back.'

Pukalski shoved at Crowe with unexpected force, making him stagger. He grabbed Crowe's coat, leaning close, his rather gauche pseudo-French cologne made worse close up and mingled with his sweat. 'We haven't got time for your shit. Talk later. Not now, for fuck's sake. We've gotta get our story straight before the cops turn up.'

Crowe pushed back. 'I've got a job to do, Pukalski.'

'What the fuck's Walker got to do with it?'

'That's what *I'd* like to know.'

Walker glared at him, trying to mask his nervousness. 'Charlie's right, Mr Crowe. Whatever beef you've got, save it for later. I'll talk to you. Make an appointment with my secretary.' He held out a business card. Crowe stared back at him, ignoring the card. Walker laughed. It was meant to display dismissive scorn, but the effect was undermined by the nervousness visible in his auburn and rather bloodshot eyes. He flicked the card at Crowe and turned away.

Crowe caught it mid-flight and stuck it in his coat pocket.

'I'll get back to you soon!' he called at Walker's back. To his satisfaction, he thought he saw the scumbag's shoulders shiver.

20

'AT LEAST THE GUN YOU WERE CARRYING WAS REGISTERED, CROWE,' Superintendent Pirran said, gazing over his desk.

'Of course, it was,' Crowe said.

During the period of confusion that followed Banger's hasty departure, he'd gone 'to check that Tansey is dead' and had taken the opportunity to search the victim's coat. Crowe's Beretta was there – Tansey would've had some plan to incriminate Crowe with it, no doubt – so he swapped it for the gun he was carrying. There was no way the cops weren't going to search them, and besides, Crowe didn't want them finding a gun registered to him on the dead man. He also collected his own car keys. At least this time Tansey hadn't left them in the car for some hood to pinch.

Hours had passed since the 'incident' in the restaurant, hours of boredom and quick-footed bullshitting. Pukalski had had a big-name lawyer in attendance practically before the cops finished unravelling their crime-scene tape, and Pukalski came over so innocent, most of them were ready to put the waitress higher up on the list of suspects than him. He'd gone off home, comforted by Walker, who insisted on staying to make sure the police were 'doing their job right'. He had said nothing more to Crowe, avoiding him with an air that exuded either fear or disdain. Crowe couldn't tell which and wasn't about to have another go at renewing the acquaintance then and there to find out. At some point, Crowe had hissed at Pukalski, 'Why're you sucking up to that scumbag?' just to see what he'd say, but Charlie hadn't answered, merely transfixing Crowe with a look that screamed 'mind your own business'.

'Pukalski had nothing to do with it,' he told Pirran. 'Tansey came in with his gun out ready to shoot. I don't know what his beef was, but he was very mad.'

Pirran sighed. 'A couple of witnesses reckon there was no gun until Jonwood pulled his.'

'They were eating their chargrilled king prawns, Piranha. Everything happened fast.'

'Sure, Crowe,' he said. 'And don't call me Piranha!'

Crowe's story went like this: he'd met Pukalski to talk about certain aspects of the Scavenger case – particularly anything relating to Skarratt's activities that might bear on it. They were getting nowhere. They hadn't even ordered lunch. Then Dick Tansey came in and headed straight toward them. He pulled a gun. Ed Jonwood – Banger – pulled his own gun in response. After much shooting, Tansey was out of the game but the general panic continued. Poor old Banger obviously hadn't intended to make such a mess, because he panicked and took off in Pukalski's Merc.

'Maybe someone had paid Tansey to get Pukalski,' Crowe said. 'Dickie's always been a mercenary thug.'

Pirran frowned. 'Well, your story matches Pukalski's – and his damn lawyer's – and there isn't any proof yet that it's a fabrication.' Naturally. They'd had plenty of time to discuss the matter before the cops had arrived. 'You sure there's nothing in it I can pin on the arrogant bastard? I'd really like to arrest *somebody*.'

For a moment, Crowe considered snitching, just to get back at Pukalski for dragging him into this mess. He suspected that Banger's precipitous 'defence' of Pukalski had made his own job even harder. Assuming Tansey really was the culprit behind the con that had been worked on Pukalski, it would have been handy to question him under more conducive circumstances than had existed in his flat.

'Leave it,' Crowe said. 'It's useless.'

Pirran nodded. Crowe had given his statement and was anxious to get away. The detective looked a little on edge and Crowe didn't want to be there if he was going to start making unfortunate connections.

'There'll have to be an inquest, maybe a trial,' Pirran said suddenly. 'If we can find Jonwood.'

'There won't be a trial. It was self-defence. Pukalski will get him off or there'll be a bargain struck.'

'I noticed he was buddies with Walker. But there *will* be an inquest. You'll have to appear.'

'Can't you get me out of it?'

'Maybe. Maybe not.'

'What is it with this Walker anyway?'

'The latest in a long line of total arseholes highly thought of by various factions amongst the conservatives. He's only about 29. Supposedly got the up-and-coming new generation appeal. For Christ's sake, he'll probably be running for the Legislative Council next year. May end up going federal before too long. Who knows? Don't you keep up with the news?'

'Not if I can help it.'

'Seems to have powerful connections. Connections willing to back him with their money. He's been rather vocal lately, particularly on certain issues that affect local business interests – in a positive way… for them.'

'Pukalski's?'

'Among others.'

'Oh? Such as?'

Pirran fell silent, perhaps considering who those 'others' might be and finding himself unwilling to tell on them. Crowe studied his own fingernails, the role of Walker playing on his mind. Who would have thought that the gormless idiot of 10 years ago could have risen so high? Who in their right mind would've given him any sort of power? The answer: someone with a lot of influence, someone who could manipulate him easily. Waldheim perchance? Crowe's investigation into Lucy's murder had been aborted so suddenly, he had never bothered uncovering what Walker's real connection with Lucy's father was. Had Waldheim been grooming the idiot for some bizarre reason that couldn't possibly be in the best interests of the nation? That's what Siegel seemed to think.

After a minute or two, Pirran woke up and looked hard at Crowe. 'Anything on the Scavenger?'

'I've barely had a chance to study those files you gave me.'

'Mrs Henry said she had a visit from you. I hope you don't intend to harass all the victims' families.'

'Too late, Doug. I've already seen some of them. But I'm a sensitive guy. I promise I only harass the wicked.'

Pirran stood up, rubbing the back of his neck. 'There's someone I think you should talk to. *Have* to talk to, actually.'

'Yeah? Who?'

'Our consultant. The shrink.' He laughed. 'Don't look so nervous. I'm sure you'll love lying on a couch and talking about your mother.'

'Really?'

'Not really. She'll drop by your office at about seven tomorrow evening—'

'After hours? Is she happy with that?'

'Sure. Why not? You think she needs a bodyguard?' He stared hard at Crowe for a few moments. Then he sat down again. 'I want you to work with her, but I don't want to advertise it too much. I think we've a leakage in this building—' he gestured toward the main work area outside his office '—and I'd rather the news rags weren't tipped off. Your role in the investigation needs to stay as under wraps as possible.'

Crowe nodded his agreement despite the general reluctance he felt. 'But when you say "work with her"?'

'Talk to her. Pick her brain. Use her as a sounding board. Whatever. At least you can keep me informed via her rather than dropping by unannounced.' He sighed. 'This whole arrangement is dodgy, Crowe. But at the moment it's an option I've been forced into.'

Crowe was still unsure exactly why the superintendent felt the need to work with him. But for the time being he'd decided to go with the flow to get whatever he could from the odd 'arrangement'.

'What's her name?' he said.

'Meera Banerjee – *Professor* Meera Banerjee. She's highly thought of in the field of criminal psychology and, in this instance, is a channel between us and various federal agencies. The point is, she's here to help and is in a good position to do just that.'

'I get it.'

'Okay.' Pirran's voice became dismissive. He flicked his thumb toward the door. 'Now get out. And try to stay away from the likes of Pukalski for the time being. I don't want his activities to make the waters any murkier than they already are.'

Crowe just nodded.

Afterwards, as the afternoon dribbled in over the city, Crowe sat in his office with a shot of the Premier 18-year-old Laphroaig single malt whisky he kept around for times like these. It made him both slow down and focus. What he couldn't help but focus on right now was Walker and his role in all this. Walker was someone who seemed to add questions to both of his current investigations – one of Crowe's prime suspects in Lucy's murder before his attention had been diverted by the revelations he'd gained from Lucy's confidante, Sara Rampen, and before the investigation was made redundant by the arrest and confession of the man the police tracked down. Now, Walker appeared to be lurking at the edges of both the haunting by Lucy and the Scavenger hunt. Maybe, just maybe, it was nothing of importance: just another example of coincidence, an over-active imagination and the endemic stupidity that characterised way too much of the political scene. On the other hand, Crowe's intuition was telling him to take a good hard look.

He checked the time on his phone. It was still within office hours. He downed the last drops of whisky, fetched Walker's business card, which described the poser as a 'personnel consultant', and dialled the number on it. After a few rings, a female voice that sounded as though it belonged to a 15-year-old who just happened to be passing by said, 'Mr Walker's office'.

'Is Walker in?'

'Mr Walker isn't available right now.'

'I'd like to make an appointment. For tomorrow.'

'I don't think—'

'I'm an old friend of his. Earlier today he said I should come for a chat. Let's say 8.30 before the day gets busy. Name's Crowe, Michael Crowe. If he's not there, I'll drop 'round to his house. Tell him! Okay? Thanks.'

He hung up before she could complain.

That night he dreamt of Lucy's sixteenth birthday party again, but this time it was different.

He finds himself drifting through the guests, paying much closer attention to them than he had when he'd been there the first time. The sun glare, the pool, the self-conscious crowd, the Tropicana band, the air of discomfort — it is all much the same as he remembered. Or it is until he sees Lucy through a gap in the crowd. She doesn't notice him. She's talking to someone. Who? He can't quite tell. He hangs back, wandering toward the duck pond, thinking he'll catch up with her later.

'Sir? Would you like a drink?' A waitress in Hawaiian dress appears out of nowhere, giving him a smile only a very sleep-deprived monk could ignore. Her tray is laden with exotic and very colourful cocktails and other more mundane offerings. 'We've got—'

'Beer will be fine, thanks.'

He takes it from her, thanks her and watches as she drifts back into the main crowd. He's feeling totally disengaged, an onlooker who doesn't quite know why he's here, let alone what he expects to find. He glances back toward Lucy and notes her father, way beyond her, in conversation with a number of older men who look as comfortable in their casual party gear as a bunch of crocodiles dressed in business suits. Waldheim keeps glancing toward Lucy, even while speaking. She's talking to a young bloke now — rather slim, taller than her and obnoxiously in her face, waving his hands around and dominating the conversation. Crowe recognises him: Waldheim's toady, Dale Walker. Back when the memory this dream was based on was being played out for real, he hadn't known him at all, though he'd seen him from a distance a couple of times, going about his business — or Waldheim's. He'd ignored him then. Now, however, his interest is piqued.

He drifts toward them, passing through the crowd like a phantom. No one talks to him, looks at him or impedes his approach. When he gets closer, he realises Walker is berating Lucy, gesticulating aggressively. She steps back to gain some distance, though she doesn't seem overly intimidated.

'I don't think you should talk to me like that, Dale,' she says.

He snaps back. 'Why do you keep pushing me away? Give me a chance, for fuck's sake.'

'Leave me alone. I don't want to go to the movies with you. I don't want to go to any clubs. I don't want to date you.'

'Why?'

'I don't have to justify myself. You just need to leave me alone.'

She begins to move away, but he grabs her wrist.

Suddenly Walker's own arm is grabbed. He gets yanked back. Crowe hadn't noticed the approach of the bloke who has suddenly become part of this scenario, but instantly he recognises him as Waldheim's driver. He's smaller than Walker but stronger. Shocked, Walker tries to extricate himself from Siegel's grip.

'What the fuck, Jim? Let me go!'

Siegel ignores him. 'I apologise for my friend, Miss Waldheim,' he says. 'He gets carried away with his own importance sometimes. I'm sure he meant you no disrespect. Right, Dale?'

Scowling and obviously in some discomfort, Walker ceases to pull against the chauffeur's grip. 'Alright! Alright already!' He looks at Lucy. 'I'm sorry. Okay?'

'Sorry, Miss Waldheim,' says Siegel with a jerk of the boy's arm.

'I'm sorry, Miss Waldheim.'

Lucy smiles weakly, looking discomforted by the whole thing, mutters that it's okay and that she's going to get something to eat, then moves away, heading for a more populated part of the grounds. As she does so, Crowe can see the shadows of death creeping over her features, blood like tears dribbling down her cheeks.

'Lucy!' he calls.

But she doesn't hear. Once again, she's leaving the world, his dream – her presence taken away by the death that is to come.

Crowe calls after her. 'Lucy! Wait! We need to talk.'

But before he could be heard, he jerked awake, staring into his benighted room and breathing slow, regular breaths to calm himself. Another dream that was more than memory. He hadn't heard the exchange between Walker and Lucy back then when Lucy's birthday party was more than a dream, more than a delusion. He hadn't been aware of Walker at all. Was this Lucy trying to tell him something yet again? If so, what exactly did it mean?

21

CROWE CARRIED THE RESIDUE OF THE DREAM WITH HIM AS HE MADE HIS WAY
to Walker's office next morning. Turned out it was in a more upmarket
part of Wollongong's business area than he would have expected; one of
Waldheim's companies had probably built the high-rise in which it was
located. Glass doors automatically opened for him as he approached the
entry. It was 8.20am. The vestibule was all open space, chrome designs
on the dark-tiled display walls, a plethora of glass, artificial plants and
abstract art works. Bland, piped music filled the space. A receptionist
took his name and scrawled it in her visitor's book, then directed him
to the lifts.

Walker was waiting for him, much to Crowe's surprise. The man was
alone, too. No looming, indifferent secretary in sight. No bodyguards.

'Can we get this over with as quick as possible?' Walker said, gesturing
for Crowe to come into his private office. His hair was surprisingly neat,
his suit expensive and in immaculate condition. Here, in his domain, he
exuded an air of confidence absent from previous versions of him that
Crowe had met.

He gestured toward a padded leather chair. 'Sit!'

Crowe almost obeyed but stopped himself in time. He stared at
Walker for a few seconds, trying to work out how to learn anything from
this meeting – how to approach it even – now that he was committed.

'Don't then,' said Walker. 'What do you want?'

'I'm currently working two cases,' Crowe said. 'Oddly, you've cropped up in both.'

'So? What *cases*?' His tone was scornful.

'Firstly, large amounts of money and a rather grotesque souvenir wanted by a local collector have gone missing and your mate Pukalski has hired me to find it.'

'What's it to me?'

'I've been wondering if the "collector" with too much money to spare might be Gregor Waldheim and that *you* are his go-between in setting up the deal. What do you think?'

Walker failed to look surprised.

'Depending on how frank Charlie has been,' Crowe continued, 'you may know some sort of internal scam lies at the heart of the missing money, though it was thwarted by the Scavenger killer bloke mid-event. Know about him? I'm thinking maybe you might be involved. Are you?'

'Me? You're fucking crazy.'

'So I'm frequently told.'

'And you think I'm behind the scam or that I'm the Scavenger?' His tone was scornful, but Crowe detected an underlying nervousness.

'Either or both will do.'

Walker sat down behind his desk, as if seeking its protection. 'Fuck, Crowe. I knew you were an arrogant bastard, but I never took you for a complete idiot.'

Crowe could almost smell his fear now. 'You're neither, eh?'

Walker just stared.

'Can you at least admit what everyone knows – that you're "sponsored" by Waldheim?'

'That's a lie. I answer only to myself and, after I'm elected, to my constituents.'

Crowe laughed. 'Okay, let's assume you *do* work for Waldheim. So, what's he want the, ah, object for?'

'I told you, I've got nothing to do with him and I don't know a bloody thing about this "case" you're talking about.'

'You've been getting lessons in political I-know-nothing protocols, eh?'

Walker glared at him for a few long moments. Finally, he said, 'And the second *case*? Is that equally ridiculous?'

Equally ridiculous? thought Crowe. *Even more so, most likely*. His basis for this one was either messages from a ghost or the scratching of his own intuition. Articulating either was unlikely to foster credibility.

'I'm looking into Lucy Waldheim's murder again,' he said in as flat and matter-of-fact voice as he could manage.

Walker produced what looked like genuine surprise and blurted out, 'You're kidding me. Hasn't Gregor gone through enough?'

'I don't know. Has he?'

'He hasn't been well since Lucy—' Walker stood, looking heated. 'I think you'd better leave, Crowe. I won't be party to any further attacks on him.'

'What about you? Have you felt any remorse?'

'Remorse? Why the fuck should I?'

'Well, I've recently learnt that your…shall we say *attraction*…to Lucy was more extreme and predatory than I realised at the time.'

'Get out!' Walker shouted. 'Now, or I'll call security and then I'll call the cops. I put up with shit from you back then, but I don't have to take it now. Piss off! Go!' He flicked the switch on the internal com on his desk. 'Security!'

'Calm down, mate,' Crowe said with a sigh. 'I was hoping we could have a nice chat. But if I've caught you at a bad time, maybe we can give it another go later.'

He strode toward the door.

'And for the record,' Walker added to his back, 'I was in Melbourne during the week Lucy was murdered, on an errand for…well, never mind who. I can give you a dozen names of people who can testify on my behalf. At least a dozen.'

With his hand on the door handle, Crowe turned and said, 'Oh, I'm sure you can. But that won't be necessary.' He gave an artificial smile. '*For the record*, Lucy sent you a message via me. She doesn't want to go to the movies with you. She doesn't want to go to a club. She doesn't want to date you.' He paused, trying to interpret the shocked expression that suddenly took over Walker's face. 'And she doesn't have to justify herself to you either. Now you'll have to excuse me. I have another appointment.'

He opened the door and exited, leaving Walker to mull over what his words might have meant. As for himself, he wasn't sure if he'd learnt a thing. But he wasn't scratching Walker off his list just yet.

After a futile day studying the files, getting bored and instead rather pointlessly interviewing a few more of the Scavenger victims' family members, Crowe prepared for the coming of Pirran's consultant by picking up a seafood pizza for his dinner, along with olives, cheese, some classy-looking crackers and red wine – in case Dr Banerjee was feeling uneasy and needed something to munch on.

Blowie's ute was waiting in the potholed parking area behind Crowe's office with what looked like roadkill leaning against the front bumper. 'Evenin', Mr Crowe.'

'Turned up at last, I see,' said Crowe as he began fumbling with his keys, balancing in one hand the boxed pizza and a plastic bag containing the other goods. 'I sensed you tailing me, again, the other day.'

'Why'd you ignore me then? What've I missed?' His hangdog seriousness made Crowe laugh, which caused Blowie to sulk even more. Crowe sensed, though, a deeper anger smouldering under the pouting. Blowie trailed him upstairs.

While Crowe drank coffee and ate pizza, Blowie chattered, ignoring the fact that Crowe was still ignoring him. Outside, the evening darkened. Crowe's mind was wandering through possibilities and scenarios, wondering what this Banerjee character would be like. He wasn't particularly keen on headshrinkers of any stripe, but who knew what she might be able to offer? It wasn't as though he was making much headway by himself.

When Blowie's screwed-up face appeared a few centimetres from Crowe's nose, he was forced to pay attention to him.

'Done nothin', have ya?' Blowie asked.

'Very little.' Blowie didn't need to know the details. 'Got a lot on right now.'

Blowie grinned and grabbed a piece of pizza. 'Let me see the police files, eh?'

'How'd you know about those?'

'Got my contacts, don't I?'

Crowe wondered who was feeding info to this unlikely journalist.

'C'mon, I'm nosy. Show me, eh? If we're workin' together, I can help ya.'

Crowe glanced at the clock on the wall. 'They're strictly confidential. Anyway, I've got things to do tonight–'

'A lady?'

'None of your business.'

Blowie grinned crookedly. 'I got somethin' for ya.' He reached into his jacket and pulled out a sheet of yellowy paper. There was writing on it. 'It was stuffed in the letterbox at ya house. You woulda got it yesterday if ya hadn't been avoidin' me.'

'I told you to stay away from my place.'

Blowie shrugged.

Crowe snatched the page and turned it over. It was crumpled and dirty, with what seemed to be a bloodstain on one corner. The writing was the same as that on the previous letter Blowie had produced and on the others in the case files. This one was addressed to Crowe.

'He's been to my house?' Crowe felt chilled deep in his gut.

'Yeah. Spooky, eh? Read it.'

It was longer than the others, the script small and tightly packed, covering very available space. Not easy to decipher.

> 'Dear Mr Michael Xavier Crowe, you are taking an interest in me now, I see. I'm flattered. How to express my gratitude? When we came face-to-face the other night, the night of Mr Skarratt's apotheosis, I recognised a kindred spirit, someone intensely aware of the weakness of human society and his own inner greatness. I am glad you survived our brief interaction. I feel excited, this is confirmation that I am on the right track, that we are on the brink of a renaissance that will force the decadent present into a glorious tomorrow. No longer need we fear for the future. The unstable nature of humanity will be at an end. Do you feel the ecstasy building, seething in the bowels of the planet, clawing towards the sun again after many ages of sepulchral gloom? I think you do. You seem a man who is more than a worm on the carcass of humankind. You, like me, are an instrument of Death, and with Death comes Change. So, you seek me. Scour the graveyards of

reality to find the truths I am freeing. You are not after the money, though perhaps you think you are. No, that illusion is a hangover from your social training. You are not even seeking the shrivelled remains of a dead whore's indiscretions, or even petty revenge, you are seeking ME! ME! Well, I am here, Mr Crowe, waiting. I will help you. I will reveal myself, slowly showing you what I really am! Have patience! Soon the saviour will walk the earth! Below is the blood of my toil. Smell it, suck it from the page, and it will bring you near to me!'

'AND THE MOON GAZED ON MY MIDNIGHT LABOURS, WHILE, WITH UNRELAXED AND BREATHLESS EAGERNESS, I PURSUED NATURE TO HER HIDING-PLACES. WHO SHOULD CONCEIVE THE HORRORS OF MY SECRET TOIL, AS I DABBLED AMONG THE UNHALLOWED DAMPS OF THE GRAVE, OR TORTURED THE LIVING ANIMAL TO ANIMATE THE LIFELESS CLAY?'

Fear ate into Crowe's spine, something that had nothing to do with physical danger. He was used to violence directed against him. He was used to pain and the threat of death. This was something different – something that came from deeper in his gut. He didn't know the source. He didn't know what it meant. The reference to Queen Marika's dead baby swept the chill into every part of him. How the hell could the Scavenger know about that? And what did it mean that he did? For a moment Crowe was afraid for more than his life, then he pushed the unwelcome feeling aside. He refused to be a victim of either superstition or someone else's insanity. 'Was this in an envelope?'

'Sure,' Blowie said, 'but I chucked it. No postmark, if that's what you're wonderin'.'

Crowe grabbed the man's jacket lapels and pulled him close. He smelt stale and earthy. 'What're you doing, poking around in my mail?'

Blowie shrugged. 'I could tell it was important! Aren't ya glad I did?'

Scowling, Crowe said, 'Don't you ever read my mail again. Understand?'

'What's the matter? Contact's been made. Ain't you happy?'

'Not so you'd notice.'

Blowie nodded, all the while squinting at Crowe with a comical look of annoyance. 'What's that stuff about money and shrivelled remains then?'

'None of your business.'

The letter did feel like some kind of breakthrough, however, though what Crowe should make of it wasn't clear. It still didn't help him find the killer. It provided no clues to the madman's identity, not that Crowe could decipher anyway. All he could do was hope this correspondence would continue, that sooner or later the Scavenger would slip up.

'What'd ya think, Mr Crowe?' said Blowie, sniffing and coughing into his sleeve.

'That it's time for you to leave.'

'I mean about the letter. What'd ya make of it? Is he mad or what?'

It wasn't the letter of someone who had all their marbles in the right place, but then, killing blokes and carting away bits of them wasn't exactly normal behaviour.

'The first letter had a quotation from some poem.' Crowe pointed at the bottom of the new letter. 'This looks like another one. Same poem, I wonder?'

Blowie looked coy. 'Nah. It's not poetry at all.'

'Where's it from then?'

Blowie shrugged again and turned away. 'You're the pro. You work it out. Got anything to drink around here?'

Crowe felt annoyance overwrite whatever pity he had for the interloper. He couldn't think straight while this particular pest was buzzing around, and if Blowie wasn't going to volunteer information he could piss off. 'No booze,' Crowe said. 'You can leave.'

'But you just got that letter. Don't ya wanna talk about it?'

'I told you, I've got business—'

Blowie screwed up his face and began to hiss through his teeth. 'You're bein' bloody trivial, Mr Crowe. A woman!' He spat the word as though it was filthy, corrupting his palate. 'This is criminal history we're talkin' about. History! You've just made contact with one of the greatest psychopaths we've ever had in this country and all you can think about is your dick. Start acting like you're *worthy*.'

'Worthy? Don't push, or you'll find yourself with fewer teeth than you've already got.'

Blowie glared, his lips trembling, shoulders tense, fists clenched. 'Ya don't scare me.'

And he went for Crowe, who stepped aside and pushed. Blowie stumbled and crashed against the wall. But he was back in an instant, landing an unexpectedly strong punch on Crowe's face. It shocked Crowe, even though it was only a glancing blow.

'That wake you up?' Blowie barked.

Crowe hit him while he was waiting for an answer. The old shithead was no streetfighter, even though there was strength in those arms of his. He screeched and fell over. Blood dripped from the side of his mouth.

Crowe rubbed the contact point on his right temple, trying to clear his head.

'You hit me,' Blowie whimpered.

Crowe dragged him up by the grimy collar and propelled him toward the door.

Blowie roared, 'This isn't the way it's supposed to be!'

'We don't always get what we want.' Crowe unlocked the door with one hand.

'I need your help,' the old guy declared. 'I won't be able to write my book without you.'

'You should have thought of that before you started stealing mail and throwing punches.'

'You need me,' Blowie shrieked.

'Like a fucking hole in the head.'

Getting him down the stairs was easy – Crowe nudged, and he stumbled. Blowie was looking a lot less sure of himself by the time they'd made it to the building's vestibule.

'If I see you again, it'll be worse than a tap on your jaw.' Crowe watched as Blowie scrambled to his feet and shuffled down the driveway to his ute, a portrait of misery incarnate. Crowe almost felt sorry for him.

He slammed the door.

Pukalski rang a bit after six. He was full of a geniality that made Crowe particularly pissed, given that the ex-PI himself had little inclination to celebrate.

'Don't be such a grump, Mike,' Pukalski said. Someone commented off the phone, and Pukalski chuckled. 'I know you'll find the bastard and get my money back.'

'I couldn't give a rat's arse about your money,' Crowe replied.

Apparently, the cops were half-heartedly pressuring Pukalski over Tansey's demise, but he'd put his lawyer onto it, and they were likely to back off, with encouragement from Dale Walker. Banger would have to give himself up eventually, once the lawyer had established a good climate for pulling a plea of self-defence. In the meantime, Pukalski was content to hide Banger somewhere in the country. 'They won't find him till I want them to,' he said.

'What's your story with Tansey?'

'That I'd just fired him for using one of my enterprises as a front for laundering drug money.' Crowe couldn't see Pukalski, of course, but he knew the Boss was grinning with self-satisfaction. 'Very handy. The federal police were closing in on that particular operation and I'm gonna use all this as a way out. Don't suppose you want to hear the details?'

'No thanks. That sort of shit will drive me back to crap '80s cop shows.'

'Careful. You'll offend me, Crowe.'

'That's the plan.'

Pukalski rabbited on about how stupid Tansey's plan had been – how could anyone get taken in by a complicated subterfuge like that?

'Clever enough,' Crowe commented. 'They played to your weaknesses, Charlie.'

'A fluke,' Pukalski bellowed.

Fluke or not, it had nearly worked. Tansey might have ended up safe, if not rich, if the Scavenger, or more pointedly Crowe, hadn't interfered. Pukalski would've maintained his paranoia to the end.

'You owe me,' Crowe said.

'I want that Scavenger first.' Pukalski's good humour evaporated in an instant. 'I'm not letting you off that one, Crowe. 200 million's still not peanuts.'

'I don't intend to get off the case. I want the bastard for myself.' For a moment Pukalski was silent, as though considering a reply. Then he grunted and hung up.

22

Dr Meera Banerjee buzzed to be let in at seven on the dot. Crowe had disposed of the remnants of pizza, showered and tidied the office. He could at least pretend to a base level of professionalism.

The consultant was tall and self-possessed. Her hair was shoulder length and jet black, her skin light brown, almost luminous. She was dressed casually – T-shirt and cardigan, jeans and sneakers – yet on her they looked like formal wear. Her nails were neatly manicured and painted a deep red. An unpretentious leather briefcase hung from one hand and a computer bag over her right shoulder.

'Good evening, Mr Crowe,' she said. 'I hope I'm not early.'

'Mike,' he said.

She stared back. She seemed wary. Not surprising, Crowe supposed, though he thought someone experienced in police work would be more used to slumming it.

'Immaculate timing.' He gestured to the office behind him. 'Come on in.'

She entered cautiously, as though she thought there might be a hungry bear inside. She took in the wooden chairs, the crummy desk, the bareness – probably wondering what the hell Crowe did here. Many people did. Crowe himself wondered. Dusty venetians on the one outside window, drawn down. Snacks, mugs and wine glasses set out on a bookshelf that moonlighted as a side table. Percolator and coffee grounds. Bar-fridge and filing cabinet. A rather out-of-date laptop that was unopened but plugged in.

'I don't normally do house calls,' she said.

'So why are you doing this one?'

'Superintendent Pirran thought it would be expedient.'

'Anyway,' Crowe added, 'this isn't a house. It's an office.'

Her gaze swivelled to the desk again, where she'd already noticed the Scavenger files.

'Drink?' Crowe asked. She looked at him blankly. 'Pinot noir,' Crowe added. 'New Zealand. A nice drop.'

'No thanks. I don't drink while working. Coffee will be fine.'

He switched on the percolator while she dragged a chair to the desk and set up her much more up-to-date laptop. 'You don't mind, do you?' she said.

Crowe shrugged indifference.

'Have you got Wi-Fi?' she asked.

'Sure. Under Corvus.'

'Cute.'

'The password is Dashiell2. Is that cute, too?'

She smiled. 'A tad predictable.'

'Can't win 'em all.'

Dr Banerjee booted up her laptop, opened various files, to reference or maybe just play for time. Once the coffee was ready, Crowe asked how she had it and presented it to her.

'Help yourself to crackers and nibbles if you get hungry.'

'I'm fine right now, but thanks.' She took a tentative sip of the coffee. 'It's good,' she said. 'You know your coffee.'

'It's essential in my line of work.' Crowe sat opposite her.

'What exactly is your line of work?' she asked.

'Surely Pirran gave you a...let's say *colourful* rundown?'

She smiled. 'Technicolour. But I wanted your take.'

'Hard to say, really. "Sam Spade Wannabee" is close enough.' He shrugged. 'My PI licence expired long ago so that's not an official title.'

'It never occurred to you to renew it?'

'It's been a while and the requirements have become rather onerous. No way I'll be going back to school to do some lame Investigative Services certificate, not at my age.'

'You're only, what, mid-40s?'

'If you insist. I didn't get along well with teachers and book study when I was 12, let alone now when I'm much grumpier and way more cynical.' He folded his arms defensively, then unfolded them when he realised what he was doing. 'Anyway, I have no great inclination to do surveillance on cheating husbands, investigate crash and bash in supermarket carparks or gather evidence on some dickhead's hatred of his neighbour's dog. Besides, there's too much paperwork.'

'So?'

'I'm a drifter, perpetually dodging both the criminals and the law, but rather adept at it. I like being an outrider. And I make an erratic living out of it. Mind you, it has its downside. I rarely have access to legal documents or police databases – unless I can find a corrupt cop who's willing to get the info I need.'

'How hard is it to find such policemen?'

He made a mock defensive gesture. 'Let's not go there. I don't want to upset Pirran any more than I already do.'

'He does respect you, you know.'

'Generally speaking, it doesn't feel like it. What about you?'

'What about me?'

'Well, how'd you get to be a headshrinker?'

'Strictly speaking that's a psychiatrist. I'm a psychologist. Born and raised in Melbourne. Grew up in Essendon. Studied at Melbourne University and various places in the US for postgrad. I did a degree in criminology, too, and then, later, gained a two-year funded study sabbatical at Quantico in the US. I teach at Melbourne University and consult for the Australian Criminal Intelligence Commission and other relevant agencies. When the NSW State Crime Command requested expert assistance on the Scavenger case, I put my hand up.'

'Why?'

'Why not? It *is* my field of study. Besides, this extreme sort of offender is so rare in Australia; this is the opportunity of a lifetime.'

'That's a weird lifetime.'

She shrugged, sipped her coffee.

'Married?' Crowe asked.

She raised her eyebrows in a mock-ironic gesture. 'Relevance?'

'I ask out of politeness, with no evil intent.'

She laughed. 'I am. We have two kids. I miss them while I'm away like this.'

He nodded thoughtfully. 'Now to brass tacks. Why me?'

'Pirran told you, right?'

'He said I'm your out-of-the box solution. But my bullshit detector is going off.'

Crowe had no doubt she knew what she was talking about, academically at least. What he wasn't sure of was why she was willing to deal with him. Okay, she'd given the official line, but what did it mean really? Why were any of them willing to deal with him?

Her eyes ran over his face, weighing up her answer.

'Pirran's not here,' he said.

Banerjee continued to stare. Crowe was finding it somewhat disconcerting. Then she said, 'He is in spirit. There are issues of confidentiality to consider.'

Crowe raised an eyebrow. 'You can trust me, and I want to trust you. But to be honest, this whole thing makes little sense to me.'

She looked away and frowned, thinking. In the midst of her deliberations, Crowe saw her attitude shift. 'All right, Mr Crowe – Mike – I *will* make an effort to trust you.' She paused, no doubt considering how to put it. 'Superintendent Pirran received a letter a few days after the Scavenger's latest bit of performance art was found.'

'A letter?'

'This was delivered to his home, which is disturbing in itself.' She removed a folded page from her briefcase. 'The original has been checked for fingerprints, fibres – nothing.'

Crowe took the paper. It was a photocopy, but he immediately recognised the Scavenger's tight-arse handwriting:

'Dear Mr Pirran,

You disappoint me. I had thought you a man of vision, but I have concluded you are not. Let me give you some advice. Help Michael Crowe. I am not a professional criminal and in no way except in spirit known to Mr Crowe. Oh, I did meet him years ago, but I doubt he would remember even if I told him the occasion. It was brief, and I was nobody then. A mere cypher. I have become much more because I know my purpose. Mr Crowe is an unpredictable and unconventional man, intrigued by me, ensnared in my work because I interfered in his current activities. I have something he thinks he wants. If anyone can find me, it will be him. He will understand. I would like him to find his way to me. In fact, he must. What I am doing is important, if dangerous. FOR SUPREMELY FRIGHTFUL WOULD BE THE EFFECT OF ANY HUMAN ENDEAVOUR TO MOCK THE STUPENDOUS MECHANISM OF THE CREATOR OF THE WORLD.'

'I met him years ago?' That was food for thought, but as an appetiser rather tasteless. Crowe had met a lot of people in his lifetime and wasn't all that diligent in remembering most of them.

'So he claims.' Banerjee gave a rather sardonic smirk. 'Clearly, you're more memorable than he is.'

'How the hell does he know about me now?' Crowe asked.

'Well, if you were there when Skarratt was killed–' she held up a hand '–which you'll neither confirm nor deny, we'll assume the Scavenger saw you then.'

Of course he did. The Scavenger's most recent missive, directed to Crowe himself, sort of confirmed this, but he wasn't prepared to share that around just yet. 'Even *if* I was there, I'd have been little more than a shape in the night. But he says years ago?'

'Yes.' She leaned back into her chair. 'That's precisely why I'm here.'

'I don't know who he is,' Crowe said.

'We believe you. I believe you. This information has been kept very quiet, Mr Crowe, and–'

'Mike.'

She gave him another evaluative glance. 'On my advice, *Mike*, the superintendent has kept some pertinent details from the media. This interest in you is the first sign of self-revelation that the killer has made. Suddenly, here he is exposing himself, potentially at least. Perhaps you do know him without knowing you do. Anyway, once Pirran was convinced you had no personal knowledge of the Scavenger, he wanted to put you under surveillance. I didn't think that was a good idea.'

'Why?'

'Isn't it obvious? With your background, it would be nearly impossible to have you watched without giving the game away. Once you noticed, we'd lose you altogether.'

'Pirran decided it was easier to let me in.'

'Make no mistake, he was reluctant. Massive political pressure's being applied to him. If it goes wrong, he'll be in trouble. He's keeping it quiet until I can determine whether or not the Scavenger's interest in you can be turned to our benefit. Meanwhile, the standard investigation goes on regardless.'

'Your job's to be my bodyguard?'

She laughed. 'Hardly. My combat training's strictly amateur level and I was never top of the class on the weapons range.'

'So, what then?'

'So I can keep an eye on you.' Her dark eyes glinted mischievously. 'No—liaison. Analysis. Any way I can be useful.'

'And what do you make of this letter in particular?'

'It indicates that the Scavenger wants to be found, at least by you. Some serial murderers are captured via confession or because they do actually want to be stopped, but I don't think that's him. He's not going to give himself up. There's more to it than that. He believes what he says when he claims he's doing something important, revolutionary even, and wants to be watched. For whatever reason, he wants to be watched by you. That suggests a connection, a relationship no matter how imaginary it might be. You're going to have to work out what his task is and where he is. I expect he'll leave you clues. I can help. In the meantime, letting me advise you will keep Superintendent Pirran off your back.'

'Blackmail?'

'Realistic precaution. I said he trusted you. The truth is he doesn't *entirely* trust you.'

That made sense enough. Crowe didn't entirely trust himself either. He stared at her. In her return gaze, he sensed an academic curiosity. It ran deep and was compulsive. No way did she intend to let this go. She would follow the trail to the very end, no matter what. In that way, she was just like the Scavenger. Or Blowie with his obsession. Or Gail with hers.

And, Crowe had to admit, rather like himself.

Scavengers, one and all.

The first thing they discussed in depth was more literature than psychology.

'*For supremely frightful would be the effect of any human endeavour to mock the stupendous mechanism of the Creator of the world,*' Crowe read aloud. 'What's it mean?'

'It was written in 1831, in the introduction to the reprint of a novel first published in 1818.'

'What novel? Would I have read it?'

'I wouldn't know. Do you read fiction much?'

'On and off. Mostly old detective thrillers.'

'Perhaps not then. But you'd know it anyway. *Frankenstein, or the Modern Prometheus* by Mary Wollstonecraft Shelley. Have you read it?'

'No, but I've seen the movie. The old one. Boris Karloff – flat head and bolts in the neck?'

'That's the 1931 film version – admittedly the most famous. But there have been lots of movies based on the book. The first one was a 1910 silent. Stage show versions were popular right from the beginning. It's fascinated people ever since it was written. Very much an analogue of the Romantic poets' view of God.'

'Interesting,' Crowe muttered.

They discussed what the scrawled words might imply but got little further than speculation that the Scavenger was increasingly obsessed by awareness of his own pretensions. Just as the fictitious Dr Frankenstein created a monster, was revolted by it and then sought to destroy it, only to be destroyed himself, so perhaps the Scavenger was doing something that he felt doomed him to divine punishment. Crowe thought there was more to it than that. He wondered whether the quotation on the latest letter was also from *Frankenstein*, but he had no intention of telling Banerjee about it in order to get her opinion. Not yet.

They dipped into the file while the night moved on and wind began roaring outside the window. Crowe watched Banerjee's face as she pondered the Scavenger's motives. Her hands moulded the air into meaning as she concentrated on a point she considered significant. She would lean forward in her enthusiasm, as though to draw him in.

Carefully, she led him through the file, supplemented by the material on her laptop: aerial shots, a socioeconomic breakdown of each site, 'victimological' information, offender risk factors, reconstructions. She developed themes and teased out significance. Patterns in the type of victim, not simply in them being male and Caucasian, but in size, too – none of the victims were over 150cm in height and they were similar in build: solid but relatively short. Traces of several paralysing drugs had been found in each body, which explained how he managed to kill them without a struggle. Banerjee called up an analysis of the 'cocktail' on her screen. It meant nothing to Crowe.

'He knows about drugs and their application.' Banerjee removed her glasses and rubbed the bridge of her nose. 'What he has done with them is original, I'm told. Fast acting and hallucinatory, designed to increase the probability of anaesthesia awareness. Indications are it's based on succinylcholine, but modified significantly to avoid asphyxia, at least in the short term. Not that there's much of a long-term involved.'

'So the victims can't move but can feel what's happening to them?'

'Exactly.'

'Nasty.'

'It is.'

'Then he's a sadist.'

'I don't think so. I think, given his complex about creation, he believes their pain, their feeling, is part of the power of what he's doing. That he's harvesting that essence as well as the body parts.' She shrugged. 'At any rate, he's physically strong but emotionally weak. He appears to act out of a sense of emasculation – perhaps he's suffered humiliation from a woman. His mother, a wife, something like that. Yet he doesn't take this out on women now. Perhaps he's scared of them and feels guilty about his behaviour in the past toward a woman who'd been important to him. Instead of dominating them physically, he demonstrates his power by dismembering other men – symbolically emasculating them. Taking a perceived female power to himself.'

'How would he act in everyday life?'

'He may be reclusive, rather withdrawn socially, but he may behave in perfectly ordinary ways. There's a possibility he's schizophrenic in the way he acts.'

'What about the size of his victims?'

'Maybe because he's short himself. A kind of suicide?'

'That doesn't fit with the witness Dernshaw's description. The man she saw Henry with was tall.'

'We can't rely on that. There's no proof it was the Scavenger or related in any way.' Banerjee shrugged. 'It's all conjecture.'

'Not much to go on, is there?'

'We know he's cunning and resourceful and, strangely for such killers, unprovocative. He doesn't want to expose himself to the general public. He hasn't contacted the papers. So far, apart from the Dernshaw woman, no one appears to have seen anything even remotely likely to give us a clue.'

'He's not only Frankenstein and a werewolf – thanks to the full-moon fetish – but he's the Invisible Man as well.'

'And Frankenstein's creation.' She repositioned the silver frames. Her eyes studied Crowe. Despite his weariness, he felt their evaluative touch once more.

'Pity we can't fit Dracula in there somewhere and he'd have the lot,' he said.

'In Mary Shelley's novel,' Banerjee continued, ignoring him, 'Victor Frankenstein collected bodies – even bits of bodies – to make a super-being, to create new life that didn't owe allegiance to God. The Scavenger collects bits of bodies, too.'

'To make a monster?'

'A superhuman,' she said, expelling breath and leaning back into her chair. 'I would guess it's metaphorical as much as literal. Simulating a process of re-creation. He's the one being created. Creator and creation fuse. As such, he's acting out of a sense of idealism – he wants to improve both humanity and himself. It's an interesting mix.'

Around 11, Crowe felt the heaviness of the day sit on his chest like congestion. Banerjee watched him yawn and slouch into the chair.

'I'd better go,' she said. 'I'm feeling rather tired.'

'It's cold and windy.' He pulled open the blind but the night beyond the glass was too thick to illustrate the point. 'You can stay here. There's a bed in the next room.'

'Yours?'

'It's a double.'

She smiled. 'Do you try to get every woman you meet into your bed?'

'You're the first.'

She stood, sliding the papers into her briefcase. Keys clanked in her pocket. 'I think you've got enough to worry about,' she said, 'without losing your virginity as well. Business, Mr Crowe. Nothing more.'

'I'm just pulling your chain. Seriously, I'll sleep out here.'

'Thanks, but no.'

'I'll walk you to your car then.'

'I can manage.'

She looked at him challengingly for a moment, then said suddenly, 'I had a chat with your girlfriend, Mr Crowe.'

'Girlfriend?'

'Gail Veitch.'

That took him by surprise.

'You've been talking to Gail? She's not my girlfriend.'

'No?'

'Well, not by any strict definition.' He scowled. 'Have you been prying into my business?'

She smiled. 'I like her. She's smart.'

'So?'

'Far be it for me to analyse your relationships or how you relate to the world, especially using such a small sample—'

'But you're going to anyway, right?'

'It's what I do. I've noticed a pattern to your interactions with everyone, but women in particular, as I'm sure you're aware. Gruffness. Lame attempts at flirtation. You display a classically stereotypical attitude I've decided is a defence, a way of maintaining emotional distance.'

'Sounds like psychobabble to me.'

'Perhaps it comes from your mother. Or your father. Something that happened to you in the past. I don't know. But it's there. It's not healthy.'

'I think I can look after myself well enough.'

'In some ways, you're a remarkably capable person. But while you're doing it, while you're playing the bad guy, don't lose sight of the things that make you what you really are.'

'And what am I?'

'An ordinary human being. A good man.'

'God save us from idealists!'

'I'm not the idealist.' She closed the laptop.

Crowe said nothing. This wasn't a conversation he wanted to have.

With her computer bag draped over her shoulder, she stopped and looked at him. 'Gail doesn't want or need a white knight,' she added. 'Or a dark knight, for that matter, as sexy as they are in the movies. Few of us do.'

With that snatch of non-sequitur wisdom, she headed for the door. 'I have some other business to take care of tomorrow. But if you need to discuss anything urgently, feel free to call me.'

She pulled the door behind her, and Crowe listened to the sound of her feet on the stairs right the way to the bottom. The outer door opened and closed. Light rain trickled against the window, but he didn't shift.

So, what do you make of that? he asked himself.

Whether the night's discussion had been a success or not, he couldn't say. But it wasn't the Scavenger Crowe's thoughts were hung up on. Rather it was Banerjee's description of him as 'a good man', despite her meagre, or at least incomplete, knowledge of both him and his past — despite what she *did* know. He had no idea if the statement were true and had little interest in pursuing it. What she'd said about Gail though… he had to admit she'd touched a sore point there. It was something he brooded over more often than he liked to admit.

Then there were his parents. Was it really them who had moulded his ingrained responses to Gail, to life, to himself? It was true his attitude toward both his parents was far from what it was ideally supposed to be. He had little respect for either, though he probably did love his mother deep down somewhere, despite her decline. In his oldest memories, she'd been a tough woman, strong-minded, loving and determined in many of her beliefs, as simple-minded as they were, but she had gradually sold out to working-class ideologies that insisted she be a diligent housewife and slave to 'her man'. She'd sacrificed aspirations such as stage acting, as she confessed to Crowe once in a somewhat drunken moment, all because 'Patrick insists it's not a respectable occupation for any wife of his'. By the time Crowe was 12, he could see how her decision had undermined her self-esteem. She'd become sadder, hating herself deep inside. As time went by, she allowed her religious leanings to become a mask to hide her disappointments. She started hearing voices. They filled her head with bland platitudes she'd repeat to him over and over again. She even took to believing in the spirit world in an overly dogmatic way and claimed the deceased spoke to her. But it was her own ghosts that haunted her, the superstitions of her Irish ancestry, her bad decisions. At the time, this had seemed obvious to the young Michael. But was that what he was doing now, himself, with Lucy?

As for Patrick, well, in no sense did Crowe love or respect the man. A self-centred tyrant, he'd been obsessed with gambling and being a right-wing, opinionated arsehole. He'd driven the family into poverty and alienated his children and many of his mates. Eventually he caused the family to break apart. Crowe's elder sister, Tara, ran away from home when she was 15 or so, blaming their father's misogynistic behaviour, though Crowe had always suspected it went deeper than that. But later attempts by him to find out the truth had resulted in bitter and irrational arguments. It provoked their current estrangement, which had lasted for years. Crowe blamed his old man for that, too. And himself, of course.

He left home when he was 16, seething with youthful anger and as ignorant as they come. He was, or so he thought, neither misogynistic nor right-wing in his leanings. But he often suspected his father's moral deficiencies formed part of his inherited DNA and sometimes came to the surface in him, or worse, were expressed in ways he was blind to. The bastard could be irrationally angry and brutal, was profoundly hypocritical in his actions and careless with his temper. Young Crowe had been happy to see him piss off in pursuit of some other woman, some different life. He died in a house fire less than a year later. Crowe's mother had grieved despite her bitterness at being abandoned but found that any going back to her long-past independence was impossible. She drank more in desperation and though Crowe tried to help her, eventually all his own self-centred wildness came to the fore and he gave up. He didn't see her again for several years. When he finally went back, she was in the terminal stages of cancer and would barely talk to him. She died soon after, alone and totally defeated. Tara, perhaps rightly, blamed him for that, too. He hadn't put much effort into looking out for her.

Meanwhile his father had lived on in him. Anger and a brutish disregard for the results of his actions had plagued his younger years, though he liked to think he had left all that behind now. Perhaps he hadn't. Not completely.

Perhaps Banerjee was right.

Banerjee? He glanced at his old radio clock. Four or five minutes had passed. It suddenly occurred to him he'd heard nothing from outside. Perhaps he'd been distracted by his brooding, but he expected he would've at least heard her car drive off. He'd heard no cars at all. What was she doing? Just as he was about to get up and check from the window, a car started up with a roar. It skidded briefly before finding a grip on the macadam. *Lead-foot acceleration*, Crowe thought, a bit surprised. But the revs calmed down and the sound disappeared in the direction of the city centre. 'Women drivers,' he muttered.

Sexist!

He smiled, hearing Gail in his head. He really should listen to her more.

He had barely begun work on the pinot noir when the building's entrance buzzer buzzed. Frowning, he went to the call box and pressed the button.

'Who is it?' he snapped into the mic.

'Dr Banerjee, Mr Crowe…Mike,' an electronically distorted version of her voice said. 'Can I come up? I think I need a glass of that wine now.'

Wind had hit Meera Banerjee like a slap the moment she'd stepped outside. Specks of rain pricked over exposed skin on her face and hands.

'Shit!' she muttered.

She retreated into the meagre shelter provided by the entrance, back against the now locked door. The sensor light on the porch was clearly not working and night crowded in. Her hire car, a smallish Mazda, was parked on the street about 20m away but she could not see it. She stood for some minutes listening to rain hitting the ground, trying to determine just how wet she'd get if she made a break for it. With the strap of her laptop bag over her right shoulder and her briefcase in her left hand, she wouldn't be doing a sprint, especially as the terrain between the main door and the road was a cracked concrete path and a lot of uncared-for ground that displayed only a threadbare pretension to being landscaped. The night beyond was misty, a random scattering of inanimate shapes, thrashing trees and bushes, and distant, indistinct movement caused by the faint streetlights beyond them.

She wasn't totally satisfied with the evening. Bowing to Pirran's insistence that they meet for the first time in Crowe's territory hadn't sat well with her, though the ex-PI had not proven to be the misogynist she'd feared. She rather liked him. Nevertheless, she hadn't handled their exploration of the case particularly well, a task that had been her sole responsibility. She hadn't got him to open up. And telling him the truth behind Pirran's decision to bring Crowe onto the 'team' might backfire on her. Would he freak out and withdraw? Would he decide he had a better chance of interacting positively with the Scavenger without being hindered by police protocols and overseen by her? Time would tell, but in the interim she needed be as focused as possible.

For whatever reason, she found herself worrying about Elias, her husband. He was back in Melbourne looking after the kids. Academic conferences and the like often took her away, and he rarely complained. But she worried how long this secondment would keep her from home. Had she texted Elias a goodnight message? No, she'd forgotten. Was she becoming too blasé, letting their relationship slip? She had to resist the urge to pull her phone out right there and then and call him from this darkened porch.

With a sigh, she reached into her pocket in search of her car keys. She'd text when she got back to the hotel. At that moment, she heard movement to her right. It had sounded like a footstep. Then the shadows coalesced into a human form and mounted the two steps leading up onto the entrance landing. A hand grabbed at her.

'Don't scream!' said a deep voice, barely decipherable through the sound of the weather. What might have been a short blade glinted for an instant then disappeared as though it had plunged into her. She felt nothing by way of pain, but instinctively she swung the briefcase in her left hand in a tight arc that connected with the head of the man before her. The impact jolted the handle from her fingers. The aggressor swore, and staggered, completely unbalanced, down the stairs, his hand falling away from her. He tried to regain stability, but the step was damp and slippery, his momentum too insistent. Gravity was on her side. He fell to his knees half on the path and half on the ragged grass beside it.

Banerjee's briefcase landed on the top step. She bent to pick it up. As she did so, the man surged up, one arm reaching out. His fingers trailed through the straggling ends of her hair as she jerked away.

'Behave, bitch!' He was still trying to rise.

Banerjee kicked up and her foot connected with what felt like a chin.

He grunted, head flying back as he lost his tenuous control over his balance. He became nothing more than a formless smudge in the shrubs and bushes along that side of the building. Banerjee considered running for the car, but she didn't know where her keys or the man had gone.

She kept to the high ground, waiting, expecting her attacker to burst from the shadows again, appearing like a homicidal phantom.

Nothing.

After a minute or so, she heard an engine start. This was followed by the sound of rubber on the damp bitumen as the driver over-accelerated, skidding in a desperate attempt to find traction. Then a long roar cut through the other sounds. Banerjee jumped down the steps and ran, trying to catch sight of the car. But by the time she'd cleared the bushes, it was a barely distinguishable shape in a drift of rain far down the street. Her own car remained parked where she'd left it.

She walked back to the porch to pick up her briefcase and computer bag, but as she reached out for the latter, she saw how much her hand was shaking. She took a deep breath to calm herself. The rain stopped abruptly, and the wind was now noticeable only in the tops of trees. The clouds over toward the city centre had thinned enough to let in the lambency of a moon that was only halfway through its cycle.

'Settle down, Meera,' she muttered. Her hands still trembled and she imagined she could feel the grip of harsh fingers on her right arm. She shook it off. 'Where the hell are my keys?' she muttered, swinging around.

The sound of jangling came from her pocket. She slid her fingers in to cradle the keys' cool metal. They'd been there all along. But she didn't feel up to driving just yet.

She pressed the intercom button for Crowe's office.

After a moment, he answered. 'What?' he snapped.

'It's Dr Banerjee, Mr Crowe…Mike,' she said. 'Can I come up? I think I need a glass of that wine now.'

23

His mobile woke Crowe about 10 the next day. Fragments of a dream hung around him like torn webbing, scraps of imagery faintly remembered. His father held him hard against a brick wall covered in metal plaques. Grey sun leaked between slits in a curtain. A knife pricked his throat. 'You're a worthless shit, boy,' his father said. Crowe could hear wind outside – and shrieking. *A woman's cries.* The wind scattered pieces of a killer, as though he was made of smoke. An elongated head roared in the air above him. To the right a hand emerged from blood-red bushes, grasping Skarratt's arm, which had been sewn onto Crowe's chest. He tried to run but had no legs. The attempt tumbled him face down in the mud. Or on a pillow. Someone screamed louder as his father snapped away. Crowe pushed the damp blankets aside. He'd been sweating. He reached for the phone.

'What?' he snarled into the mouthpiece. Line noise merged with the words.

'Mike? You sound like death warmed up.' Gail.

'I was asleep.'

'I was wondering how things were going. Haven't seen you for days.' She sounded strange, alien, and something in her tone made him uneasy. He remembered what Banerjee had said.

'Things are fine.'

'You're cross with me?'

'You were talking about me to the cops.'

'What? No.'

'Banerjee told me.'

'Did she? Well, we hardly talked about you at all.'

'What *did* you talk about?'

'The region's problems. Crime. Being a journalist. She wanted to know about my relationship with Pukalski.'

'And you told her?'

'Sure. Why not? I've arranged to interview her – you know, as a female criminal shrink – once this case is over. I like her. She's smart.'

So, it was a mutual admiration society, an all-round girl crush. Great!

'Well, don't talk to people about my business. Okay?'

'You know I don't. What's the matter with you?'

'Nothing. I haven't had any coffee yet.'

'For the record, you're an arsehole without a layer of caffeine between you and the world.' He said nothing, so she continued. 'Listen, I rang the other number first. The Mt St Thomas one. Someone answered, I assumed you, but they didn't say anything.'

'I've been sleeping in the office. An acquaintance and his girl needed someplace to hide out and I let them use the house.'

'Oh, yeah?'

'They've been there nearly a week. Burger's not a great conversationalist.'

Silence. Waiting for her to say something more. Outside, Crowe thought he could hear echoes of his dream, but it was only wind humming in the power cables.

'Have you got a woman with you, Mike? Meera Banerjee maybe?' Gail asked out of the blue.

By the time he'd walked Banerjee to her car, it had been close to 1.30. Amused as he'd been at the thought of her judo kicking some scumbag in the chin then round-housing him with her briefcase, he was still concerned. The impenetrable nature of the night meant she'd had no chance of giving an exact description, but at least something might be forthcoming with a bit of a push by the unit's portrait artist. When Crowe had urged her to mention the attack to Pirran, she'd refused, claiming the attack was random, some lowlife taking a chance. She didn't want to give Pirran a reason to confine her to the station or give her some watchdog 24/7. 'Besides,' she'd added, 'the Scavenger doesn't target women.'

'Maybe he's changed his mind. You need to be careful,' Crowe had said.

'I'm always careful.' She'd tossed her bags into the back seat of the Mazda. 'Killers like him don't suddenly abandon their well-constructed *modus operandi*. I'll ring you about our next meeting. Thanks, Mr Crowe.'

'Call me Mike. Or just Crowe.'

Banerjee had given him a slight smile as she settled in behind the steering wheel. He'd watched her drive off. There'd been nothing more between them.

'What if I have?' Crowe snapped at Gail. He didn't quite know why he was being a prick.

Gail did, though, no doubt. 'You're acting strangely, Mike.'

Suddenly he wanted to talk instead of scream, to pick through the shit careering around in his skull. Maybe Gail could melt the dream remnants away.

'I should've rung you before this. There's stuff to discuss. But not on the phone.'

'Can you come over?'

'Some things I have to do first.'

'Me, too.' She paused. 'I'm in the Gong.'

'I figured.'

'I have an interview in an hour. This afternoon okay? After lunch.'

'Whatever.'

She said nothing more and he nearly hung up. Then, 'Mike?'

'Yeah?'

Pause.

'Oh, nothing.'

'Okay then.' This time he did hang up. He figured she'd been going to say she missed him or something equally sentimental. He couldn't take that sort of trouble right now. How had it gone so far? Emotional entanglements made you weak. Life was hard enough without having to live it for two.

He grunted at his own thoughts. That was his father speaking.

Something had changed. Part of him wanted to ring back. Desperately.

He pushed himself across the room and found some Panadol Forte instead. He had places to go.

The wind coming in from the southwest carried memories of snow.

Death. I think about it sometimes as I sit here in my bleak, shadowy cell, and wonder why it no longer scares me. It used to, when I was younger. I'm still young, I guess, but time has ceased to have any meaning to me as my past and dreams for the future shift and fade and disappear, only to come back when I least expect them. Most of my time is spent in the shadows, though on and off I get intimations of a terrible transition, not into the oblivion of eternity – which means nothing to me, except a welcome release from this place – but a different future in which I'm born again, this time in a corpse, and must live an undead life feeding the desires of…of…I don't know who. Somebody. Somebody who has meddled in the natural processes of living and holds the key to my passing. An evil man, who might think he is doing the right thing but is instead sowing the seeds of an unnatural, tormented existence.

That's what I fear most. That's what I need to stop.

And that's why I need my friend's help. I was close this time, close to communicating what he needs to know. But again I was dragged away. I couldn't hold onto the moment. The words slipped away from me before I could utter them. I forgot what I wanted to say.

Why does memory come and fade and drag me back?

There must be a way.

24

ILLAWARRA BOOKS AND RECORDS AT THE EASTERN END OF CROWN STREET in the centre of Wollongong had an old copy of *Frankenstein* hidden in a pile of mostly black-embossed paperbacks with titles like *The Bad Place*, *Carrion Comfort*, *The Scream*, *The Doll Who Ate His Mother*. Crowe handed over three bucks and returned to his office to read it, picking up some Thai takeaway first.

The book was pretty dull – to Crowe it seemed an over-wrought frenzy of Gothic images, self-flagellation and big words. The writer seemed unable to get to the point. Not Crowe's cup o' tea at all. But on the title page was something familiar. An epigraph:

> Did I request thee, Maker, from my clay
> To mould Me man? Did I solicit thee
> From darkness to promote me?
> *Paradise Lost* [X.743-5]

So, the Scavenger had been quoting from *Paradise Lost*, yes, but via *Frankenstein*. Did that make a difference?

Crowe made some coffee and read on, chewing occasionally on a mash-up of massaman curry and larb. The novel took a long time to get moving. It was narrated by several people: a sea captain, Victor the mad doctor, even the monster. Mostly Doc Frankenstein rabbited on about modern science (meaning electricity), agonised over half-baked moral dilemmas and drifted toward medical radicalism. By page 50 he was sewing together a monster made from bits and pieces of corpses. That was where Crowe came upon a familiar passage – words the Scavenger had quoted in his letter to Crowe: 'And the moon gazed on my midnight labours...Who should conceive the horrors of my secret toil, as I dabbled among the unhallowed damps of the grave, or tortured the living animal to animate the lifeless clay?'

Another connection.

All the killer's letters – all three Crowe had seen at any rate – quoted from *Frankenstein*. Was the book merely a metaphor for his obsession with dismemberment? Or did he see himself as somehow creating new life? Was there some other insane meaning? He was aping Dr Frankenstein but taking it a step further by vandalising the living instead of the dead.

By the time the monster was lurching around the countryside taking his despair-driven and well-articulated revenge, Crowe had ceased to see any relevance in what he read. Whatever was useful was in the first half of the book, he was convinced.

He switched to the police files, churning once more through now-familiar facts as the weather got fouler in sympathy.

He wondered when Gail would arrive.

'Crowe?'

He'd drifted off into a nap. The phone had dragged him back to the world, his mind heavy with phantom emotions.

'Yeah?'

'This is Pirran.'

'What d'you want?'

'How's the search going?'

'Well, I know who we're looking for,' he said wearily.

'Who?'

'Frankenstein.'

'Frankenstein? You going to take this seriously at any point?' His pitch went up a notch and Crowe remembered the pressure the superintendent was under.

'A joke, Doug. The Scavenger's got a thing about the novel *Frankenstein*.'

'How do you know?'

'It's this idea we're working on,' he said. 'Based on some of the quotations.' He was careful to be vague so Pirran wouldn't know Banerjee had shared the contents of the letter Crowe wasn't supposed to know about.

'Sounds a bit pointless. You're wasting your time.'

'There are MO similarities.' Crowe recalled Blowie's comment the first time they met: *The Scavenger's like a mechanic, scrounging together bits of a car in order to build a better one. Frankenstein scrounges bodies, in the book. What if that's his plan? To build a better man.*

Pirran made a sceptical noise. 'How does it help?'

'Look, every crazy has his logic though it might not be obvious to everyone. We know he uses drugs to make his victims compliant, so a doctor maybe? Someone with access to pharmaceuticals. If he's building a monster, gathering body parts over nearly a year, he'll have knowledge of preservation techniques. And he's got to have access to a cold room. That implies location, resources—'

Pirran sighed. 'What does Dr Banerjee think of this theory?'

'Meera put me onto it, but I've expanded the idea. Ask her yourself.'

'She hasn't been in yet. You keep her up late, did you? Or is she maybe still there?'

No wonder Banerjee had slept in. Exhaustion, aftershock, wine. He tossed up telling Pirran about the attack, decided against it; both he and Banerjee were withholding information for fear it would constrain how they did their jobs. She'd said she had something to do. He'd give her a call later if he didn't hear. No point disturbing her after last night's events.

'She went back to where she's staying about two, Piranha,' Crowe said. 'It was pretty intense.'

'What was?'

'Our brainstorming.'

Pirran grunted.

Gail's black leather skirt was so new it made little creaks as she moved. She shrugged off the designer cloth jacket and dropped it over a chair, then kicked off her high heels with a relieved sigh and came to stand close to him. Her short hair was windblown, but her makeup looked fresh.

'Rough out there?' Crowe asked.

She moved even closer. 'You in a better mood?'

'Let's find out.' He stood and their bodies met, starting at the mouth. His hand slipped under her blue tank top. Beyond the walls, wind began screaming again.

'I was hoping for a cup of coffee,' she managed.

'When?'

She lifted her hand and caressed his forehead and temple. 'Sometime in the next two hours?' He felt her other hand moving down his back.

'No worries,' he said, fingers stroking the satin of her skin. 'It's on the boil.'

Flesh pressed into his fingertips. Warm, burning. The weight of her thighs increased the ache. Crowe touched smooth skin under her left ear, feeling its quickening pulse. A wisp of hair on his face. Sweat and perfume.

She leaned closer. Shallow gasps. Lips open, lids shut. He ran his free hand down her shoulder, around the soft curve of her breast. Lips and tongue teased her there.

'Now,' she said. Her breath mimicked the whisper of their bodies rubbing against each other. Crowe removed his fingers from between her legs, smearing moisture on her skin. His tongue licked at her other breast. She pushed hard against him. Breathed out, thrusting suddenly. Crowe eased into her. Into her heat, wet and comforting.

'Can you love me, Mike?' she said.

Crowe was unable or unwilling to speak. He made a low sound that might've meant anything.

'Charlie and I were never together,' she whispered. 'Not like this. He wanted to show me off, that's all. Wanted me to touch him sometimes. Just *seem* to be his. He thought it gave him authority. Me? I was after stories.'

It didn't matter. Crowe hadn't been thinking of Pukalski and didn't know why it should matter. The fact was a curiosity, and he knew the subject would never be mentioned again. But in that moment as her words died away, he was intensely aware of her, who she was, what she was. He wondered how she had come to be there. He wondered what she wanted. Him? Why on earth would she want him? And what did he want? What was he afraid of? He listened to her voice, though she said nothing more. Saw her face, though his eyes were closed against her chest. She moved gently. He groaned. For the first time in a long while the darkness behind his eyes wasn't fraught: no phantoms, no voices, no serial killers. Everything that threatened was overwhelmed by Gail's presence. Crowe put his hands on her buttocks and pressed them in hard, so they were locked together.

'Let it go,' she said.

The release came from deep inside him. Crowe shuddered, over and over. As it passed, he felt tremors in her body, like feather touch on sensitive skin.

For a moment, there was no enemy.

Later, Crowe shared the *Frankenstein* theory. Gail wasn't impressed but fetched the book and began reading. He saw it catch at her imagination. He made coffee, poured it into mugs and brought her one.

'This is good,' she said, gesturing with the book. 'I'm surprised I haven't read it before this.'

'Not well written,' he muttered.

'What would you know? Seems perfect to me.'

She sipped and read, and Crowe watched her, the elegant curves of her neck, her breasts and belly, one leg pulled up so she could lean the book on it, and he could see into the shadows between her thighs. Her mouth would twitch occasionally as though she was repeating something silently to herself. Her lack of self-consciousness was extremely arousing. He played with a few erotic thoughts then started idly flicking through the Scavenger file again.

'Graveyards,' she said a bit later, looking up from the page.

'What?'

She rose and came toward him, pointing to a passage in the book.

His gaze focused past her finger.

'Stop perving and read page 50 on.' She handed him the book.

'I've read it already.'

'Really?'

'I can read, you know.'

She shook her head in mock amazement. 'You said there was a graveyard near where one of the victims met his end. Around here.'

'There was a cemetery at Bulli, too.'

'Where's my laptop?'

'You didn't have it with you.'

'Must be in the car.'

While he read page 50 again, she pulled her clothes on and went to fetch her laptop. Once it was up and running, she tapped away at the keyboard, muttering to herself. Then she nodded, making a satisfied noise intended only for herself.

'Why'd you want me to read this?' he asked, waving the novel about.

'There's a lot in there about graveyards. This bit...' She grabbed the book and read: '*Now I was led to examine the cause and progress of this decay and forced to spend days and nights in vaults and charnel-houses.*' She looked up. 'That's where he gets all the bits to construct his creature. Graveyards. *I collected bones from charnel-houses; and disturbed, with profane fingers, the tremendous secrets of the human frame.* All the Frankenstein movies have scenes in graveyards. Bodysnatchers. Stuff like that.'

'So?'

'So graveyards are a significant part of the imagery of the story.' She grunted. 'Don't be so bloody obtuse and literal, Mike, or you'll never catch him.'

'What are you getting at?'

'I think it's a metaphor.'

'What?' He remembered Banerjee making a similar observation.

'Where were the victims killed?'

'All over.'

'Show me.'

They went through them, one by one, checking against a map of the Illawarra she'd called up on her screen. None of the victims appeared to have been killed in a cemetery, but in each case, there was a cemetery within easy walking distance.

'You think it's just a coincidence?' Gail asked, clearly not thinking so herself.

'Maybe not. What d'you think it means?'

'Let's say the Scavenger does think of himself as Frankenstein, as all those quotes suggest. So, he's collecting bits of bodies but not from dead people. Maybe he wants to go one step further than the good doctor. Frankenstein's monster simply destroyed its creator, which might have been appropriate because it was a creature of death, made from dead things. The Scavenger's making his creature out of "live" bits. I bet he thinks he's accumulating life for later use by cutting pieces off his victims *while they're still alive.'*

'You're making this up as you go along.'

'I'm trying to *think* like him. If you follow the logic, it makes sense. What did he say in that first letter? Something about transforming his victims?'

Crowe grabbed the letter from his files. *I am not making my colleagues less than men. I am transforming them, helping them and myself to become something greater.* He looked at Gail, suddenly feeling they were starting to understand the bastard. 'And in the second letter...' He fetched it. 'He talks about greatness and apotheosis, shit like that. And here. Something being freed from *the graveyards of reality.'*

'What if he sees his purpose in those terms?' Gail continued. 'Making a single creature out of a whole lot of different men – living men – because he wants his creature to be not only an accumulation of bodies but of individual life forces, too. And what if his fantasy is so strong, he starts the search each time where he can associate with Frankenstein?'

'In graveyards.'

'Yeah, graveyards. Life from death. Sort of kick-starting himself. He goes to cemeteries late at night. After all, he doesn't want to be seen. Then he waits for someone to show – not in the cemetery, but nearby. He probably wanders around till he finds one.'

'It could take days to get the right conditions. No one else about except the victim, the right weather, the right bloke – they've got to be shortish, apparently.'

'Why?'

'He doesn't like large guys?'

'The point is, he doesn't have to rush. He can wait. There's plenty of time. Maybe he plans ahead. Yeah, that'd be the way it goes. He identifies his victim early on, then watches to see when's the best time to get him in the right place.'

Crowe shrugged. 'It's possible. Sometimes, maybe. Some of the victims were doing things they always did, others were just a fluke. McCartney had got up to pee–'

'But didn't you say his wife claimed he had a weak bladder? He probably got up every night.'

'Okay. What about Lester Henry? He just couldn't sleep.'

'Same thing. He'd been restless for some time. He liked walking on the golf course and frequently went there after late shift.'

Crowe referred to his notes. 'Cecil Stambridge. Killed at Shellharbour. He'd had a blue with his mates, who were drinking at the club. He left alone because he was pissed off. That's not something that happened every night.'

Gail huffed. 'Probably near enough. Most blokes are predictable, Mike. Even you.' She smiled knowingly, but he didn't bite. 'Late-night habits, drinking at the club, coming back from an evening shift...whatever. I'd guess most of them were caught doing things they could be expected to do. And the timing doesn't have to be that precise. The Scavenger could take him earlier. Or later. He could afford to miss nights, too. He's working the full moon, but it's more or less full for, say, four days.'

'There was one from Adelaide. Killed in Kiama. That had to be a fluke.'

'Flukes are okay. No reason why he can't be flexible. Maybe he had some other reason for wanting that guy. Maybe someone he'd had in mind for that area didn't turn up, but the writer did. If he watched too closely, took the easiest options, he might get caught. Maybe, with that one, time was running out and he didn't want to miss the full moon. So he just took the first opportunity. From memory, Williams doesn't quite fit the profile.'

'You're implying, though, that he generally researched his victims?'

She stood and wandered toward the window. 'To some extent. I don't know. It's possible, even likely, given the fact he hasn't been caught, hasn't been seen much. It suggests he's been careful. But beyond that, I have a nagging feeling it's graveyards you need to focus on, not just in regard to victims.'

Crowe was about to reply when she gestured him to silence. She was looking out the window.

'There's someone been watching the place, Mike. In a Falcon ute. He was there when I came in and still is. He's just sitting. You know him?'

'Old bloke?'

'Yep. It's that Blowie character, isn't it?'

Crowe went over to her. Blowie was parked further down the street, between some other cars.

'I saw him because he turned and watched me rather closely as I drove up,' she said.

'He reckons he was a journo once. Len Bugden. You know any journalist by that name?'

'Not that I remember. What paper?'

'The local. But the *Herald* earlier. Reckons he came up with "Scavenger" as the killer's name.'

'Got a camera with a decent lens?' she asked.

He did, for surveillance work. It even had a telescopic lens. Gail checked the batteries and crouched, propping the camera against the window frame.

'What's this for?' Crowe leaned over her to look out the window.

'I can check his story,' she said.

Crowe left her to her peeping and made coffee. Wind battered the outside of the building, more furious than ever.

A hand. Rope lowers through its pale fingers, stark against a background of black suits. An old woman. A grey-haired man, comforting her. Both stare downward. A child with a scarf around its neck. A young woman weeps and wipes at her face. Other mourners. All staring down. A grim priest holds a funeral emblem – an ornate, ceremonial lantern. The hint of a cross, then a skeletal figure stonily leaning on a sword.

From behind metal spikes leers a pair of manic eyes in a round, dishevelled face, scarred and pitted. Nostrils flare. Fingers claw against the metal. Then another face, this one long, white and well-groomed, appears behind the first. 'Down, down, you fool!' it says.

The first face disappears, but the second, belonging to a dark-haired, brooding figure, lingers, watching as the mourners slowly depart. The priest with the lantern wanders away. Left behind is a large man in a suit. He carries a spade. Against a grey, two-dimensional sky, he slams it into the mound of displaced soil, then removes his jacket and, in his waistcoat, begins to dig. Dirt streams into the grave, covering the sharp edges of a barely seen coffin. Soon he is finished, compacting the mound he has created with the flat of the spade. He puts on his hat, lights a cigarette, looks at his handiwork once more then walks over the edge of the horizon, holding his coat and his tools.

The two faces — one manic and goggle-eyed, the other grimly intelligent — appear from behind the spiked-metal fence, which, it turns out, surrounds a tombstone. A huge, naturalistic crucifix towers over them, stark against the moody clouds. 'Now, come on,' says the intelligent face. 'Hurry, hurry!' Together the two men approach the newly filled grave and, watched by the cloaked skeleton leaning on its sword, they begin to dig.

Time passes and the hole gets bigger. 'The moon's rising,' says the one who is obviously master. His hunch-backed servant stares upward. 'We've no time to lose.' Soon they have bared what they seek. 'Careful,' says the master. They struggle to lift the coffin from its bed. 'Here he comes!' An unadorned geometric shape appears from the hole, and they strain against it until it stands vertically, like a lightless, alien crystal growing from the earth. The master leans against its surface. His hair is less groomed than before.

'He is just resting,' he says, 'waiting for a new life to come.'

Crowe resets the DVD. Gail has gone back to Sydney and he's alone with Frankenstein and the wind.

25

WITH GAIL GONE, HE'D SLEPT BADLY AGAIN. WHATEVER PROTECTION HER presence had offered left with her. His office seemed cramped and uncomfortable, creaking and groaning under the threat of some vast evil pushing against its boundaries. There were times when he felt the line between sleep and wakefulness disappear, so he was never sure whether the faces forming in the shadows were real or phantoms of memory. Sometimes he thought they were going to become Lucy. They didn't. That was a relief, but the uncertainty was giving him the heebie-jeebies.

At least Blowie's ute had been gone by the time Gail left, and there'd been no further sign of the old pest.

Crowe had called Pirran and passed on Gail's theory about cemeteries, suggesting that it might be worthwhile to have some of his underlings do sweeps through the local bone orchards, see if they couldn't turn up a sign that the Scavenger had spent time in them. Chances were too much time had passed for there to be anything useful forensically, but you never know. He might have left deliberate messages. At any rate, on the next full moon it'd be sensible to keep an eye on local cemeteries. Pirran remained sceptical but kind of desperate. 'What does Dr Banerjee think of this?' he said.

'I haven't talked about it with her yet. It was Gail's idea.'

'Hasn't she called around?'

'No. Must have really slept in.'

'Well, if you see her, tell her to call me, asap.'

As Pirran left the phone, Crowe could hear him calling instructions to some minion. He grinned, then wished he hadn't: the motion made his head hurt. He hung up.

Crowe put the coffee on, then drifted to the window. No purple ute, but there were a few cars parked in the street: a white Cortina, a blue Daihatsu, a grey and a silver Commodore and an old, dirty VeeDub. Nothing to worry about. The wind was still up, tossing the branches of trees about as though annoyed by their refusal to break.

Staring into the street, he wondered yet again why the Scavenger believed Crowe could find him – *wanted* Crowe to find him.

A flickering bolt of light hurt his eyes and he blinked. He angled his head and began to move away even before he realised it wasn't someone's side-mirror reflecting up at him that had caused the glint. The window in front of him shattered. Crowe felt tiny shards of glass sting his face and hands. A bullet spat into the ceiling on the far side of the room. A second shot came, lower. But he was already on the floor.

He stayed put until he heard a car accelerating down the street. He swore, stuck his head up and watched as a silver Commodore turned east. Didn't get a look at the licence plate. He pulled himself to his feet, considered the starburst hole in the glass pane, then the pucker mark against the ceiling. The coffee began to bubble. Crowe's headache felt worse.

The day did not improve. Crowe was still tossing up whether to tell Pirran about the shooting and whether to take it seriously himself – was it the Scavenger? Pukalski trying to hurry him along? Even Blowie, trying to scare Crowe after their falling out? Or some other as yet unknown malefactor determined to fuck up Crowe's life? Crowe swallowed another Panadol Forte and followed it with a shot of whiskey, then went to collect his mail.

Back upstairs, with another coffee, he tossed out the junk mail and circulars and set aside a bill for payment. The second letter he came to shot all other considerations to oblivion.

> Mr Crowe, you disappoint me. I had great faith in you, faith
> that you would understand me, not scorn me. Faith that in
> you I would find a kindred spirit. I wrote to the police so

that they too might know that you are special. I told them you would find me, though I knew that you would not turn me over to their secular and profane clutches. You belong with me in this project.

But you are trivial like the rest, it seems. What are you doing? Dirty things with women! Meaningless pleasure when you should be finding me! Perhaps you do not understand the magnitude of what is happening around you. You don't understand, just like the rest. Time is short. You must find me soon.

I have left a message for you at your house so that you might understand. Go there now. Don't let the police follow you. (Do you know that they follow you sometimes? I have seen them – while my eyes were following you from afar.)

THIS WAS THEN THE REWARD OF MY BENEVOLENCE! I HAD SAVED A HUMAN BEING FROM DESTRUCTION, AND, AS A RECOMPENSE, I NOW WRITHED UNDER THE MISERABLE PAIN OF A WOUND, WHICH SHATTERED FLESH AND BONE.

Crowe sat back, let the page dangle from his fingers.

This letter was a print-out, not hand written. What might that mean? Did it reflect his annoyance? Crowe had of course been aware of the cops following him at times; he lost them when he needed to. There was Blowie on occasion, and he wasn't subtle. Could the Scavenger actually be the driver of the Commodore? Had he taken a shot at Crowe to get his attention? Who *was* this bastard? Chances were Crowe had seen him, perhaps brushed across his presence on the street.

He rang his home phone number, letting it buzz for a few minutes. No one answered. Maybe Burger and Sandy were out. Or doing what came naturally.

Crowe picked up his gun and shoulder holster, grabbed a coat and headed out.

After parking out front of his house, Crowe checked the mailbox for any 'messages' from the Scavenger. Nothing there except a book of

Domino's Pizza vouchers and the desiccated corpse of a small frog. The house looked quiet from a distance, no obvious sign of trouble. He glanced around for prying neighbours, but there was no movement anywhere, except as supplied by the wind, its roars and whistles filling the silence of the street.

As he got closer, he realised the front door was open, just a crack, less an invitation than a threat. He moved quietly around the back. The door was shut. As he approached, an indistinguishable shape crossed the window. Crowe leaned closer and peered through the dirty glass. Nothing except the empty and untidy kitchen. Could it have been a reflection on the pane, trees tossing in the wind? Probably. Standing to one side, flat against the wall, he turned the door handle. The lock disengaged. He pushed gently.

Nothing happened. He waited for a moment, trying to sense an ambush, but all he could hear was the wind and a dripping tap. Once inside the doorway, the smell took over. It was sickly sweet, meaty and overpowering.

Emotion died in him, an objective coldness taking over. He moved through the kitchen, following the stench.

It was coming from his bedroom. Before going in, he checked the rest of the house. No one. He shut the front door, locked it and turned off the TV, which was flickering away silently. A half-eaten kebab and several hamburger wrappers lay on the lounge, along with empty glasses that used to have beer in them. Lots of other rubbish. Hooper and Sandy wouldn't win any Homekeeper of the Year awards. Crowe feared they wouldn't be winning anything ever again.

They were on the bed, which had soaked up so much blood the sheets might have been red silk, except they'd blackened and in places dried out, becoming matte and crusty. Both were naked, though it hardly mattered. They'd been slashed and hacked about, Hooper in particular. The skin was barely recognisable as such. The big man's strength, Sandy's youthfulness: neither was relevant anymore. Neither had prevented their deaths. They were just butchered meat now. Only their faces were intact, contorted by their last experience of pain. Sandy looked almost pleading. For what, Crowe wondered. Restoration to life? Or a quick death?

The killer had hacked off Hooper's head. It lay separated from the ragged stump of his neck, neatly arranged on the pillow. Sandy at least had been left in one piece.

As he looked away, appalled and trying to push aside the fury he was feeling, he noticed a message scrawled in blood on the creamy wall above the bedhead: THIS IS THE END OF ALL HUMAN LIFE. ONLY ONE IS IMMUNE. SCAVENGER.

What the hell was that supposed to mean?

He tried to compare the writing to his memory of that on the Scavenger's handwritten notes. But the surfaces on which they were written were too different. The styles seemed separate from each other, but also too much the same: the message was the *content*.

He got out of the bedroom, wanting to escape the smell. Shut the door and tried to think, but emotion rushed back into him, making it too hard. Rage welled in waves, but there was no target within immediate reach, and the anger was forced to pull back, becoming a deep ache in his chest. He breathed evenly. All that did was draw the smell more sharply into his nostrils.

For a moment, he saw Sandy, alternately childlike then provocative. And Hooper, bullish and naive.

Another body superimposed over the top: Lucy's. The blood-splatters on the shed wall above her so clear in memory he could pick out the wetter patches of red. It seemed to form words this time: HE WANTS ME BACK. What the hell? That wasn't real. There'd been no words, not then, not ever. Why now? And what did it mean?

He shook his head and the images disappeared.

None of it was useful. He was going crazy. He had to think.

A sound came from the bedroom, audible even through the closed door. A groan. Something dragging. A footfall. Was the killer still here?

He kicked the door open, gun in hand.

What he saw, for one long instant, was too unnatural to be real. Sandy's body had pulled itself upright, rolling off the bed with a dull squelch of bare foot on bloody floorboards and a low tearing noise – the sound of her skin, stuck down with dried blood, now separating from the sheets.

She was still alive.

Unable to act, Crowe stood watching as strange spasms trembled through her waxen, torn flesh. How could she possibly have survived? There'd been no sign of life.

Her face turned toward him. Her eyes were dull and empty.

'*Help me!*' she moaned. '*You…must…stop them.*'

Her head jerked unnaturally, one arm flailing in a spastic tremor that caused her to stagger. Crowe rushed to her, grabbed her shoulders, and she collapsed against his chest. As he felt her dead weight in his arms, a wave of intense nausea rushed through him. Vision fragmented, the carnage swirled away into a torrential blackness. He lost grip on himself…

'*Stupid girl!*' *Thud of fist against flesh. A demonic snarl. Terror, panic, an intense aching despair well up inside him.* '*You have to love me.*'

Light and shadow across the blades of a pair of shears.

'*Please! No!*'

'Lucy!' Crowe cried out.

The man glances toward him, as though he can sense Crowe's presence. His face is obscured but for the eyes, and Crowe can't tell their colour or proper shape, distorted as they are by rage. The man turns away again, his right hand reaching up to grab the shears off the wall.

'*I love you. Now I'll teach you to respect me!*' *he yells, the words morphing into animalistic snarls even as they fade. Shadows slash the air, turning to red as they strike the wall.* '*You never really see me. I can't take it anymore.*'

A woman cries out.

'*Lucy!*'

Crowe groaned, trying to force himself awake, conscious that he was caught in a nightmare.

But the nightmare merely changed.

'*No, Daddy! Please!*'

'*But I love you, my precious baby. I love you so much.*'

Flesh and sweat. Caressing fingers. A different pain, smothering, burying.

Then the world darkens, and all Crowe can hear is a distant call he is unable to ignore. It urges him to return, though he doesn't want to. Here in the dark the pain is dulled, and he feels some measure of peace. But the voice calls, plucks at his skin, demanding. It is love. A demanding love that insists he return.

An invisible finger runs down the side of his head.

Car beams flash across his eyes. A squeal of brakes. Hands grasp but are torn away as metal and cries and blood and the demands of an endless prying multitude swirl into nothingness again.

Cold, dead flesh. Weight of agony in his arms.

Crowe burst from the kaleidoscopic vision with a hard cry of defiance, staggering back, releasing the burden that weighed him down. He slipped on patches of partially dried blood, fell. His hand slid as he levered himself up.

For a moment, Sandy stood impassive, then her body tumbled forward with a groan, crashing lifeless to the floor.

I don't know where I've been. All I have are fragmented memories fading around the edges, struggling unsuccessfully to remain clear. For a few minutes, I wasn't here, was in another prison, one of cold and dead flesh. Not my own, a body impossible to endure for long. Snatches of another's life, truncated now in a tsunami of violence and agony – so similar to experiences I felt I owned but could barely recall – scurried across my mind like spiders in a mindless panic to escape the descending image of a predator. I know there is blood and there is violence.

And he is there. My only friend.

'Help me!' I cry. 'You...must...stop them.'

For a moment, I feel his touch, his arms around me, trying to support me. I reach up and rub a finger down the scar on his cheek.

The past I must own takes over with a despairing power I cannot withstand. It flings me away from the moment, and from his arms...

...and I am back in my prison. Waiting. Waiting for something worse than dying.

Alone.

26

CROWE HAD NEVER BEEN AFFECTED LIKE THIS BEFORE, NOT BY ANYTHING, not enough to lose his grip on reality. Had the last few moments been some absurd hallucination? But he could feel Sandy's weight, smell the rancid blood.

And Lucy? How did she figure in this?

His head throbbed. He shut and locked the back door. If he went to the cops, he'd be held up in investigative red-tape for days, maybe weeks. Though the house was Ed Rice's, if he were there in person, it wouldn't take Pirran long to work out who Ed Rice was, and then his involvement would likely be long-running and acrimonious. He had no patience for the interrogation that would follow and none of it would help Sandy anyway. Or Lucy. The Scavenger was really pushing at him, and Crowe wanted to find him even more than he had before. He considered burning the place down, but, in the end, he simply left the bodies for someone else to find. He could act innocent if they ever came to him about it. Right now, he just wanted to get out of there. He'd washed his hands. Spatter was drying on his cuffs, but he didn't want to waste time changing. He'd burn the shirt later.

Not wanting to risk being seen near the house, he left through a gap in the back fence after erasing his hand marks from the blood he'd fallen in. He hadn't spent much time on the scene, but it was his house and there'd be plenty of incriminating fingerprints around the place. He'd have to deal with that later, if it came to light. Right now, he had to go. The yard butted onto an area of bushland, and he hiked through it along a path he'd used several times in the past to avoid people he suspected might be waiting for him out front. Wind was still pummelling the trees, so the bush was alive with creaks and moans and sounds of anguish.

Sandy staggering up from the bed.

Red splatter on a wooden wall. Lucy's mangled body sprawled in dirt and blood.

Those manic eyes.

He pushed the images away. Why was Lucy plaguing his thoughts like this? What did she have to do with Sandy? And who was the man he had seen in his vision?

A figure stepped out onto the path ahead. It was solid, dressed in oversized clothes that hung on it like rags. For a moment, Crowe didn't recognise who it was although he did recognise the shape of an old-fashioned shotgun in its hands. He tried to duck behind a tree, whipping his gun up as he did. The figure came forward.

'Stay where ya are!' Blowie's tones. The loopy ones. Crowe lowered his weapon.

'What the hell is this, Blowie?' he said.

Blowie stiffened, his cheeks twitching oddly. 'Don't try anything, Mr Crowe.'

Crowe looked warily at the shotgun. He didn't recognise the make, but he was sure it was three shots at most before reloading was needed. A break-action 12 gauge. It had the battered appearance of an old, much-neglected hangover from hunting days out on the farm. Chances were it hadn't been kept in prime condition. But then again, Crowe suspected Blowie wasn't as generally careless as he made out.

'Whatever you say, Blowie.'

'Throw ya bloody gun away!' he snapped.

'Forget it. I keep it. If you don't like it that way, we can see who's the more efficient killer.'

Blowie said nothing. His skin was blotchy with broken veins across the nose and cheeks. His broad shoulders tensed, his whole body focusing on the shotgun.

'How old's that gun anyway?' Crowe said softly. 'Haven't seen one like that since my previous life in the Old West.'

Blowie glanced at the gun, as though surprised to find it in his hand. His eyes came back to Crowe.

'My father's…' he hissed uncertainly. 'Duck hunting.' Then, sounding like a wounded child, he added, 'Ya won't talk to me.'

'So?'

'Ya pushed me around, Mr Crowe. That wasn't nice. I've just been helpful, and ya tell me ta piss off. I told ya, I'm writin' a book. This is an angle I wanna see.'

Crowe said nothing.

The big man looked past Crowe toward the house, then whispered, 'Ya found 'em, I suppose.'

A branch groaned above Crowe as wind tugged at it.

'The Scavenger's mad at ya, Mr Crowe. I read the message.'

Two intense eyes in the filth of night. The shadow in which they hover moves fast and the weight of it slams into Crowe, pushing him backwards from a low trajectory.

Crowe gasped. Another memory of when he'd found Lucy. But not now. Desperately, he shook it away.

'Somethin' wrong?' hissed Blowie.

'Did you do it, Blowie?' Crowe growled, just to see the man's reaction. 'Did you kill my friends?'

'Really? You serious? How can ya even think that?'

'Because you're here and my friends are dead,' Crowe said.

'Me? You're the one who's pissed him off.'

'You're the one poking your nose in where it isn't wanted.' Crowe glared at the man. 'Pity it isn't *you* in there with your head disconnected from your body. None of this is any business of yours.'

'It *is* my business. I'm in it whether you like it or not. I'm a chronicler, I am. I watch. This story is gunna be big. It'll put me back on top! But you won't help!' The man's madness swirled in his eyes. Crowe wondered how much Blowie had actually lost to unhinge him like this. Hopefully, Gail might be able to fill in the blanks.

Crowe moved closer. 'Look, Blowie, I got mad, that's all. Watch from the distance, stick your nose in the Scavenger's business all you like. But keep it out of mine. I don't want you bugging me.'

'I can help.'

'What you're not getting into your head is, I work alone.'

'You're workin' with a dame.'

'Dame? This isn't the 1940s, Blowie ol' mate.'

'Ya know what I mean.'

'Okay then. I just don't want your help. So piss off!'

With a sudden cunning look, Blowie balanced the shotgun with one hand while he reached into his pocket with the other. It came out with a bit of folded paper. 'I found this in the house,' he said. 'Near the bodies. It's for you. I was helping, see.'

As he held it out, Crowe, in a move he would question later, swung his hand up to grab the shotgun instead. Blowie tried to bring the barrel back and for a few moments, they grappled with it. Suddenly the journo pitched forward, head-butting Crowe. Something seemed to fragment behind Crowe's eyes. He tried to keep hold of the gun barrel, but his grip had been loosened, which allowed Blowie to swing the weapon around. Crowe's own gun went off harmlessly as metal crashed into his face. He staggered and fell.

Part of him was expecting an explosion that would tear a hole in him. Instead, the butt of the gun thudded into his shoulder, and then his head, and the trees around him flared from green to red to black. In the blackness, more memories came, like nightmares in an uneasy sleep.

The cops are making general disclaimers on the radio. Crowe listens to detective Sergeant Someone-or-other giving nothing much away, though he comments that certain fingerprints have been found and that they are currently being compared against sex offender files. He says a vehicle was seen leaving the Merryvale road late. The whole issue of the missing body is being kept from the press. 'We're hoping the driver will come forward to answer questions,' he says. 'A local resident is helping us with our inquiries.'

Sara Rampen is behind the counter of a small pharmacy in the main street of Mittagong, sticking labels onto bottles. A pharmacist. She doesn't want to talk to Crowe.

'You're not a cop,' she says, poking at his licence. 'And this is out of date.'

She's a short woman with wild, black hair and eyes that constantly appear to be evaluating what's before her. She looks as though she has Asian genes somewhere in her ancestry. A long way back. Her white uniform has a hand-made ceramic brooch pinned to one breast – a pop-art toucan.

'Just trying to find Lucy Waldheim's murderer,' Crowe says.

'Well, you're looking in the wrong place.' She ostentatiously tidies the shelves behind her, straightening bottles and rattling the pills in them.

'You were buddies with her,' he says. 'Been suggested that the two of you were in a relationship.'

She glares back at him but doesn't respond.

'Is it true?' he asks.

'What business is it of yours?'

'Lucy was murdered. Maybe that makes it my business. Then again, maybe it's irrelevant. How will I know unless you tell me?'

She turns around fully and leans on the counter. 'I loved Lucy,' she says. 'I met her in here, we talked, became friends. Sometimes I saw her at weekends. She'd come over to my place, we'd have lunch, talk some more.'

'That's all?'

She nods. 'Not that you'll believe me. I'm a lesbian, so you think I'm morally bankrupt. An easy equation to make you feel safer. But it's not lesbians that rape and brutalise—'

'Can we drop the politics? I just want to know if Lucy was a lesbian.'

She pushes herself back. 'It's not a disease. Not every woman I meet turns into one.'

'Just asking. It might be important.'

Finally, her eyes seek out Crowe's. 'Who are you working for?' she says, glancing around to check that the shop is empty.

'Lucy's father.'

This time anger becomes hatred. 'Then talk to him! You want to know who might hurt her, ask him.'

'He hurt her, did he?'

She moves away. Her shoulders and arms tremble. 'What's the use telling you? All you'll do is cover up for him.'

'I liked Lucy. I want to find her killer.'

Before disappearing into the preparation room at the rear, she turns, staring Crowe down. He doesn't retreat. 'Did he tell you what he's done to her for years?'

'You tell me.'

She comes closer, gesturing in a way that's almost pleading. Her hands shake. 'Look, Mr Not Really a Private Eye. Lucy wasn't a happy girl. She came to me because she wanted advice about avoiding pregnancy.'

'She was seeing someone? A name?'

Rampen doesn't respond to that. Only her eyes reveal her feelings. 'I referred *her to a doctor, but she came back and eventually we got to know each other. We talked a lot, for months, on and off, avoiding the real issue, and it was going on the whole time. She only told me last week.'*

'What did she tell you?'

Her eyes lower – there's sadness but also intense loathing. 'Men can't help themselves, can they? Every woman is ripe for the picking, no matter who.'

'I get it, okay? We're bastards. So, what did she tell you?'

'Gregor Waldheim – businessman, pillar of the community, good father and loving husband – was raping his own daughter, that's what.' She looks at Crowe accusingly. 'He's been doing it since she was about 12. Maybe earlier. I don't know. Lucy had repressed a lot of it. Can you believe that, Mr Tough Guy? How's that fit into your world view?'

Her words hit Crowe hard. He feels rage building deep down in his gut and struggles to keep it from getting out.

'Was it true?' he says.

Sara Rampen laughs bitterly. 'True? Her anguish was true. I saw the torment she underwent.' Suddenly there's only sadness in her voice. 'He'd told her it was normal, just something loving daughters did for their fathers, and she'd tried to believe that, even though in the beginning it had torn her up. She knew he shouldn't make her do it. But heaven help her, she actually loved the bastard! Wanted to be loved by him. She thought he wouldn't love her anymore if she made him stop, especially after her mother died. I said, "No. That's bullshit. If he really loved you, he'd see what it was doing to you." But she wouldn't listen to that. She couldn't listen. She just blamed herself for feeling so filthy.'

'Why'd she tell you?'

'Because I was there. A woman who wanted to understand her. Someone who cared.' Rampen rubs her hand across her face. 'I don't know. But something burst in her, not long before she ran away. Something burst and she told me everything.'

Crowe didn't think he had been out long. It didn't feel like it. Maybe not at all. The blow to the head had been a glancing one. Perhaps he'd been hallucinating, but if so, the images were strong and eerily tactile and showing no sign of becoming unreal.

Sandy's body staggers toward him, falling into his arms.

He gasped. For a moment, he couldn't remember what had happened.

A corpse. Staggering up from the bed.

Help me!

Visions of…what had he seen? Lucy again? This time her murder. And another vision that seemed to be a mish-mash of different traumas? Hers and Sandy's? Whose nightmare was it? Had any of it been real?

Crowe could feel thick moisture oozing from broken skin on the side of his head and scrapes across his cheekbone, where the pain was strongest.

Memory of his failed investigation into Lucy's murder was recurring. Why now? Was it a coincidence? It had felt deliberate somehow, as earlier memories had been. As though he was being forced to remember.

Remember, Mr Crowe. You must remember.

Lucy again?

Blowie was gone. Movement caught Crowe's attention, but it was only wind in the undergrowth. His gun was still in his right hand. Something was crumpled into his left. The Scavenger's note.

He holstered the gun but could hardly focus as he staggered upright. The exertion or the change of altitude caused his headache to concentrate into a nauseous surge. Suppressing it, he slumped against a tree. He touched the side of his face. Blood greased his fingertips.

Moments passed and he didn't try to stop them.

He's on a headland, where wind and rain roar in his ears. Skarratt's ahead, running full belt for a clump of trees. Crowe tries to follow, but something solid, something with eyes bright and intense, pounds into him. He hears a grunt. Feels wind and rain.

Crowe raised his hand to his face, avoiding the spot where the butt of Blowie's shotgun had connected with him. He rubbed his forehead. The pain diminished. When he felt a bit better, he unfolded the note and read it. His vision was slightly blurry. Hopefully that would pass. He was getting too old for this.

This note was handwritten, the scrawl matching that on the other Scavenger missives.

Mr Crowe, the time of the Great Ceremony approaches. Will you be ready? Do not take me lightly, sir. I will become angrier. My anger is something you could not bear. All around you are helpless before me. None can help you. There are things you must do, something you must find for me and not for that criminal, Pukalski. The last part of what is needed. You know what it is. Find it. Find the source of power quickly. But at the same time watch and strive to attain perfection, and I will spare your friends pain and guide you to me. It begins where first we met.

SHE DIED CALMLY; AND HER COUNTENANCE EXPRESSED AFFECTION EVEN IN DEATH. I NEED NOT DESCRIBE THE FEELINGS OF THOSE WHOSE DEAREST TIES ARE RENT BY THAT MOST IRREPARABLE EVIL.

Spare his friends pain? It was a bit too late for that, he thought bitterly.

27

When Crowe got back to his office, there were two messages blinking on the answering machine. The first was a curt 'Ring me' from Pirran, the second a more frantic-sounding one from Pukalski of roughly the same substance but more ill-mannered: 'Call me back, you fucker'.

He ignored both. He had to talk to Gail.

Crowe sank into his chair, dropped his head into his hands and thought. Whatever had happened in his house, whether Sandy had been clinging to life for a moment or whether it had been something more supernatural, the visions he'd had clearly meant something. His subconscious mind had been working away on the case without him. Now it was starting to speak out.

At the same time, memories of Lucy had been on the rise. She haunted him, however you looked at it. He was close to believing the haunting was real and that his mother's superstitions had been justified. Lucy's ghost, or some unstable remnant of her being, was trying to show him the route he had to take. It seemed limited in what it could do and say. But ghost or not, her presence was everywhere.

The more Crowe thought about it, the more he felt Dale Walker had something to tell him. He was the one who provided a clear connection to both Lucy and Pukalski. The connection was perhaps that he worked for, and had been groomed by, Waldheim, but was there more to it?

And that bit from the Scavenger's last note: 'There are things you must do, something you must find for me.' Although it seemed an age ago that this had all begun, what Crowe was looking for was Pukalski's money and Queen Marika's foetus. He'd assumed that the Scavenger already had the money, but why would he want the foetus as well?

He thought of all Gail had said about the thing being a nexus of power, of it being a 'container' in which life might be stored or created. Perhaps the Scavenger wanted it as a supernatural kick-starter for his creation.

Crowe sat back. He'd always thought that the Scavenger's attack on Skarratt had been purely a crime of opportunity, a matter of chance. But was it a coincidence that a body-part-collecting serial killer just happened to be at Wilkinson's Bay the night an eldritch object was meant to change hands? Was Queen Marika's dead unborn baby what the Scavenger had wanted all along? Or was he the mysterious millionaire who'd forced Pukalski to get the foetus? That last bit would make sense, but only sort of.

How did it all connect? Crowe could spitball until the cows came home, but what he wanted – needed – was facts.

'Damn it!' he yelled and slammed his fist into the wall. It hurt, but he didn't care.

He opened the safe, determined to go through the Scavenger file with a fine-tooth comb. On top of the folders lay the invoice he'd grabbed days ago from Tansey's flat and promptly forgotten about the moment he'd closed the safe door on it. The name scrawled at the top caught his attention, and a recollection lit up somewhere in his brain.

Walker.

'Dale Walker,' Crowe said into his phone. 'You know him?'

'That grovelling little weasel? Sure,' Gail replied impatiently. 'What's he got to do with anything?'

He'd interrupted her during an interview with some popular reality TV star – a victim of *Love Island*. Gail wasn't particularly pleased, and Crowe could hear the annoyance clearly in her voice. She hated being interrupted even more than she hated covering the shows. Crowe's swift explanation about Walker's connection with Pukalski, however, stopped her from hanging up.

He then told her about Hooper and Sandy and started to talk, albeit cautiously, about ghosts. At which point her conciliatory tone let him know she was trying to figure out how to get him to sign into a high-care psychiatric ward.

'The corpse seemed to get up and you've been having visions relating to an old case,' she repeated, her tone even. 'And what do you make of this, Mike?'

'A bit less than you do, I suspect, and a bit more. Look, forget about whether there really was a ghost or not. The point is, I reckon someone – my own subconscious, if you like – is trying to tell me a thing or two. And I need you to do me a favour.'

'Oh?'

'I need some background on Walker.'

'That's easy, he's a candidate in the upcoming state elections–'

'I know all that. I need to know who his connections are, who his powerful friends are, who he's in bed with. How the hell did he get where he is today? No way he could've done it himself. When I knew him a while back, he was a complete loser.'

'Being a loser's no hindrance in politics.'

'Well, he was some sort of lackey of Waldheim's back in the day, and I suspect he still is.'

'Waldheim?'

'Yeah. Dig as deep as you can. I also need you to find out what happened to the bloke who was tried for the murder of Lucy Waldheim.'

'What's going on?'

'It's a long story. Seems to be a connection between Lucy's death and what's happening now. God knows what – but it's…' He paused, reluctant even now, to say the words. 'It's …it's Lucy's ghost I keep seeing. She's been talking to me, Gail.'

'Oh?'

'She begs me to help her.'

'She's been dead for quite a while, Mike.'

'You think I don't know that?' he growled. 'It's crazy. But it keeps happening, over and over again. I can't ignore it.'

You must stop him, the corpse had said. But stop who? If it really had been Lucy in Sandy's body, why would she be concerned about the Scavenger?

'I think you need a long medically enhanced rest, Mike.'

Crowe grunted. 'I'll rest when I'm dead. And maybe not even then, the way it's going. Look, just find out what you can. And quickly. Things are hotting up and I don't think we have much time to work this out. And Gail?'

'Yeah?'

'Be careful. Meera thinks the Scavenger hates women. That might put you in the firing line.'

'I thought he only targeted men.'

'Given what happened to Sandy, I'd say his MO's changed. It'd probably be best if you stayed away.'

Someone honked outside in the sparse traffic. 'Where are you?' Gail asked.

'On my way to Sydney.'

'You do know it's illegal to use a mobile phone while driving?'

'Sure. I'm in control.'

'It's stupid, Mike.'

He didn't reply.

'Where are you going now?'

'To see a man about a mummy,' he replied.

He thumbed off the connection before she could protest. He felt the pressure of responsibility – of guilt – pushing hard against his chest, digging into his thoughts, weighing him down. The Scavenger had done in Hooper and Sandy certainly. Not Gail.

Stay away from Gail, you bastard.

I dream of a girl, one whose life ends in violence and bloodshed. I feel the fear that tears through her, struggle with her as she tries to stand, share the pain as the knife plunges into her chest, tears her skin apart, carves its incoherent messages into her flesh. Her screams flood through my own throat, and though I try to release them I can't overcome the weight of the death that drags her into the Dark. Instead I scream my own words, words whose meaning dissipates as they echo around my prison. In an instant, they are gone.

But as the immediacy of the dream fades, the terror turns to hope.

He has begun to understand. I sense a shift from denial and pointless recrimination to an acceptance he has not felt before. For a moment, the feeling verges on elation.

'Mr Crowe,' I whisper. 'Stop them. Stop them, please.'

Perhaps if I say it often enough, even though unheard and echoing dully from the stone walls of my prison, he will find a way to free me, to save me.

The pick-up address on the invoice he'd pinched from Tansey's place was that of Speed Logistics, situated obscurely in one of the more industrial areas on the banks of Sydney Harbour. The afternoon felt inappropriately pleasant given how shitty his day had been: lots of winter sun and a rustling breeze with just enough oomph to tease at his hair like an indifferent lover's fingers. Crowe drove in through the open chain-link gate and followed a series of handwritten signs that pointed toward a loading bay marked 'COLLECTION' in peeling yellow paint.

As a business, this warehouse looked more like a dump than a transport firm. Rubbish lay everywhere, most of it an unaesthetic mishmash of twisted metal, faded paintwork and rust.

Crowe honked and a small window opened in a red-ochre patch of wall. A weary gaze stared out at him.

'I've come to pick up a consignment for Macca's Curios.' He held up the crumpled paper. Macca's Curios was the name on the invoice. It was a long shot, but the name seemed appropriate. Crowe couldn't think of anything much more curious than a pickled celebrity foetus – if that's what the invoice was for.

The window slammed shut, something screeched mechanically, and the bay doors began to rise with a ratchet hum. The wait seemed interminable but eventually the metal roller-door disappeared to reveal a cluttered interior full of boxes and containers. A largish woman dressed in a workplace-branded windcheater, khaki shorts, long socks and scuffed black shoes appeared from around the corner. 'Authorisation number?' she snapped at him.

Crowe read the numbers off the invoice. The woman frowned. 'What is it?'

'Miscellaneous knickknacks,' he said. 'Brought in from Europe.'

She reached out. He had to exit the car to hand the paper to her. Snatching it, the woman squinted intently at the fading scrawls.

'I remember this,' she said. 'Someone picked it up maybe three weeks ago.'

'Damn,' Crowe said. 'You sure?'

She stared at him, as though analysing his features.

He stared back.

'You the owner?' She squinted suspiciously.

Crowe paused, considering his options.

'Nope,' he finally said, deciding on an 'outsider' stance. 'Private investigator.'

'Not a cop?'

He flashed his licence at her. 'Private commission.'

'You working for the owner?'

He got the notion that a lot hung on his answer. 'No,' he said, taking a punt. 'The owner's AWOL. His wife hired me.'

She nodded thoughtfully, as though her fears had been confirmed. Then she glanced right and left, as though checking for spies. 'Couple of other blokes were asking about this consignment just last week. Didn't like the look of 'em.'

'And you like the look of me?'

'Not particularly. But more than them, yeah.' She grinned. 'This whole deal's been worryin' me, and I reckon it's time I gave it up. I'm not sure I did the right thing, you know, so I'd rather it wasn't here anymore.' She shrugged. 'Boss wouldn't like it and I can't afford to lose my job.'

Crowe shrugged. 'No problem there. I have short-term recall problems.'

Behind her, an indistinct form moved amidst the angular chaos of the warehouse. By the time Crowe had focused on the spot, the only shadows were flat and unmoving. There'd been something familiar about the way that half-seen shape had held itself.

'Thing is,' the woman said, 'the bloke that came to pick up the consignment first time paid me to hold onto it for him.'

'Hold onto it?'

'Yeah. I filled out the paperwork, so officially he took it from the premises. But in fact–' she made that surreptitious spy-check movement again '–it's still out the back.'

Crowe perked up at that.

'He said he'd fetch it in a day or two. Never did.'

'And you didn't tell the others?'

She shook her head, making her short but tangled brown hair quiver unnaturally. 'No way. Showed 'em the sign-off sheet. They immediately assumed the consignment was gone.' She huffed. 'But they reckoned they worked for the first bloke – de Mora was his name – and I figured if they *did* they'da known he left the stuff here…unofficially.'

De Mora. That rang a bell, though Crowe couldn't think why.

He described Tansey to her, and she confirmed it sounded like he might have been one of the pair.

'Thing is,' she said, 'someone named de Mora was killed in a hotel in Balmain just after the first guy had come to collect the consignment. Saw it in the papers. There was a photo, not a good one, and it looked like him.'

Ah, yes. That's where he'd heard the name before, from news reports at the time. Was the man's murder Tansey's work? Given he'd intended to abscond with the $180 million in Pukalski's metal case, and he clearly wasn't in possession of the foetus, there had to be someone else – an outsider – who was responsible for handing it over on behalf of the actual owner. So Tansey and his conspirators had intercepted this de Mora bloke. With the foetus in hand they could've simply made the drop-off and taken the money, thus avoiding a bloodbath and no one the wiser. But Tansey and his mates weren't overly subtle in their methods of interrogation. Humans are both resilient and fragile, and it's easy for goons like Tansey to forget that. They clearly killed de Mora trying to get the location of the foetus from him then found themselves unable to muster the requisite brain cells to figure out what he'd done with it.

'That's one thing,' the woman said, grabbing Crowe by the arm and dragging him inside the building. 'But it's more than that. Whatever's in that box out back, I don't think it's right, ya know? Gives me the creeps.'

He shot her a quizzical look.

She shrugged. 'Checked back over the paperwork and just can't figure how it got in the country, ya know? Never went through Customs, that's for sure. What if it's drugs?'

'You didn't open it?'

Her stare widened in horror. 'No way. I'm far enough in already without being an accomplice to somethin' bad. As it is, I just bent the rules a bit. I can say I had no idea and it'd be the truth.'

'You willing to hand it over to me?' Crowe asked. 'If it's what I think it is, it's not drugs. Nothing illegal. At any rate, if you do, I can guarantee your part in this ends here.'

Crowe guessed what governed her decision was the fact she'd been fretting about it for a long time rather than any inherent feeling of honesty emanating from him. That she'd told him as much as she had indicated her choice had already been made.

'Happy to see the back of it.'

She gestured for Crowe to follow, and they wound their way through corridors of crates and sparsely packed shelving. Crowe felt rather pleased with himself, thinking he was finally making some progress but also weighing up his options should this consignment prove to contain what he suspected it did. Perhaps he could use it as a lever to get closer to Pukalski's client. He was beginning to think talking to that particular man of mystery might offer insight into how Queen Marika's dead baby, Pukalski, Lucy Waldheim and the Scavenger were connected.

A sense of presence imposed itself on him, some vague awareness of indefinite shapes that didn't belong. He glanced to his left down a long, dim space between crowded shelves. At its end was a figure watching them. It was slight and girlish.

'What's up?' the woman he was following asked, drawing his attention. When he looked back into the shadows, the figure was gone.

'You alone here?' Crowe asked.

'The boss is away on business.' She pointed toward the back of the warehouse. 'Coupla blokes – Joe and...forget his name – do the heavy lifting, you know. But they're on a job at the moment. No one else. Why?'

'Never mind. Lead on.'

Their destination proved to be a small room with all the ambience of a disused lavatory. The woman switched on the exposed globe as they entered, revealing cardboard boxes of tatty files crowded around a few rusted cabinets. She heaved one pile out of the way and opened a panel in the exposed wall. Then she stepped back.

'You can get it,' she said. 'I'm not touchin' that bloody thing again.'

Crowe peered into the narrow space. A shape was nestled there, about the size of a small suitcase.

'This it?'

She grunted and stepped back further. Crowe reached in and grabbed it.

Someone screaming...a man. Sudden flash across the ceiling.

Crowe jerked away.

'You feel it?' the woman whispered.

Mr Crowe! Stop him! Stop them!

At that moment the lights went out, leaving the space lit only by the scraps of daylight that managed to get through a small dirty window at the rear.

What the hell was going on?

The woman groaned. Crowe looked up in time to see her dropping, face contorted in a moment of shock. Something moved behind her. Crowe tried to focus on it, but the woman's weight crashed into him and forced him to the floor. Moisture splashed along the side of his face. Warm and thick. Smelt like blood. The woman was trembling, groaning.

He swore and moved her aside. A fist emerged from the shifting gloom and ground across his forehead. A glint, sharp in the gloom. Knife blade.

'It's mine,' a gruff voice snarled.

Crowe fumbled for his gun. The woman was still obscuring his view, confusing him. He sensed someone looming, saw hands reaching for the box. Crowe's gun pulled free and he brought it up fast. The Scavenger – it had to be him – only a featureless blur, jerked away, howling. The safety was still on. Crowe shoved against the woman as he thumbed it off and squeezed the trigger desperately. In that confined space, the sound was deafening.

Had he hit the Scavenger? The attacker shouted something, but it was more the shriek of an angry animal than a cry of pain. Crowe fired again, blindly. A box of files crashed over him. As he pushed them away, he heard running feet.

By the time he'd extricated himself from the rubbish, the phantom was gone. For a moment Crowe considered taking off after him, but he had no idea where the bloke had disappeared to, and the woman clearly needed help. Given the Scavenger's history, he was pretty adept at hiding and making quick getaways. Meanwhile, Crowe had the box and its contents to consider – he wouldn't outrun the Scavenger carrying that thing and had no intention of abandoning it. He gave the woman a glance and saw her chest heave. A cursory examination revealed that the Scavenger's knife hadn't touched her; she'd just hit her head as she fell. She was semi-conscious but would be okay.

With difficulty but determination – he wasn't leaving the prize behind even for a minute – Crowe carried her and the case into the main area and made her as comfortable as he could, staunching the blood flow with bandages from a first-aid kit he found on a nearby wall. He called an ambulance from the office phone. Though loath to leave her lying there alone, Crowe had no time to worry about the niceties. She'd be fine. He hefted the box again and stumbled out of that place.

No one was around to see him leave, at least no one visible.

28

INSIDE THE BOX, CROWE FOUND A LARGE METAL CONTAINER, WIRED SHUT and locked. Barring violence, it wasn't going to open, not here, not now. No way was he stopping en route to deal with what was inside. Blood had splattered on his coat and pants – for the second time in so many days – and he looked like someone a good citizen would report to the authorities without a qualm.

Besides, there was always a chance he was being followed. He made a few tricks-of-the-trade manoeuvres, dodged and weaved through suburb after suburb, and kept an eye out for suspicious vehicles on the long stretches of freeway between Heathcote and Wollongong. At the top of Bulli Pass, he turned off his usual route, wound down through the graded curves and stopped out of sight on the lee side of a particularly abrupt corner. A few cars passed, but they contained working stiffs heading home for the afternoon. Nothing suspicious. Finally, he felt confident that he wasn't being tailed and kept going toward the Gong.

He couldn't go back to Rice's house, and his office was an obvious place to wait for him to show up, so he decided to stop in a motel for the night, the first one he came to, provided it wasn't too conspicuous or too upmarket. He needed to get this box open, check the contents, talk to Gail. He'd freed himself of the Scavenger for the time being and was sure he had the much-coveted foetus. It was only a matter of keeping his shit together until he could figure out his next move.

Unfortunately, he wasn't as free to choose as he thought.

'Mr Pukalski wants to see you,' said a dull, business-like voice coming from a dull, business-like face. The face belonged to a bloke dressed in a silver-grey suit, baggy and slick like something straight from the Gucci trendy-exec catalogue. His tie was tinged green to match his expensively dyed hair. This vision of uncool pretension yanked open his door. How the hell could Pukalski have found him so quickly? Crowe had only just pulled into the nearly empty parking lot of a crummy-looking motel in the backlots of North Wollongong.

'Tell him I'm busy,' Crowe said, staring up at the goon. 'He can make an appointment through my secretary.'

'You don't have a secretary,' the man said humourlessly.

'She pretends to be an answering machine.'

Mr Middle-Management didn't smile, which was fine by Crowe. He reached out. Grabbed the door to close it.

'Mr Pukalski will be very cross if you don't come.' Obviously with Banger off-line, Charlie-boy had been reduced to hiring from rent-a-heavy.

'Should be used to it by now.' Crowe stuck the key back in the ignition but changed his mind about turning it. Middle-Management had a gun in his hand and was pointing it at him. *Give me a break*, he thought. How many gun threats did he have to put up with in any given two-day period?

'We'll go in my car.' Middle-Management glanced in the back seat. 'And bring the package with you.'

They drove in silence. Middle-Management's underling – a chubby-faced Somewhat-Lower-Management type who reminded Crowe of a grown-up Lou Costello – steered their Volvo while Middle-Management himself kept an eye on Crowe in the back seat. He was too close, and Crowe might've taken him out several times, but there didn't seem any point. The man was a pro and the attempt would be unlikely to have a tidy outcome. Crowe needed to speak to Pukalski anyway.

'There's a tracking device on my car, I assume,' he said by way of conversation.

Middle-Management said nothing but gave him a smug smile.

They turned right off the main road just past Warrawong and followed the curve of the lake for a while, stopping at the front gate of a place that must've had a great view of the murky water. A high, bleached-brick fence surrounded the house and its large yard. Lower-Management pressed a button on the dashboard and the gate swung open. The house looked like the result of a collision between a second-rate Roman temple and the Kirribilli Yacht Club.

Pukalski kept Crowe waiting in his front vestibule for maybe 15 minutes. The latter shuffled his feet impatiently, but the two heavies were impervious to boredom. Finally, they took him through to an Italianate room that Pukalski apparently used as an occasional office. The man himself was standing, studying Crowe's entrance.

'What're you playing at?' Crowe growled.

'Shut him up!' said Pukalski calmly. Middle-Management shoved him and at the same time gouged his gun across Crowe's neck.

'Did he have any weapons?' Pukalski added. Lower-Management shrugged. 'Well, check, for fuck's sake.'

While Middle-Management held his .38 against Crowe's temple, the underling rifled through his coat. The search yielded Crowe's Beretta, but there was nothing he could do about it. Did Pukalski know what was in the parcel? So far no one had attempted to take it from him. But Pukalski wasn't very happy, and it was Crowe he wasn't very happy with. Charlie-boy had not been weathering the waiting game well.

He strode toward Crowe, his hands cradled in his coat pockets. As he approached, he motioned the heavies to one side with a shake of the head.

'This is wasting my time, Pukalski,' Crowe said.

'Someone been expressing their dissatisfaction with your work, Crowe?' He poked at the bruises on Crowe's face and cast a critical eye over the bloodstains.

'You could say that.'

Pukalski did the circuit around him as though Crowe was some sort of strange sculpture he needed to examine from all sides. Crowe didn't turn to watch him. And didn't say anything. If this were a game, he wasn't going to play till someone told him the rules.

'Have you found the Scavenger yet?' Pukalski said from behind him.

The way he said 'Scavenger' told Crowe plenty. It dripped with scepticism, so that he might as well have asked if Santa Claus was in town.

'I'm working on it,' Crowe answered.

'Like shit you are!' Unexpectedly, his foot rammed into the back of Crowe's knees so they bent and he stumbled. Middle-Management joined in, and Crowe found himself sprawled on the floor. Pukalski's Italian-leather shoe thudded into his ribs. Crowe tried to grab Pukalski's foot, but a gun barrel appeared in close proximity to his right nostril.

'What is this, Pukalski?' he growled.

'*Mr* Pukalski to you!' He kicked Crowe again, then stepped back to study the effect. He sounded slightly disappointed. 'I've put up with as much shit from you as I intend to. It's time you knew your place.'

'And where might that be?'

'Six-foot under, dick-brain.'

He moved around so Crowe could see him. Crowe started to get up. 'Stay down!' Pukalski said. 'On your knees.'

'Get fucked!'

'Jonathan!' He gestured to Middle-Management. There was a gunshot and searing pain scored through the muscle of Crowe's right arm, midway between shoulder and elbow. The impact and his reaction sent him flying. He swore, holding the wound as blood seeped out through the torn cloth of his jacket.

'Next time he might miss and get you somewhere serious,' Pukalski said.

Crowe struggled to his knees. Pain was like a knife slicing to the bone.

'This was my favourite jacket, you mad bastard,' he muttered.

'You won't be needing it for long.'

Great. We're in full gangster mode now, Crowe thought. 'What's this about?' he managed. 'I thought you were going to be patient, Charlie. Let me do my fucking job.'

Pukalski stood over him, hands on hips like a diminutive colossus. 'It's about you and me, Crowe. It's about deceit. It's about the scam you were pulling with Tansey. It's about your treachery.'

'Me and Tansey? Are you out of your mind? I don't know what you're talking about.'

Pukalski snarled, trembling with anger so much he almost looked like he had Parkinson's disease. 'Scavenger, my arse. It was you killed Skarratt and the others. You took my money. You and Tansey set up the whole business, and I thought you were just bloody clever to work out what they'd done. Well, none of it was clever. It's not even believable.'

'What's brought this shit on?'

'Putting two and two together, that's what.' He finally acknowledged the presence of the box, which was sitting right where Crowe had dumped it. 'Found the merchandise, I see,' he barked. 'Right where you left it, I assume.'

'I think you've added up incorrectly, Mr Genius. That box contains personal items relating to my great-aunt Cecily. I'm writing up the family history.'

Pukalski snorted. 'You must think I'm a fool, Crowe.'

Crowe nodded whimsical agreement.

'A little birdie tells me you've often involved yourself in matters that were none of your business,' Pukalski continued. 'Sensitive matters. A while back you deeply offended a good friend of mine, it seems. He was willing to leave you alone then, but now I know about the connection, I can smell your guilt. He wants what he paid for.'

'Yeah? I've pissed off lots of people in my time. Can you be more specific?'

Pukalski shrugged. The smile that trembled over his lips was like a seismic tremor through porridge.

'You don't mean Gregor Waldheim by any chance, do you?' Crowe added.

Pukalski stared at him, neither confirming nor denying. But from the look on his face, Crowe knew the truth of it. That was the least likely of his speculations confirmed.

'You're not going to tell me Waldheim is the one you're working for, the one that scares the shit out of you?'

'No, I'm not,' Pukalski replied. 'And he doesn't scare me.'

'You were trembling enough when you hired me.'

'I was angry, and I respect him.'

'Waldheim's a pathetic nobody, a simpering bastard—'

'A pathetic nobody with more money than the fuckin' government and with powers you can hardly imagine.'

'Powers? What sort of—'

Pukalski gestured at Middle-Management, who came forward with a leer. Crowe tried to defend himself, but it was useless. How much abuse could his skull stand up to anyway? He guessed he was about to find out.

Crowe visits Gregor Waldheim after talking to Lucy's friend, Sara Rampen, rage propelling him through a gang of servants that try to keep him out. 'Mr Waldheim's ill. Mr Waldheim's still in shock. The doctors say Mr Waldheim shouldn't see anyone.'

True, Waldheim looks like a broken man. His mousy hair hangs languidly over his ears and forehead, his shoulders droop. He sits at a large desk, scanning business papers, and glances up with an air of paranoia when Crowe barges in. Behind him, paintings full of vaguely demonic imagery stare down on him with a disapproving scowl. A faint pungency hangs in the air, rising from the ashtray where he's recently stubbed out the last in a long series of cigarettes.

'Well, Crowe,' he says. 'Have you got something positive to tell me at last?'

'You're a bastard, Waldheim,' Crowe growls. 'That do?'

'What?' Waldheim straightens up, flushing red. 'How dare you!'

'What've you been doing to your daughter?'

'What's wrong with you, Crowe?'

'I know, Waldheim. I know what you did to her.'

'Are you accusing me of killing her? You must be mad.'

'I don't think you killed her. Not that.'

Waldheim stares at Crowe for a long moment, then slumps in his chair – he's interpreted the disdain on Crowe's face. 'How'd you know?' he whispers. 'Her diary? I haven't been able to find it.' He shakes his head. 'It's all wrong. She was making it up.'

Crowe had expected denial, but Waldheim isn't able to dredge up a scrap of conviction. He'd never been overly strong, just enough to fool the less perceptive of his clients, and his money and business acumen always managed to intimidate the rest. But this–

'Don't even say it,' Crowe growls.

'You don't understand what it's like, Crowe.' He almost stands in order to plead more effectively. But being behind the desk presumably feels safer, so he stays there. 'I really loved her. I kept seeing her, so gentle, so womanly...so like her mother. I missed Gloria and Lucy was all that was left of her. It seemed... it just seemed natural. I–' he licks his lips, anxiety and guilt heaving in his chest '–I couldn't help it.'

'Bullshit!' Crowe moves closer. 'Did anyone else know?'

'No, I swear. It was our secret, just Lucy and me.'

'What about Eleyn?'

Crowe senses movement, spins around and reaches for his gun. But it's

Farnestine herself, her face hard and emotionless. 'Oh, I knew, Mr Crowe. God forgive me.'

Crowe glances at Waldheim as he makes a sort of gargling sound and, if possible, sinks further into his chair.

'I thought it was our secret,' he whispers.

'No, Gregor,' Farnestine says. 'I worked it out. From the way she reacted, the way you did. It wasn't hard.' She comes no further into the room, as though there's something dead in there she doesn't want to smell. Who can blame her? As if the weird paintings, the shelves of old, leather-bound books and the gargoyle figures that line the top of huge mahogany bookshelves against every wall aren't bad enough, there's the sheer stink of Waldheim's guilt – and her own – to deal with.

'Why didn't you do something about it?' Crowe almost howls with disgust.

'I wanted to help her. I wanted to help Gregorius.' Farnestine gestures nervously. 'What could I do but wait and hope I could stop it somehow.'

Waldheim whispers, 'Lucy agreed it would be our secret.' As he speaks, he reaches for his cigarettes, flicks one from the packet on his desk. When Crowe sees it, he remembers where he'd last caught a whiff of that foreign tobacco smell. The feeling that surges through him is so close to dismay, he can barely ask the question.

'And that's why you killed her?' he manages finally. 'To keep it secret?'

Waldheim's up like a sprinter off the starting block, though whether fear or anger compels him, Crowe can't tell. Waldheim grips the edge of the desk so tightly Crowe thinks he might break the wood. 'I wouldn't do that. Never.'

'But you'd rape your daughter for – how many years was it?'

'Rape? No. I'd never hurt her.'

'Call it what you like. What were you doing at Merryvale the night she was murdered?'

'I wasn't–'

'You were there. So were the ashes of one of those cigarettes you smoke. Imported especially, are they? How many people in Merryvale smoke those things, do you think?'

Waldheim glances at the unlit cigarette as though it's something he's never seen before and can't understand what the hell it's doing between his fingers. 'I...um... don't know.'

'Gregor!' Farnestine cries from the doorway. 'Tell him he's wrong!'

He looks at her and they hold that position for what seems like minutes. Then he folds forward over his desktop. Papers rustle to the floor. 'Ye...' Waldheim moans, 'Yes.'

'Yes?' Suddenly anger is like a hot poker rammed through Crowe's chest. 'Yes? Yes, what?' He grabs Waldheim's hair and wrenches his head back so his face is exposed. The eyes are dull, as though he's forcing awareness out of them, retreating from the world. 'Don't pass out on me, Waldheim! I want you here, damn it. Here where it hurts!' Crowe smashes the man's face down on the desk, hard, but the man only groans.

'Mr Crowe!' Farnestine leaves the threshold at last, enters the room properly. Her hands clamp on Crowe's shoulders, try to pull him back.

Crowe ignores her. 'What were you doing there, Waldheim?'

He groans again as Crowe pushes him back into the chair. Blood dribbles like snot from his nose. Crowe throws Farnestine off and comes around the table. Waldheim's eyes follow his movement.

Crowe grabs him. 'Tell me, Waldheim, or I'll mash your face into dog food.'

'Mr Crowe! Please!' Farnestine has trailed Crowe around the desk.

Waldheim says, 'It's what I deserve, Eleyn. Let him punish me.'

'Tell him you didn't kill Lucy, Gregor. Please.'

He meets Crowe's gaze. 'We'd argued, Mike,' he says, 'Lucy and I. She said coming to her room at night had to stop. "I'm ashamed," she said, "it can't be right, if I'm so ashamed." I...I...' He lapses into a trance, so Crowe shakes him. 'I hit her...' he says, dazed, as though Crowe has woken him from a deep sleep. 'I struck her, and she ran away. That's when I called you to find her. I was afraid what she might do.'

'Oh, Gregor,' Farnestine whines.

'What then?'

'When you asked about Merryvale, I knew she'd be there. I went to talk to her, but she was irrational about it. She said there were laws.' He looks at Crowe. 'I was afraid she didn't love me anymore.'

'You argued again?'

'I was only there a while.'

'There were signs of an argument, Waldheim. You tossed a beer can across the room.'

Puzzlement flickers over his face.

'You fought with her,' Crowe presses.

Tears fill his eyes and his lips tremble. 'Yes. I...I'm sorry. Sorry.'

'You killed her. Admit it.'

Waldheim collapses, sobbing and muttering to himself. To Crowe's surprise Farnestine kneels beside him and takes him in her arms. Crowe is still so angry *he wants to kick the shit out of him, but the peak moment has passed and now there's only room for numbness.*

'Then you came back and took her body away, right?' he says. 'Why do that? And where did you take her?'

Waldheim looks up at him with eyes wet and red. 'No, no!' he cries. 'I didn't. I didn't–'

A discreet cough draws Crowe's attention toward the doorway.

'Excuse me, ma'am,' the intruder says. Waldheim's personal assistant shimmers in the doorway – a thin, quiet woman who's been with him for years.

'Not now, Joyce,' Farnestine says wearily.

'But Mrs Waldheim,' the woman says, as though she thinks the scene that greets her can be resolved by what she has to say. 'It's the police. They've arrested a man. He's confessed to killing Miss Lucy.'

'What?' Farnestine says.

'Yes, ma'am. It's good news, isn't it? It doesn't bring her back, but at least there's some justice done.'

Farnestine looks at Crowe for explanation. Waldheim is still sobbing.

'There must have been a mistake,' Farnestine says.

'No, ma'am, he's confessed. And they found the implement which…which did it.'

'Shears,' Crowe says.

She nods. Then adds, 'And they found Lucy's fingers, too.'

'Not her body?'

'No, sir.'

'There must have been some mistake,' Farnestine repeats.

Waldheim mumbles for amnesty to himself or whatever God had abandoned him.

As Crowe groaned his way out of darkness and bad memories, what he saw was Waldheim's gaunt, broken expression, breathing words across the desk as though there was some way they could change things – as though he could weave a spell to drag the present back into the past and somehow make things right again.

Then he was gone, and Lucy stood against the far wall, blood streaming from her eyes. The shock threw Crowe back. He felt his mind slipping away.

Her lips moved as she held out her hands, pleading. This time Crowe couldn't hear her, though he knew well enough what the words would be.

'I don't know how to stop him,' he whispered.

He tried to stand, to go to her, but he couldn't get his legs to work. Slammed his fist against the wall, wanting the pain to bring him back, to stop him from fading completely. There was no impact. No pain.

'Why does your father want with the foetus?' Crowe managed.

He thought she said something, but he heard the words as though they were carried by a passing wind.

'Lucy? Why does he want it so much?'

Lucy began to fade. *He wants...me...to...*' Her voice hissed in his ears, but the words lost coherence as Lucy was consumed by shadows.

Crowe lapsed into oblivion.

When he woke again, there was pain in his skull, not his fist. Lucy was gone.

He'd become so used to headaches over the previous few days, the one he had at this point seemed like an old friend. Luckily the light in the room was low wattage. Besides, other parts of him felt much worse. At least one rib was broken or pretending to be, and he couldn't use his right arm at all. It was as though someone had locked the muscles from working. That thought made him wince.

He was trapped somewhere in Pukalski's house, waiting for the next round to begin. They'd tried to beat the whereabouts of the money from him, but as he didn't have a clue, that led only to more violence – and then Pukalski was called away. Middle-Management had headed off to search Crowe's office and Ed Rice's house. Banger was with him. Without admitting anything, Crowe had led them to deduce the money might be there. Lower-Management would stay behind to make sure Crowe didn't decide to leave.

'We'll be back, Mr Crowe,' Middle-Management said.

Crowe was convinced that Ed Jonwood – Banger – was the one who had soured Pukalski on him. Jonwood had come into the room while Middle-Management laid into Crowe and stood silently watching like a block of chiselled granite. 'He'll admit it,' Pukalski said to him, 'eventually.' Cunning lurked in Banger's eyes. Crowe wasn't about to admit that Banger wasn't as stupid as he'd always taken him to be, but he was definitely more involved. The longer he stared at Crowe, the more Crowe became convinced it was Banger and Tansey who'd been working together. Guided carefully, Banger would've been a useful spook in Pukalski's organisation – always there, barely noticed, trusted, like a piece of sturdy but mediocre furniture. Crowe's mind went back to the shooting of Tansey in the *Harbourview Restaurant* – Banger's edgy awareness of what Crowe was saying, his fast reaction to Tansey's presence. He'd panicked, afraid that Tansey might reveal his part in the scheme. He decided to shoot first and decisively. And Tansey's 'What're you doin'?' had been directed at Banger, not Pukalski, as though the huge bodyguard's defence of Pukalski was unexpected.

Now Banger was out to get Crowe as the one responsible for the whole thing going south. Maybe there was still incriminating evidence lying about and he'd had to double-shuffle in order to divert suspicion from himself. Probably he'd been the one to snipe at Crowe through his office window. After all, a dead Crowe couldn't peck at any scraps of carrion that might have been lying around.

Meanwhile, Crowe knew they weren't going to kill him, not deliberately anyway, or not yet. Waldheim apparently wanted to see him, and clearly Waldheim's hold over Pukalski was still functional – more so than ever, perhaps, thanks to the latter's recent stuff-ups. Well, Crowe wanted to see Waldheim, too, but he wanted to do so not as a prisoner but on his own terms, as someone with leverage. After all, he personally owed Waldheim nothing and he had what the man wanted.

He glanced toward the corner of the room. The foetus-preservation container was on a desk pressed up against the plain windowless wall. Pukalski's lot had obviously been told they were not to touch the merchandise. Crowe was the one who had to take it to Waldheim.

You must stop him.

Lucy had clearly been trying to warn him about her father the whole time. But what was he up to?

There was only one way to find out.

But first, Crowe had to get out of this place. He pushed himself up, testing his wounded arm again. He could move it after all, just barely, and it hurt like hell, but it didn't feel like it was broken. Hopefully the bullet had only scratched past the muscle, traumatised it but not torn it.

He nearly fell over several times. Perseverance won out though. By the time he made it to the door, he was feeling like he could keep going. He tried the handle. It was firmly locked. No surprise there.

Over the years, he'd learned many useful skills, not the least among them lock-picking. The lock on this door was old-fashioned and simple, the sort he'd been able to open when he was 14. He just needed something firm and thin to slide into the hole. He glanced around the room. It was not usually used to house prisoners, he guessed. Hard to say what it was used for. It was small, with no windows and occupied only by the desk, which came with a lamp and a chair. He checked the desk's single drawer – empty except for a half-used writing pad and a pen. His eyes rested once again on the box and he had an idea. He opened it and studied the container that was still waiting to give up its esoteric contents. The wire bound around the top wasn't part of the container's primary security measures; it was simply there to hold a metal tab with a line of numbers stamped on it. Having forced the tab back and released one end of the wire, he proceeded to break off a piece the length of his finger. He tested its strength, then went back to the door.

One ear against the wood, he could hear dull, soundtrack-type riffs and distant voices. Sounded like *Sex in the City* reruns. Gail had made him watch an episode a while back – clearly not because she liked it, but because she wanted to destroy whatever belief in humanity he still had.

After a moment or two he thought he heard footsteps moving away. Perhaps whoever was out there was restless. A good time to act. He inserted the length of wire along the inside of the doorjamb and moved it upward at an angle. The lock clicked open after a few attempts with barely a scrape.

Carefully he eased a crack between the door and the jamb. He was in luck. Lower-Management was on the far side of the room, making himself a drink at the tiny bar there. Obviously, he didn't expect Crowe to be awake let alone making a break for it. Lower-Management's back was to him, but there was no way Crowe could get to him before he turned. Then Crowe saw a hand-gun lying on a chair facing the large TV, roughly halfway between him and the goon.

Crow reacted quickly. Lower-Management had finished pouring his beer and was dropping the empty bottle into a bin. He turned. As he did, Crowe flung open the door and stumbled toward the unattended weapon. Lower-Management yelled something and flung his beer aside. But he'd been taken by surprise, and it slowed him. Despite Crowe's aching legs and the fiery pain that jabbed through his chest and down his sides, he got to the chair first and made a grab for the gun – a Colt. Good enough. Lower-Management's flailing leg toppled the chair and the pistol grip brushed across Crowe's fingers and slid away.

Lower-Management grunted something incoherent. Crowe sprawled after the gun, forgetting the state of his right arm. Pain made him jerk back at the last moment and Lower-Management's leg collapsed over him, his knee digging into Crowe's back. Crowe swore and tried to throw him off. He could smell the man's sweat and the stink of his aftershave. He'd been smoking, too. 'Give it up, Crowe!' the man grunted. Crowe twisted as much as he could. Lower-Management laughed at the grimace Crowe let flow over his face.

But the poor bastard should've gone for the gun straight off. Instead, his base-level sadism had given Crowe breathing space. He drove his left elbow into Lower-Management's groin and, as the goon roared in pain, bucked him. Then Crowe had the gun in his left hand and was rolling and pulling the trigger. Lower-Management's body shot backwards, leaving an after-burn impression of red as he fell. He struck the TV then the floor with a dull thud and began to spasm. Crowe had aimed for his right shoulder but had hit the poor bastard fair in the chest.

Crowe crawled to his feet.

Lower-Management was screaming and crying, tears and blood running down his jowls. 'Shit!' he groaned, repeating it over and over, in a wheezing voice that was failing quickly.

'Lie still!' Crowe said. 'I'll get help.'

Who was he kidding? Crowe could hardly call the police or an ambulance, and from the look of him the poor bastard was bleeding internally. He'd die, and soon. Crowe walked over to him.

'You going to last?' he said.

Lower-Management tried to speak, but his mouth was suddenly full of blood. It dribbled out over his lower lip. Terror filled his expression.

'Sorry, mate,' Crowe said, but the man wasn't listening anymore.

The part of the house Crowe was in seemed empty, not that he made a thorough search. He hoped his Beretta was around somewhere, but it remained elusive. No doubt the 'guys' had taken it with them. Lower-Management's Colt would have to do. What he did find was a phone and with it he called Pirran's office. He left a message to suggest the cops go to the Ed Rice address if they wanted Banger.

'Tell him now!' Crowe said. 'The perp won't be there long.'

He figured Banger and Middle-Management would be arriving at his house any minute. If Pirran sent a car quickly, they might meet, and the results could be interesting. At any rate, it would muddy the waters.

'Can you give me your name, sir?' the cop on the end of the line asked.

Crowe hung up. He then called a cab and gave as the pick-up point an intersection he remembered passing on the way to Pukalski's, maybe half a kilometre away. He reckoned he'd be able to make it that far.

29

WHILE CROWE WAITED AT THE CORNER, LEANING ON A TELEPHONE POLE and clutching the container to his chest, the sky went out of phase, as though there were problems with the circuitry. Clear night sky became cloudy.

Skarratt running.

Rain, a viscous film, is flung across him in shreds. Trees squirm. Crowe feels his fingers pressing into mud and soaked grass as he struggles to regain his feet. There's a dull pain in one shoulder where he was hit by the briefcase. For a moment, the night seems to form phantom shapes, threatening the presence of many enemies. Glancing right and left in a delirious motion that fails to grasp onto anything – to find a stability that will give him direction – he loses sight of the fleeing Skarratt. He dismisses the phantoms. Skarratt is his target. He's getting away. Crowe spots a movement in the rain and staggers toward it.

Immediately his motion is broken mid-stumble. An area of milky gloom proves more solid than he'd expected. He hears a deep grunt and feels an impact on his chest. He stumbles again, grabbing for support. His fingertips brush against something that isn't a tree. Heavy breathing under the howl of the wind. He focuses on a patch of night. Two eyes surrounded by wet, textured cloth. A balaclava. Black. Perhaps navy. The eyes are barely visible. They hover about shoulder height above a barrel chest that blends weirdly into the rain. There's a band of phantom material to one side. The strap of a carry bag or a backpack. And a sharper sliver held in a pale hand.

His attacker comes at Crowe again. Over his head, as Crowe braces against the impact, he notices something. An incongruity. About 2m away, the shadows are translucent, as though a ghost is moving around to get a better view of the action. A denser drift of mist? Or Skarratt?

But the sliver he'd seen is a knife. As the Scavenger hits him, Crowe ignores everything except the blade. The fabric of his jacket parts. He struggles to bring his gun around, aware of a sharp pain in his arm. Blood flows.

Waiting for the taxi, his side aching and his arm throbbing toward numbness, Crowe wondered about that memory. Why would Skarratt have come back? Some sort of connection between him and the Scavenger? It didn't seem likely, but then not much of this seemed likely.

And Crowe thought, *Yeah, there mighta been somethin' else too.* That's what the old bloke at Bulli Beach Holiday Park had said.

Somethin' else.

Or *someone* else? Two people had been there that night. One the Scavenger, sure. The other? He was starting to suspect.

The honk of the taxi shook the memory from Crowe's mind.

Luckily his BMW was still where he'd left it, even though the key was in the ignition. It took him all of five seconds to find the tracking device that Pukalski's lot had been using to monitor his movements. He crushed it under his boot, cursing himself for being careless enough not to check before this. Next, he headed to his office, where he took time to clean up and to examine the 'merchandise'.

The metal container opened under the influence of his probing screwdriver. Inside was a tubular, translucent jar sealed tightly at the top but offering a good view of the contents. The thing in there looked like a mutated pup. Its wizened features, conveying an incongruous ancientness, stared out at him with bemused indifference. It looked as though it might have been about four months along when its mother died. Crowe tried to see if it had been destined to be a boy or a girl, but there was no way he could tell, and he didn't fancy opening the preservation jar to inspect the thing more closely. Let it stay right where it was. Watching it suspended in that murky fluid gave him the creeps. He pulled back, convinced it was going to move and scare the shit out of him.

Don't let him have it! whispered Lucy's voice.

At any rate, Crowe had confirmed that, genuine or not, this was what Waldheim had been after. That Lucy didn't want her father to have it left him wondering why.

He cleaned up, packed a few clothes, picked up the Scavenger files and put the lot in his BMW with the re-locked and re-sealed container. The office wouldn't be safe anymore. At this point, Crowe felt he couldn't trust leaving the thing out of his sight.

He knew what he had to do next, but he needed to be sure Gail was safe. He tracked her down in the office of *Manhunter*, the Sydney magazine she had occasionally wrote for.

'Pukalski's likely to be after you,' he said.

'Pukalski? What've you done, Mike?' She sounded weary.

He told her, which produced none of the acrimony he'd expected.

'But the salient points are these,' Crowe said. 'One, I have the foetus. Two, I know who paid Pukalski to get it for him.'

'Who?'

'Waldheim.'

'You sure?'

'Totally.'

'It wasn't the ghost of your friend Lucy who told you that, was it?'

Crowe couldn't tell if she was mocking him or not. He assumed she was.

'Pukalski himself. Not directly but close enough.'

'I might've known your intuition would give up the goods.' She didn't wait for him to say something. 'You asked me to check on Dale Walker and Fred Creedy, remember?'

'Creedy?'

'Lucy Waldheim's murderer.'

'Right. What about them?'

'Dale Walker has well and truly been given a leg up the greasy pole by Waldheim, who's a major contributor to party funds. Walker still has a reputation for being Waldheim's lackey – not that anyone's too forthcoming about it.'

'I asked him about that. He denied it vehemently, of course.'

'Of course.'

'And Creedy?'

'Creedy's dead. He died about a year after being committed to the high-security wing of a psychiatric hospital. Found in his cell one morning, slit open and guts removed, most of which had been arranged into some sort of occult motif on the floor. One of the warders was blamed, but he cleared out and no one's heard a thing about him since.'

'Sounds like a ritual.'

'Exactly. And get this, Mike. Waldheim's something of a guru in fringe religious circles these days. In a big way.'

'What? Really?'

'Leader of an esoteric branch of spiritualism called the Ancient Cadre of El Hareen. He's written a book on practices relating to raising the dead and controlling spirits. What's more to the point, I tracked down a copy of his book, and there's a whole chapter on the magical use of aborted foetuses.'

'All that ghost-trapping shit you told me about?'

'And more. Much more. Some cults encourage members to eat the brains of aborted foetuses in order to gain immortality.'

'Hence the bastard's interest in the Queen Marika trophy.'

'I'd say so. Waldheim's the sort of guy who'd want to live forever. And he sounds like he'd arrange for the punishment of his daughter's killer, too.'

Crowe reckoned she was right. It filled in enough gaps to be true, even to the extent of Waldheim paying out $200 million to acquire the foetus. Such an acquisition would, he imagined, cement Waldheim's authority among his fellow cultists. And maybe he genuinely believed he could gain immortality.

Don't let him have it! Lucy's voice seemed to resonate through his bones.

But why would Lucy care?

Now that the foetus was in Crowe's possession, the sensible thing would be for him to destroy it. But that wasn't likely. Crowe had to see Waldheim but on his own terms. And he had the means to dictate them. Crowe had what Waldheim wanted and it would get him in to see the man. Otherwise, he reckoned he'd have a rat's chance in hell.

'This guru rep Waldheim has acquired,' he said. 'Is it serious? Pukalski seems scared of him—'

'And even so, he tried to cheat the man?'

'Well, he didn't see it as a cheat. He figured Waldheim wouldn't give a damn who ended up with the money so long as he got the foetus. Waldheim's always seemed rather weak to me, in person, but of course you don't need to be a thug to have power. Money can make people do anything. Waldheim worries Pukalski financially now that the foetus has gone AWOL, but maybe this makes it worse for him. Could Charlie be scared of Waldheim's cult, too?'

'Well, Waldheim's deep into the occult and, I'm told, is considered a high-level, very powerful sorcerer by his believers. I reckon Charlie's superstitious enough to believe the man has genuine arcane power and can summon Satanic forces.'

'And can he?'

Gail laughed. 'Well, you suddenly believe in ghosts. Why can't Waldheim have his demons?'

Why indeed? Crowe thought. But he'd had quite a bit to do with Waldheim and had never seen any sign of supernatural powers. All he'd seen was self-centred megalomania, business nous and moral weakness. Anyway, ghosts were one thing, demons were something else entirely. He'd never seen one and the only evil he'd ever had to deal with was decidedly human in origin.

'You know Waldheim's current address by any chance?' he asked Gail.

She knew the general area and, when she told him, Crowe knew just where to go.

He was about to hang up when she said, 'And Mike?'

'Yeah?'

'Your old mate in the purple ute?'

He'd almost forgotten the photos Gail had taken from his office window. 'What about him?'

'Len Bugden *is* his name. And he used to work for the *Herald* before heading down to the Gong. Mainly crime reporting, some features. He was good, too, could bring a story to life, extract information from interviewees like magic.'

So the old weirdo hadn't been lying. 'I'm sensing a but.'

'But he had a rep for throwing tantrums. A friend of mine knew him, and she said he got worse as time went by, whenever he thought he was being disrespected, which was pretty much whenever he didn't get his own way. Turned into a scary bastard, one minute so laid-back you'd think he was asleep, next minute on the verge of going supernova.'

Crowe muttered, 'That's him all right.'

'Apparently, he went too far. He beat up a couple of people he was supposed to be interviewing – cut some drug pusher who told him to piss off. They suspended him for a while. Put him on real estate or something. Then he chucked a keyboard at the editor's brand-new monitor and they sacked him.'

'Any reason he went crazy?' Crowe felt wiped out but tried to keep his mind alert. It slithered about, legless.

'A feature series he wanted to do – the editor told him it wasn't on. This was, let's see, in mid-December last year, about the time the newspapers were figuring there was a serial killer loose. His proposed opus was on rogue criminals of the South Coast region. One of the central stories was about the Scavenger – and Bugden *was* the one who named him. My friend told me he had been going on about it for a while. Very obsessive.'

'Huh.' Obsessive didn't even begin to describe Bugden's major malfunction.

'Oh, and Mike?'

'Yeah?'

'He really doesn't like women. Doesn't like them in the workplace, doesn't like answering to them. Misogynistic as fuck.'

Crowe was quiet for a moment, recalling Blowie's comments when he'd accused Crowe of being 'distracted' by Banerjee. And he hadn't heard from her since then. She'd promised to call, but she wasn't even listed under Missed Calls and hadn't left any messages. Suddenly he was worried for her safety. 'I'll see you in a while.'

'My place in Sydney?'

Crowe suggested it wouldn't be a good idea. She shouldn't go back there herself. Better to book into a hotel – somewhere inconspicuous they could use as a safe house. Her first choice was the *King Cross Hilton*, but Crowe suggested the *Southern Hideaway* instead, a tacky '60s-style motel just south of Sydney. Gail said she wouldn't be seen dead in a place like that, and again Crowe didn't feel like arguing about it.

'When will I meet you there, dead or alive?' she said after he'd expressed a disinclination to haggle.

'Tomorrow. I've got some business to take care of first.' Crowe glanced at his watch. He would rather like to get to where he needed to go before sunset. 'Besides, I don't think the Scavenger's through with me yet. We're playing some sort of a game.'

'Be careful, Mike.'

'Careful's my middle name.'

Gail made a mocking sound.

After he'd rung off, Crowe called Pirran's office and left voice mail: the superintendent needed to check up on Dr Meera Banerjee as soon as he got the message.

As he headed south along the highway, the Scavenger pondered the merits of this action. He knew what Crowe was carrying, and though he wanted to get his hands on it he was reluctant to expose himself in person just yet. Certainly not on the highway or on ordinary suburban streets. Never in plain sight. He assumed Crowe was taking the Object to Gregor Waldheim, and stealing it from that man's hands might prove even more problematic than getting it from Crowe's. He had left Waldheim alone, despite his knowledge of the man's search for the unborn offspring of populist celebrity Marika Kucera. He knew Waldheim's purpose in seeking to obtain it, too, and found him undeserving. It would be better if the Object was in the Scavenger's hands, as his need for it – indeed, the moral importance of its power to him – was more immediately vital. Much was at stake, as his experiment in the creation of Homo-Superior was reaching its culmination. What he had to do would inevitably succeed, for the sake of humanity's future and in honour of his lost innocence. The legacy of Marika Kucera's accident might be the final item needed to ensure success.

However, it was a bloody shame he'd found out Crowe had the Object too late to organise a more convenient theft. His lackey had let him down in this regard, as he so often did. Nevertheless, that Michael Crowe had the Object was justification of his faith in *that* man to get him what he wanted – what he needed – despite Igor's naysaying.

As for retrieving the Object from Waldheim, he would have to go against his own best practice and ad lib.

Igor advised against it, of course. His nature was always contrary, much to the Scavenger's chagrin. He claimed it was an irrelevance, a distraction from his own real purpose. 'Real purpose?' What did the minion really understand of his purpose? Oh, yes, he had a vague idea, the sort of conceptualisation the mainstream media would grasp without any problem. But much lay behind it, realities that Igor had no ability to understand. Esoteric knowledge, deep thinking, experience and ancient wisdom told the Scavenger he needed to do this and that he would succeed, whatever the odds. This was the inevitable next step in human evolution.

As Crowe left the highway, the Scavenger knew his guess was correct. Crowe was definitely heading to Waldheim's current residence. The Scavenger had seen the monstrosity in the early stages of its construction and was convinced he could get in without being seen. In fact, he had prepared for it, long ago. At any rate, if Crowe could get in, so could he.

He followed, careful to keep out of sight.

That Waldheim had chosen to build a home in Merryvale, right on the spot where his daughter had been brutally murdered, struck Crowe as ominous at best, and the drive there gave him plenty of time to stew over just how perverse it was. The black magic connections only served to exacerbate the feeling. Crowe remembered demonic imagery – paintings he'd barely glanced at – on the wall of Waldheim's old study and ornaments with a similar esoteric, cabalistic look to them. At the time, Crowe had thought them weird decorations, but he realised now that he'd been in the man's personal shrine. Clearly Gregor's leanings had always been toward the occult, only now it had blossomed from a curiosity to a full-blown obsession. How else could you explain his willingness to pay out hundreds of millions of dollars for an aborted foetus? What people did in the name of belief never ceased to amaze Crowe. He hoped God, if he deigned to exist, was equally amused.

The Kilcairn Creek Road was a tad more upmarket than it used to be, with a relatively new bitumen surface and decent side drainage. Yuppie developers had finally arrived in the township itself, but the surrounding land remained as under-developed as it had been in 2008, with ancient gums crowding the road on either side and giving it an air of being on the way to nowhere.

At the turn-off Crowe passed a spot he recognised, where he'd unknowingly spied Lucy's convicted killer, Creedy, standing on his porch. The house looked as though it had been burnt to the ground, with nature consuming the leftovers. All that remained was a blackened chimney and charred wooden framework here and there, along with piles of debris mostly overgrown with weeds and the encroaching bush.

Don't take it to my father! Don't let him have it! Lucy's voice echoed in Crowe's brain.

He glanced into the back seat at the tattered container. Even given that he intended to speak to Waldheim – and possibly do a lot more than speak – perhaps it would have been better to leave the foetus hidden someplace where neither Waldheim nor Pukalski could find it. Who knew what Crowe would be up against once he faced the bastard? But Waldheim wasn't a criminal overlord, just a ruthless businessman, and Crowe didn't believe in real, non-metaphorical demons, should Lucy's father feel the urge to summon one. Waldheim was just another sick, twisted little pervert billionaire, and he didn't scare Crowe in the slightest, despite Pukalski's obvious fear of him. Creedy's fate, and the ritualistic nature of it, suggested that Waldheim was capable of ruthlessness. Money, and religious fanaticism, could buy you a lot of payback without bloodying your own hands. At the very least, the weird souvenir of Queen Marika would get Crowe past whatever defences Waldheim might have with a minimum of fuss.

Besides, it seemed to Crowe that the Scavenger was after this particular curiosity as well, and that being the case, it was safer right here with him than it was likely to be anywhere else. Did it really matter if it ended up in Waldheim's possession?

Don't...hi...m!

Lucy again. She was persistent, he'd give her that. This time, however, her words were strangely fractured.

'I'll be careful, okay!' he muttered. 'No way I'm going to give it to him. Trust me.'

As his words faded, he caught a movement out of the corner of his eye. A figure sat next to him in the passenger seat. He glanced sideways. An adrenaline surge went through him.

Lucy. Pale, gaunt and dishevelled, blood dribbling like tears from her eye-sockets. The shock nearly sent him off the road and into the bush. He pulled over onto a rough patch of gravel. Lucy stared at him sorrowfully. He should, he thought, be used to it by now.

Her lips moved, but he heard nothing.

'Lucy?'

Again, her lips trembled, but this time her voice became a tinnitus hiss, that morphed into...*don't...*

'Don't what?'

Give...him.

'The foetus?'

Help...me, plea...

'How, Lucy, how can I help you?'

Her image began to flicker. *Don't let...*

'Lucy, I swear–'

Can't talk...dark...closing in...barrier...

'Lucy!'

But even as he said her name, she was gone.

For a moment, he sat gripping the steering wheel tightly, fingers whitening from the pressure.

While his pulse calmed, he stared into the bush, wondering how much more of this incursion of the supernatural into his life he could take. He was used to threat and to danger, but this was so subversive to the way he had always understood existence, he wasn't sure he could cope. But if it was what it seemed to be, then Lucy needed his help. He knew he'd failed her last time. He wouldn't do it again.

'Lucy?' he said tentatively, as though mere speech could fracture what was left of reality. 'Are you there?'

No answer. For a moment, he thought movement in the trees might be a sign of her return. 'Lucy? Is that you?' But after a few moments, the disturbance subsided, having been nothing more than the wind.

'Perhaps you can hear me.' As he spoke, he swivelled his head around, watching for her to materialise. 'I hope you can. I know you're worried. I don't understand everything that's going on, but I'm guessing your father wants to put the foetus to some nefarious use or other. Immortality or whatever. And I guess you're not keen on the idea. I can't imagine what might happen or what it might mean for you, but...' He had begun to feel foolish, as though talking to himself. 'But, no matter what,' he continued after a moment, 'I won't let him have it. Okay?'

She didn't reply.

'I won't let you down.'

The silence made him feel stupid. It filled the car as he turned back onto the road and continued toward Waldheim's estate. As he did, he thought he heard a car coming up from behind and glanced into the rear-view mirror. Nothing. He stopped to get a better look, but still there was still no sign of movement. Clearly his nerves were on edge.

He continued, albeit more warily.

30

THE MANSION WAS, AS MIGHT BE EXPECTED, QUITE SPECTACULAR. ALL SIGN of the previous cottage, and the shed in which Lucy had been murdered, were gone. Yet the new building looked a bit too much like a mausoleum for Crowe's taste, with several wings and stark walls devoid of Gothic statuary. It would have cost plenty and, as Crowe expected, it was designed to keep unwelcome visitors out. A surrounding concrete fence, higher than usual and topped with razor wire, emphasised the exclusionist principles underlying its construction. Security cameras squatted at intervals along the fence. There was a guard station to the right of the main gate. Unwelcome entry would not be easy.

Crowe had no intention of being coy about this. He stopped the car in front of the huge, wrought-iron gates and watched the camera there focus its cyclopean eye on him. He honked the car horn several times.

A grille in the wall beneath the camera crackled.

'Crowe, is it?'

'Gregor, nice to hear you after all this time.'

'Why are you here, alone?' Waldheim said. 'I have no reason to think you wish me well.'

'If I'd been going to kill you, Gregor, I would've done it back then, while my blood was on the boil. I've come now because Pukalski, bless him, reckoned you wanted to see me.'

'He caught you and you escaped him.' It wasn't a question.

'You do realise he's an incompetent fool, right?'

Waldheim said nothing. Perhaps Crowe had taken him by surprise and he was trying to work out what to do.

'You going to let me in?'

'I don't think that would be a good idea.'

'I have what you want, Gregor.'

'You brought it?'

'Why not? You paid for it, didn't you? It's yours now.'

'Show me.'

Crowe leaned into the back seat, dragged the container around to the driver's window and held it up. Something that felt like cold, spectral fingers gripped his arm, trying to force his hand down.

'It's okay,' he whispered.

The pressure subsided.

'Pull back the covering,' Waldheim ordered.

Crowe did as requested, revealing the metal box. Its lock, which he had replaced, had a certain convincing arcane quality to it.

'There should be some numbers engraved along the lid. Read them out to me.'

Crowe hadn't even noticed them before. He read them out. They were different to the numbers he'd seen on the bottle. Did that mean something?

After a pause, the gate mechanism emitted an electronic buzz, and the gates began to swing open. Crowe waited until they were completely out of the way, then headed up the winding driveway toward the front entrance of the house. No one emerged from the guard station. No minions had appeared. As he approached, he noticed someone standing at a window on the upper storey, shadowy and indistinct. Waldheim?

No. Waldheim was waiting in the open doorway. Crowe glanced back at the window. Whoever had been there was gone.

He had been expecting a bodyguard, someone not unlike Banger, or at least a butler. Guard dogs or an elite team of ninjas. An evil dragon maybe. Something. But there was just Waldheim, looking frailer and more weather-beaten than Crowe remembered him. Much of his hair, shoulder length and unkempt, had gone completely white. He sported a short, trimmed beard and a full face-load of wrinkles. A tall man, he'd been solidly built when Crowe first knew him, but now he was gaunt and lacking in whatever presence he used to wield. Life hadn't been treating him well.

'You look like shit, Gregor,' Crowe said once he'd climbed out of the car.

His host shrugged. 'Who cares what I look like? I don't see anyone much these days.'

'But your money still impresses, I assume.'

'More than ever. Just bring the container.'

'No heavies to make me behave myself?'

'I no longer have a need for bodyguards to protect me. I have other means of doing that.'

'Demons, I assume.'

'The belief in them, at any rate.'

That was it for pleasantries. Crowe followed him along the entrance hall and into a close replica of the study he'd used as a meeting room back in the good ol' days.

'You alone here?' Crowe asked, conscious of the apparent lack of staff.

'Just me, my secretary and far too many memories, Mike,' he replied. He glanced around, as though attempting to recall something. 'People come and go.'

He retreated behind his desk, casting only a side-glance at the box Crowe was carrying. Sighing, he collapsed into his chair. His eyes rose to meet Crowe's, and only then could Crowe see the iron determination that still lurked in him, buried but alive.

'Ms Farnestine?' Crowe asked.

'Gone, I'm afraid. No one stays with me by choice.'

'At least you have your money,' Crowe deadpanned.

Waldheim grunted. 'Money, I find, can buy you stockbrokers, business agents, police, political allies, criminal aid and even a degree of fame...' He gestured at the bookcase behind him, which housed books with his name on the spines, as well as endless rows of books by other maniacs. Crowe couldn't recall having seen them years ago, but perhaps Waldheim had been more secretive about his leanings then. All the books appeared to concern themselves with primitive religious practices and black magic. Some of them seemed very old and expensive. 'What it can't give you is a woman who will stick by you, no matter what, or friends who give a damn.'

'What about health?'

'I have severe rheumatoid arthritis,' he said. 'And a prostate that is succumbing to cancer.'

Crowe dumped the box on the desk in front of him. 'Is that what this is about?'

Crowe could see the desire begin to burn.

One skeletal hand reached out, its fingers edging toward the wooden box. 'You know what it is?' he whispered.

'Of course. Bizarre, I must say. Some would say perverse.'

'I told Pukalski not to tell anyone.'

'He's not very reliable.' Crowe gestured mock distress. 'And he *is* very greedy. I must say, though, I'm impressed by how much you control him, Waldheim.'

'He's a superstitious man, Mike, and I have a certain, shall we say, tenebrous reputation among those in the know. That and the threat of legal attention directed toward various of his business interests were enough motivation. However, I clearly miscalculated the depth of his commitment.'

'Greed wins out over fear, it seems. Tell me, did you kill Creedy?'

'My daughter's killer? Why wouldn't I want him dead? But alas, there's no way I myself could get to him.'

'But your money could.'

Waldheim managed a restrained smile. 'Money can be deadly, true, and there were demons that needed to be appeased.' He gestured toward the chair in front of his desk. 'Please, sit down. You look uncomfortable.'

'Thanks, but I'll stand.'

'Whatever you wish.' Waldheim's eyes fixed on the container. 'So, have you seen it?'

'Sure. Ugly little weasel, I must say. Why don't you take a look?'

He nearly did; he leaned toward the box, his hand touching its edges. But then he pulled back.

'No. No, not yet.'

'What's wrong?'

'It must be done properly. There are protocols, mystical requirements. You will want payment, a reward for finding it. I am a man of honour, Mr Crowe. I pay my debts.'

Crowe watched him for a moment or two, aware of just how

obsessed he was. Whatever this thing represented, it was fundamental to his plans, the incarnation of emotions that had tormented him for a long time. In his head, there was a ritual involved in dealing with it, and he'd stick to that no matter how illogical and impractical it was.

'Are you afraid of dying?' Crowe asked.

Gregor snorted, his line of sight shifting from the container to Crowe. 'If I were afraid for myself, would I have let you in the door, Michael? I know you hate me. When I heard that Pukalski had brought you in on this, I was angry at first but not afraid. I simply thought you'd spoil it. I never suspected you'd be the one to bring it to me.'

'You're after immortality, aren't you? That's what this thing is for.'

'I have no interest in living much longer.'

'What is it you want then?'

He half rose, leaning on the desk and eyes blazing. 'I want her back,' he said. 'I want my daughter back. *She* will be my legacy.'

Guilt. Responsibility. Innocence. How are they determined?

'I'm sorry,' Crowe says to Sara Rampen. She's the only one of them he really feels sorry for. Lucy doesn't need his pity anymore, as ineffectual as it had been.

Crowe is on Rampen's front step, dodging the overhanging grape vines. He figures she deserves to hear the story from someone who'd cared for Lucy rather than from the TV news. She listens, shakes her head, turns away.

'It shouldn't have happened,' Crowe says.

She looks at him again, as though somehow he's to blame.

'She's been avenged,' he adds. 'It's over.'

'You don't understand, do you?' He sees the sorrow in her eyes, though there is disdain in her voice. 'It's not over. You're a scavenger like the rest of them, so how could you possibly understand? All this?' Her gesture encompasses the world. 'It's a feast that never ends.'

Then she withdraws into the interior of her house.

She'd been right, of course. It wasn't over. These things rarely end at all, let alone with such ironic tidiness. Lucy – radiant, kind-hearted Lucy – was still at the centre of her father's fantasies.

'You won't accept it, Crowe, but I loved her, more deeply than I have ever loved anyone, even myself.' Waldheim's manner was studied, the words rehearsed so often they'd nearly lost meaning. 'Her death and my part in it have haunted me ever since.'

Does he feel he has to justify himself to me? Crowe wondered.

'Bit late for regret now,' Crowe said coldly. 'You tormented her, violated her when she was alive, and one way or another drove her to her death. If she hadn't been at Merryvale, alone—'

'I loved her.' Waldheim's manner blazed with sudden fire. 'Yes, I was weak and did the wrong thing, but it came from love.'

'Either way, you're a total….' Crowe paused. 'I was going to say 'arsehole', but that's an insult to arseholes.'

Waldheim stared into Crowe's eyes. His were wet with tears. 'I want to right the wrongs.'

'You can't. She's dead.'

Waldheim paused, making sure he had Crowe's attention. Then he said, 'She needn't be.'

Crowe didn't reply.

Waldheim licked his lips, as though his own absurd words had dried them out. He gestured at the container on his desk. 'Believe me, Crowe, I haven't sought this to give myself a better life. Or more life. It's for her; I've done it all for her.'

'What the hell are you talking about?' Crowe said, though he suddenly understood why Lucy might want him to stop her father's – her tormenter's – insane ambitions.

'Surely you realise what *this*–' Waldheim pointed to the container '–represents. The power of Marika Kucera's life, death, legend. Her unborn daughter, empty of life yet filled with its potential. With an empty shell this potent, this vital, with this much drawing power, I can call life from death. Crowe, I'll bring Lucy back. I just needed the vessel.'

Gail had been right. Waldheim had taken on-board generations of superstitious bullshit and was planning on undertaking some stupid ritual to assuage his guilt. In his mind, Lucy's spirit could be drawn back from the grave into the shell of a cultural icon's unborn child.

The voice called, plucked at his skin, demanding...

Waldheim intended to force Lucy to live again.

'You believe in all this paranormal guff?' Crowe asked.

'You'd be surprised what esoteric knowledge can achieve,' Waldheim said, a faint smile like a nervous twitch slithered across his face.

Help me, Mr Crowe! Don't let him do this! He'll damn me to an eternity of suffering.

The voice was loud and desperate and clear to Crowe, as this conflation of moments had apparently given it the strength to break through whatever barriers stood between it and the living world. Crowe glanced around, feeling disoriented. Once he would never have believed Waldheim could achieve his goal. But Crowe had totally succumbed to the belief that Lucy's ghost had been communicating with him, so why should he doubt that Waldheim could achieve this transmigration of a spirit – Lucy's spirit – into a mystically powerful foetus? Lucy feared it. He could barely imagine what the consequences of that would mean to her.

And he knew then she'd been right. He should never have brought the foetus here. He certainly wouldn't hand it over.

Waldheim lowered his head into his hands as though it were aching. 'Do you comprehend now that I'm not a bad man? That I want to make everything right?'

'What if your daughter doesn't want this?' Crowe said. 'What if bringing her back hurt her more than you could imagine? Would you still do it?'

Waldheim looked up, surprised.

'What are you saying?'

'She's been unable to move on, Gregor. She's told me as much. She's been begging me to stop you.'

'You're lying.'

Lucy suddenly spoke clearly in his head. *He forced himself on me back then, Mr Crowe, with claims of love and false appeals to duty and respect. Now he wants to force me to return to him. He'll never leave me in peace. Do I have to feed his weakness forever?*

And he's not the only one.

'Well? Answer me, man!' Waldheim yelled at him. 'Why would you deny me this? Why would you make up these lies?'

'She's speaking to me now.' Crowe sounded hollow.

'Why can't I hear her then?' Waldheim stood. 'Why wouldn't she tell me herself?'

'I don't know how this works. You're supposed to be the expert. Maybe you've become toxic to her. Maybe you've locked her out by your own actions, your own selfishness–'

'All I want is to make amends.'

'This isn't the way to do it. We all failed Lucy once and now you're about to make it worse.'

'But I...I just–'

He broke off. Crowe watched as Waldheim focused past him in surprise, perhaps shock. 'What are you doing here?' the man cried.

He wasn't talking to Crowe. Crowe heard a footfall behind him. Began to turn. 'Who's–'

Something jabbed into the base of his neck. Hands shoved against him, sending him crashing onto Waldheim's desk. The container tipped over, tumbled and slid toward the edge.

'No!' Waldheim reached for it.

Crowe kicked backwards, feeling a strong chemical numbness stealing through his muscles, sapping his ability to control them. Weakness spread fast. His foot connected with someone but without enough strength to achieve anything useful. Talon-like hands held him down. Cold breath shivered across his neck.

He bucked, hoping to throw the weight from his back. A fist pummelled his head, slamming his face against the table.

'Get the hell off me!'

Another needle jab. Tendrils of light were bleeding into the room, oozing through holes in the walls.

Crowe tried to lash out against the encumbrance and the numbness. It was no use. Despite his best efforts, he could barely move.

The room slipped away, dimming. His mind dimmed with it. He was forgetting what he was here for, who he was.

Mr Crowe?

He turned his head sideways. Shadows against the far wall became the figure of a young woman emerging from nothingness. Lucy, barely visible. She moved closer, leaning toward him, whispering.

My father isn't the only one, she said. *The other is here.*

Her pale hand, with fingers still missing, reached toward Crowe.

'Lucy...' he began.

Her face was clear at last: the pale skin, green eyes, black lashes, wisp of hair across her forehead.

But as he watched, its lines tightened, skin stretching over the bones beneath. Flesh became dry and ancient, hair faded. Her orbital sockets filled with blood while her lips shrank, baring skeletal teeth. Crowe pushed away. This time he overcame the weight of the thing on his back and made it to his feet.

He struggled to remain standing, flailed at the fog obscuring the room. The demon shrieked in his ears.

Screaming curses, Waldheim had grabbed the container that held Queen Marika's offspring. Clutching it to his chest, he stumbled toward the door.

Crowe tried but couldn't find his gun.

The thing's breath scoured across his cheek.

'Stop him!' Crowe pleaded. 'He's the one you want!'

He felt the demon look up. It moved on his shoulders, its claws gripping, its centre of gravity shifting.

'Don't let the bastard get away!'

It lifted off him, the sienna bloodiness of its hide sweeping past like a monstrous bird caught in his peripheral vision.

Emitting a bone-scratching cry, it swept toward Waldheim.

Waldheim glanced back, his face contorted in horror. His attacker swirled around him.

And Crowe pitched forward into a vast nothingness. Lost in a corrupted memory.

He rubs his hand over the wound on his arm. The room has filled with chaos, a seething miasma of disjointed images. Blood mixes with rain and dirt, awareness of lacerated flesh dulled by cold. The demon slashes with its claw, which cuts through misty rain like a splinter of lightning. Crowe dodges, unbalanced. His left arm sweeps around, missing his attacker completely. A gun roars. Nearby vegetation thrashes under the impact as though resisting slaughter.

Was that noise only wind? A cry? Someone swearing? It might have come from the bushes.

No time to listen. The demon strikes, forcing Crowe back from the arc inscribed by the knives of its claw. He falls back, bashing his head against a wooden wall.

'You can't ignore me!' the demon cries.

Crowe stares it in the face. It isn't a demon — not fully anyway. It's a man. The man's face is distorted in a primeval and uncontrollable fury, so volatile that snatches of humanity and monstrosity morph in and out of each other, fighting for dominance. His features are perpetually transmuting, so it's impossible to get a fix on him.

In his hand, he grips a double-bladed weapon.

'It's because I'm not tall enough, not handsome enough, isn't it?' he cries. 'I'm unworthy. You see me as a nobody. Well, you're wrong. I have power. Power over life and death. The future is mine.'

The blades, already limned with blood, descend toward him, striking again and again. Blood splatters the wall behind him.

Crowe screams. But it is Lucy he hears.

For a while Crowe didn't know who he was or whether he even existed anymore. The world was lost, torn aside and replaced by a reality crueller and more absurd than the one he had always known.

He had been part of that abandoned world. He had gone with it into the night.

Movement shivered through the muscles of his back.

No, he hadn't gone completely and nor had the world. He felt soft roughness under his fingers. He was lying on carpet.

Unable to move much more than that, he gazed along the floor – straight into staring eyes. Waldheim's face was bleached white, contrasting with the garnet pool in which it lay.

It took Crowe a while to recover. By the time he did, and discovered that Waldheim was dead, his throat cut and genitals mangled, the Scavenger was long gone, along with the withered prize Waldheim had wanted to use for himself. Crowe lay there on the carpet for a longer time yet, able to move but without the will to do so. He listened for the wheezing sound of his own breath, strained to hear a footfall, waited for the spectral voice that would tell him who he was.

Mr Crowe.

Mr Crowe.

Wake up.

'He's dead, Lucy,' he whispered into the carpet, as loudly as he could. 'Gone. He can't harm you now.'

He sensed someone bending over him. He shifted his head to see who it was. A hand, missing three fingers, touched his forehead.

'I made a mistake, Lucy,' he said, delirious. 'But it's okay. Your father can't hurt you anymore.'

A face drew near, focusing into features he remembered, but dark-eyed and bloodied.

But the other can... The voice echoed in his skull.

'Who–'

…trapped in a madman's dream…

'Where can I find him, Lucy?'

…madman…don't know where, she answered, but her voice was now so far away he could barely make out the words.

'It can't be your father? Surely he's no longer a threat.'

The face began to fade, too, becoming a mere smudge on the carpet.

…world is full of…scavengers.

'The Scavenger's a danger? Because he's got the foetus?'

Silence hissed in Crowe's ears. 'Don't go, Lucy. Tell me who he is, where I can find him.'

Crowe thought he heard her say something, even as the hissing faded in tandem with her voice. He could barely make sense of the words.

'Lucy!'

*What my father wanted to do…delusions…won't work, only…*Her voice faltered again.

'Where are you, Lucy?'

He forced me away…don't let him force…me…

A long silence fell, heavy with anticipation. He listened but heard no more voices, no whispers, no hissing – only the growing chatter of his own thoughts.

It was the Scavenger she feared.

No. Impossible. She'd been murdered long before the Scavenger arrived on the scene.

One thing was certain, though. The Scavenger remained his target. His job wasn't over yet.

Not for Pukalski and, more importantly it seemed, not for Lucy.

31

Meera Banerjee had been taken in the *Novotel's* underground carpark. Such places, with their concrete floors, thick pillars and erratic lighting, were claustrophobic at the best of times; at 2.30 in the morning, they achieved a new level of creepiness.

But she was exhausted from the attack outside Crowe's building, the glass of wine had relaxed her, and the last thing she was expecting was to be slammed face-down on the hood of her car. A needle slid into her neck as she struggled under her attacker's grip. She tried to fight back, kicking him in the groin, which clearly annoyed him. All she got was the impression of a bearded, scowling face, wrinkled-up eyes and untidy brown/grey hair before he struck her in the face. Flung backward against the hood of her car, she tried to regain her balance, but whatever had been in the injection was already taking effect.

'What do you want?' she said. 'Money?'

He didn't reply. She tried to move but couldn't.

'Please, you...don't...' she began. The words had become fuzzy. Meaningless. Banerjee felt the strength draining from her muscles, the world fading around her, her thoughts turning to fog. Yet she could feel the pain of her bruised face and the warmth of the car hood through her jeans, and smell the mix of petrol fumes, oil and dampness endemic to all such places. She slid down until she was sitting on the concrete floor.

The man slipped a cloth bag over her head then lifted her easily. She was dumped into the back of a vehicle – a ute? – and then they travelled, she bumping around, sliding helplessly, trying to gain some sense of where they were going. It took maybe three-quarters of an hour and ended on a rough road somewhere, though by then she had absolutely no idea where. She could smell the bush, the salty tang of the sea.

Her captor dragged her out of the truck and carried her across what sounded like rough stones and scrub. He put her down and she heard him fiddling with a lock. A door creaked open. She was hauled up again. He lugged her down some stairs, treading tentatively, as though her weight made the descent difficult.

Sounds and smells of the outside bled away, becoming duller, staler. The temperature dropped noticeably, and she wondered how far below ground level they were. She tried to squirm, to make his task more difficult, but she still couldn't move. They turned several corners, and occasionally her feet rubbed against walls, suggesting a series of corridors. Finally, he stopped and opened another creaky door. He carried her across a stone floor and set her down reasonably gently in a corner.

Banerjee could see pinpoints of light beneath the bag covering her head. When he removed the bag, quickly, like a magician with a flourish, she was briefly blinded by the light of a single globe hanging in the centre of the stone ceiling. She tried to look around to get a better sense of this space but again couldn't move.

'I'll leave ya now,' the man said. 'You'll be in the dark most of the time. Sorry, but that's the way it's gotta be. When the drug wears off, you'll find water on your right. Don't spill it while ya gropin' around. I'll bring food if ya behave yaself. That means, no yellin', screamin', tryin' to break out. There's no one around to hear anyway. I got stuff ta do.'

She couldn't turn her head to see what he was up to but was aware that he grabbed her hair. That was followed by the peculiar chewing sound of scissors with a mouthful.

'That's enough,' her gaoler muttered.

She heard him turn and walk out the door, feet scraping in the lazy pattern she'd noticed earlier. The door slammed. It sounded metallic and heavy. After a moment, the light disappeared. It was several hours before the paralysis wore off, but before then she'd drifted into a shallow, restless sleep – a sleep that offered no rest from nightmares.

Banerjee woke with no idea how much time had passed. She could see nothing. The rough grit of a long-neglected stone floor scraped under her hands as she pushed herself up, using the wall as support. Parts of her ached but she didn't think anything was broken. She was alive. Perhaps she was lucky. If her kidnapper was the Scavenger, he might well have dismembered her on the spot. But that made no sense. None of this did. Banerjee wasn't a middle-aged, white male. Nor did the killer take his victims home with him, not whole anyway. Had the nature of his obsession changed and along with it his long-established, rigidly adhered to *modus operandi*? Could he change so much, so far into his immaculately devised campaign? Psychologically, it didn't seem likely. But in this atmosphere of madness, anything was possible. It wasn't very scientific of her to think so, but what else was she to do?

Then she remembered what he'd taken: her hair. She ran her fingers through what remained and felt the loss sharply. Elias loved her hair. Her assailant had cut off several centimetres. What the hell did he want that for? A souvenir?

A wave of near panic washed over her, causing her to tremble. Then tears overtook her – stupid, pointless tears, as much from frustration as sheer terror. She let an insistent catalogue of grim possibilities play out dozens of R-rated scenarios in her mind, hoping they'd exhaust themselves and leave her free to think more clearly, to devise some action that might give her hope of escape.

Nothing presented itself, so she decided the best thing she could do was to explore her environment. For almost an hour she felt her way around every part of the room like a blind woman: rough stone walls; no windows, locked or otherwise, except for a small outlet high up on one wall that seemed to be a duct allowing air to flow into the room. It was barely big enough for a rat to escape through. The door was heavy and locked tight. It had a small window at face level with a strong steel grille. She pressed her face to the grille, tried to look out into the corridor, but there wasn't a skerrick of light to relieve the darkness. In the most distant corner of the room, she stumbled upon a metal table.

It was dented and rusty. Nearby was what felt like an old chamber pot, obviously intended to act as a latrine, and a pile of blankets that smelled clean enough to have been placed there recently.

On the table was the jug her captor had mentioned. Was the water in it poisoned? No. Why use water to kill her when he'd gone to the trouble of bringing her here and providing basic amenities? She drank a mouthful to no ill effect.

The room itself was larger than the average bedroom, but not by much. She imagined it to be dungeon-like. Located underground. Her mind filled with medieval imagery. She wondered if there were guards outside in the corridor. No, this killer more likely worked alone. But how had he found this place? Where was it exactly?

Time passed. She sipped water. Peed into the pot. Obsessively poked at the door, seeking a weakness. On and off, she shouted, demanding release, sometimes pleading. She hated doing that, but it came unbidden. Finally, tired out, she slept, again not peacefully.

Flaring light woke her, followed by the grinding sound of the door opening. At first, she couldn't see anything as her vision adjusted.

'Comfortable?' he asked mockingly.

'Who *are* you?' Banerjee said, pulling a blanket around her shoulders, a pointless protection. 'Why are you doing this to me?'

'You were lookin' for me, weren't ya?' He laughed. Then, with a weird change in tone: 'Well, I thought I'd oblige.'

'So you're the Scavenger?'

'Cut a fine figure of a psychopath, don't ya reckon?' He gave a humourless laugh. 'I know I look like some deadbeat crazy. All part of the act, I assure ya.'

He came closer, a tall, slightly stooped presence silhouetted against the globe in the ceiling. He was carrying a leather tool bag.

'You're gonna help me get what I want,' he said.

'And what is it you want?' Banerjee asked. 'Maybe I'd be willing to help. If you tell me—'

Was that amusement on his bearded face?

'I know what you are, sniffin' around Mike Crowe like a bitch in heat.'

'Is that what I'm doing? Do you resent it? We could go somewhere more pleasant and talk about Mr Crowe and my sex drive, if you like.'

'No talk, Mizz Headshrinker.' He scowled. 'I hate your lot. Know-it-all mind-parasites.' He shrugged. 'Even so, I'm sorry I gotta do this. I really am.'

He loomed over her. She began to rise but was in too vulnerable a position. He shoved her down with one foot. When she tried to grab his leg, he kicked up, hitting her on the side of the head. Dazed, she fell back.

'That's for the boot ta the head ya gave me last night, darlin'.'

Banerjee tried to clear her mind of pain, of fear, of the sense that nothing she said or did could help her here and now. 'Please, I–'

Then he was on her, crouching on her abdomen, hard enough to force the air from her lungs. He slammed her left hand onto the stone floor, holding it down with his own. His grip was strong, stronger than anything she could muster. She struggled to force him off, raising her knee in an attempt to catch him in the crotch. But she couldn't get enough leverage. Her free hand slashed at his face. He knocked it away easily and slapped her on the side of the head where he'd hit her before, hard enough to knock her skull onto the stonework. Her squirming became frantic.

'This'll hurt a hell of a lot more if you make a fuss.'

What if she went limp? Maybe then he'd relax enough for her to roll him off...

Her captor raised his right hand to punch her again, but he stopped when she went quiet.

'Much better, m'love,' he said, lowering his hand and using it to draw something out of his tool bag. She couldn't quite see what it was. 'A minor sacrifice on your part, that's all I need–'

'What sort of sacrifice?'

He grinned. 'You'll see.'

She began to struggle again, fear sweeping over her.

'I can assume you're not gonna make this easy?' He shook his head like a disappointed parent. 'Okay, I'll give ya a break.' He dropped whatever he'd been holding; a metallic clang echoed through the room. He reached into his bag again. This time he brought out a bottle of liquid and a cloth. Holding her down with his knees on her stomach and chest, he opened the bottle and poured liquid onto the cloth. She recognised the sweet, pungent smell: chloroform.

'Just a special cocktail I've acquired for this sort of occasion. It'll be better this way.'

'Administering anaesthesia drugs can be dangerous. That stuff will kill if you don't know what you're doing.'

'Well, if the worst happens, it'll make the job even easier, right? And you'll be beyond caring.' He chuckled again.

She made another concerted effort to push him off, but he pressed down so hard the struggle hurt her. Then the cloth was on her face. The smell intensified. She held her breath. Or tried to. His weight on her made it impossible to maintain.

'None o' that!' he growled and pressed harder. She gasped.

Her fingers went numb first. Her sight failed, blackness creeping in from the edges. Her tormenter said something she couldn't make out. She felt herself slip away.

Sometime later, she woke to pain in her left hand and a deep awareness of loss.

What the hell had he done to her?

PART THREE
FACES OF A MONSTER

32

BELMORE BASIN AND THE OCEAN LOOKED DIFFERENT IN THE SUNLIGHT. THE slope from the carpark where Crowe had found Skarratt's body was more open, not quite the wasteland it had seemed that night. No one was about despite the relatively fine weather. He locked the car and made his way to the spot where he'd first come face-to-face with the Scavenger. Crowe still ached; he would for a while. Middle-Management's bullet had sliced through the outer layers of flesh, but his whole upper arm was bruised, right to the shoulder. His head hurt, internally and externally. Driving hadn't been easy; without power steering, it would've been a hell of a lot worse.

He stopped, facing a cluster of trees from which the Scavenger must have come. The ground dipped, then rose again and disappeared behind salty, windblown scrub. Turning south, he could see the path that led away to the main road. Further around, the steelworks were visible in the distance. Whitish smoke rose in an atomic pillar from one of the stacks. There was fire in the heart of it.

To his left lay a few paces of open ground, then bushes. He'd been forced into those, and past them, and down the slope. In daylight, he could see how close the tangle on his right was – enough to hide someone until they were within arm's reach.

'Big man!' the Scavenger cries.

Crowe hears the words and for a moment fails to understand. Is it scorn? He takes it as scorn.

'Big man!'

The words might be mocking, but there's something else in them. A cry for help?

His eyes stab at Crowe. Wind and rain follow, as though the storm emanates from inside the Scavenger's head. Crowe backs away, flailing at him. The gun is knocked aside.

Crowe stumbles further, turning his foot on a thick stem, feeling the touch of tossing bushes – a bottlebrush, not yet in flower. The Scavenger pounds into him. Crowe steps back, grabbing at the leaves and the rain.

Then there's another push.

He tried to focus on that moment. Something important lurked in it. Wind, slighter than on the night when he met the Scavenger, whistled in his ear.

Something rushes from a wall of shadows. Hunched a little, moving fast and yelling. Crowe can't understand what it yells. It pounds into his side, completely unbalancing him. The gun fires into the ground. For a moment, he sees a face. It's not wearing a balaclava.

He's seen the face before.

Then he falls.

Crowe blinked the images away. He'd forgotten that glimpse. But it was there now. Like a ghost.

He hadn't known it at the time and hadn't put it together before this, but the face was that of Len Bugden. The ex-journo had been there that night. Or Crowe imagined he had. Was it another imposed memory? Was his recollection of that encounter – obscured by the speed of events, by rain and wind and the messy tumble that followed, warped by dreams and drug-induced delusion – merely playing games with him, like the Scavenger himself? How could Bugden be the Scavenger? Crowe had always assumed the Scavenger was short because, well, that night he'd seemed so. Banerjee's theory confirmed it because of the uniform height of his victims.

Could Crowe have been fooled by the way his attacker moved then, bent over, hitting low? Possibly. But maybe the idea that Bugden was the Scavenger, though he had dismissed it many times, had been lurking in his subconscious and had now worked its way through to his reflections of that night, changing them. It wasn't as though his memories had been particularly accurate lately.

Maybe he was simply losing his grip. After what had taken place in Waldheim's mansion, that wasn't an unlikely possibility.

The Scavenger.

He'd done what Lucy wanted. He'd stopped her father from using the foetus to resurrect her. Or rather, the Scavenger had. But it seemed he had created something worse. He was sure the nightmares he'd experienced at the time and since then held truths he needed to understand, but so far he could make little of them. The one fact he was clear on was that the Scavenger, and his absconding with Marika's unborn child, threatened Lucy as deeply as her father had. Somehow the two were connected. The urgency to find him was personal now.

Crowe walked across the slope toward the withered line of under-tended vegetation into which he'd fallen. Looking for what? He had no idea. Just something to help him put the pieces together. He expected no material evidence but half hoped that being here, where it had started for him, would cause some suppressed memory to surface or his subconscious to cough up an insight that had so far eluded him completely.

Neither of these things happened. Instead, as he stood on the edge of the slope, looking out across the buildings being erected along the foreshore, something caught his eye, almost at his feet. A box of some kind lay in the undergrowth. It looked new. He moved closer and knelt to get a better view. It was a red cardboard shoebox. *Slickers*, it said in white letters across the lid. It was tied with a piece of string. It was neither old nor sodden; it had to be a recent addition to the décor. It wouldn't have lasted in this condition in the weather the way it had been lately for longer than an hour or two.

Crowe spun around, scanning. The far edge of the grassed area disappeared over the slope westward. Trees and shrubs were shifting nervously. He couldn't see anyone.

Removing the string, he cautiously slid the lid off the box. Inside, there was hair. A lot of it. Long and black. Nestling on top of the silky pile was a note. Feeling the hair wisp against his fingertips sent a prickly ache right along his arm. He glanced up, sensing someone watching him, yet no one was in sight.

The note was similar to the ones he'd seen from the Scavenger, though there was something wrong with it. The handwriting was clumsier, the tone right off. It was like a carefully, but not carefully enough, written forgery.

When I was young, my cousin and I used to participate in paper chases. You like paper chases, Mr Crowe? As an underworld 'facilitator', you are familiar with the search, and chasing information on bits of paper isn't so far removed from your normal method of working. Tidier, I suppose, but tidiness is a virtue. I respect it. It gives pattern to reality. Like counting how many holes it takes to fill the Albert Hall. To fulfil desire through an intricate ordering of the world. Here in this box is a piece of something you desire. I'll send you a more significant piece soon. Be on the lookout. It will offer you a clue. Think your way to me. Isn't that what detectives do? Are you being a detective now? I suspect that Sherlock Holmes would have found me already. What's up with you?

THE NECK'S BROKEN, THE BRAIN IS USELESS. WE MUST FIND ANOTHER BRAIN.

Bugden had Banerjee. He would cut her up and send her to Crowe bit by bit until he found the Scavenger. A body chase. Did he intend to use her brain for something, maybe to aid the Scavenger in creating his monster? Was that what the final quotation meant? The idea filled Crowe with dismay.

Then it hit him. This had been left for him, but as his coming here wasn't something Bugden could have guessed in advance, the box must have been put in place since he'd arrived. If that was the case, Bugden had to be nearby. Watching.

Crowe looked up as a gust of wind swirled around him. Something moved in the distance. The figure disappeared even as Crowe saw it. He ran, the impact of each step sending pain through his side right up to his brain. Land fell away quickly, so he had to go maybe 100m before he could see far enough to spot Bugden easing himself into the purple ute, which was illegally parked at the bottom of the slope. It started up as Crowe stood there looking down, taking deep breaths to ease the wrenching in his gut, to settle the dizziness still haunting his skull.

The ute began moving and he tried to anticipate its route, hoping he'd be able to get some clue as to where Bugden was headed. He expelled breath calmly.

Then the ute disappeared behind buildings along the foreshore. It could be going anywhere.

Again, Crowe cursed the man. He was being manipulated at every point in this investigation, dragged helpless to some preordained end. He was getting nowhere, except to where Bugden, and presumably the Scavenger, wanted him to be. He had no idea where it would end up but, he suspected, it would be nowhere good.

He took a deep breath and called Pirran's number. Time to pay the piper.

33

GAIL'S RED MAZDA WAS IN THE PARKING LOT OF THE *SOUTHERN HIDEAWAY*. That was good. Crowe felt utterly buggered. If he didn't lie down soon, he'd keel over where he stood. It wasn't just bodily injuries, nor Waldheim and his fate. It was Lucy. He'd failed her a second time.

But the truth was, he couldn't get rid of the notion that what he did now would be important to both Lucy *and* Banerjee. The problem of Dr Banerjee and the Scavenger beyond her was perpetually on his mind – a sort of frenzied frustration he couldn't settle – and it wove itself with thoughts of Lucy. He was to blame for whatever was happening to Meera Banerjee and if he couldn't find her, and quickly, both she and Lucy would suffer. Assuming ghosts could suffer, in Lucy's case. From all he'd experienced, it was apparent they could.

All the way up the Illawarra Highway, his anxiety had grown, becoming more and more urgent. The superintendent had hit the roof when Crowe finally spoke to him; after the message he'd left on the way to Waldheim's place, Pirran had had all hands looking for Banerjee. Her briefcase and laptop had been found on the concrete floor of the hotel carpark, beside the open door of her abandoned vehicle. Her mobile had been in her briefcase. Whoever had taken her had been careful to scope out the security cameras so his attack wasn't recorded, but there was footage from an external camera showing a purple Falcon ute roaring up out of the garage not long after it showed Banerjee arriving in the small hours. The number plate of the ute had been obscured.

Now, having learned about the box of hair, Pirran went so silent Crowe thought he might have died on the spot. When he finally spoke, he didn't even sound angry as he told Crowe to come to the station immediately. He'd gone beyond rage into some state Crowe couldn't define. Crowe knew if he turned himself in, chances were Meera Banerjee would be dead before the law let him out again. The only new clues were the ones Crowe had been given, clues *he* was most likely to be able to use. And Crowe hadn't mentioned Waldheim either. Sooner or later someone would find the man's mangled corpse, and that could only make things worse.

Meanwhile, would Bugden stop at hair? Killing women wasn't part of the Scavenger's MO. This taking of Banerjee, and the murder of Sandy for that matter, would have surprised Crowe if he wasn't already convinced that Bugden was somehow involved. Gail had said Bugden didn't like females in positions of power. Bugden...the Scavenger. How exactly did everything Crowe knew of them both fit together?

He politely declined Pirran's offer and hung up as the superintendent began making a noise like a kettle left too long on the stove.

At the hotel reception, Crowe was faced by a bleak man of anywhere between 30 and 70, dressed in jeans, a crumpled white dress shirt and a carelessly placed black bowtie.

'My, ah, wife took a room here,' Crowe said. 'She's expecting me.'

'Name?' the bleak man said with a lack of interest so complete Crowe thought he might wander off if not answered quickly.

'Byrd,' Crowe replied.

'Just overnight, is it?' The receptionist held the pen in an odd manner between his forefinger and thumb, as though he was afraid it might leak on him. 'She didn't know.'

'Indefinite,' Crowe said. 'Let's start with a week, eh?'

'Okay.' He wrote something then looked at Crowe earnestly. 'Just the two of you?'

'Yeah.'

He frowned, not deeply though, more like an afterthought. 'You want to order any videos? Thirty bucks base rate for a week. Movies five bucks each. We got some good ones.'

'Videos?' Crowe said. 'Bit archaic, aren't they? No thanks.' As he spoke, he leaned against the desk and scraped his side. He winced, feeling the blood flee from his face.

'You hurt?' the receptionist said, showing little concern.

Crowe had cleaned up the damage as much as possible, but it still showed. The effort of driving here had caused an eruption from the bandaged wound. A wet stain was visible on his sleeve.

'Car accident,' Crowe said through gritted teeth. 'It's okay. Forget it. Room number?'

The receptionist told him, and he slumped toward the stairs, which were hidden behind a drink machine. 'Your *wife's* got company already,' the receptionist added. Crowe stopped and looked back at him. The man sighed, his mind barely holding onto this last thought. 'They can't stay, you know,' he went on. 'Room's only a double, even though there's an extra bed. They'll have to pay.'

'What company?' Crowe said.

But he'd already guessed. Pukalski appeared from around the drink dispenser. His right hand was in his deep coat pocket.

'Hi there, Mikey,' he said. 'We got here quicker than we thought. Hope you're not put out.'

'Just a bit surprised.'

Pukalski smiled grimly. 'We won't disturb this gentleman further,' he said, nodding toward the receptionist, who might've been calculating their compatibility rating. 'Gail's waiting with our mutual friend.'

'Right.' His subtext sank over Crowe like a net. He didn't have the energy to fight, even if he'd thought he had a choice. He moved up the stairs, keeping his hands in the open.

Pukalski's precise footsteps followed him.

As they entered the room, Crowe saw that Middle-Management, looking peeved and dishevelled, was indeed watching Gail. Closely. Along the barrel of his gun. The room was small, its cement-rendered walls painted yellow and green, with a double bed facing a TV and lots of artificial-wood trim. An internal door led into the bathroom. Gail sat in a cane chair. Middle-Management rubbed at his shin and stood a cautious distance away, which suggested he'd already learned how far her legs could reach.

'Ah,' Crowe said, 'old-home week.'

Gail gestured casually, but Crowe could see she was worried. One foot was missing a shoe, and her coat lay draped over the end of the bed. Papers were spread out there, as well as a writing pad and her laptop. She'd obviously been working when the uninvited guests dropped in.

'How long've you been entertaining this lot?' Crowe asked her.

'Booked in just after three,' Gail said. 'They burst in about half an hour ago. Very rudely, too.'

Pukalski shoved him into the room. Crowe stumbled as the door slammed.

'Watch it, Charlie-boy!'

'You watch yourself, Crowe.' Pukalski was no longer as civil as he'd been at reception. 'I'll have the gun,' he added.

'What gun?' Crowe said. 'You took my gun already.'

'Whatever fuckin' gun you've still got.'

Crowe grinned, grimaced at the resulting pain, and drew the Colt carefully from his inside coat pocket.

'That's Gary's.' Middle-Management stepped closer.

'He didn't need it anymore,' Crowe said.

Middle-Management took it. From the expression on his face, Crowe thought for a moment the thug was going to shoot him.

'That's enough!' Pukalski barked.

Middle-Management glared.

Pukalski glared back without flinching.

Reluctantly, the goon returned to his position near, but not too near, Gail.

Crowe sat gingerly on the edge of the bed. 'Don't have much luck with your employees, do you, Charlie?' he said. 'Do you specifically advertise for dumb-arses?'

'Just shut up!'

'Surely you didn't shepherd me in here so we could sit around and count each other's worry-lines.'

In a studied manner, Pukalski took a cigarette out of a silver case and flamed it with a fancy lighter. He balanced the cigarette between the second and third fingers of his left hand, so that his other fingers covered his face when he drew on it, as though he was trying to hide. He didn't look to be in any mood for a full and frank exchange of views. Crowe thought he'd take a crack at it anyway.

'You had someone tailing Gail, eh?'

Pukalski said nothing. Smoke curled from his nostrils.

'Where's Banger?' Crowe asked.

'You bloody know.' Pukalski loomed over Crowe. 'He'd just left your place when the cops arrived. Jonathan got away.'

Middle-Management preened.

'Bloody hell, Crowe,' Pukalski said, 'was it you did that?'

'You mean Hooper and his girl? Johnno saw it, eh?'

From Charlie's queasy expression as he nodded, Middle-Management's description of the scene must have been rather vivid.

'I work cleaner and you bloody well know it,' Crowe said. 'And I don't shoot my friends. That was our mutual pain in the arse, the Scavenger's work.'

Pukalski turned away. 'He's real?'

'Did you think I made it up in league with the newspapers and the cops?'

Pukalski's mouth puffed like a fish trying to kiss the glass of its tank. 'I thought you were conning me. I thought the whole scam was yours. Banger said—'

'Jesus, you're taking advice from fucking Banger now?' Crowe shook his head. 'Use your bloody brain for a change, Charlie. You dragged me into this kicking and screaming! Remember?'

Pukalski leaned against the support for the TV. 'It was Jonwood then?'

'Yeah, it was bloody Jonwood.' Crowe got up and paced toward him.

Middle-Management straightened as if under threat.

Crowe ignored him. 'The way I figure it, Banger was dangling on Tansey's strings. Tansey had the brains, such as they were. Banger provided muscle and inside info because *you* talked in front of him like he was some fricking rock. When I came to you at the restaurant, and then Tansey turned up, Banger panicked. He thought it'd all come out and the shit'd hit the fan.'

'It would've.'

'He didn't trust Tansey to take the blame without spilling, and why would he?'

Crowe turned away. Gail was watching them all, carefully evaluating the state of play. He had to admire that she still looked like the poster girl for cool, calm and collected. 'You all right?' he asked. 'These pond scum get up to anything scummy?'

'I'm fine,' she said. 'You look a mess.'

'Yeah, I dressed especially for the occasion.' He pointed at Middle-Management. 'Thanks to that arsehole and the Scavenger.'

'You had another run-in?'

He nodded, taking care not to do it too energetically. 'Yeah. At Waldheim's place, when I went to give the Great Man back his... merchandise.'

Crowe thought Pukalski's head was going to explode. 'You saw Waldheim? You bastard. Did you tell him anything?'

'You mean about your fuck-up?' Crowe laughed. 'Trust me, Charlie. He knew you were a prize turkey already.'

'Shit.' Pukalski turned in circles like a malfunctioning wind-up mouse.

Crowe laughed again, which reminded him of how much his head hurt. 'But it doesn't matter what he knew. He's done.'

'What?'

'Scavenger got him. Made him laugh from ear to ear.' Crowe made the cut-throat gesture.

Pukalski rubbed at the back of his neck. 'But you got the bastard, right?' he asked. 'And you got the money back?' No doubt about it, Charlie kept his focus.

'Scavenger escaped. But he left me a message.'

'What message?'

'Hair.'

'What?'

'A woman's hair. She's working with the police. On loan from the Feds. So you see how much he likes people who interfere with his plans.' Charlie didn't need to know that Bugden had left Banerjee's hair and that the Scavenger was probably a separate entity.

'Oh, god!' muttered Gail.

Crowe thought Pukalski might suck himself inside out. 'He's going to send her back to me bit by bit until I find him. Incentive, yeah?'

'Why's the fucker care about you, for chrissakes?'

'I think your takeaway from this, Charlie, should be that he doesn't like people interfering. You're one of those people. You're about the right height, too.' He paused to let Pukalski absorb the implications of that. 'And now that he's taken the policewoman, the cops are going to be scouring everyone even distantly involved. No doubt you'll be on the list.'

A ripple passed through Pukalski's body. He came at Crowe and gripped his lapels. 'I'm out, as of right now. You get me, Crowe? Out of it. Mention me to anyone, including the cops, and you're dead.'

'My lips are sealed.'

'Out of it!' He dropped the material of Crowe's coat as though it burned. He jerked his head toward Middle-Management. 'Come on!'

Gail and Crowe watched them perform a comedy routine at the door, trying to get past each other. Once right of way was sorted out, Pukalski looked around. 'If you get the money back, Crowe, you can have 20 per cent. But I don't think you'll get it back. I think you'll be dead.'

'You might be right.'

'You can't control this, Crowe,' he said. 'If this bloke got the better of Waldheim, then...Waldheim wasn't some cheap crook. He was–'

'Yeah, I know. A sorcerer. But apparently his guard-demons had the night off.'

Pukalski grinned sourly. 'Good luck. I'd say see you again soon, but I doubt I will.'

'Pukalski's right, Mike,' Gail said later. She'd got the receptionist to locate an ancient first-aid kit by sheer force of charm, then cleaned up Crowe's wounds with a modicum of sympathy. He'd filled her in on the events at Waldheim's estate, though he left out all the really weird bits.

'The police can't get this Scavenger. Looks like he's too much even for the experts. What can *you* do?' she asked.

Crowe got up and made them both cups of instant coffee that tasted a bit too much like bed-dust for his liking.

'I think I know how we can find him,' he said.

She stared, her expression an odd mixture of fear, excitement and something else. That would be her curiosity. She had the scent of a story.

He told her in detail about finding Banerjee's hair, about Bugden and his suspicion that the journo was working with the Scavenger, not just trying to report on him. 'He's been fucking involved from the start.'

'Are you sure he's not the Scavenger?'

'It crossed my mind. But I don't think so. The psychology's wrong.'

'Psychology, eh?' Gail dug into the chaos of notes and other papers she'd been working on before Charlie and Middle-Management had so rudely interrupted. She held up what she'd been looking for. 'So, I got my hands on this – no, don't ask how, a good journalist doesn't reveal her sources. Have a look at Bugden's outline for the feature series he'd pitched. Check out who else he was interested in from the start.'

She handed Crowe a bundle of photocopied pages and he moved to the window to read them. Bugden's name was on the top. Crowe skimmed through the lead-in and found the journo's list of possible subjects. There was a smattering of South Coast identities, including an ex-mayor and several businessmen, going right back to the development of the first coal mines established in the Illawarra in the early 19th century. But the main stories centred around Charles Pukalski, the Scavenger and Michael Crowe. Crowe raised an eyebrow. His name appeared, along with Pukalski's, under the heading, 'Skirting the Edge of the Law'.

'See what I mean?' Gail walked over to him. 'He knew you all right, Mike. He was writing about you before you met him in the library. I haven't got any copies of what he was writing, but I'm pretty sure he'd started. God knows what he's done with his research.'

'He's still writing this stuff,' Crowe said. 'A book about the Scavenger, he told me.'

'And that's why he's been bothering you. He wants you in it. You think he's orchestrating this whole thing?'

Crowe nodded wearily. Gail's hand rubbed across his shoulder. She began kneading. The strength of her fingers relaxed him almost at once but paradoxically focused his thoughts. 'Obviously, he'd been keeping an eye on Pukalski, too, and Charlie's supposed to be a cleanskin. Is he weaving Charlie-boy into this Scavenger scenario as well? It'd be a neat tie-in.'

'How could he?'

'I've been wondering about the Scavenger being at Wilkinson's Bay that night. It's a bloody big coincidence. Did the Scavenger know about the set-up? If so, he's got to have a contact within Pukalski's organisation or know someone who's got one. Bugden kept going on about his contacts. He might have known what was on and thought it'd make for good drama. What Bugden wanted dovetailed with what the Scavenger wanted.'

'Which was?'

'The foetus. I doubt the Scavenger had any interest in the money. What if offing Skarratt was just a crime of opportunity? What if the Scavenger was there that night because he knew about the foetus? What if he took the briefcase attached to Skarratt's arm because he thought it contained what he really wanted? He was disappointed then, but he's got it now, thanks to Waldheim. And me.'

'And you? Did he know you'd be there at Wilkinson's?'

'Someone told Bugden, Bugden told the Scavenger. Maybe he followed me. I wonder whose idea it was in the first place.'

Gail's fingers rested on his shoulders. 'So, Bugden couldn't have known the Scavenger would be there unless…'

'He's working with the bastard.'

Gail made an *ipso facto* gesture.

Crowe grunted, reached into his pocket and pulled out the note he'd found at Wilkinson's Bay. 'Bugden left this with Banerjee's hair,' he said. 'I saw him. At least I'm pretty sure I did. But more than that, he's been around every time I got one of the Scavenger's notes. And going to Wilkinson's Bay again triggered something – I saw him on the night Skarratt was killed. Again, I *think* I did. So, yeah. I'm pretty sure he's not the Scavenger, but collusion with him is not a bridge too far.'

Gail read the note. 'This is from the Scavenger, right?'

'It's supposed to be?'

'Bugden's handwriting?'

'Well, it didn't look the same, but maybe he was faking. Do the different sides of someone with split personalities have different writing styles?'

'It's called dissociative identity disorder. And while it can involve some physical changes, height isn't one of them. Not unless it's Jekyll and Hyde territory.' She pointed at the note. 'You know what this is though, don't you?' Her slender finger scored along the meaningless words referring to holes filling the Albert Hall.

'What?'

'Reference to a Beatles' song, from the *Sgt Pepper*'s album. 'A Day in the Life'.' Then she sang the key lines.

When she finished, she grinned. 'You told me Bugden sang bits of that song to you when you first met. Clever of me to remember, eh? That's another tick in favour of *this* letter being from Bugden, not the Scavenger.'

'So, we've got a tag-team of killers, but we don't know if the Scavenger knows he's got an offsider or that Bugden is just doing all this to make sure he gets a good story.'

They were silent for a moment, contemplating the kind of obsession that might inspire Bugden to act as he had.

To break the tension, Crowe grabbed the note, dragging Gail closer as well. 'Here's some more trivia: THE NECK'S BROKEN, THE BRAIN IS USELESS. WE MUST FIND ANOTHER BRAIN. What's that, Miss Smartypants?'

'I think I could guess. The movie.'

'Yeah, fuck it, Karloff's *Frankenstein*. I know because I watched it the night before last. The doc says those exact words just before he sends his servant off to find a brain. Unfortunately, the brain the klutz picks is, by chance, a criminal one.'

'Then if the Scavenger's following the pattern set by the film versions of the Frankenstein story, he'd want a minion, an Igor.'

'Right. Which is Bugden.'

'Makes sense. And maybe he'd want a criminal brain for his monster, too. Maybe he'd like Pukalski's. Pukalski is a shortish bloke, after all, like most of the others.'

'It's an idea,' Crowe said thoughtfully. 'I wonder if it's occurred to him.'

34

THE GRUESOME FIND AT THE MT ST THOMAS HOUSE WAS REPORTED ON THE late-night news. Crowe and Gail watched reporters playing chicken with cops and crime scene tape, regurgitating the fuck-all that had been given in the press briefing, then adding their own little flourishes: was it related to the Scavenger? Or some kind of mob-related payback? Then there was a cut to Dale Walker, giving his law-and-order campaign piece, saying that if he were elected 'good' people wouldn't have to live in fear anymore. Crowe turned off the TV to avoid throwing it out of the window.

'An anonymous tip-off, hey?' drawled Gail. 'Well, you're not going to be able to live there again.'

Crowe didn't bother to answer.

Later on, Crowe tried to sleep, but every fragment of information he'd collected kept circling about in his head. Gail had no such trouble and breathed gently beside him while he lined up the facts and the speculations, trying to separate them from absurd images of patched-up monsters and ghostly delusions or visitations or whatever they were. Pukalski and Tansey and Banger. Bugden and Waldheim and Banerjee. An endless array of possibilities. Bits of songs and novels. Scavenged poems and pictures, and human bodies, obsessive journalists. His mind shuffled the ideas about, made new combinations, got nowhere. At some point, he must have dozed off because he found himself at Wilkinson's

Bay again, walking toward a huge shoebox. Inside was Meera Banerjee, carved up into neatly labelled pieces.

He eased himself out of bed and rang Pirran. He figured the superintendent wouldn't be leaving the office in the current climate. Probably sleeping under his desk.

Pirran picked up on the first ring.

'It's me,' said Crowe.

'I notice you've failed to surrender yourself,' Pirran said equably, then, temper getting the better of him, yelled, 'Where the fuck are you?'

'Don't shout, Doug. I've got a headache.'

'You'll have more than a headache if I catch up with you. What do you think you're playing at?'

'Survival. So far today, I've been beaten up twice, shot in the arm, drugged—'

'The Scavenger?'

'Among others. You get Jonwood?'

'He escaped.'

'You've got to be fucking kidding me.'

'The uniforms thought they had him trapped in the house. Another bloke had legged it into the bush over the road. But when the back-up arrived, no sign of Jonwood inside.'

'Jesus.'

'What about that couple? In the house. Did you know about them?'

'They were friends of mine. It was the Scavenger sending me a message.' Easier to bundle Bugden and the Scavenger into a job lot. Crowe paused. 'Anything on—'

'Banerjee? No sign as yet. I think we can take it that she hasn't just got sick of her current life and taken off for sunnier climes.' Pirran cleared his throat. 'I want you in protective custody. Tell me where you are. I'll send someone to get you. Better still, I'll come myself.'

'Can't do that, Doug. I've got to keep at it.'

'You're just being stubborn. Pride, isn't it?'

'I've got a better chance than your lot.'

'Crowe, for Christ's sake—'

'He *wants* me to find him. If I'm in protective custody that'll just put a crimp in his plans, and I don't want to think about what he might do to Meera if he gets frustrated. Sorry.'

'Crowe?'

'Yeah?'

'If Meera Banerjee dies, I'll nail your fucking hide to the wall myself.'

'I know you will, Piranha, I know you will.'

It was only as he hung up that Crowe realised he hadn't told Pirran about Bugden's involvement in any of this. Was the cop right? Was it pride? Or just plain arrogance?

He paced toward the window and looked out, scanning for any sign of a purple Falcon ute sitting there like a bruise against the night. The streetlights cast yellow pools over unfamiliar cars, but what he was seeking wasn't there.

Suddenly a thought occurred, and it made him nervous. What if Pirran had traced the call? It's what Crowe himself would've done.

He woke Gail and told her about the phone call. Beyond a heavy sigh, she said nothing, just rolled out of bed and started to pack her stuff, quickly and efficiently. He told her she had three minutes. She gave him some side-eye.

But Pirran and any possible phone traces weren't the only reason for the move. Crowe knew the Scavenger was out there. Bugden, too. He intended to do some fancy driving to make sure no one was on his tail. So far too many people had been too successful at following him. Way too successful.

'Turn off your phone,' he said, turning off his own, 'just in case. And gimme your keys.' Taking her car would throw off anyone looking for the BMW. He dragged on his soiled clothes, vowing to burn them when he had a chance. His shoes seemed several sizes too small. Gail disappeared into the bathroom.

'I'll take your computer and papers, meet you at the car.'

Outside, the air was colder than Crowe had expected. The breeze held rain. He glanced around, but the only movement was a woman heading purposefully and anxiously for the safety of the next streetlight.

Opening the back of Gail's Mazda, he tossed in her stuff then glanced toward his old BMW, which was parked in a nicely sheltered spot where it should be safe enough for a few days. But even from a distance, he could tell the driver-side door was open.

Cautiously, he moved toward it, reaching into his coat. No gun. Pukalski hadn't returned it, the bastard. But there was no one in the car or nearby. He pulled the door fully open and leaned in to flick on the internal light.

On the driver's seat, like a dead mouse left as tribute by a cat, was a finger. Small. Delicate. Severed. The blood on its ragged end was dry. The nail polish, a bright red, was the one Meera Banerjee had been wearing.

Was Bugden watching from somewhere? Or did he just drop crumbs and scamper away laughing, knowing Crowe would follow him? He glanced around quickly. Nothing moved except for wind-rattled trees and bushes. A car drove past.

Taking a deep breath, Crowe looked at the finger. It was a grotesque bookmark on his old-fashioned *Gregory's* South Coast street directory, which was open to Maps 2 and 3. Wollongong's northern suburbs: Austinmer, Coledale, Wombarra, Scarborough, Clifton, Coalcliff, Stanwell Park.

Another message.

Look there, it said. Find me. I dare you.

'That's just what I intend to do, you bastard,' he muttered under his breath.

Crowe wasn't with him when Pukalski got home. He was dodging late-night traffic with Gail Veitch, trying not to think about Lucy's corpse, trying not to superimpose Meera Banerjee's face on top of it, trying not to imagine little parcels of body parts arriving at regular intervals. Crowe was also dodging the fear that Gail might be next.

As he drove, he kept glancing in the rear-view mirror to see if he and Gail were being followed. He used manoeuvres he'd picked up over years of street life, anything he could do that might throw off a pursuer.

Yet even when they were curled together in a cheap double-bed in Sutherland, his arms tight around her, he still couldn't shake the feeling that Gail was about to be carried off into a bloody twilight.

So, Crowe wasn't there when Pukalski's bodyguard opened the front door and thus knew nothing about Charlie-boy's fate. But he heard about it afterwards.

The night in Lake Heights is wild. Banshees whistle at Pukalski from the eaves of his house. Jonathan slams the car door behind him and rushes up the stairs, jiggling loose the front-door key from the crowded keyring. 'You should've let me finish him,' he's saying. 'He mightn't have shafted you, Mr Pukalski, but he killed Gary.'

'Gary let himself get killed. Tough shit. You can clean up the mess. In memoriam.'

'In what?'

Momentarily the wind dies. The night is quiet, except for traffic on the distant main road. Pukalski looks around as Jonathan fits the key into the lock. No lights show through the windows, which is to be expected as his wife Anna has taken the kids to her mother's for a week.

But where's the housekeeper? Pukalski thinks belatedly as Jonathan opens the door. As he does, he squeals, surprised. A large figure stands in the doorway. The figure is holding a gun.

'Jonwood?' says Pukalski, recognising the shape. 'Is that you?'

'What?' growls Jonathan, relaxing. 'Banger? For god's sake—'

The gun points at Jonathan's chest. A sharp detonation erupts from its barrel. Pukalski's minder cries out as the bullet tears into him, lifting him from his feet. He tumbles backwards down the stairs like a broken doll thrown by a petulant child.

Pukalski screams obscenities, springing for the nearest cover.

But as he moves, his arm is grabbed by fingers that feel like steel claws. Something sharp is forced into his shoulder. He screams some more, staring into a face wearing a balaclava.

'Relax, Mr Pukalski, I've come to take you to your money…and to make you into a better man.'

And already Pukalski feels the drug beginning to work.

35

THE ILLAWARRA ESCARPMENT TOWERED ABOVE CROWE AND GAIL LIKE A huge prison wall that had been breached once too often, abandoned and then overgrown by bush. On their left, the land fell away sharply to a grey seascape, its surface chopped by cross-currents and a wind that had swung around to become south-easterly. There was no rain, not yet. The sun had disappeared behind the western cliffs but a clear blue sky still lingered overhead. A cloudbank further north along the coast, however, rose like a mountainous threat, relatively low and ominously dark. Crowe was ready to see that as an omen of things to come.

They'd taken the route through the national park, heading south from Sydney toward Wollongong, and were now travelling along the coast road at Coalcliff. Gail slowed the car as they passed gates marked 'Illawarra Coke Co'. A sign warned passers-by to watch out for trucks. If Crowe was right, however, it was psychopaths they had to worry about.

'It's over that way, I think,' Gail said, pointing into bush that scurried up over the cliffs, pushed into nervous motion by the wind. 'The other side of that ridge.'

Crowe was feeling marginally better after some patchy sleep and some painkillers. Gail had strapped his ribs and changed the dressing on the bullet wound in his arm, and his head ached just a little less.

After leaving the *Southern Hideaway*, they'd found a hotel closer to

Sydney and managed to hunt down some decent breakfast and coffee that didn't make Crowe want to punch someone, while he went through Gail's notes and the papers she'd collected on Len Bugden. Blowie's archive was a study in paranoia. Scribbled messages to himself and the *Herald*'s editor accused politicians big and small of personal vendettas against him. He saw undercover cops lurking in every failure and traced organised crime into so many corners the Mafia would've had to work triple time just to handle the paperwork. Many of the notations were nothing more than trivia and ravings. However, one item caught Crowe's attention: reference to a cemetery somewhere on the escarpment at Coalcliff. It was because the Scavenger had so determinedly chosen his killing fields in proximity to cemeteries that Crowe noticed it. Blowie called this particular boneyard 'Stony Ground' and mentioned it in connection with a black-mass cult he claimed had functioned in the area during the 1960s. Three young women had been ritually slaughtered there during the early part of that decade, and police finally arrested an ageing miner who reckoned he was a witchdoctor and was trying to conjure Beelzebub to wreak havoc on the colliery for sacking him. Blowie's submission claimed that, even today, you could find black-magic talismans and the entrails of freshly killed animals among the graves.

'It's not in my *Gregory's*,' Crowe had said while Gail sat in bed drinking tea. 'Or Google maps.'

'Maybe it doesn't exist.'

'He made it up, you mean?'

'Or maybe it's old, like, so old it's stumbled off the map?' She grinned.

Crowe knew full well it was a long shot, but the more he thought about it, the more he came to accept that checking it out would be worth the effort. At least he could give the idea a run. It wasn't like they had any other leads.

Lightning visits to the Lands Department and the State Library unearthed an old map and the information that the graveyard had been attached to a Trappist monastery, back when religious folk had felt inclined to lock themselves away from the world's temptations. When the urge toward sanctity passed, the monastery was abandoned. A long time after, in 1958, it was repurposed as a psychiatric hospital. They could find no notice of closure, but the lack of references to the place after the late '80s didn't bode well.

'What'd you reckon?'

'I reckon if you're a mad scientist who wants to be a latter-day Frankenstein, or a rebel journalist looking to hide out, what better spot than an isolated and long-forgotten asylum?'

'Let's go!' Gail decreed, eagerly.

'You're not coming,' Crowe said. Too quickly. He recognised the look on her face.

'And why not?'

'Might be dangerous.'

'And so far everything else has been a tiptoe through the tulips, I suppose?'

'Just find somewhere to lie low,' he said, aware he sounded like a man who'd already lost the argument.

She crossed her arms across her chest and glared. 'I'm a grown-up. I'm also a journalist,' she said. 'There's a story here. If you don't let me go with you, I'll just follow on my own. Either way, I'll have my camera with me... you know, to record your impressive bravery.'

'For fuck's sake, it's not a job for a—'

Her scowl stopped him dead mid-sentence. 'Look, Mike,' she said with all the tolerance of an impatient executioner, 'I can bloody-well take care of myself. You don't have to worry about me.'

'Who said I would?'

'Then what's the problem?'

He sighed. 'Just try not to get killed.'

After Crowe arranged to obtain a gun from one of his shadier acquaintances – a much older model of his favourite Beretta being the best he could do – and Gail made sure her camera was ready to go, they set out for the South Coast.

Coalcliff Colliery looked like the decaying skeleton of a huge alien spaceship half-buried in a field of ash. Towers poking up through black soil were connected to dumps, loaders and processing plants by segmented pipes and strips of rusted metal. Maintenance and storage buildings squatted between them and on either side of the railway line that ran through the sprawling complex. There were no lights, no cars, no sign of activity.

The old map had identified an entrance road but hadn't placed the monastery-cum-loony bin very accurately. Sure, it was on a long, black line called Stony Creek, beyond the abandoned coal-mining operations, and a road was supposed to run behind the colliery and back along the coastal escarpment to the south. But Crowe and Gail couldn't find it. The scrub around them was thick and unforgiving; the lack of signage seemed a personal affront. All of the bush-cleared avenues they investigated led to dead ends.

'What do you reckon?' Gail looked back over the mud map she'd scribbled during their research trip that morning.

'Don't know, but my gut tells me we're getting close.'

She pointed back behind them. 'Try that way.'

They drove south. At the base of a gully, a sign read 'Stony Creek'. Crowe pulled into an old road to the left, parking on crumbled bitumen where a chain blocked further access. Beyond the chain, the road disappeared under gouged-up dirt and lantana. They both got out of the car to investigate, walking along the track with quick, quiet steps.

The creek emerged as liquid muck from a concrete, man-sized hole. Further up the hillside, Crowe could see the top of a green building with 'Coalcliff Mine' stamped on it. It appeared old and faded. A pipe dripping water ran down to the creek bed. Stony Creek had been dug in under the railway lines and even the mine buildings. Its other side wasn't in sight and it possibly ran underground for hundreds of metres. Who could tell?

A Wormald security car waited for them back beyond the chain. As they approached, a large man in uniform adjusted himself into an imitation of authority. Crowe's nerves were so on edge, he reached into his coat for his gun, but Gail stopped him.

'Let me handle this,' she said. 'Let's not get carried away.' She headed toward the bloke at a brisker pace. She pulled back her shoulders so the material of her shirt was forced open above her breasts.

'Hi there,' she said.

'It's private property,' he snapped.

'Oh, is it?' Gail looked along the fence line. 'There were no signs.'

'That's why there's a chain.'

'Sorry, I didn't mean to break any rules.' She smiled at him, showing him her open face. He wasn't a young bloke, in his late 50s or so, but he wasn't lacking in active hormones. Gail stepped close to him, edging into his personal space. 'I'm from the university,' she said. 'I'm writing a history of the area.'

'Oh yeah?' He moved away slightly, but Crowe noticed he'd softened.

'Dr Karen Judge,' she added, holding out her hand so he was forced to shake it. 'This is my research assistant.' Crowe nodded at him. 'I'm actually looking for an old monastery that's supposed to be around here. On Stony Creek. It's proving rather elusive.'

'Monastery? You prob'ly mean St Aloysius – it was a nursing home.'

'Nursing?'

'Yeah. You know, for nutcases. Wasn't very popular. Having it in the area, I mean. They closed it down in, oh, I don't know, the mid '80s, I guess.'

'I see. Where was it exactly?'

He glanced southward. 'Over that way. Well into the bush. They wanted privacy or something.'

'And how can I get to it? It's so easy to get lost!'

The bloke scratched at the side of his face and pointed vaguely south-westward. 'There was a road running behind the colliery, but it's been blocked off since about 2013.'

Crowe watched the man study Gail out of the corner of his eye, notice she wasn't looking at him, and glance down at her cleavage. Then he realised Crowe was watching, coughed and reddened.

'About halfway to Stanwell Park,' he said, barrelling on. 'Just a dirt track, probably overgrown now. The first part of it is still used by Transport NSW for track maintenance – goes to a depot. After that it winds around, pretty steep. Two, three kays. Maybe more. It's bush all the way.'

'How come they've hired you to guard the place,' Crowe asked, 'if the colliery's abandoned?'

'For the Railway Authority mostly. There's equipment stashed here and there. I drive up and down, keeping an eye out.'

Gail smiled. 'Well, thanks for your time.' She stepped away. 'Be sure and look me up if you're ever in the vicinity of the uni.' Then she added mischievously, 'I specialise in sexual deviancy during early colonial history. Might interest you.' She turned and strode toward the Mazda.

He watched her intently as she moved.

'Don't make academics like they used to, eh?' Crowe said.

The bloke's pale face flushed red again. He saw Crowe was smiling and relaxed. 'Hell, no,' he muttered.

Crowe slapped him on the shoulder. 'Thanks for your help.' He followed Gail to the car.

The track was rough and pitted; now and then they came to places where gravel had been dumped into eroded runnels and splits in the earth. Sometimes the road was wide enough for two cars, but only just. At other times, it was barely wide enough for one. If they ran into anyone coming in the other direction, there'd be no way they could hide. One thing was for sure: it had been used recently and often.

The road followed the shape of the land, winding all over the place. At times, the gradient was so steep, the tyres barely gripped the loose surface. They were surrounded by bush almost all the way. After about 15 minutes, the slope flattened and they came to an old stone pillar. A weathered, barely legible sign announced: 'St Aloysius Sanatorium'. Another sign, hand lettered, was beneath it: 'Keep away. Dangerous area'. On the opposite side of the track stood a pile of broken stones that had been a twin of the pillar: gate posts. Crowe noticed a rusted metal framework buried in the undergrowth.

Gail parked down a side track that might have gone somewhere once but was now a cul-de-sac. It gave enough coverage so that from the road the car would look like just another piece of long-abandoned junk, if it was seen at all. Then they walked. Whatever heat the day had held was fading fast and the wind had sprung up again, making the bush around them toss and twitch. All that peripheral movement made Crowe nervous.

St Aloysius Sanatorium wasn't in the best of repair. It was a double-storey building the size of several large houses, made of massive sandstone blocks, soiled, broken in places and badly eroded, with sculpted window ledges and other weather-worn ornamentation. A short wing stuck out the far side at a right angle was burnt and skeletal. The surrounding kikuyu lawns hadn't been mown for years and there were clumps of weeds a T-Rex could hide in.

On the left, several hundred metres away, the land curved down toward a spot where trees grew thicker and greener; undoubtedly it was where Stony Creek or an offshoot flowed. Crowe could just pick out a sectioned-off area, overgrown and mangled, that was probably the Stony Ground graveyard.

They circled around that way through the bush, keeping out of sight of the building as much as possible, aided by the obscuring walls of dried-out, necrotic vegetation.

The cemetery was surprisingly spread out. It swept down a slope that led to the creek and along it for 100m or so. Crowe wouldn't have thought a place as isolated as this would've had call for so many graves. It was surrounded on most sides by smaller trees – grevilleas and wattles, rather than gums – but taller trees were scattered through the place. Many of these had died and were now dried-out monoliths poking up from among the gravestones. On some graves were odd man-made objects: images constructed from feathers and the skulls of small animals, braided grasses and leather hangings. Several raised grave slabs looked as though they'd been used as altars. There were vases of dead flowers, bowls – the contents of which were now discoloured, desiccated lumps – and scratchings that might've been occult symbols or just graffiti.

'I don't like the look of this,' whispered Gail.

Neither did Crowe, but at least it all seemed old and unfrequented.

'Let's get this over with,' he said.

36

'PLEASE!' MEERA BANERJEE WHISPERED TO NO ONE, A POINTLESS, DESPAIRING gesture that did nothing to comfort her but one she'd repeated nonetheless. Darkness and isolation were eating at her resolve. How long had it been? Two days? Three? More? Time passed erratically, racing by or dragging on according to the level of pain and discomfort she felt. She didn't know how much more she could take without going crazy.

The air was cold, infused with a stale, subterranean mustiness. Perhaps she'd die here. Perhaps all that would be found of her would be her bones sometime in the future when this place – whatever, wherever it was – had been marked for demolition. Maybe they'd identify her by her missing finger.

Or all her missing fingers, if it came to that. She wondered when he'd come back for another.

'God help me,' she muttered. Her hand had begun throbbing again. She needed proper medical care. Much longer and infection would be inevitable. Her captor had made an effort to bind the stub of her finger to staunch the blood flow, but it wasn't a great job, and who knew how sterile the whole thing had been. Not that he cared. He didn't intend to keep her alive long term, but it ensured she was 'fresh' each time he sliced bits off and sent them to the target of his schemes: Michael Crowe.

What had possessed her to take on this job? Why had she continued with it? She knew why: she'd taken the job simply because it was a chance to make a name for herself by orchestrating the capture of Australia's most unique contemporary killer. And she'd suggested Pirran take Crowe into the fold, use him as a stalking goat, because the Scavenger was so interested in him.

In her lowest moments, she blamed Crowe. She blamed Pirran. But mostly she blamed herself. What could she tell Elias that justified her dismemberment and death? What would her children think of her? Would she ever get to speak to them again? Even if she did, there was no way she could make them understand when she didn't understand herself.

'Stupid! Stupid! Stupid!' she yelled, her weakened tones echoing around the room like the whispering of phantoms. 'And what's more, *I'm hungry!*'

The ghosts repeated her words, mocking her as the sounds faded into the gloom.

The outbuildings – a shed, a stone cottage and a large garage – looked abandoned. The day was beginning to fade. No lights had come on inside the main building, so Crowe felt more confident they were alone. He hoped their luck would hold. If this was where the Scavenger and/ or Bugden spent his/their time, then it seemed they'd both gone out grocery or body-part shopping. Gail took a picture and the slight digital click the camera made echoed uncomfortably loudly.

The front door wasn't even locked. They edged along a dank, gloomy corridor, past a small vestibule area and several big rooms, all completely gutted. There was nothing except junk pried out of the floor and walls or carted in by vandals. The sanatorium's fittings had obviously been removed long ago.

'What was that?' Gail whispered.

Crowe hadn't heard anything in particular. Wind rattled loose panelling somewhere above, making a scratching noise like rats' feet across the walls. His own breathing was a dull drone. Their shoes scraped on a floor covered with debris despite the fact they were being careful. Nothing else.

'Don't get jumpy,' he said. 'It doesn't look like anyone's been here for ages.'

'You don't believe that any more than I do.'

The ground floor proved to be deserted and unused, but upstairs they found two cell-like rooms that were in use. Both rooms were too gloomy to see into, having no external windows, so Crowe felt around for a light switch and tried it. Nothing.

'Use your phone,' Gail whispered.

He activated the torch function on his Galaxy. It wasn't much but would have to do. In one room, there was a mattress on the floor and lots of other stuff – books and papers (a dictionary, a thesaurus, a report by criminologist Paul Wilson on serial murder in Australia, a current almanac, Capote's *In Cold Blood*, a well-thumbed hardback copy of Mary Shelley's Frankenstein novel, and a pile of true crime magazines), an old manual typewriter and a collection of messy A4 pages with typing on them. Bugden's book on the Scavenger? Crowe flicked through the pages, but it was all nonsense – garbled sentences relating to designer viruses or drug deals in inner Sydney or occult rituals in the suburbs. There were also some clothes. These were dirty and crumpled, but one item he recognised – a windcheater he'd seen on Bugden. Well, the crazy journo at least was hanging out here, but did he have company?

In the second cell were lots of newspapers. Also an old TV with a VHS recorder/player attached, a beanbag and a filthy lounge chair. Neither the activation light on the VCR nor its clock was on, even though its power lead was plugged into a wall socket. Tired of wasting the battery on his phone, Crowe tried a light switch. There didn't seem to be any electricity. Not surprising, as the place was so isolated and officially no one lived in it anymore. He was willing to bet an unmarked video cassette lying on the floor near the TV was Karloff's *Frankenstein*. In the far corner were a half-empty carton of wine bottles and a plywood cupboard full of non-perishable food. Seemed like Bugden ate chips, drank and sat around imagining that the TV worked.

'This is definitely Bugden's shit,' Crowe muttered. 'No sign of the Scavenger yet.'

'No body parts anyway,' Gail said. 'What do you think he'd do with them if he hung out here?'

Crowe shrugged. 'Store them somewhere cold?'

'A cellar,' she said. 'Didn't monasteries always have wine cellars and cold rooms?'

I found someone today – a woman. Perhaps I've seen her before and simply haven't remembered. Such things are not at all implausible. It happened while I was wandering the corridor, looking idly through the grilles in some of the doors. There she was, trapped in a room I don't recall ever noticing before. Due to the gloom, the woman was little more than an anomaly in the shadows, and at first I thought she might be a ghost. I stared, wondering if she would see me.

'Hello?' I said carefully. She didn't move or acknowledge me. 'Can you hear me? Please answer.'

I thought she twitched then, raised her head and looked around, so I tried again. 'I'm a prisoner here, like you.'

She pushed herself onto her knees.

'I'm at the door,' I added, excited that the woman seemed to be responding.

But after a moment, she lowered herself again, muttering words that sounded like 'Now I'm hearing things'.

Urgently I told her she wasn't imagining it, that I was here. I was talking to her. I'm sure I was. Why couldn't she hear me more clearly? I grabbed at the door handle and pulled, but as always was unable to make the lock turn. 'I'm sorry,' I whispered as my hands dropped away.

She said nothing. The darkness thickened until I couldn't see even the ill-defined shape that had first drawn my attention. It was as if she'd faded away like the hills at dusk.

Then I…then…I feel the memories disappearing now…

Where am I? Oh, yes, in the near-dark of my own space and…

What was I thinking? It's gone, whatever it was. Gone. It remains only as a sadness, an emptiness, I cannot name.

I think it was important, but it's no use trying to recall it. Like all my recollections, it has retreated deep within me, too deep to be salvaged. Perhaps it will rise to the surface again, though I don't know why I think that. Anything that may have clarified in my head has already drifted away, so I can't even remember whether I've forgotten something.

Why does my past fade so quickly? Or did it never really exist? It's like I'm nowhere, adrift in a space that is without substance, without meaning. A space where meaning is fleeting and reality a dream I continually wake from.

All I know is I am trapped here, perhaps forever.

I must try harder to hold to my purpose.

Whatever it is.

37

Entry to St Aloysius's wine cellar was through a door hidden in the kitchen's walk-in pantry. Crowe pulled up the latch and it came easily. The hinges had been recently oiled. The stink emerging from down there was rank – the sweet stench of decaying meat. He wondered that it wasn't worse, considering what he expected to find.

'Mike?' Gail whispered.

A noise from behind them. Beyond the kitchen door. Crowe spun around, yanking his gun from its shoulder holster. A faint echo of something moving. They both listened. Still. Silent. Nothing followed.

'What did it sound like to you?' Gail asked after a moment.

'Footstep,' he replied. He edged through the door and looked around.

'I'm liking this less and less.' Gail came up behind him, holding the camera as though it were a machine-gun.

'Must have been an animal or something,' Crowe said. 'Or a branch falling against the wall. The wind's getting pretty fierce.'

'Yeah,' she said. 'I suppose so.'

'Well, there's nothing else.'

She didn't look convinced.

The stairs led into blackness. A hint of texture – a brick wall maybe – lurked in the shadows.

'I can't go down there,' she said.

'Hey, you insisted on coming.' It sounded a lot like *I told you so.* 'Stay here then.'

'You can't leave me, Mike. What if Bugden's around?'

'You'll hear his ute long before he turns up in the flesh. Give me a yell and I'll come back. Okay?'

'If Bugden *isn't* the Scavenger, the actual Scavenger might turn up—'

'There's no one here. I won't be long. How big can the cellar be?'

'Big enough to hide a bunch of corpses and the loony who offed 'em, I'd guess.' She stared at him for a moment, then gave a sardonic smirk. 'Okay then. What're we waiting for? An invite?'

She gripped his arm – the wounded one – and he pulled away. 'Look,' he said, 'no one's up here and there'll be no one down there either. I'll go down. You stay here.'

'Alone in the Entrance to Hell? Are you kidding?' She glanced around. A grubby black panel of four switches was on the wall near the door. 'Maybe one of these will make things clearer.'

Crowe was about to say the power was off but wasn't quick enough. Her finger toggled the switch, and a piss-weak glow came on in the pantry. There was a naked 40-watt bulb hanging on a cord.

'Maybe this one,' Gail said. She flicked another switch. Suddenly the cellar was radiant. 'That's it.'

The stairs went down perhaps 20 steps and disappeared around a bend. Crowe frowned.

'What's the matter?' Gail said, looking at him quizzically.

'I tried the switches upstairs. There was no power then.'

'Maybe the globes were blown?'

He frowned. 'Stay here. Give me a yell if anyone turns up.'

She glanced nervously out from the pantry at the growing gloom, the shadows building into suggestive lumps of darkness.

'Take this,' Crowe said, handing her the Beretta.

A dry, below-ground chill grabbed him as he descended. Rotten-meat stench seemed to leak from the walls and was heavy in the air. Other smells mingled with it, chemicals Crowe wasn't educated enough to identify.

The first room he came to – small, poorly lit by light spilling from the corridor – was used for storage. It was untidy and disorganised, though the remnants of order were still visible, left over from a time when the place was a functioning sanatorium. Labels were stuck here and there, peeling away from the stained wood and pitted metal struts. There were bottles of various sizes, most of them close to empty, some containing liquids, some pills; a few surgical implements, scalpels, needles and unidentifiable stainless-steel tools, as well as skeins of thread, cloth, nails, and coils of electrical cabling. A few larger receptacles held body organs – a heart big enough to be human, fingers, something like liver, an intestine. Shadows spread out from corners; the electric light seemed increasingly feeble. He pulled back, unsure of shapes lurking on higher shelves or what was behind him. He felt claustrophobic.

No one was here. He knew that. He tried to take a deep breath to calm himself, but the taste of the air was nauseating. It started him coughing.

'What's going on, Mike?' Gail's voice trickled down from above.

'Nothing,' he shouted. 'I won't be long.'

Narrowness widened suddenly into a large, open area. In the first instant of seeing it, the space was a clutter of exotic shapes and thick shadows: benches, objects hanging about the walls, a tangle of wires and beams like a gigantic web. He blinked and took it in, and his heart seemed to speed up, sending a rush of heat through his body.

'Jesus Christ on a bike!' he muttered, though no one was there to hear him. Especially not God. He didn't hang out in Hell.

Hung on the far wall was the most grotesque sculpture he'd ever hoped to see. It might've been made of clay and leather and bits of old rag, but even from this distance he could see it wasn't. It was a conglomeration of human bodies. Or body parts, at any rate. It was taller than Crowe – even allowing for the fact it wasn't touching the ground but was suspended by wires and cables that seemed to emerge from its limbs, chest and thighs. There were four arms that Crowe could see. Its skin, which was leathery, differing in colour and texture in sections, was peeling away here and there, torn, curling, patchy. On its left side, Crowe could see bones showing through. At other places, the epidermis bulged, as though internal structures had gone astray. There was stitching all over it. How many men were its parts scavenged from? More than the nine he knew about.

Only one body had been included whole. Right where the monstrosity's heart should be, the chest was open and a large cavity exposed. Into the cavity the Scavenger had slotted the foetus he'd taken from Waldheim. The withered form was scrunched up as in a womb with wiring inserted into it, trailing out to join with surrounding machinery.

Crowe went closer. The smell was ghastly, nauseating. He covered his nose and mouth with his hand. It didn't work. Obviously, the Scavenger had taken measures to preserve the bits of his monster – embalming perhaps, tissue dehydration, smoke-curing, pickling...who knew? But it didn't help. Crowe thought for a moment, head thick with the smell and the absurdity, that he was dreaming, that this was a nightmare. But only for a second. The sensory reality of it was too much. He staggered back, coming to rest against a bench.

His hand squelched into a pool of blood. He grunted and pulled away. Something made him glance up at the thing's face then.

Had it spoken?

Had *they* spoken?

He blinked. Not face. Faces!

It had three heads. One was so far buried in its chest, it might've been some sort of a petrified creature being weathered out of stone. Another was more normally placed above the left shoulder and sewn into it. This one had close-cropped blond hair. But the head had been stuck on at an angle, staring at the wall behind the creature. It looked almost skeletal, as though its skin was rotting off the bone. The third head was obviously intended to be the main one. It was facing the right way and was centrally placed, perhaps even connected to the backbone. It was fresh. Blood dripped from it and a needle and thread still dangled from the base of the neck where the head was being stitched onto the body. No attempt had been made to preserve that one.

The dead face was familiar, though for a moment its unnatural situation drove all recognition from Crowe's mind. The thick lips appeared to be pouting, and Crowe was filled with an overpowering conviction that they were about to speak. His breath faltered. After perhaps a minute, when no sound came, he breathed out and moved further away from the creature, dizzy and ill.

That face had stared down at Crowe like this before.

Crowe's kneeling, his arm aching and bloody. 'I've put up with as much shit from you as I intend to,' the other says.

Now Crowe was standing, but the face was still staring down at him. He'd grown taller.

Pukalski gazed at Crowe from the creature's wide shoulders.

Crowe's mother – a stern Irish matron – was a God-fearing woman, in her own way. 'Don't expect life to make sense, Michael Xavier,' she'd say. 'God likes his little jokes.'

God the comedian. Crowe had pictured the joker-God as a squat, pimply kid hunched over the Earth, waiting for his opportunity to be a smart arse, or pointing a magnifying glass at an anthill. Throughout history, He'd indulged in some pretty diabolical jokes.

And maybe He was only getting warmed up.

A frantic yell from Gail pulled Crowe from the grip of Pukalski's death-mask stare. He blinked, shot the monstrosity a nervous glance and turned toward the entrance. Quickly, he stumbled back the way he'd come, negotiating the stairs in a defensive crouch.

'What's up?' he said, finding words difficult, as though the air below had damaged his lungs.

Gail gestured for quiet. She leaned toward him as he rose above pantry-floor level. 'I heard it,' she whispered.

'Heard what?'

'A car. Sounds like a ute.'

Crowe listened. No sound for a moment, except for the wind. Then a door slammed. A car door.

'He's coming inside.'

The door slammed again. There was no point being hesitant about this. Whether Scavenger or willing accomplice, Bugden was a killer. Of that, Crowe had no doubt. Seeing that monstrosity in the cellar drove away whatever residual lawfulness might have lurked in him. He had no intention of risking his own life, and certainly not Gail's, just to give the lawyers something to do during a protracted trial.

'What did you find downstairs?' Gail asked.

'Stuff you wouldn't believe and don't want to see.' He put a hand on her shoulder as much to steady himself as her. 'Wait here.'

'You'll need this,' Gail whispered, and she handed him the gun. Crowe let the weight of it press into his palm. 'Be careful!' she added.

Crowe switched off the lights before edging through the pantry door. He crept across the dusty gloom toward the front of the building where Bugden had parked his ute. He was aware of Gail behind him as he entered a large room that gave out through French windows onto a long verandah running the length of the sanatorium's central building. Dried-out boards and rotting cloth randomly covered a wall of dirty, cracked glass.

He waved Gail back, thinking he could hear Bugden say something. The weirdo was muttering to himself. Swearing at…what? The world in general?

Bugden's feet stepped up onto the stone verandah. His shoes ground on loose rubbish. Crowe positioned himself near a gap and peered out. Bugden had stopped a few metres away and was picking his nose. As he did so, he turned and looked out across the overgrown lawn. The sun was disappearing behind the escarpment, spilling only a dusky evening light in patches on the weeds. Wind battered the middle-distance trees. Bugden muttered something. Still no sign that anyone was with him. Crowe wasn't sure if that was good or bad. Obviously, he was expecting someone.

At that moment, Gail yelled a warning and the room behind Crowe lit up, splashing yellow-blue light onto the walls. A deeper, male voice growled something as he turned. His eyes clear, unaffected by Gail's flash-unit because he'd been looking the other way, Crowe plucked the scene out of returning shadows in an instant. A large bloke holding a gun was striking at Gail, who moved back out of his reach. He'd come through a side door and was momentarily disoriented by Gail's flash, but his gun was waving about, uncertain whether to point toward Gail or Crowe.

This latest arrival was Ed Jonwood. The gun wasn't Banger's usual revolver. In fact, even in the gloom, it looked like Crowe's own Beretta. He was pleased to see it, despite the circumstances.

Banger blinked and the decision was made. Crowe would be his target. Before Banger could aim, however, Crowe fired, rolling to one side. His gun spat twice, and so did the one in Banger's hand. Bullets thudded into the floor near Crowe, then shattered a pane of glass that had somehow survived for years. Only one bullet of Crowe's found its mark, but one was enough. Banger stumbled, shocked, as the small hunk of metal slammed into his side. Crowe got to his feet while the big thug tried to steady himself. Banger fired again, but the projectile missed Crowe by an arm's length. Crowe returned fire and another bloody hole appeared in Banger's chest. His stare was wide and fierce but also bewildered. He collapsed onto his knees, muttering to himself. Gail came up beside him and took the gun out of his unresisting hand. She recognised it and clicked on the safety, then poised to toss it to Crowe.

Crowe gestured for her to keep it. Banger wasn't a threat anymore, but the element of surprise was well and truly blown. Where was Bugden? Crowe turned back toward the window. The old bastard was just reaching his ute, no doubt going after that shotgun he'd already used on Crowe, albeit as a club. Crowe kicked at the French window, splintering the wood as though it was papier-mâché. It was hollow with termite holes. The pieces turned to dust and splinters of glass, blowing out into the wind.

'Leave it, Bugden!' he yelled.

The ex-journo ignored him. He pulled open the front door of the ute, using it as a shield. Crowe couldn't get a clear shot. He ran along the verandah.

When Bugden's shotgun let loose in Crowe's general direction, Crowe had registered the fact he had it in his hands a second before. He was already dropping, down and to the left, behind the verandah's low railing. Buckshot hit the wall above him. He felt splinters of stone and wood on the back of his neck.

Quickly he crawled to the edge of the railing and fired around it. A slug clanked into the ute's rust-pocked duco. Crowe ducked back as the shotgun bellowed again. That was two shots. Was that the limit? Maybe, maybe not. Crowe took the chance and leapt up, took aim, and shot at the glass of the car door. It shattered into a web. He squeezed on the trigger once more as Bugden scrambled into the ute and began fumbling below the dashboard. Crowe's shot ricocheted. He fired again. A hole punched into the windscreen. Bugden yelled something but was still working away, just out of sight. Then his head appeared again, his eyes catching Crowe's an instant before the latter fired.

He ducked and Crowe's bullet hit what glass was left, this time turning the remnants of the windscreen opaque. Bugden was a phantom behind the milky weave.

Then the ute's engine roared to life with a shudder and an explosion of white smoke from the exhaust. Bugden rammed the gear stick into reverse as Crowe jumped down the stairs. He fired, putting another hole in the hood. The ute was moving fast, backwards along the rutted drive, raising dirt for the wind to whip away in thin ribbons. Tyres skidded as Bugden's foot over-revved the old heap, the vehicle wobbling about as though drunk. Crowe ran on, trying to aim alternately at Bugden and the tyres.

Once he'd made some distance, Bugden stopped and put the ute into a forward gear, which meant Crowe found the grinning grille above the rust-spotted front bumper suddenly coming at him, despite the ute's deflating wheels. He fired again and leapt aside, rolling into long grass full of sharp twigs and stones. The ute swept past, then turned in a wide circle and headed toward the gate. Crowe hit one of the ute's back tyres. The old Falcon swerved, struck a ditch and veered into the grass. Suddenly Bugden was headed toward the graveyard, bumping over rocks and crushing bushes like a juggernaut. Clearly still in control, he jerked the Falcon to one side to avoid a larger tree, managing to only sideswipe it.

Crowe pulled a spare magazine from his pocket and rammed it home. Bugden couldn't get far in that direction. As Crowe ran toward him, the ute reached the graveyard fence, rammed it, broke partly through and collected a headstone under the left wheel. It ground to a halt. Even before it did, Bugden was scrambling from the cabin. He peered at Crowe, screamed an obscenity and raced away through the scattered graves, ducking and weaving like someone navigating a minefield. Crowe followed.

Before Crowe could get a clear shot at him, however, the ex-journo reached the downhill side of the cemetery and leapt into the bush. An overgrown track led off across country and downward along the dried-out creek bed. Crowe guessed the path made its meandering way toward the coast, cutting across the rugged terrain where the road had twisted and dog-legged endlessly just to travel maybe one or two kilometres as the crow flies. The sun was low, almost obscured where the bush tangled in on itself. Soon he'd never be able to find Bugden. And what then? More harassment? More bits of Banerjee?

Crowe leapt the low fence defining the boundary of the cemetery's spoilt ground, hoping he'd be able to follow Bugden, that he'd see him once he rounded the next corner. Then the next. He took in as much as he could of the scrub to either side, not wanting to miss if Bugden tried to leave the track. He saw nothing. Not ahead; not in the thrashing shadows growing within the thickets of lantana; not among the groves and clumps of bush. After a few minutes, he stopped to listen. Wind was still raging in the treetops, muffling whatever noise Bugden might've been making.

'Bugden!' he yelled, frustrated. His voice was lost in the swish and creaking of wind in the trees. The sky became overcast, the air stormy.

Crowe ran on.

At the base of a shallow corridor between two rock outcrops, the path opened into a clearing. Beyond it, the bush continued, thicker than ever. No sign of Bugden. He'd made it across without Crowe seeing him, and he might've gone any of a dozen ways. Crowe doubted his ability to follow the trail. The air had thickened into a liquid grain, dripping darkness across the matted foliage. A cockatoo flew overhead, a white spectre shrieking its harsh metallic warning against the blue-grey clouds.

Useless. He'd lost the bastard.

38

INCREASINGLY, BANERJEE HAD BEEN HEARING THINGS — PHANTOM movement and ghostly voices. They were never clear, never meaningful, always garbled and incoherent. They were the cries of her own fears.

Once, though, a voice had caught her unawares, when she was half asleep. *Can you hear me? Please.* Banerjee was so out-of-it, she'd barely registered the sound. She looked up.

I'm a prisoner here, like you.

The words had, at that moment, seemed so real, so present, she'd pushed herself onto her knees to look around. She could see nothing except for the few vague shapes allowed by her night-adjusted eyes, all familiar now.

'Who's there?' she called but got no reply. It had to have been a dream. She fell back against the wall, pressing her hands to her ears, but the voices in her head continued unabated.

Hours went by.

The ghosts were still screaming when Banerjee became aware of something new: a series of staccato noises.

Gunshots!

That meant a glitch in her captor's plan? Crowe? The police? Something else entirely? Whatever, surely she could take advantage of it. Somehow.

She stumbled blindly toward the door. She began thumping on the steel barrier with her right hand and calling out for help. Useless. No one would hear.

What if it was the police? She had to let them know she was here.

On the other hand, was she willing to risk the possibility that her captor, the Scavenger, was still alive and free, and would inevitably come for her? Then she realised that the noise had stopped. Instead of being demoralised, she was energised. Now more than ever, she needed to have a contingency plan. She needed something to fight back with.

She shuffled through the dark over to the metal table she knew was there; one time he'd left food on it. The food had been stew, cold and nasty smelling, but she'd eaten as much as she could stomach to bolster her strength. Somewhat to her surprise, she hadn't thrown the muck up.

She hadn't gained much strength from it, of course, except maybe a stronger determination to get out of the dank hole. If he hadn't been shot by police, the Scavenger would be dropping by soon, probably to finish her off. She'd need to do something to escape once he opened the door. If Crowe or the police had taken him down, she needed to draw attention to her plight. Chances were they didn't even know she was here, wherever 'here' was.

The table was solid enough but not too heavy. She dragged it to where she calculated was the centre of the room. Her right hand bore most of the effort as any attempt to use her left, with its four remaining fingers, caused muscle strain that made her wound ache badly. She felt new blood leaking from the makeshift bandages. Ignoring it, she climbed onto the tabletop, shakily stood and began waving her good hand around in the dark, even as her brain kept telling her she was about to fall.

The globe was somewhere there, dangling on a short cord. She's seen it in those moments when the globe had been turned on. Her questing fingers found nothing. She shuffled warily along the table. Still nothing. She went back the other way. Still couldn't find it. At the edge of despair, she gave an extreme flourish: her fingertips feather-touched something. She swiped again, hooked the globe and tugged. It came out of its socket with a protesting snap, and Banerjee tossed it aside. It shattered somewhere in the dark.

Feeling a little more hopeful, she climbed down. The next part of the plan was more problematic: pulling the table closer to the door. More effort, more pain, more blood. When she felt around to make sure it was close enough, she took a deep breath and steeled herself: lifting the table and tipping it on its short end required both hands, and the agony in her injured limb made her nauseated and faint. But she positioned the table so it was hopefully out of direct line of sight of anyone opening the door. Then she fetched the metal water jug, went to the window in the door and called for help as loudly as she could while banging the metal jug against the grille. Hopefully the banshee noise would vibrate through the corridors loud enough to draw attention. Anyone's. She wasn't very hopeful about that, but even a small chance was worth taking at this point.

The rhythm became almost hallucinatory after a while, the screams and the clanging morphing into a chant, like some ancient evocation. It boiled up from deep inside her – a primal paean that, without intent, brought the forces of the dead into the real world.

She saw a young woman standing in the corridor just to the left of the door. Banerjee shouldn't have been able to see anything as the lights were all out and the corridor was dark. But there the figure was, staring at her with an unworldly stillness. For a moment, it wasn't odd at all, that figure, as though it was meant to be there and Banerjee was meant to see her. But then reality wiped away the sense of inevitability and Banerjee stopped striking the door with the jug, overcome by irrational terror.

'Who are you?' she whispered. 'What do you want?'

The present was only what she made it out to be, wasn't it? Reconstructed from the remnants of the past still lingering in her back brain? Ghosts that were the manifestation of memories crying out for resolution? Pleas for help or screams of vengeance given form and substance, urging her to understand, to do something, to live?

'Who are you?' she repeated.

The spectral figure held up one hand. Three of her fingers were missing, and in that moment Banerjee could see blood and torn flesh and slashed clothes.

He's coming, the girl whispered.

Banerjee jerked back in surprise, closing her eyes as she did. She opened them again immediately, and the phantom was gone.

He's coming.

Another hangover from her earlier delirium? Banerjee pushed down her fear, pulled back the tears that were swelling.

Okay then. Ghosts or not, she was getting out of here.

'Come on, Ms Phantom!' she yelled. 'I get it. You're real! Help me now!'

Wait! What was that? Footsteps?

Banerjee reined in her imagination and listened. Someone *was* coming. The distinct, irregular gait echoed from somewhere along the corridor.

It was him.

Bravado blossomed in her. 'Let me out of here, you brain-dead maggot!' she screeched. 'Drop by for a chat and a cuppa tea, and we'll *talk* about it, eh? Talk, talk, bloody talk! It's what cunts like me do, isn't it? Talk!'

He was close. She struck at the door with the jug again.

'Who've you been shooting at? The cops maybe? If I keep this up will someone hear—'

Heavy steps. Right in front of her. The corridor lighting came on, splashing its dull lambency across the walls. A face was suddenly there, in the gaps between the metal bars – a maleficent phantom.

'Shut it!' he growled. 'I haven't got time for ya right now.'

'Oh? What's up? Crows squawking at the door?' She banged the jug again and screaming obscenities.

'Shut the fuck up!'

'Don't feel like it! Why don't you go chew on your shrivelled balls? All they're good for, is my professional opinion! I've never met a more emasculated piece of shit than you in my whole career.'

He drew back, making a noise deep in his throat. 'I was gonna deal with ya later, but now will do just fine—'

Banerjee heard the click of the switch in the corridor, but her cell remained a place of shadows.

'Oops!' she said. 'No light in here. How's your night vision?'

He swore and began fumbling with keys.

She stepped back, quickly manoeuvring herself into position between the legs of the table, then tilted it until it was balanced *just* on its top edge. The lock clicked. Banerjee's left wrist was wracked with searing pain, and she could feel blood dribbling down her arm. The door began to creak open. Her muscles strained, shifting the table just past tipping point.

'Don't ya go frettin' now, honey!' the man said. 'I'm only gonna put ya out of ya misery – and mine!'

The door was more than half open and he hadn't noticed what she was doing. She shoved on the table. It toppled.

The table crashed down, striking first the edge of the door then hitting her tormenter. He howled. The noise echoed around the stone walls, rebounding along the corridor and disappearing into the distance like an exorcised demon. The man stumbled back, swearing, lost his balance and fell. Banerjee ran forward, hoping to get past her captor while he was down. But even down he was too fast. He kicked back against the upturned table, which Banerjee had been trying to climb over. She lost her balance when it shifted, and her captor was suddenly in front of her. He pushed her back, hard.

'Stupid slag!' he snarled.

She crawled into the thicker darkness, away from the pale, distant illumination coming from the corridor.

There was the sound of grinding: he'd kicked the table away from the threshold. 'Can't hide from me, bitch.' The man's silhouette loomed in the doorway as he crooned, 'Come to papa! C'mon. Okay, who doesn't love a bit of hide 'n' seek?'

Banerjee remained silent, not giving him any way to easily locate her.

'I'm gonna enjoy—'

A bell rang. Loud. It sounded electronic, its pseudo-peal vibrating through the guts of the building like a high-pitched, oscillating whine. A warning siren.

Banerjee said nothing. Didn't move. Didn't breathe.

'Fuck!' her captor growled, clearly annoyed. 'I gotta go. But ya might as well make ya peace with whatever deity you've sold your soul to, 'cause you're dead now, baby. I'll be back.'

He dragged the door shut. It banged against the lintel as though it didn't fit. But he wrenched it violently and it ground shut with an ominous metallic echo.

'Don't wait up, honey!' Then he was gone, footsteps moving fast.

The bell must have heralded something important, but the weight of her failure drowned any curiosity. That futile escapade had been her last chance to get out as nearly in one piece as possible. He wouldn't fall for that sort of ambush again. Next time he'd have light. A gun. As it stood, Banerjee was as good as dead.

Sobbing, she clambered over the upturned table to the door and started banging on it with her uninjured fist. She stuck her fingers through the grille, gripped the bars and pulled. She had no intent, no expectations – it was a purely physical expression of her anger and frustration.

And the door shifted. She let go, startled. For a moment, she stood staring at it. Dim light still drifted through the corridor beyond, but with something of a shock, Banerjee realised some of that light was visible in an erratic line between the door and the jamb, at the level of the handle and lock.

She leaned down and peered into the gap. The impact of the table had bent the door out of shape and the locking mechanism couldn't quite latch.

She put both hands to the grille, bit her lip, and *pulled*. Hard. The metal door made a grinding, snarly groan, and opened. She stumbled back, cursing momentum and the sudden escalation in pain in her left hand. Breathing heavily, *easy, easy,* she tried to calm down. The pain receded. She breathed out. In. Out. Calm.

What now?

'Well, Not-Dead-Yet-Meera,' she said, 'let's get the hell out of here.'

She stepped into the corridor.

At that moment, the corridor lights started to fade. Must have been on a timer. The shadows began to engulf her. She almost welcomed them.

Somewhere above, thunder rumbled, sending shivers through the building.

Which way? Left or right. The killer had raced off to the left, but he had come from the right. Had he just returned from somewhere outside the building? Perhaps. But at least she could, for a while, assume if she went right she wouldn't run into him by accident.

She headed off into the darkening passageway.

39

No lights were on in the sanatorium when Crowe got back. That made him nervous. He couldn't imagine Gail was happy to crouch in the growing gloom with Banger, who was surely a corpse by now. Gail was tough, but not so self-confident she'd scorn the reassurance of light.

A storm flickered in the distance beyond the trees and ridges. Its breath swept over the escarpment and slammed against Crowe, making him falter as he approached the main building. He was tired. Tired of the uphill hike, tired of the irresolution. Where was Bugden now? Could the ex-journo have returned before him? Would he bother, considering how little spunk he'd shown in confronting their unexpected incursion? Crowe didn't know. But hadn't getting Crowe here been his plan? Crowe checked the cabin of the man's ute. The shotgun was still there, so he took it with him. No point leaving it lying around. It was a two-shot gun and empty, but he found an unused cartridge under the front seat. Bugden must've dropped it in his panic to get moving. That's what he had been feeling around for. Crowe could find no extra ammunition in the ute, but that one shot might be of use.

No one was in the front room where he'd left Gail and Banger, and that pushed Crowe's weariness into unease. The only evidence of Banger's demise was the streaks of blood on the floor, an indication he'd been dragged off. By Gail? Unlikely. The place was quiet, though when he listened hard, he realised the wind had dropped, and faintly, back behind the residual rustle of air brushing the outside of the building, there was something else, and not the blood in his temples. It sounded like an engine. An electricity generator? Someone must have started it after they'd entered the place. That would explain the sudden presence of power where before there'd been none.

And then Crowe saw the spill of light in the hall beyond – just a smear, a trail left behind by some giant slug. Maybe it was coming from the kitchen? Or beyond that, the pantry. That's where Gail would wait for him.

He moved quietly. She had his Beretta, and he certainly didn't want to surprise her into shooting him, yet something kept him from calling out. He wasn't confident all was well. There were few obvious sounds and none close by, but in a moment of unusual stillness, he thought he heard someone screaming. And banging. But the noise was so distant, so faint, he couldn't be sure it was more than a night bird squawking or his strung-out imagination.

One thing he was utterly conscious of was the stale, rotten smell permeating the building. It made him even more nervous. He held his gun in his right hand, ready to shoot at anything, and the shotgun was cradled in his left, jammed into the crook of his arm, his finger taut on the trigger. He stopped just outside the kitchen door and listened.

An alarm went off, an electronic screech that echoed around him like a banshee filling the building with its fury. Shock knifed through him, flattening him against the wall. It seemed to go on forever.

Then, just as suddenly, the alarm stopped. The silence stunned him nearly as much as the noise had.

'Won't you come in, Mr Crowe?' a voice whispered from deep within the stillness.

Crowe froze. He held his breath. Had that happened? The voice had been there, yeah, though for a moment Crowe wasn't sure if he'd imagined it.

'It's a pleasure to have you here,' said the voice. It sounded slightly familiar, but not like any manifestation of Bugden.

'Do not be afraid, Mr Crowe! We are waiting, your lady friend and I.'

The voice continued to linger at a nexus between reality and memory, tenuously grasping at sense. Crowe didn't move, breathing in shallow gasps, his mind playing with possibilities. For all he knew Gail was already dead. No, he didn't dare think that!

'Mr Crowe,' the voice continued, 'you are not a fool, generally speaking, so try not to act like one. Please come around the corner of the door. You will be able to see us. The woman is safe, for the moment, though I am holding a scalpel at her throat, and if I get impatient, or if you threaten me, I *will* kill her. You might kill me, but you would lose her, too. I know you care for her enough to be made predictable. It's a weakness, albeit a commendable one.'

The words skidded through Crowe and turned into a muscular tension that began aching in his shoulders. This had to be the Scavenger.

'Throw the gun aside, please,' the voice continued. 'Why take chances? If you attempt to shoot me, the woman dies before I do.' He laughed, a low snicker that was almost a cough. Crowe could tell there was no way this man, whoever he was, accepted even the possibility of his own death. 'You see, I don't believe you will sacrifice her. I don't think you are so afraid of me that you feel we can't talk. After all, we've had some pleasant exchanges in the past.'

Crowe tried to think. Was there any way of taking him by surprise?

'Please, Mr Crowe,' the voice continued. 'I have so looked forward to meeting you face-to-face yet again, in the open this time, without subterfuge – to work together, discussing how you can help save mankind.'

Meeting face-to-face *yet again*? *Other pleasant exchanges*? There it was: the claimed familiarity.

'Is that you, Bugden?' he said.

The voice produced a brief snicker. 'No points there, Mr Crowe. You know I'm not him. My Igor isn't here right now, though he's on his way.'

'Whatever you reckon,' Crowe said, tossing the shotgun into the open doorway so the Scavenger could see him cooperating. 'But why should I talk to a lunatic?'

'Lunatic?' His voice flared for a moment, hard with indignity. 'You don't believe that. You're teasing me, testing.'

'Why don't you tell me how the hell it's sane to build a sculpture out of corpses?'

The Scavenger chuckled. 'Now I know you're joking. *That* is something you must surely understand.'

'Tell me about it.'

'Like this? Around a corner, hiding like a frightened mouse? Face me like the man I know you are?'

'Let's just say I'm not very trusting. How about you start talking and maybe I'll join you when I'm ready – face-to-face?'

'This is about more than trust, Mr Crowe. This is about respect.'

Crowe listened for him to keep talking, intent on ducking out the front way and dashing around to the kitchen when he did. But his peripheral awareness latched onto something behind him. He began to turn and was struck hard across the base of the neck. Pain lanced through him – sharp, like knives – as he slammed forward against the wall. He tried to steady himself but was hit again. The impact flung him across the open doorway and, as he fell, he saw two figures, one in a chair – Gail. She was slumped forward as far as her bonds would let her. Behind her, bending over her, was a stubby figure dressed in what looked like a lab coat. The man's face was covered by a surgical mask. Crowe tried to point his gun toward him, confused about how the man had managed to slug him, but he couldn't be sure he wouldn't hit Gail and he groaned instead. She might still be alive. Crowe rolled, but something weighty slammed onto him and a stink he recognised told him Bugden was right there at his back.

His mind began to drift as though he'd been drugged yet again. He hadn't felt any needle – or had he? He struck out at the large shape looming over him, but his fist moved as though through mud. Suddenly a gun barrel was pushed hard against his forehead. His own?

'Bye bye, Crowie,' someone said.

'Don't hurt him!' demanded the other voice.

'Just wanna knock him out. Safer than way.'

'I don't want his brain injured, fool. Can you not see how helpless he is? Bring him to me.'

Rough hands grabbed Crowe and dragged him into the room.

An image of himself being consumed by the Scavenger's grotesque creation flashed across Crowe's mind as he slipped into hallucinatory numbness, hoping the fucked-up monstrosity would at least get indigestion.

He stared into a pair of familiar eyes. They were deep, as though containing a new universe of possibilities, a vast emptiness awaiting the Big Bang.

I know you, he wanted to say, but he could no longer form the words.

'Your coming was preordained, Mr Crowe,' the man said. 'There's a storm brewing. My course is now clear. Tonight, everything changes.'

40

BANERJEE HAD PASSED THE DOOR OF THE CELL NEXT TO THE ONE SHE'D occupied and had reached another door, largely invisible in the deepening gloom, when she heard a voice whisper: '*Help me!*' Startled, she pressed back against the wall opposite.

'*Please, help me!*' the voice said again. It was faint. Might have been an echo of the voices that had been shouting inside her head for the past few days. Yet there was something more immediate about it. It clearly belonged to a young woman. '*I need you to help him.*'

Help him? Calming herself, though uncertain whether this were real or not, Banerjee whispered back, 'Is someone there?'

'*You know him,*' the voice said, trembling in her ears, '*Help me! I need Mr Crowe. Bring him to me—*'

Mr Crowe? It wanted Mike Crowe?

The voice stopped abruptly, as though there was a limit to how much it could articulate each time. Against her better judgement, Banerjee approached the door. It was open but not by much. The gap didn't reveal what lay beyond. She peered in through the grille. It was too dark inside to see anything and too far from what remained of the corridor lights, which were almost completely gone now. She felt around, hoping there was a switch near her. There was, but did she dare flick it on? What if her captor noticed and realised what it meant?

'*Help me!*'

The lighting appeared to work in sections along the corridor, and the alarm had no doubt summoned the Scavenger out of this network of rooms altogether, taking him into the main, ground-level building. She decided to risk it. A life could be at stake. She located two switches and flicked the first. Nothing happened. She tried the second. A dim light filled the corridor.

Banerjee peered through the grille into the room. As in her prison cell, there was little spill of light and the place remained largely in blackout mode. But here the bulb was directly in front of the door and enough of its illumination got through to show her a shape in the shadows. It seemed to be a woman leaning up against the wall.

'Are you okay?' Banerjee asked, instantly cursing herself for directing such a stupid question toward this victim. Of course, she wasn't okay.

The figure didn't answer. Nor did she move.

Taking a deep breath, Banerjee grabbed the handle and pushed inward. The metal door opened easily, surprising her so much she jerked her hand away. The door creaked to a halt.

Okay, Banerjee thought, looking in at the light-streaked shadows that filled the room, *now I have to go in*. Very carefully, she edged the door further open and with even greater caution stepped into the space. She glanced around but could see very little. A few more steps, however, allowed her to establish the shadowy body of a young woman tied to the wall. Banerjee knelt beside her and leaned closer, stretching out her hand to touch the woman's arm. As her fingers met the cold, leathery skin, a sense of total loss swept over her – a terrible awareness that there was no life here and hadn't been for a long time. She pulled her hand away.

Seen close-up, even in the prevailing gloom, it was obvious the corpse had been 'preserved' by an attempt at taxidermy and a poor one at that. Visible skin on her face had been slashed, more so over her arms and legs, and the wounds sewn up with little skill. Three fingers were missing from her right hand. The clothes too had been poorly repaired. The stitching and bloodstains on them suggested that massive damage had been inflicted on the victim's chest and stomach. The original damage must have been horrendous. From what Banerjee could see of her face, the victim had been in her late teens. Her eye sockets were empty, but her hair had been carefully combed and spread over her shoulders. The 'expression' on her face was terrible in its artificially made-up, unnatural stillness.

Banerjee asked herself what sort of monster could have done this, but she knew exactly who it must have been and what sort of monster he was. But why? The fact that the corpse had been reconstructed and embalmed to make it last made this seem like a shrine. She noticed an array of markings on the wall behind the corpse. Leaning close and squinting at them, she could see that some were mystic signs; she had seen their like before but didn't know what they meant. Some seemed meaningless. Just decoration. Her knee knocked against a vase with dead flowers in it. She winced, as though touching it was a further violation.

She moved away. This display somehow held the key to the genesis of the Scavenger's mania. But she had no time or stomach for answering such questions right now.

But what of the voice she'd heard earlier, calling to her? If not the fetishised corpse, then who? She stood and stared into the darkness, trying to see the darker shadow of a figure lurking in the gloom. Nothing.

'Is there anyone here?' Her voice trembled with a barely suppressed dread of what might answer, but there was no response. She backed toward the door. Stepped out into the corridor. By this time, she'd convinced herself that the voice had been in her head, a delusion like the other times she'd heard voices. As for the coincidence of stumbling upon a preserved corpse, she preferred to dismiss it. If this was the lair of the Scavenger, she could expect to stumble upon body parts. But not whole bodies, mummified. And not a young woman. It didn't fit the Scavenger's MO. So, what did it mean? Suddenly Banerjee was filled with a renewed urgency just to get away.

Darkness thickened and became mustier as she left behind the diminishing light. She continued along the corridor, shuffling through the growing gloom like an old, blind woman. She felt her way past a few more doors but heard no voices. Her journey through the dark seemed to go on forever, though she was sure there was a psychological factor at play, a metaphorical claw scratching at her brain, confusing her. She was moving too slowly. Maybe, just maybe, she was stopping without realising what she was doing. Stopping and staring into the darkness, thinking she was moving but in fact merely staring into her own mind, shuffling along an inner labyrinth that was filled with a drifting fog as the outer darkness leaked into her. It was the same darkness that had shown her the corpse, and the ghost, of a young woman.

She shook herself free of the paralysis. She was better than this. Stronger. She had to keep going. A lot – her life, if nothing else – was at stake.

Almost immediately (if her sense of time was still working at all), while dragging her aching left hand lightly over the wall, the stonework disappeared, leaving an unexpected void. She turned to look. Stairs. She could barely make them out, but they went upward, like floating phantoms. At the top, a low, yellowish light smudged the murk, enough to make the stairs vaguely discernible. Above the top step, the dark was textured. A door?

Tentatively, she felt her way up the stone stairs. The door at the top was wooden and old. Not very large. About two-thirds her height. She squinted and could make out a handle. She turned it. It didn't budge. Swearing, she took the corroded metal ring and put all her weight into turning it. A stab of pain shot through her injured left hand. She didn't let up. After a moment, with a grinding snarl, the handle moved and the bolt released. Slowly, she opened the door. Outside, the night was wet and windy, her path blocked by vegetation. It smelt like freedom.

They need help.

A voice? It had sounded like the one she'd heard earlier, but the words had been muffled and indistinct. She looked around and could see no one. Her subconscious thoughts were bubbling to the surface again. But who did her subconscious think needed help? A distant flash of lightning drew her attention. The towering escarpment showed above the trees. What she could see before her was a cemetery, an old one. Lightning flashed again and thunder followed – not immediately, but more contiguous with the lightning than moments ago. The storm was moving toward them, heralded by rolling black clouds. The landscape was going to get even darker very soon. A rough path ran through the cemetery, so she followed it.

Nearer the far side, she caught sight of what looked like a battered ute, its wheels jammed among damaged headstones. It appeared to have smashed through the already shattered fence that had been trying to keep out both the encroaching vegetation and vandals for a long time, totally without success. One headlight flickered a dull beam across trees and nearby graves. She cautiously moved toward it. It could very well be the vehicle that had brought her to this place. What had happened? She felt panic beginning to grow. She backed away from the vehicle and the cemetery where it had met its end. Deeply afraid, she hurried through the bush, veering from a building she could see through the trees. Wind pounded against her and she cringed as a flash of lightning over the escarpment was followed immediately by a burst of thunder that vibrated in the ground under her feet. Rain began to lash her. The moon disappeared completely behind a huge wave of cloud.

Another burst of lightning sparked off something in the bush to her right. It was red and metallic, its outlines too defined not to be man-made. She crouched down, hiding from it behind an enormous clump of cleavers weed. Cautiously she watched–

They need help!

Again? The barely heard words almost made her lose her balance and fall backwards. She steadied herself and listened. All she could hear now was wind howling in the trees.

After a moment, she crept toward the spot where she'd seen the partially visible object. Nothing leapt out from the bushes. No one spoke. As she drew close, lightning flashed again and for a moment she could see what the hidden object was. A car. A Mazda, to be precise. A red Mazda. She'd seen it before. Or one like it. It had belonged to Gail Veitch, the journalist. What was it doing here, hidden amongst the trees?

Afraid of what this might mean, she glanced around, half hoping Crowe and Veitch would miraculously appear and stop her current train of thought, the demands of responsibility, from growing stronger. But she knew what she had to do. Crowe and Veitch were in the Scavenger's lair, and they were in trouble. It explained why things had gone silent after the Scavenger quit his attack on her, why he'd rushed away, summoned by some sort of alarm. It's why she'd heard no ongoing sound of conflict, had detected no evidence of Crowe's presence. No police sirens. Nothing. After the initial shootings, it had gone quiet. She'd known all along.

They need help, her memory whispered.

And there was only her available to give it.

41

CROWE WAS IN HELL AND REALISED HE'D BEEN THERE BEFORE.

A sickening grotesquerie hardened into focus. At first, he panicked, thinking it was alive and coming for him. He squirmed against bonds that held him hard on a flat surface. The smell made him cough and choke.

'Give him a drink!' a voice said.

Not the monster. That stood on its network of wiring against the far wall, more dead than any corpse Crowe had ever seen. It was the epitome of dead. A glass of clear liquid, held in a scrawny hand, appeared in front of Crowe's face. The glass tilted against his lips. Water. It tasted metallic.

'Piss off!' he coughed.

'Ya too negative, Mikey.' Bugden's voice was rich with knowing irony. 'So determinedly ungrateful.'

'Untie me and I'll reconsider it.'

The madman giggled. 'Don't think so, mate.'

Crowe lay strapped to some sort of gurney, one of those things they always had in old mad-scientist movies. From what he could determine out of the corner of his eye, the one he was on was makeshift, a fake or at least old, like everything else in this B-grade mad-scientist 'lab'. A few metres in front of him, fiddling with the wires that hung around the monster like a web, was a figure dressed in cloth pants and a lab coat.

'Who are you?' Crowe demanded.

'We've met,' a voice said. 'Several times. Surely you remember.'

The man turned, hunching slightly. He was solidly built and familiar. As he straightened up, he pulled down the surgical mask. Crowe recognised him at once. At the same time, he realised how deeply wrong he had been all along.

'Jimmy Siegel. You're the fucking Scavenger?' he said.

'I've been reluctant to adopt that moniker.' Siegel came closer, a sombre look on his face. 'If I must have a nickname, I'd prefer to be known as the new Doctor Frankenstein.'

'You're out of your fucking mind.'

Siegel smiled. 'A deliberately provocative remark, Mr Crowe. We don't need to go straight into abuse, surely.' He turned to Bugden, who was standing to one side. 'Is he tightly restrained?'

His accomplice grunted reassurance.

Siegel moved to stand next to Crowe, upright and close, so Crowe could see the anarchic mania in his eyes. How the hell had he not seen this in him before? True, he'd only spoken to the man a couple of times and in very different contexts, but Crowe's intuition had been completely fooled. As Waldheim's employee, Siegel had been ordinary, kindly, even likeable.

'You were Lucy's driver,' he said. 'I thought you were a good man, decent. Why this?' He glanced around the room.

'I'm still a good man, if flawed, like all men. Indeed, I seek to become a better man, one more worthy of Lucy.' He looked sorrowful. 'I know she would have wanted this. She gave me Mary Shelley's book to read, for me to improve myself. What I do, I do in her honour. It is clearly what she wanted.'

'And Blowie?'

'This is totally his show,' Bugden said. 'As I've told you, I'm a Watcher, a biographer, if ya like. I keep records.'

Crowe couldn't see his face clearly, but he heard the mockery and knew that Bugden had been feeding ideas to the man, playing on his madness. And of course, he'd done some killing himself.

'You, Mr Crowe, are here to witness me create new life,' announced Siegel, his voice serious and firm. 'In Lucy's name.'

'That thing is the epitome of your new life?' Crowe nodded as best he could toward the monstrosity on the far wall.

'My beautiful, astonishing New-Man.' Siegel looked at the aggregated corpse as though it wasn't coming to bits, rotting, splitting along the seams, a clumsy monstrosity that was about as aesthetic as an open sewer.

Crowe wondered what he saw when he looked at it.

'Humanity transformed,' the Scavenger said, answering the unspoken question.

'Transformed into what? It's a mess.'

'You *look* but you don't *see*.' Siegel said. 'It is imperfect now, yes, but when I give it Life, the imperfections will disappear. All its parts will be integrated. The Life I offer is both a scientific and spiritual miracle. It will make my creation into something beautiful.'

'Right,' Crowe said. 'It looks like a bunch of zombies that've gone through a blender.'

Siegel's eyes stared coldly. 'You can mock,' he said, leaning over Crowe. His breath smelt incongruently fragrant, as though he'd been eating mints. 'But you will nevertheless be witness to the greatest event in human history since the coming of the Messiah. The next stage of evolution is about to be enacted.'

'So, you're God now?'

'I've become the Creator's tool. I take old life and, with it, achieve apotheosis of the flesh.'

'You're a murderer and what you've made is a god-awful mess, a bunch of dead people and misery for those who loved your victims.' Crowe focused on the object embedded in the monster's flesh. 'And why the foetus?'

'It's a focal device, Mr Crowe. I believe it will allow me to succeed where my predecessor failed. It gives me what the original Frankenstein never had: a powerful spiritual conduit. When I discovered it existed and was in this country, I understood it was a gift. It will give my creation the ultimate power – a soul, a binding spiritual force. I knew I must incorporate it into the Work. The Universe offered it to me. I knew I had to take its advice.'

'You're as crazy as Waldheim.'

Siegel looked at Crowe sadly. 'I thought you of all people would understand. I am nothing like that moral degenerate. His medieval Satanic ways are not mine, though I admit I learnt a lot from his research. Yet to a degree he was kind to me, and it's thanks to him that I could gain some education.'

'Did you kill Creedy for him by any chance?'

'Creedy? Of course not, though I was more than happy for the man to die. Walker got that job.'

'Walker killed him?'

'Orchestrated it. A favour for Waldheim and a way up the ladder. I was glad.'

He turned away and wandered back to his creature, where he lovingly fiddled with wires and other pseudo-scientific paraphernalia that surrounded it.

'Watch what ya say.' Bugden leaned close, as though whispering sweet nothings in Crowe's ear. 'He's unstable. Mad as a cut snake.'

'As distinct from you, eh?'

'Oh yes, indeedy. I at least know what I'm doing.' He looked back at Siegel. 'As it is, he wants you alive to witness his triumph. Bait him and maybe he'll just add you to the mix.'

'Your preference, I assume.'

Bugden grinned.

'Where's the woman?' Crowe asked.

'Your bitch journo?' Bugden made a careless gesture toward the side. Crowe twisted around as far as he could and saw Gail there, stretched out like him on a gurney. Just beyond her was another gurney with a figure laid out on it. Banger. 'I convinced him she could be of use,' Bugden whispered. 'It wasn't hard. He has a thing against dishonouring women. I think his mother loved him.' He laughed. 'Yeah, I know. Hard to believe. Anyway, once the *creature* lives and Victor's virility is transformed, he'll want someone to prove it on.' He paused, grinning sardonically. 'Or so I argued.'

'Is she dead?' Crowe growled, a seething fear within him waiting to burst in his chest.

'Dead? What'd ya think we are? Perverts.' He laughed.

'Jonwood?'

'Done for, I'm afraid. You saw to that. Not that it matters. His usefulness has ended.'

'Enough of this chatter. Prepare him!' The Scavenger's voice echoed around the room, grabbing Bugden's attention. 'It's getting close.'

Bugden turned back toward Crowe, tossing an annoying grin his prisoner's way. 'Certainly, Master,' he said.

'And get me another Hagedorn needle from the supply cupboard,' Siegel said. 'This one is not working to my satisfaction.' He held up a bent needle, glaring at it as though it had let him down.

'Righto, boss.'

'And hurry!'

This time Bugden scowled, unseen by the Scavenger, who was once again absorbed in whatever he thought he was doing. He grunted and whispered to Crowe, 'I'm under-appreciated, as you can see.'

'You're both crazy,' Crowe muttered.

'We do our best.'

Bugden bent down and began turning the ratchet that tilted the tabletop. The mechanism growled and whined. Crowe found himself at a 45-degree angle, forced to stare straight across the lab toward the patchwork monster and its fidgeting creator.

'It's front-row visuals for you, ol' mate,' Bugden said, adding, 'And then, no doubt, the thing will eat you for breakfast.' He laughed and strode off, disappearing out a door on the far side of the room. The Scavenger glanced up, gave Crowe an accusing look and went back to his pottering.

'Hey, Siegel!' Crowe yelled after a few minutes. 'What the hell is supposed to happen now?'

From somewhere above, thunder rumbled.

Siegel glanced at the ceiling. Then he turned to Crowe. 'The time is approaching. I have much to do.' He straightened up. 'You think I'm just a publicity seeker, don't you? Taking a journalist like Bugden on-board?'

'I think you're a psychotic madman. You've been killing innocent people, Jimmy.'

'I've been carefully following procedures barely hinted at in many of Mr Waldheim's books, books I took from the older parts of his arcane library. Those, and deductions of my own, have revealed long-sought-after knowledge into the essence of not only understanding the origins of life, but creating it. I'd explain, but it is, I'm afraid, beyond the ability of most of humanity to comprehend. But what it means is, I have not been "killing" these men but have been taking their vitality hidden in folds of weak flesh and indifferent bone.' His eyes widened, his hands gesturing extravagantly, miming his words. 'Put together like this, the men I have recruited will not die. They'll become something so much greater than any of them individually. And as they are transformed, so am I. My soul will be taken into the creature, through the powerful conduit of an unborn child—'

'Why those particular men?'

'They were the Chosen. I saw a likeness in them. Mostly small in stature, they were yet large in spirit, restless and constricted by their lives. They had a passion for more.'

'You watched them?'

'Many of them. Some Igor would seek out for me. I would go, study them, learn about them. When the time came...' He shivered. It wasn't coldness doing it, but a tremor of joy. Tears glistened. 'I would approach them with my offer, at night, under the full moon. They would always accept. No, Mr Crowe, I was never a murderer, never a killer. The police couldn't catch me because they were looking for a psychopath. I'm a scientist. I never murdered anyone. The universe is on my side.'

'Yeah, yeah, sure. What about Sandy and Burger, the couple at my house in Mt St Thomas, eh? That looked like a massacre to me. What the hell did they do to deserve that?'

For a moment, the Scavenger seemed puzzled. 'Sandy?' he said, dismissively. 'You're mistaken. I do not use women in my work. I do this in their honour. I do it for Lucy.' He went back to whatever he'd been doing, clearly disturbed by Crowe's question.

Bugden reappeared, carrying a needle much like the one the Scavenger already had, and a box full of other equipment. 'The storm. It's on the way,' he said to the Scavenger, who looked past Crowe. 'You were right, Master. We've been lucky.'

'It's not luck.' Siegel strode forward. 'See, Mr Crowe? See how the heavens cooperate. It is ordained. God sets his seal on my Great Undertaking, and soon Lucy will join us in glory.'

'Lucy?' Crowe said. 'That's the third time you've mentioned her. What's she got to do with this?'

Siegel ignored his question and moved away. 'Have you finished making those connections?' he asked Bugden.

'Yes, they're done,' the 'assistant' replied in a formal tone.

'Well, come and help with these attachments. We've lots to do.'

The Scavenger began adjusting dials and pulling wires taut. He bustled over to the monstrosity and poked at it yet again, flattening out lumps, smoothing tears in its flesh, connecting loose wires. Crowe noticed Pukalski's head had been fully stitched onto the enormous shoulders.

'If this storm develops as I hope, you'll have plenty to be afraid of before the night is over,' Siegel muttered as if to himself.

'What's he going to do?' Crowe asked.

'Do?' Bugden replied, opening his arms in an encompassing gesture. 'This is the Great Moment. The beginning of the ritual. Old Vic there is gonna bring his boogeyman to life.'

'Sure he is.'

Bugden chuckled. 'What's it matter what you or I believe will happen? What a story, eh? It's what I've been preparin' for.'

'What'll he do when it doesn't work?'

'God knows, but it should be entertaining. The story will grow some bigger, hairier legs perhaps and make me famous!'

'Infamous, more likely.'

'Whatever the outcome, I was ready to end this. It's gone on too long. I hoped your presence would be a catalyst. And I was right.' He grinned. 'The timing was perfect. There's even a storm outside. A bloody great electrical storm, miraculously predicted by the weather bureau.' He turned and, raising his voice, declared, 'The storm is vital.'

Siegel looked around, deadly serious. 'This storm will be magnificent,' he screeched. 'All the electrical secrets of Heaven!'

'It's the Frankenstein movie,' Crowe suddenly twigged. 'That's the ritual!'

'Great, isn't it?' whispered Bugden, leaning at him. 'He's so crazy his brain's gonna explode and we're all here to see it. Sadly, I doubt you'll survive the night.'

Another crash of thunder tore through the walls, louder this time, not overhead, but close. The Scavenger reacted by leaping up and shuffling toward Crowe.

'It's time,' he said, standing face-to-face, no longer hunched over, pinning Crowe with a look. 'Time for you to play your role.'

'Role?'

Siegel, totally immersed in his performance, came closer. Crowe felt fear squirm into his belly as the madman shoved his face up against his. Now he smelt rotting flesh. Had he been eating parts of his victims?

'You must witness everything,' Siegel said, 'for you're to become part of it, as you were always destined to be, ever since you talked to me in the days following Lucy's death, and confirmed it when I met you again in the pub. You clearly loved and respected her. You'll bring her here to me.'

'Bring her?'

'She's nearby, you see. She's ready. I can feel her spirit coming closer.'

Crowe pulled against his bonds. They wouldn't give. 'You'll never get away with this,' he said. 'The cops will find you eventually.'

'What do I care for the police?' Siegel mugged to a non-existent camera. 'What's the meaning of Law? I'm transforming the society that makes the law. When my creature is walking in the open air – and I'm within it, huge and fearsome and virile – what will the police matter to me then? I'll have atoned for my sins by ushering in the future of mankind.'

Right on cue, a rolling tremor of thunder shuddered into the cellar from above.

'See? One man crazy,' Siegel cried, 'three very sane spectators!'

42

As it happened, four spectators were present, though Banerjee would prefer the lunatic who had sprouted the words to never discover that fact. She was more scared than she'd ever been, crouching just out of sight behind the half-open door. She had crept into the building, searched and finally followed the voices she could hear as little more than an auditory anomaly underlying what should have been only wind and the occasional crack of thunder. The intermittent sound led her down into the building's below-ground level via the kitchen – a different set of rooms to those she was already familiar with – until the susurration became coherent, if delusional, sentences. She'd glanced through the gap between the door and its jamb, seen Crowe and Gail tied down on archaic operating tables, her tormentor and another man dressed like a 1930s mad scientist, and the huge pile of body parts sewn into the rough shape of a man-monster hanging on a web of electrical wires, and found terror had sapped her mind of acceptable psychologist jargon, if not rationality itself.

'When my creature is walking in the open air–' the Scavenger said, in front of Crowe, who was tilted nearly upright on his gurney '–and I am within it, huge and fearsome and virile, what will the police matter to me then?'

At least her predictions about the man's obsession with Frankenstein had been correct, just as his use of the term 'virile' suggested the sexual guilt she'd diagnosed as his primary psychosis. That was some comfort.

Thunder rumbled.

She needed to act, to do something positive. If she'd had a gun, maybe a straightforward confrontation would have been feasible. But all she had was a lump of wood she'd picked up on her way into the building. True, she had driven off her tormentor with a physical attack, but she doubted it would work again – especially in this context. Even Crowe had proven to be no match for both her gaoler and the actual Scavenger. Crowe, however, might be the only one here with even the ghost of a chance of taking them down. Maybe if she could somehow untie him? That would involve sneaking into the room.

'In 15 minutes the storm should be at its height. Then we'll be ready,' the Scavenger pronounced.

Fifteen minutes? Ready? What will happen then? Banerjee wondered.

Whatever it was, she didn't expect it would be good.

She had to do something.

Gail groaned and shifted on her gurney as though the Scavenger's pronouncements were too much to swallow, even when you were more or less unconscious. Like Crowe, she was strapped down, though unlike the thick leather thongs that kept Crowe in place, hers appeared to be ordinary rope.

'I gave her a stronger dose than I gave you,' Siegel explained to Crowe. 'But she's waking now, in time for the Great Ceremony.' He looked at the ceiling and what he imagined lay beyond it. 'In 15 minutes the storm should be at its height. Then we'll be ready,' he quoted.

Crowe strained against the bonds, making the bench rattle. Hopeless. 'You can't bring dead people back to life, Jimmy. Especially not when they're in bits.'

'I told you, Mr Crowe. They're not dead. Only sleeping. They were sedated, like you, like your woman, and like her they'll live again. Only they will awaken in one body, multiple-souled, a giant!' He shuffled close again, so Crowe could see the sallow, almost transparent quality of his skin. 'I've been trapped in a pall of insignificance for too long. I've been ignored because of it. No more. I too will be there when the Creature wakes. I'll see through its eyes, feel through its skin, crush with its hands. I'll be with my one true love once more, who in her turn will be given new life, and our progeny will bring back the race of *gods*. You're a man of power, Mr Crowe. Surely you understand. That's why you're here.'

'Why pick on me for this privilege?'

'You were kind to Lucy.' He condescendingly patted Crowe's cheek. His touch made Crowe shudder. 'And I know she liked you.' A crooked smile sped across his face before he turned back to his 'preparations'.

'Actually, it was me who suggested bringing you in,' whispered Bugden, appearing beside him and leaning close. Crowe looked into Bugden's eyes; they were seething with ironic messages. 'Clever of me, eh?'

'You knew Skarratt was going to be at Wilkinson's Bay that night?'

'More or less. I got close to old Banger, used to get inside info from him when I was writin' shit for the papers. Not as stupid as he seemed, and he had ears and could keep his mouth shut. He knew about Skarratt, though not everything. Bit of a cock-up in the end. He didn't know what was really goin' on. He didn't know about you.'

'Did he tell you he was working a con with Skarratt and Tansey?'

'Was he? There ya go. Double dipping. More cunning than I woulda given him credit for.' He sighed. 'Guess he wanted the money for himself.' He gestured toward Jonwood's corpse. 'We'll never know for sure what he was really up to.'

So, Crowe reasoned, Siegel recognises Crowe that night and recognition starts him off on a new tack. He discusses it with his 'Igor', who disapproves at first, but in the end approaches Crowe, trying to draw him in. The mad reporter decides he likes the synchronicity, threads weaving together from his previous research – the killer, Pukalski, Crowe. But he turns resentful when Crowe is less than cooperative. That's when he kidnaps Banerjee.

'Where is she?' Crowe said, rather loudly. 'The woman you kidnapped. You cut off her finger.'

Siegel must have heard. He looked back, frowning, but silent.

'Shush!' Bugden glanced at Siegel. 'We don't know what you're talking about!'

'The hell you don't!'

'There's no such woman,' he added, his rheumy eyes glancing toward the Scavenger.

Something twigged. The old fool was scared, Crowe realised. But of what? Had Banerjee escaped him?

'She's a consultant with connections to the federal police,' Crowe said. 'You're messing with the big kids. It won't go well.'

Siegel came over and touched Crowe on the chest. In that moment, Crowe felt a sensation that was almost pain. He tried to pull away.

'I told you, Mr Crowe,' Siegel said gently, 'I don't kill women and would never condone such a thing. Such criminality runs counter to my purpose. If women have been hurt, it was not related to my experiment.'

His intense stare drilled into Crowe, as though searching for something inside him. Would he find what he was looking for? And if he did, what would he do with the knowledge? Crowe felt an uncharacteristic terror growing like a cancer in his gut. This was certainly not the Siegel he had known. This one had, no doubt, always been there, but only as a potential. Something had let it out. Perhaps forced it out. With a grunt, he pushed the terror back into an inner darkness where there was nothing for it to feed on, and smirked at the Scavenger with calculated insolence.

'Well, you sure don't act like a man who gives a damn about women,' he said.

Siegel pulled away, a sharp and barely contained anger contorting his face. The hand that had been touching Crowe's chest turned into a fist.

'You know nothing of me,' he growled. 'Who are you to dictate how I should act? If women have been hurt, I had nothing to do with it.'

At that moment the man's words and something in his anger sparked a memory in Crowe. For perhaps the first time he saw not only driver Jimmy Siegel but the face of a killer. Memory exploded in his head.

The flashlight pulls away, revealing meaningless splatter on the wall behind Lucy's corpse. He throws the beam back across her face. Her eyes are dull, flesh leached to wax. Blood lies in runnels on her cheeks as though she's been crying. His guess is, she's been dead for several hours at least.

He raises the torch, and for a moment the meaningless blood splatters seem to change, forming rough lettering over the wall. This time it spells out a name.

In the aftermath of that distorted memory flash, he felt his mind fill with more memories – memories that weren't his at all.

Siegel's snarling face looms above, eyes seething with anger. Behind him, the space is dark and claustrophobic, though spill from the one dim light hovering slightly to the right illuminates him enough and causes the dim images of tools, shelving and other indistinguishable objects to form a ghostly texture in the shadows.

'You owe me, Lucy,' he growls. 'I've been patient, but your persistent denials, your disinterest, are more than I can take. I love you. You must know that.'

'Leave me alone!' says a young woman's voice, wavering with fear.

'I've been friendly.' He leans closer. 'I've been kind. I defended you. I gave you presents.' The madness is clear in his face now, despite the dim lighting. 'You didn't throw them away. And you helped me imagine a different future for myself and for you. But you won't let me touch you. You rejected me when I made my love clear. Now you seek to hide from me—'

'I thought you were doing your job. I've always tried to be polite, but now you want too much, Jimmy. You won't leave me alone. You're just as bad as Dale—'

'I'm nothing like that scumbag.' He sneers. 'I defended you. But condescension, that's all you give me. You look at me and you see a weakling, someone who can be easily dismissed, someone you think you are above, someone you pity. You refuse to love me. You laugh at me behind my back. You must understand I'll always love you.' As he speaks, he leans in, as though to kiss her.

'I liked you. But you want something I can't give you.' Young-woman hands push out, shoving him back.

He staggers but immediately comes at her, one hand spread, slapping hard across her cheek. She cries out. 'Stay away, you creep! My father—'

'He'll do nothing!' Siegel's voice has taken a different tone. It's venomous and uncontrolled. He's let loose the Scavenger in himself. 'He has no power over me, and no more do you.' He glances around and grabs at something on the wall. 'I love you,' he says. 'I will always love you! But I need time—'

'No! Please!'

'I'll make you understand. You'll need to rely on me to live again.'

Lengthy blades come down, over and over. There's a flash of reflected light on metal.

Blood splatters through the light and shadows.

The young woman screams. Screams again and again, until she chokes on her own blood and falls silent.

43

BANERJEE WATCHED ANXIOUSLY.

'If women have been hurt, I had nothing to do with it,' the Scavenger said. He stepped away from Crowe, who at that instant cried out and started to thrash against the gurney, as though he was convulsing. Both the Scavenger and Bugden stared at him, bemused, perhaps shocked. After a moment, Crowe stopped straining against the straps that kept him captive. He began breathing heavily, in gasps, trying to force himself back to normal.

'What *is* your problem, Mr Crowe?' said Siegel.

'I saw–' Crowe spluttered. Then he stared the killer in the face. 'It was you.' He pulled at his bonds but still couldn't break them. 'I saw it and didn't realise–'

'Saw what?'

'What you did to Lucy, Siegel. I saw it all.'

The Scavenger stepped away from Crowe, surprised and indignant.

'She is my one and only true love,' he said. 'I would not hurt her. I wanted to save her.'

'Save her?'

'Save her from herself. Save her from making the biggest mistake of her life.'

'You're fucking delusional.'

'She'll see what I've achieved and will come back to me.' He gestured toward the monstrosity. 'Though silent for years, she'll return. She'll understand I do all this for her. I've kept her close to me – very close – so that she'll know she can once again be with me. You should shut up!'

'Or what, Jimmy?' Crowe glared at him with barely contained anger. 'You'll kill me with the shears you used on her?'

Siegel waved dismissively, eyes blazing. 'I've no time for this nonsense. I'll make everything right, as I always intended.' He turned to Bugden, his voice calming, becoming more practised. 'Help me check the wiring. The time is nearly here.' He moved toward the monstrosity on the wall.

Bugden had been watching the Scavenger intently as his accomplice spoke. Banerjee recognised the apprehension in his glance. Whatever atrocity the Scavenger had committed in the past, he'd now dedicated himself to creating new life in atonement, and the lives he took to achieve that end had been assigned only to men he perceived wanted new lives themselves. Other killings, and the mutilations committed on herself, the death threats, they were Bugden's doing and the journalist was scared the Scavenger would find out. A rivalry seethed deep down in their relationship. To Bugden, the Monster was not simply a physical concoction but a whole network of power he was able to build through the Scavenger's passion, guilt and madness. His hidden agenda rose close to the surface, and it was one the Scavenger himself wouldn't like.

We could use this, Banerjee thought. *It's risky, but what alternative do we have?*

Taking advantage of the two killers' distraction, she ducked from her secure spot outside the room and crept toward Crowe. Hopefully, her bare feet would not be heard under the background noise of wind, rain and thunder, and the hissing and crackling of various pseudo-scientific machines attached to the Monster.

'We must hurry,' the Scavenger said with an air of Shakespearean authority, looking skyward. 'The celestial powers are approaching their peak alignment.' Banerjee stopped, holding her breath and crouching as low as she could behind a table covered in a mish-mash of metal and wire. But the Scavenger spoke without raising his head from the old-fashioned computer terminal he was poking at. Bugden's attention stayed on his 'master'.

Gail Veitch, who was quite conscious now and in a position to see more of the space than Crowe, glanced Banerjee's way, her expression, dulled by drugs, a mixture of surprise, hope and inevitable anxiety. Banerjee gestured at her to wait, to hold still.

The Scavenger and Bugden were still looking away from her.

But as Banerjee drew close to Crowe, he must have sensed her movement. He tried to bend around. She scrambled over the final few steps and grabbed Crowe's left arm, which was straining against the straps.

'Don't speak,' she whispered.

He nodded, turning back to a relaxed position.

Banerjee bent to one side to check on the Scavenger and his lackey around the edge of the upright gurney. They were both focused on the Monster, exchanging ludicrous pseudo-scientific jargon about 'axillary nerve clusters' and the 'neurological coordination of multiple brain stems'.

'Mike, listen.' She was as close to him as she could get without revealing herself. 'Focus on the killing and molestation of women. Poke at him about it. It's a violation of his project's purity. Just trust me in this. Use me if necessary. It might give us a chance–'

But she'd said too much. Taken too long. Suddenly Bugden stepped around Crowe, his face red with fury beneath his wiry beard.

'Well, who have we here?' he said.

Banerjee backed away. She tried to control the trembling in her legs and arms.

'One of your victims,' she replied.

Bugden huffed. 'I know you, girlie.'

By this time, Siegel too had realised there was an interloper in their midst. He strode over, pushing Bugden aside.

'Interruptions!' he yelled. 'Why am I being interrupted? This is a vital time, and any delay could result in failure. I can't tolerate it.' He moved around Crowe's table. 'Why are you here?' he growled at Banerjee, who backed further away.

'I'll get rid of her,' Bugden said and made to grab her.

'It's Dr Meera Banerjee,' said Crowe, looking straight at Siegel. 'Surely you recognise her. You kidnapped her.'

'Shut ya mouth!' Bugden screeched, stepping closer and punching Crowe in the face. The Scavenger shoved him aside.

Siegel glared at Crowe. 'What are you saying?'

'Don't listen to him! He's a liar!' Bugden tried to reach Crowe again, but the Scavenger wouldn't have it. He grabbed Bugden by the arm.

'Don't you dare interfere with me again!' he snarled. He seemed larger.

Bugden froze. The Scavenger pushed him away and turned back to Crowe.

'What do you mean *I* kidnapped her?'

'She's an academic consultant in the pay of the police,' Crowe continued. 'You kidnapped and abused her. Had you forgotten?'

'I did no such thing. I'd never–'

'Sure.' Crowe spat out the word with added venom. 'I've seen one of the women you supposedly haven't killed. A young woman named Sandy. Carved up like some meaningless carcass. At the start of life, murdered along with her lover, who was a colleague of mine. You wrote a note on the wall above her – after you'd mutilated her body. You *signed* it with her blood! It was pure, senseless, misogynistic slaughter. But she wasn't the first young woman you've murdered, was she?'

Siegel pulled back, stepping away as if to escape Crowe's accusations. 'I never–'

'You cut off handfuls of this woman's hair,' Crowe continued, nodding in Banerjee's direction. 'Sliced off her finger as a warning to me to back off and then to entice me here.'

'I agreed to none of this.'

'Really, Mr Siegel?' said Banerjee, moving toward him, despite her fear. 'I was kidnapped by your minion and locked in your dungeon. I've been tortured. Do you think I cut off my own finger?' She held up her bloody hand. Then pointed her uninjured hand toward Bugden. 'Your lackey did this to me. And he blamed you. I knew he was going to kill me, until I tricked him and escaped. But it all comes down to you!'

The wannabe Dr Frankenstein – a pillar of misguided idealism – glared at his treacherous Igor.

Crowe watched with bitter amusement as Siegel turned on Bugden with one of the most inhuman snarls he'd ever heard come from a human mouth, realisation hitting the madman like a bolt of the lightning that even then sent thunder to rattle the walls of his 'lab'. 'You!' he screamed. 'You killed and tortured when I said you should only humiliate. You spoiled everything.'

Bugden's face seemed to collapse like a deflated balloon. Terror washed over it. 'They're lying!' he yelled, backing off.

But the Scavenger was no longer moving. He'd stopped, slightly bent, gazing at the journo from under his eyebrows. Then he growled and straightened up, scarily calm now. 'You argued we should do just what this man has described. You went against me. You slaughtered, hurt women, and you have put the blame for it on me.'

'Look, ah, Victor, old mate. I—'

'My redemption was to have been without moral blemish,' he yelled, anger welling up like it was going to explode him. Crowe heard Gail stirring, pulling at her restraints, but her muffled grunting didn't distract the pair from their confrontation. 'My Super-Man must be a thing of life, not death. It must be born in purity. How else can I gain redemption? How else could my lover return to me?'

Crowe took the opportunity to gesture for Banerjee to come closer. 'Go!' he whispered. 'Get out while you can. Who knows where this is going?'

'Not while you two are here.' Banerjee began pulling at the leather straps on his wrist.

'Take Gail and run.'

She kept trying to loosen his restraints.

'Forget it,' he said as forcefully as a whisper allowed. 'No time. The straps are too strong—'

'I can try—' She looked around, then made to go fetch a scalpel on a nearby table but stopped after a few steps when Bugden roared.

'Bugger this!' He had pulled himself together, dredging up a good dose of bluster and throwing it at Siegel. 'Look, you brain-dead fool,' he said, 'killin' was a good idea. We're not muckin' about with some fantasy here. It's murder, good old-fashioned bloody mayhem. I'm not interested in your goddamn *redemption*. Or your imaginary lover. Your destiny is to be a serial killer, the craziest serial killer this country's ever had, not some bloody romantic miracle-worker. I'll make you into a legendary *nightmare* in an age full of horrors.'

Siegel's eyes were bulging.

'I created you,' Bugden went on, careless. 'I made you what you are. If I wanna cut up women on your behalf, I damn well will.'

Siegel roared and leapt. But the old man already had a gun out — Crowe's Beretta. He waved it at the enraged madman and started to yell for him to stay back. Siegel didn't stop. Thunder rattled the house, like a monster trying to break through the walls. Then he jerked as the first bullet ploughed into the right side of his chest. Blood flashed in the yellow light. But it didn't stop him. Momentum and his ferocity carried him to Bugden before the ex-journo could fire again. The Beretta went off but to one side. Crowe watched a bullet ricochet from the wall about a metre away.

Siegel had Bugden by the throat, strangling him with one hand. Crowe remembered how wiry-strong Bugden was, but the Scavenger bore him to the floor with ease. The old man was gagging and choking, trying to swear, trying desperately to bring around the gun, but he couldn't do either. Siegel slammed Bugden's hand against the floor and smacked on his wrist. The journo's fingers jerked open, dropping the weapon. He made a noise that was as much despair as pain. It did him no good. Crowe could just see his throat – Siegel's fingers pushing into the windpipe so that Bugden's withered, yellow skin tore. His eyes bulged. Siegel roared.

After a few moments of thrashing, Bugden's body went limp. Siegel stood back from him, his fingers dripping blood. 'If you've destroyed my work,' he muttered again, 'I'll kill you!'

Bugden didn't answer. Not easy to say anything without a throat.

Another roar of thunder echoed around them. This time it sounded as though it was directly overhead and moving fast. It lingered in the stone floor and the walls. Siegel glanced up, from Crowe to Banerjee and back. Pain and grief and madness sparked in them. 'I must...' he began. He looked confused.

'Hurry?' Crowe suggested.

'Yes, yes. Hurry. The storm is at its peak.'

The wound in his chest was bleeding badly. He clutched at it, licking his lips as though they'd gone dry. Slowly, breathing heavily, he moved toward his creature, poking stupidly at the wires.

'Siegel!' Crowe tried to get his attention. 'Doctor Frankenstein!'

Siegel glanced back, eyes wide and mad. 'What?' he wheezed.

'You're hurt. You'll need help now your assistant's gone.'

Unscripted words found very little grip in the madman's head. He frowned, concentrating on them. His face was shiny with sweat. He'd wiped a streak of blood across his brows.

'Yes,' he muttered. 'Help.'

'Untie me,' Crowe said, trying to sound as innocuous as possible. 'I understand your purpose now. I want to help.'

The Scavenger looked his prisoner up and down, as though trying to remember who he was.

'Trust you?' he said at last. He shuffled closer and whispered, 'You know my…my secret shame.'

'And I know why you seek redemption because of it. I understand.'

'But you hate me for it. I can see that. I can't trust you.'

'Sure you can. Everyone trusts me. I'm a really trustworthy guy.'

'You are a liar and a thug. Igor…he said so. You are here—' He coughed, choking on his own innards maybe. 'You are here to watch,' he managed, once the fit had passed.

'Hey, you're not going to believe everything Blowie told you about me, are you? He was a fool and he lied about the women he killed. There's no way you should've trusted him.'

'Minions, they are always a problem,' Siegel muttered.

Thunder rumbled through the building again. Gail gasped in response. She coughed and threw up – the effect of her heavy dose of drugs.

'Listen, Doctor,' Crowe said to Frankenstein-Siegel, who was moving toward his dials and levers. 'You think you can't trust me, but what about the woman, eh? That one.' He gestured as best he could toward Gail. 'She's not like me. She understands. Tell her what to do, she can help.'

'What are you doing?' Banerjee said. As best he could, he gestured for her to stay out of it.

'You need help, Doc. You're injured.' He sent a look of what he hoped was assurance in Gail's direction. 'She's a journo, too. Blowie's out for the count, so who's going to record your triumph, eh? She could, couldn't you, Gail?'

Her voice was slurred, but Gail managed to snatch up the ball quickly enough. 'Yeah,' she croaked. 'Sure I can. I can…I can get you all the publicity you…deserve.'

Siegel looked at them. His eyes seemed full, as though he was crying, but with tears that couldn't flow. 'It is an important event,' he muttered. 'Changing history. It should be seen.'

'You have a responsibility,' Crowe continued. 'Surely you need to make your perfect creature known to all mankind!'

'Responsibility,' Siegel said, speaking almost to himself.

'Make Lucy proud.'

'Yes, yes. Lucy.' Siegel's voice was a shallow whisper.

'Just let the woman go. She'll promise not to run away, won't you, Gail?'

More thunder. Siegel looked up, flustered, almost panicked. Banerjee, seemingly invisible to him, moved around the lab, poking at equipment. Siegel stared straight at her once or twice, but his eyes skirted over her, seeing her as an unwanted stain on the cloth he was weaving. He didn't want her to be part of his narrative.

'All right!' Siegel yelled, 'Hurry!' He hobbled past Crowe, still ignoring Banerjee. Out of the corner of his eye, Crowe watched him release Gail's bonds. He didn't bother waiting for Gail to stagger to her feet, which she did, sounding nauseated and ill. In a moment, the Mad Doctor was back at his wires. This time he headed for a roughly put-together contraption like a fuse-box. Bits of coloured cable hung out of it. It connected to a power gauge with a needle wobbling about behind its glass face.

'Got a generator out the back, eh?' Crowe asked. 'A big one?'

Siegel nodded. 'Two. And we...I've put a lightning collector on the roof. It will harvest the storm's power. The power of Creation.'

Gail was fiddling with the leather strapping at Crowe's left while Banerjee, who had fetched the scalpel, hacked at the right side. Siegel wasn't taking any notice of her.

'Hurry,' Crowe whispered.

'Give me a chance. This stuff is stronger than I thought it'd be.'

Suddenly the Scavenger emerged. He whipped around, his finger pointing. 'Don't touch him,' he screamed at Gail, 'or I'll kill you both!' Gail jerked away from the bonds. Banerjee looked straight into the Scavenger's eyes as they passed over her. But he ignored her as before and turned back to Gail. 'Get the video camera! It's in that box.' He pointed at the junk Bugden had fetched earlier. 'Do your job!' He had a knife in his fist now, a big one. Gail shot Crowe a glum acknowledgement and moved away. Banerjee, her hands shaking, paused.

While Gail was fetching the video camera, Crowe tested his bonds. They were tight, but Banerjee had made some headway. He tried to work on them by stretching them, but whoever had put them on him – Bugden, no doubt – had known what he was doing.

'I'm getting there,' Banerjee said.

'You should go.'

'He's not even seeing me. His mind has blocked me out.'

Thunder rumbled. Close. The room shook.

This time it sent the Scavenger into a frenzy. He began flicking switches. Whatever he did had some effect because the air filled with a low hum and the lights dimmed.

'Are you ready?' he asked Gail.

'Is this thing automatic?' she asked, holding up the old video camera.

'Are you ready?' he screamed, much louder.

'Sure,' she said, realising the realities of filming weren't important to him. 'Whatever you say.'

Siegel put his shaking hand on a larger lever. 'This is it!' he screeched, wheezing under the strain. 'With the next bolt of lightning, mankind's childish reign comes to an end. The New Man will be born into greatness. I...*I* will be redeemed.'

The place went dead quiet except for the hum. Crowe yanked at the leather straps with all his strength but stopped when Siegel turned to him.

'Are you watching?' he said, still ignoring Banerjee. 'Can you feel the power of Creation?'

More thunder roared. Though that meant the lightning flash that accompanied it had past, Siegel took it as his cue. He pulled down the switch. Current must have diverted into the grid of wires surrounding his creature; the lights flickered lower and parts of the grid began to glow, like the elements of some enormous globe. The doctor rushed over to his monstrosity, standing under it and gazing up adoringly.

'Come, my creature!' he yelled, 'Live! Live!'

Nothing happened. Suddenly conscious that a disappointed lunatic was likely to want a scapegoat, Crowe pulled frantically on his bonds. The one Banerjee had been working on gave under pressure. He yanked his arm free and used it to work on the other. Banerjee moved to his remaining strap and cut at it with the scalpel. It was slow going. At that moment Gail appeared, holding some sort of hand-held electric bone saw.

'Look what I found,' she said. 'I could take off your hand, but let's try the strap first.' *Good to see she's still got a sense of humour*, Crowe thought ruefully. If only he could retrieve his own.

The saw went through the strap, as well as the large one holding down his feet, in seconds. Crowe stepped off the gurney, stretching his muscles. 'Okay, let's–' he began.

Crowe's movement must have registered with Siegel, cutting through the man's delusions, because he turned, a small, angry figure hunched beside the larger one crucified on an electric grid. In places, glowing wire was making dry skin and cloth smoulder.

'You!' he growled.

Crowe leapt toward his Beretta, which was still lying where Bugden had dropped it. He couldn't let Siegel get there first. Stumbling over the dead journo's corpse, he fell face down on the floor, feeling the metal slip under his fingers. He reached again, grabbed, held the gun tighter. Pushed himself up and turned toward Siegel. As he did, he called out, fully believing it was the right thing to do, calling to the one whose spirit was most at stake, suddenly knowing he could free her: 'Lucy!'

Time seemed to slow, consumed by the moment, grinding to a halt.

A shadow formed in the space between Crowe and Siegel. It was only as the shadow took on substance and detail that he realised it was her. In that instant, he found himself accepting the reality of it without his normal scepticism providing any sort of relief.

It was a Lucy filled with sorrow and anger. Yet there was compassion, too. He could see it in her face, beneath the bloody wounds and beyond the spectral trauma that had held her captive for so long. He called her name again. The shadowy figure glanced toward him in silent acknowledgement then turned to face her murderer. Siegel stared directly at her, a look of puzzlement, then terror, distorting his face.

'No,' Siegel cried. 'You can't be here. Not yet.'

'But I am,' she said. 'Brought here by the only man who ever really cared for me. The only one who cared for me without wanting anything, the only one who wept for me – not just through his eyes but in his heart. He opened the way for me to escape my prison.'

Siegel collapsed to his knees.

'I wept for you,' he said, his tone pleading. 'I didn't mean to hurt you.'

'You wept for yourself. Just like my father, who obtained that poor unliving child–' She indicated the foetus trapped in the dead flesh of the Scavenger's monstrosity. 'Not really dead because it never really lived – just so he could drag me back, to trap me in it to ease his own guilt, to control me. You – you took many lives to soothe your own guilt.' She gestured toward the Creature. 'It ends here.'

'Please,' Siegel moaned. 'I've always loved you. Please forgive me!'

Crowe raised his gun, intent on shooting the bastard, but Lucy signalled for him to stop. Reluctantly, despite himself, Crowe lowered his weapon.

'I must give my creation life,' Siegel pleaded.

Lucy glided closer to him. 'I'm sorry. It's not possible. It was always a delusion. Move away now or you'll be destroyed along with it.'

'I won't abandon it!' Siegel cried. 'I can't. This is my Great Work–'

Lucy began to fade. 'It's your choice, Mr Siegel.'

Crowe blinked as what seemed like a sudden flash of lightning crashed around the room. Thunder shook the building.

The foetus burst into flame.

'Mike! Look out!'

Gail grabbed Crowe and pulled him back. Sparks shot up, exploding from the machinery that surrounded Siegel's obscene handiwork. The explosive roar of the thunderclap shook right through to his bones.

'What the hell?'

Something moved on the wall. The grid-wires, most of them sparking, shifted and pulled against the burning flesh. Siegel, still on his knees, heard the crunch of bone on bone and glanced around. A raging fire had consumed the foetus and was spreading through the rest of the carcass.

'It's alive!' the remaining shreds of Victor Frankenstein cried enthusiastically as his monster shifted under its own weight, its support wires melting and giving way. 'It's alive!'

A large section of the wiring flared up, spouting flame like a dragon.

This time the Creature really did move. The loose mass of burning flesh and bone seemed to strain against its metal bonds, tearing bits of itself away. 'It's alive, it's alive, it's alive!' Siegel-Frankenstein shouted. 'You were wrong, Lucy. I did this for you.' He glanced around, then appeared frustrated that the phantom he'd been talking to was no longer there.

In that moment, the Creature came down on top of him, sparks flying as electrically charged wiring broke and danced about. Siegel embraced the tumbling monstrosity for a moment, current hit him, and he shrieked. He thrashed about under the dead weight of his New Human, which was burning in patches.

Banerjee ran toward the control panel and pulled the main switch to OFF. But by then the Creature was smoking in earnest and Siegel wasn't moving. An oppressive smell of burning flesh filled the cellar.

Crowe looked around through the rising haze, seeking Lucy. She was nowhere to be seen.

Banerjee stared at him. 'Are you okay?' she asked.

He said nothing.

Gail grabbed his arm. 'Come on! We've got to get out of here.'

'Did you see her?' he said.

Gail stared at him for a moment then pulled him toward the door. 'Not now, Mike. Now's not the time. Come on!'

44

THEY GOT OUT AS QUICKLY AS THEY COULD. THE STENCH WAS APPALLING and would've choked them if they'd stayed any longer. The kitchen remained unlit. Wiring throughout the house must've fused out, because none of the lights would work, even though Crowe could hear the generator pounding away in the shed out the back. For a while the three of them stood in the cool, open air, breathing it in, saying nothing. The night was still windy, and lightning flickered along the tops of the trees silhouetted against the sky to the east and distant thunder gurgled like an old man dying.

'Is it over?' said Gail at last.

'I think so,' Crowe replied, and he moved closer, listening to the natural sounds of the bush. He put his hand on Gail's shoulder. 'At least we made it out more or less intact,' he said. He acknowledged Banerjee. 'All of us.'

Banerjee smiled weakly, exhausted by lack of sleep, pain, and too much adrenalin to do anything else.

'I mean it,' Crowe added. 'I doubt I'd be alive now if you hadn't been here. You unhinged him.'

'Yeah, you owe us big time,' Gail said. 'You can shout us dinner somewhere very expensive, once my memory of what went on in there fades a bit. I'm not sure my stomach will be up for much for a while.'

Crowe nodded, but he was barely listening. 'Did you see her? Did you see Lucy?'

'I was hoping you wouldn't ask me again.'

'But did you see her?'

'See who?' Banerjee asked.

Crowe stood silently for a moment or two, eyes lowered.

Gail turned to Banerjee, a resigned look on her face. 'A rather persistent delusion,' she said.

'No delusion,' Crowe growled. 'She was there. I saw her clearly and so did Siegel.'

'Well, *I* didn't,' Gail said. 'All I heard was both you and the maniac talking nonsense. How about you, Meera?'

'I didn't see anyone except us, that Blowie character and the Scavenger.' Banerjee stared at Crowe suspiciously. 'Who didn't I see? Who was the Scavenger talking to?'

Gail answered for him. 'A young girl named Lucy. A young girl who was murdered ten years ago. Mike found her body, though subsequently it disappeared.'

'She was there.' Crowe walked a few metres away, his back to them, staring into the shadowy trees. 'She spoke to me. She spoke to Siegel, too. Confronted him. He was the one that killed her.' He turned back. 'I saw it. The murder, I mean.'

'Lucy is a ghost,' Gail told Banerjee, her tone ironic. 'As a shrink I'm sure you have definite opinions about why people see ghosts. Self-delusion motivated by what – guilt? Grief? Mike has been suffering from both for some time.'

Crowe frowned, saying nothing.

Much to his surprise, though, Banerjee didn't confirm Gail's take on the subject, not initially at any rate – a take he would have totally agreed with before this. Instead, she looked at him, not the way you look at a lunatic, but as though she wanted him to elaborate. He resisted for a long moment, staring into her eyes.

'Look, I know it's crazy,' he said. 'I've never been a superstitious man. Not even religious. But I know Lucy was there, for real, and for better or worse, I'm convinced there was some sort of connection between us, a bonding that gradually allowed her to get free of whatever force was stopping her from…fuck, I don't know, from moving on? At first the connection was distant, conveyed through distorted memories. But as I got closer, emotionally closer, she began to manifest.' He stared into Banerjee's eyes. 'I'm out of my mind, right?'

Banerjee looked thoughtful for a few moments then said, 'Bugden locked me in a cell down–' she hesitated '–down under the main building.' She pointed. 'Over that way. I escaped and while trying to find the exit I stumbled onto a body in one of the rooms. Someone – the Scavenger, I assume – had tried to preserve the corpse. It was a young woman. She'd obviously been stabbed many times. It looked like some sort of shrine.'

Crowe stared at her, aghast.

Gail opened her mouth to say something but must have decided better of it when Crowe caught her eye.

'I think,' Crowe said, 'I'd better go have a look.'

They found the cell in question easily enough, using a torch they fetched from Gail's car – her Mazda was still intact, though with its tyres slashed – and guided by Banerjee through the back door on the far side of the graveyard. The two women remained in the corridor while Crowe stood silently, unmoving, illuminating the young woman's corpse with the torchlight. After a few minutes, he turned away, leaving the room in darkness. 'It's her,' was all he said. He wouldn't discuss it further, despite Gail's attempts to engage him. They returned to the building's main entrance and stood staring into the gently moving bush and the clearing sky.

Later, after the burning diminished, Crowe searched the place as best he could, even down in the madman's lab. Siegel's creature was still smouldering, glowing inside as though life had indeed been sparked in it. Now that life was fading again. No sign of recovery from Siegel, though. Crowe got hold of one of the prostrate figure's arms and tested for a pulse. Nothing.

He found plenty of evidence, none of it Pukalski's money. The leather case was there, still attached to Skarratt's wrist, but it was empty. In a sealed cold room buried deeper in the cellar, there were bits of bodies, bones with the meat scraped off, skin in the process of being cured, even the wallets of the Scavenger's victims. He'd written out charts detailing information about them, and next to each name was some piece of identification – driver's licence, credit card, mobile phones, sometimes a photograph of family or friends. Amongst them, he found his own phone, and Gail's. That was something. But no money. Obviously, Siegel or Bugden had removed the money from the bag, but they could have done anything with it after that. Used some of it to finance their 'experiment' perhaps – one of the generators was new and recently installed. But they might have thrown the whole stash away, for all Crowe thought they were likely to act like ordinary people. Money didn't seem to motivate either of them.

Behind the building, Crowe stumbled upon a car – a station wagon with black-out windows – which hadn't been there the last time he'd checked. No doubt it had been Siegel's personal transport, perhaps given to him when he quit his role as Waldheim's driver – and its presence raised his hopes that they could drive out using it. But there were no keys he could find and it resisted his attempts to get it going using other means. He suspected Bugden had scuttled it.

So, resigned to being unable to drive away from this place, he rang Pirran.

Pirran's office woke the superintendent at home and before too long he turned up with a bunch of other cops. He was visibly relieved to find that Banerjee had surfaced, and if not for her, would probably have been a lot more sceptical about the grotesque and rather ridiculous tale they had to tell. They'd saved the more ludicrous details to last, and really, he wasn't all that content to believe any of it until he went down into the cellar and eyeballed the mess there. He was a lot whiter and sicker when he came out.

'And we solved yet another crime for you, Piranha,' Crowe said. 'Two for the price of one.'

'Oh?'

'Meera found Lucy Waldheim's corpse. Remember that case?'

'Closed long ago. Her murderer was–'

'Not the one that confessed to it and was ritually slaughtered in prison. That was a set-up. It was Jimmy Siegel – the Scavenger. He'd worked for Waldheim and was obsessed with his daughter. He killed her in a fit of anger when she rejected him. All this–' he waved his hand toward the sanatorium '–the Scavenger/Dr Frankenstein gig, all this was intended to assuage his guilt.' He didn't add, *And to bring her back, just like her father too had wanted.*

'Is this true?' Pirran asked Banerjee.

She nodded. 'It seems so,' she said. 'Certainly the girl's body is there, set up like some sort of shrine. I've seen it.'

Pirran didn't comment.

'What happens now?' Gail asked. They were waiting on the sanatorium's front verandah while the cops poked around downstairs. Banerjee was having her wounds attended to.

'They'll harass us for a few hours back at HQ,' Crowe said, holding Gail against his body – they both craved the warmth. 'Then members of the press harass us, and after that, the cops have another go. We give statements that completely avoid all mention of ghosts. We'll be able to stop thinking about it in a few months, if we're lucky, after the inquests. After Lucy gets a proper burial.'

'It was a close thing...crazy.' A look of ironic humour crept over her face. 'Siegel was crazy. What sort of love acts the way he did?'

'At least he had the decency to kill himself in the end,' said Crowe. 'Let me off the hook.'

Gail was silent.

'Are you okay?' Crowe asked eventually.

She turned from him so he couldn't see her face and stared out over the darkened bush. Then, 'This'll make a great story,' she declared at last, a deliberate tangent. 'Hope I can get my camera back. Maybe I should find it now and take some pictures of the monstrosity.'

'If they'll let you.'

That sounded like a challenge, and in the space of a breath, she'd gone to tackle it. Crowe remained where he was, turned off, recuperating. Some rookie offered him coffee from a thermos. It was good enough.

Gail came back some time later with Banerjee, whose hand looked a lot tidier and less swollen. 'They've got a lot to examine,' Gail said, 'so there was no need for them to see this.' She patted her coat pocket, which was bulging somewhat. Crowe glanced at Banerjee, who faked an innocent look. Rather gruesome shots would eventually appear in *Manhunter,* and they were exclusive. By the time other journos started to arrive, as light was creeping up over the horizon, Pirran had got his act together and managed to keep them away.

Much to Crowe's chagrin, however, Pukalski's money was discovered when they moved the bodies, and the autopsy boys began the task of identifying what bits belonged to which victim. The Creature's stomach was full of the stuff – Siegel-Frankenstein had used it as padding. Some of it had been burnt, turned into an ashen, bloody mess, but some of it survived. Didn't do Crowe any good. They didn't know to whom it belonged and he could hardly tell them. In the end, most of what was left went into a government-backed fund to aid the victims' families. Crowe was fine with that. He didn't want Waldheim's blood money.

In the weeks that followed, police investigators pieced together the story, most of which Crowe had already figured out through guesswork. Bits of information about Siegel were found, but mostly all it showed was a man who couldn't get his act together even when given the chance. How he'd set up at the old sanatorium, how he'd started on his career as architect of the New Man, Crowe would never know, though in the aftermath there was plenty of speculation. Grey areas are popular with journos – you can say what you like, and no one can prove you wrong. And they had to make parts of it up, just so it all made a modicum of sense.

Siegel's involvement in the death and disappearance of Lucy Waldheim was kept quiet, however. It would come out eventually but for a while no one talked about it. Perhaps she could rest in peace at last. Crowe hoped so. At any rate, he never heard from her again.

The book about the Scavenger that eventually appeared was more or less a work of fiction, even though the writer had had access to Bugden's notes. Crowe wasn't mentioned in it, not by name. The writer was overcome by a conviction that he should play down Crowe's role – the barrel of Crowe's Beretta stuck up his nose was the decisive argument. Pukalski's widow used similar methods to keep speculation on her husband's affairs to a minimum. No one at any point mentioned a burnt foetus being found amongst the carnage of the Scavenger's cellar, and Crowe chose not to ask about it. The role of Queen Marika's aborted offspring in both these events and the death of Gregor Waldheim did not appear in police reports, though much later something similar was hinted at in various conspiracy-based Facebook and Instagram groups. Where the idea originated remained a mystery, and who in their right mind takes such things seriously?

Pirran reckoned Bugden had found the Scavenger the same way Crowe had. He'd written a couple of articles in various journals, and it was quite possible that Siegel, seeking publicity, had got in contact. Perhaps the first letter from the Scavenger that Bugden had shown him was the key. Pirran thought it possible that, as he'd claimed, someone in Bugden's debt within the department had intercepted it – the man had had quite a network for a lunatic.

Crowe never got involved in the diplomatic upshot of Meera Banerjee's capture, though he realised it meant some smoothing of ruffled feathers had to take place among the pollies. Banerjee had commended Crowe for his role, much to the chagrin of many. Pirran's department underwent an 'investigation', though Pirran himself came out of it with a commendation. After all, there'd been a lot of clout hanging on the Scavenger's capture.

'I don't know what you did to Banerjee to make her so forgiving,' Pirran said to Crowe after one intensive grilling. 'I guess saving her life helped.'

'Saving her life? To be honest, Pirran, she saved mine. You must've read my statement. She was amazingly resourceful and brave. She can have the credit.'

Pirran nodded. 'But, damn you, Crowe, you weren't very open with me. If you had been, maybe we would've got her back with 10 fingers.'

'I doubt it.' He gave Pirran a serious look. 'But I solved the case, didn't I? I did what you asked. What more do you want?'

Anger propelled the cop off his chair. 'What more do I want? How about a sense of responsibility? Don't think I haven't connected you with Waldheim's death. Some fingerprints that match yours were found at the scene.'

'Waldheim? Honestly, Piranha, it was Siegel who did him in. You know that as well as I do, and I know it for sure, even though I wasn't there. Any prints were no doubt from previous visits.'

'What about Pukalski's minder?'

'Jonwood? Turned out he was in Bugden's pay.'

'And Creedy?'

'You can put that one on Dale Walker, under orders from Waldheim.'

'You're kidding me?'

'I have it on good authority. Not that you'll be able to prove anything. The authority is dead – Siegel himself.'

'Jesus Christ!' Pirran rubbed his hand across his forehead. 'I haven't got time for mavericks, Crowe. I'm not enamoured of your methods.'

Crowe raised his eyebrows calmly. 'I fulfilled my part,' he said. 'Solved more cases than expected. Don't be so ungrateful.' He shrugged. 'It'd be too bad if it came out you didn't fulfil your part of the bargain. Right now, I'm not sure to what extent those blokes investigating your department even know it was you who took a maverick on-board.'

Pirran grumbled, sitting down. 'Are you blackmailing me?'

'How could I? Surely you haven't done anything wrong.'

He sat silently glaring at Crowe. 'Damn straight I haven't,' he muttered.

'Sure. You wouldn't get busted or anything. Some might question your wisdom though.'

They looked at each other, bloodshot eyeball to bloodshot eyeball. Finally, Pirran laughed. 'Damn you, Crowe. I should just take your bluff and ride it out.'

'It's a possibility.'

'But I won't. You actually did okay.'

Crowe stood. 'See? Your judgement's on the mend already.'

'Don't push your luck.'

Crowe looked at him reproachfully. 'For fuck's sake, Doug,' he said, before turning to leave, 'what's a man got to do to satisfy you? You really should learn to appreciate your friends more.'

AFTERMATH

WHEN LUCY WAS FINALLY BURIED, IT WAS A LOW-KEY AFFAIR, ORGANISED BY Crowe and Gail in the absence of known or at least sympathetic relatives. Investigations into Waldheim's murder incidentally uncovered stacks of paperwork detailing his illicit activities over the years, and court action by many of his victims saw much of his estate handed out by the court as compensation. A will was also found, leaving the house and what was left of his wealth to his daughter. Given that Lucy no longer had any need for anything her father could offer her, Waldheim's estranged wife, Eleyn Farnestine, ended up claiming much of it. Beyond that, Crowe had no idea and even less interest where it went.

Lucy's coffin was lowered into the ground, watched only by Crowe, Gail and Father Joseph Calder, whom Crowe had approached to give Lucy a proper send-off. Father Joseph had been Crowe's mother's priest for several decades and, though Crowe had abandoned religion long ago, he still remembered the priest with some fondness. His scepticism regarding the Church and its spiritual teachings was, however, as strong as ever, though recent experiences had left him with a mind more open than it had once been. Just a bit.

After the priest finished his prayers for the dead, and Crowe and Gail dropped the first dirt onto her coffin, they walked slowly back to Gail's car. It was a pleasantly warm day, with only a few ragged clouds ambling across the sky on high-level currents. At ground level, the air was calm. Gail took Crowe's hand.

'You okay, Mike?' she whispered.

'Sure. Why wouldn't I be?' He smiled ironically. 'Why are you whispering?'

'Actually, I don't know.'

'Lucy's not going to hear you.'

'So...' Gail stopped, forcing him to stop as well. She stared at him, searching. 'You don't think she's still around?'

He shrugged. 'No need for her to be. That was the point of all this.' He glanced toward the grave then brought his gaze back. 'I still remember things about Lucy, good and bad, but they're just memories. Real ones. I haven't had any of the other distorted kind since that night.'

'So, everything's back to normal?'

'Normal?' He began walking again, bringing Gail along with him. 'To be honest, I'm not sure what *is* normal anymore.'

Gail huffed. 'Let's go get a beer or three then. Maybe that'll remind you.'

He nodded thoughtfully. 'Excellent idea. My shout.'

ROBERT HOOD

Robert has been continually published in Australia and overseas since his first professional sale in 1975. His genres of choice are: horror/weird fiction, crime, fantasy and science fiction.

He has published over 140 short stories, a number of novellas, a few novels, lots of kid's books, and other strange stuff – including an opera libretto, some poetry, and a promotional kid's book (for the manufacturer of a certain hazelnut-based chocolate spread).

Robert has won several major Australian awards, including the 1988 Australian Golden Dagger Award, the 2014 Ditmar Award (Best Novel) for *Fragments of a Broken Land: Valarl Undead*, and the 2015 Australian Shadows Award (Best Collected Work) for *Peripheral Visions: The Collected Ghost Stories*. His stories have also found their way into Year's Best anthologies in Australia and overseas.

Robert was once referred to as 'Aussie horror's wicked godfather' in a magazine article on Australian horror.

ACKNOWLEDGEMENTS

Scavengers has taken a long time to become the novel I wanted it to be. Thanks must go to Kaaron Warren for reading an early version and helping me to believe in its value; Angela Slatter for doing a professional edit and giving me advice on how to improve it; and Jason Nahrung for undertaking the final edit. Ultimate thanks to Lindy Cameron of Clan Destine Press for her enthusiastic acceptance of the book for publication.

Thanks as well to Cat Sparks (and her father, Cameron Sparks) for the excellent cover.

Scavengers is set in Wollongong, NSW, on the Australian coast, as it seemed an ideal setting for the story, not because it is a place full of gruesome crime (it isn't), but because the environment was perfect for the story. Most of the settings in the story exist; some don't. All the characters are fictional, however.

Mike Crowe, Gail Veitch and Charlie Pukalski first appeared in 'Bloody Hide', a short story I wrote for *A Corpse at the Opera House*, a collection edited by Stephen Knight in 1992. Crowe then reappeared in 'Sandcrawlers', written for *Case Re-Opened*, edited by Stuart Coupe and Julie Ogden in 1992.

Both were received extremely well, and I always intended to write a novel about Crowe. It took a while before I got to work on Scavengers, but once I did, it grew and grew into the book you are holding. I had a lot of fun writing it. I hope you enjoyed it, too.

If you did, I intend to write more about Crowe.

CPSIA information can be obtained
at www.ICGtesting.com
Printed in the USA
BVHW040902260922
647977BV00028B/103